W9-DHH-223

THREE WEEKS LESS A DAY

a novel by Gary D. McGugan

◆ FriesenPress

Suite 300 - 990 Fort St
Victoria, BC, V8V 3K2
Canada

www.friesenpress.com

Copyright © 2016 by Gary D. McGugan
First Edition — 2016

All rights reserved.

No part of this publication may be reproduced in any form, or by any means, electronic or mechanical, including photocopying, recording, or any information browsing, storage, or retrieval system, without permission in writing from FriesenPress.

This book is a work of fiction. Names, characters, businesses, organizations, places, events, and incidents are the product of the author's imagination or are used fictitiously. Any resemblance to actual persons, living or dead, events or locales are entirely coincidental.

ISBN
978-1-4602-9325-6 (Hardcover)
978-1-4602-9326-3 (Paperback)
978-1-4602-9327-0 (eBook)

1. FICTION, THRILLERS

Distributed to the trade by The Ingram Book Company

garydmcguganbooks.com

For Monty,
Read Winters?)
Enjoy the read!
Gary [signature] 07-08-18

For my wife, Linda,
who planted and nurtured the idea of writing a novel.

Congrats on Ironman 2018 season.
Love,
Mom.

wow.

05.02.18

2018

MULTIMA CORPORATION
John George Mortimer
Founder
Chief Executive Officer (CEO)
Chairman of the Board

MULTIMA LOGISTICS
Wendal Randall
Division President

MULTIMA SUPERMARKETS
Suzanne Simpson
Division President

MULTIMA FINANCIAL SERVICES
James Fitzgerald
Division President

ONE

Head down, eyes shaded with stylish Serengeti glasses, Wendal Randall bounded down the broad concrete steps. Engrossed in an intense cell phone conversation, he scarcely noticed the tiny wisps of high white clouds accenting a brilliant blue sky. He nodded curtly, then watched as a uniformed limousine driver made eye contact, quickly swiveled around with surprising agility, circled behind the vehicle, and opened the rear door with a grand flourish precisely as his passenger arrived.

Wordlessly, but with a cheerful smile of appreciation, Wendal ducked into the rear compartment, cradling the tan jacket of a tailored Armani suit over his left arm. The driver closed the door and then, within seconds, the luxury German-engineered sedan was on its way while Wendal continued his Bluetooth conversation.

"That time and motion detector is really over the top, Ricky," he said. "I've never seen an app convert data so quickly with such little information. Let's be sure the patent attorneys get the paperwork finalized today."

"Already on top of it, WR. You surely taught me that lesson. I may not be as quick as you, but I'll never come up on the short end of a ground-breaking invention again," Ricky Technori responded with a laugh.

"Don't sell yourself short. We both know there's no one in the business who can churn out code as quickly and accurately as you. And I note that you thoughtfully remind me about that little MIT incident every time we have our chat about your performance," Wendal responded lightheartedly.

"Don't you think those nice five figure bonuses more than compensate for your one tiny oversight way back then? Keep coming up with great ideas like this app, and those bonuses will soon have another zero added!" he continued.

"Now, can you summarize all the new benefits in a PowerPoint I can use at that technology conference next week? It's sure to get us tons of media coverage and maybe even some new business. Can you get it to me by Sunday so I can build it into my presentation?"

"Consider it done," Technori replied to finish their call.

Relieved to end the call quickly, he could now fully enjoy the tranquility of this short ride from his office just off Biscayne Boulevard to Miami International Airport. Wendal usually diverted incoming calls to voice mail while he traveled, and with some slick computer programming, delayed all incoming email and text messages for thirty minutes. Only a few pre-qualified names could override the complex coding to disturb him in real time. He valued such rare opportunities to escape the constant torrent of telephone calls, emails, and personal meetings that came with his role as president of Multima Logistics, the technology and logistics division of Multima Corporation.

He used these few moments to lean back in the car's comfortable rear seat, stretch his long legs, and take a deep breath. He performed the same ritual almost every trip to the airport. Relaxed, he could spend a few minutes thinking of upcoming challenges or past successes.

That made the sudden, intrusive buzz of an arriving text message an annoying interruption. With a sigh, he dutifully reached for his device and read:

Confidential. JGM to leave at FYE. Call me tonight. Cell. H.

"Holy shit!" Wendal blurted aloud, attracting his driver's momentary glance in the rear-view mirror. This was big! Those cryptic words carried important news. Instantly, he started processing the startling message. 'JGM' referred to John George Mortimer, founder and chief executive officer of Multima Corporation. Wendal's boss, this legendary CEO was considered one of the richest men in America with untold billions in personal wealth.

Mortimer's apparent intention to leave the company at Multima's fiscal year end was almost unfathomable. Without a doubt, it would have incalculable implications. Whom would the board of directors choose to replace Mortimer? How would the board make such an important decision? Where would Wendal fit in their plans?

'H' was Howard Knight, an influential director on the board of Multima Corporation. He was also on the board of powerful Venture Capital Investments, a large private equity fund based in New York, and there was some history between Randall and Knight. Their first encounter took place almost ten years earlier when Wendal owned a small company experiencing dire financial difficulties.

These converging bits of information sent Wendal's heart rate racing, causing him to think about his promising career and the dramatic upheaval he had already experienced in such a short time. It seemed like a whirlwind had engulfed him since the day he graduated college.

Those years at Massachusetts Institute of Technology were truly impressive. In fact, Wendal cultivated his earliest exciting ideas at MIT, where he graduated *magna cum laude*, earning a master's degree in business administration with a major in computer science.

His classmates and professors considered him a genius with almost any aspect of computer technology. Throughout six remarkable academic years, Wendal was also a master electronic gamer, an adventurous hacker, and a creative dreamer. In classes, he listened intently to professors' lectures about all aspects of international business, then undertook research on his own.

As his college education progressed, Wendal conjured up almost unlimited opportunities to earn money and achieve status. Eventually, he came to realize that companies everywhere move trillions of dollars in goods from factories to distribution warehouses and customers in every corner of the world. He envisioned a compelling need to track all these manufactured products to ensure timely delivery with minimal damage or theft.

He learned that companies also tried to minimize inventory in transit or storage by precisely scheduling shipments of goods to arrive as needed by customers, a concept originally pioneered by Japanese business with just-in-time deliveries.

Wendal grasped that a software package allowing companies to track their shipments accurately could have enormous benefits for purchasers, manufacturers, and all those involved in the many stages between a factory and a customer.

He devoted every spare moment of his last two years at MIT and leveraged from classmates all the expertise he could coax or cajole to invent a miniature tracking device. The result was a work of art. As thin as a sheet of paper and the size of a postage stamp, the device could easily attach to cartons or individual packages with an adhesive. Once the goods entered an area equipped with Wi-Fi, this tiny device would send a signal to a satellite. With the Internet, data could instantly flow to computers around the globe.

Wisely, Wendal secured patents on the tracking device. He and his friends also wrote, tested, and perfected code for a unique and innovative software program they could license for a fee.

After graduating, he recruited three classmates whose brilliance in technology approached his, and they all set out for the Sunshine State. In Miami, they founded Worldwide Logistics Corporation, commonly known as WLC. It was a minuscule business with a grandiose name, but also with a spectacularly unique product.

After just three exciting years, Randall and his colleagues had grown WLC into a multi-million-dollar enterprise doing business with companies on every continent. Then the problems started. Unfortunately, internal expense controls were no match for either the creative genius of its software programming or Wendal's penchant for expensive marketing schemes. Poor financing decisions further compounded problems. Debts piled up fast. Lenders gradually became unwilling to lend.

Eventually, it appeared WLC was teetering on the precipice of bankruptcy, with Wendal about to lose all of his invested money, his business, and his dreams of success.

At that desperate juncture, investment banker Howard Knight suddenly appeared. It was apparent he knew all about Wendal Randall, even before their initial contact. He was well aware of his outstanding education, intellect, and technological genius. The crushing business debt was no concern. Surprisingly, Knight seemed sympathetic to his dire financial circumstances. He said he'd seen it all many times before.

He offered a solution. "Sell WLC to a much larger and financially stronger company, one that can take over the debts. Such a sale will provide a life-saving financial solution for your struggling company."

Further, Knight implied there might even be an opportunity for Wendal to continue managing his venture after the acquisition. "Success is still achievable. You just need the financial umbrella of an already well-established and profitable company."

At that point, Wendal had few other options. Given the impending fiscal disaster, it all looked incredibly elegant. They started discussions to sell Wendal's faltering company to John George Mortimer and become part of his formidable enterprise, Multima Corporation.

Howard Knight served as intermediary and talks progressed well. Mortimer had been looking for technology expertise to improve the critical logistics of his sprawling Multima Supermarkets division and was also prepared to let Wendal continue to manage the business, just as Howard Knight had predicted.

Mortimer's offer to purchase came with three conditions. He would appoint a new chief financial officer to better control company finances. The WLC name would immediately change to Multima Logistics. And, most importantly, Randall must understand that the supermarkets division of Multima Corporation would become his number one focus.

Their deal closed within months, and John George Mortimer created a new operating division—Multima Logistics. Wendal Randall became its relieved and debt-free president while Mortimer became Wendal's first-ever boss.

Their transaction proved to be brilliant. Multima Logistics continued to grow its sales dramatically over the next ten years. Its innovative technology helped Multima Supermarkets become a leader in shipping, warehousing, deliveries, and inventory management. In fact, Multima Supermarkets gradually became one of the lowest cost operators in all of America's intensely competitive retail industry.

Meanwhile, Wendal continued to advance his sophisticated GPS technology to include other valuable customers such as car rental outlets, heavy-equipment suppliers, and finance companies.

Wendal Randall and John George Mortimer also became close friends, despite a thirty-year gap in their ages. Randall's genius with technology constantly intrigued Mortimer, who in turn repeatedly impressed Wendal with his unrivaled business acumen.

As Wendal's limousine glided into the private jet section in a corner of Miami International Airport, his thoughts returned to Knight's earlier text message. Much was about to change. If Howard Knight's secret information proved correct, within a few months an entirely new business era would be underway at Multima. With that sobering thought, Randall felt an odd tingling sensation on the back of his neck. His few moments of quiet time were over.

Jolted back to real time, a newfound conviction seized him without much more consideration. He must find a way to become Multima Corporation's leader and define the company's future. That evening's call with Howard Knight promised to be an interesting one.

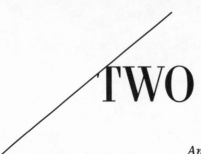

TWO

An office tower near Wall Street, New York.
Late night, February 18, 2016

Howard Knight reached for the ringing smartphone.

"Knight here." His tone was soft yet intense.

"Wendal Randall returning your message. Sorry it's a little late. I expect you didn't want our conversation overheard by a driver and thought it better to call you from the privacy of a hotel room."

Knight nodded in silent agreement, acknowledging that Wendal was showing improved judgment with such sensitive matters. He assured Randall the late hour was not a problem and added that this conversation would likely be his last, after a long sixteen-hour day of constant focus.

Although anxious to get on with the purpose of the call, Wendal was apprehensive about how best to proceed. Howard Knight was, after all, a powerful director of the company. Moreover, their prior conversations had not always been pleasant.

"Your text message today was certainly unusual," Randall said tentatively.

"Yes. This new development is interesting for all of us," Knight responded. "In fact, some of us on the board have been expecting it and waiting patiently for it for some time now. John George Mortimer is a business legend, and there's no doubt he's developed a successful company, but he's aging and seems to be losing his competitive edge. Some of us think Multima Corporation would benefit from someone new running the company, someone more creative and energetic."

Interesting start, Wendal thought. "Sounds like you may welcome a leadership change," he said.

"Some of us think that might rejuvenate the business," Knight responded. "And let me say, Wendal, some of us are thinking about you as a potential CEO candidate. Do you want it?"

Wendal tried to suppress an audible gulp for air as the resounding importance of this question registered.

Desperately, he tried to process both the suggestion and its implications to structure an appropriate response. Of course he wanted the job. Virtually every business executive in America would covet such a role. But he knew he should not appear too anxious or the price of Knight's support might go up.

"I wouldn't use the term 'want' because I remain satisfied working with my team in Miami. However, if offered such a position, a division president of Multima would be foolish not to consider it seriously," Wendal responded.

Right, Howard Knight thought. *He's trying to play the reluctant leader. We'll dispense with that crap immediately.*

"Let's not waste each other's time, Wendal. Those of us who are considering this issue have no time for games. If the board offers you the CEO position at Multima, will you accept it or not?"

"I might like to discuss a relocation of the corporate headquarters to Miami and perhaps other details, but I'd be very interested in the job," Wendal conceded.

"Good," Knight replied. "Pleased to learn you're willing if selected. But it's going to be imperative that we handle your succession to the CEO role very delicately if we want to win support from the entire board. Let me explain what's going on and how we'll need to prepare.

"This whole matter must remain totally under the radar. No information shared with anybody. Mortimer had us all sign some ridiculous binding confidentiality agreements. We're not supposed to disclose any details about his planned retirement. Sharing this with you already puts me in violation, and if anyone traces it back to me, there will be severe consequences. Are we clear?"

Wendal swallowed hard and quickly responded that he understood the ground rules. He had experienced some of Knight's 'severe consequences' a few years earlier. He certainly didn't want that to happen again.

As he listened, Randall was disarmed and surprised by both Knight's candor and his open declaration of apparent support. Tentatively, a broad smile took form as he digested both the extraordinary new information and implied assistance to catapult him into the most powerful position in the company.

There didn't seem to be any strings attached, and he couldn't immediately identify any new costs. It certainly appeared that Knight had become a secret ally in Wendal's career progression efforts. This development was truly a dramatic departure from bygone days.

"Now, Wendal," Knight said. "Tell me about some of the exciting new projects you and your team are working on down there in Miami."

Without a moment's hesitation, he began. For the next fifteen minutes, Wendal articulated an idea that had been incubating in his mind for several weeks. It was a radical plan, an idea he had previously been reluctant to discuss with his CEO because he knew Mortimer would have serious reservations.

This conversation created an opportunity to move that far-reaching idea forward. Now, he could ferret out waste and duplication of human resources that cost Multima enormously every year. Should his ambitious idea win the support of the board, hundreds of millions of dollars more would flow to the bottom line profits every year. Not a bad circumstance for a new CEO.

Wendal sensed this might be an ideal time to enlist the support of the board to re-engineer basic operations in the Multima Supermarkets division, realizing profits dramatically higher with advanced technologies. As he outlined his idea to Knight, Wendal grew convinced this opportunity was the golden chance he had been seeking. Further, the exercise would showcase the diverse talent and technical brilliance of management throughout his division.

Most crucially, it might also be an opportunity to move right to the top of the Multima organization chart in a role he unquestionably deserved.

THREE

Venture Capital Investments' offices, New York.
Almost midnight, February 18, 2016

Howard Knight was relieved to be back in his office after an exhausting business day. Using the VCI business jet, he started with a three-hour flight from New York early in the morning, then another three for his return from Fort Myers. In between, he had participated in that momentous meeting of the Multima board of directors when John George Mortimer divulged his shocking and company-changing retirement plans.

His conversation with Wendal Randall concluded this unusual day in a peculiarly satisfying way.

Mortimer's disclosure of his imminent retirement as CEO of Multima Corporation was a development Knight had privately predicted and anticipated with increasing eagerness for more than a year. He had detected small signs of fatigue starting to appear in Mortimer's facial expressions and body language. Further, he wasn't entirely satisfied with some of Mortimer's recent decisions. The CEO was aging, and with the onset of advancing years, even the most successful business legends lose a little of that intangible mystique that sets them apart.

Howard Knight knew his call with Wendal Randall involved high personal risks. Nevertheless, he was certain Randall would keep it confidential. That was not a problem. The real issue was Randall's judgment. It had some major flaws.

Knight grimaced as he recalled with distaste a nasty issue back in Wendal Randall's college days. That unsavory problem had gurgled to the surface during the delicate negotiations with Multima Corporation to buy Wendal's failing company.

Of course, some understandable factors led to the incident. Wendal was the consummate geek throughout his teen years. Addicted to technology and electronic games, he barely experienced what most people would consider a normal social life. In fact, he never learned how to relate to women. He had never dated, even in college. So it was somewhat understandable that his one college sexual adventure went terribly awry.

It was a shame Randall hadn't been able to adequately contain the damage. Instead, Knight was forced to use external resources to make the problem go away. He was now out of pocket more than one hundred thousand dollars. Of even greater importance, he also owed The Organization something in return. This new development with Multima might help to settle that lingering obligation. After a decade of patience, the Multima Project appeared ready to bring those lucrative investment returns The Organization desperately craved.

It had been a long time coming. Knight originally conceived his idea to acquire Multima Corporation more than a decade ago while laboring in his office at Venture Capital Investments. For months, he meticulously toiled through detailed investment research to absorb everything he could about the Multima empire.

First, he pored over corporate presentations, annual reports, and analyst recommendations. Then, he learned the company structure, who owned shares, how the board of directors governed the company, and even how John George Mortimer's thought process seemed to work. Additionally, he thoroughly investigated the personal backgrounds of all senior members of Multima's management team.

Knight scrutinized Multima's many business successes and even managed to identify a few strategic errors. Back in those days of mind-numbing research and investigation, Howard Knight probably knew more about Multima than any individual outside the company. Moreover, he liked what he saw.

When Knight learned about Wendal and his struggling company, he recognized he might have the desired investment carrot to entice Mortimer. He had been confident that Mortimer eventually would agree to almost anything to gain control of that tiny, failing logistics firm headed by an owner who also happened to be *the* technology genius of his generation.

It had been a grinding process to put the transaction together, but his prediction had proven correct. Mortimer eventually agreed to surrender a good chunk of Multima's ownership control to acquire Wendal Randall and his little technology company.

VCI's billion-dollar investment to purchase fifteen percent of all Multima Corporation preferred shares had been steep. To date, the return on that investment had been adequate. However, The Organization didn't invest its money to earn just adequate returns. They expected stellar results every time.

Now, it looked like a genuine payoff might be around the corner. With Mortimer relinquishing day-to-day management of the company, Knight was poised to implement some drastic new corporate operating policies that could genuinely benefit The Organization. Wendal Randall would become an essential component of such changes, and his ascension to the position of CEO was crucial.

With more than $150 million per week flowing through Multima Supermarkets, he could only imagine the limitless opportunities to move and conceal money that otherwise might be problematic. The Organization already had a patchwork of solutions to hide and launder cash, but this opportunity might become the golden goose they had craved for an entire generation—a respected and visible company where no one would suspect money laundering activities.

At last, the ultimate success of his plan to control Multima Corporation appeared achievable. Of course, Knight would need to ensure that Randall and his colleagues performed well in the little management transition charade Mortimer was trying to stage.

Knight would also need to do some work with other members of the board of directors to influence the outcome. Nevertheless, he knew his plan to please The Organization required Wendal Randall to become chief executive officer. For the next few months, at least, Knight vowed to keep a close eye on him to avoid any further nasty surprises like that sordid mess with the college girl.

His mission would be to ensure there were no surprises at all. The Organization didn't react well to bad news, and Howard Knight had no desire to test the patience of the powerful interests he served.

FOUR

Fort Myers, Florida.
February 23, 2016

John George Mortimer confidently strolled towards his car parked outside his elegant home on Caloosa Drive. It was ten minutes before the scheduled start of his meeting with the three division presidents and small executive staff at Multima Corporation's headquarters.

Initially, some found it curious that Mortimer chose to relocate to a somnolent locale like Fort Myers. Many considered the mid-sized city on the west coast of Florida mainly a community catering to seasonal 'snowbirds' seeking relief from the miserable weather of their northern habitats. But Mortimer loved to spend time at his waterfront home on the slow-moving and aimlessly winding Caloosahatchee River. It was only a mile from the picturesque locations Thomas Edison and Henry Ford had both selected to build their winter estates a century earlier. He considered it an honor to reside in the same neighborhood those legendary icons of American business once called home.

John George had purchased his property several years earlier. Initially, he had used this home as a seasonal retreat until he made the big decision to relocate permanently from Atlanta. He loved the year-round Florida sunshine and warm, almost tropical, climate. Plus, he favored the idea of locating Multima's corporate offices away from the three operating divisions to reduce his personal involvement in day-to-day operations.

Lightheartedly, he had noted that Fort Myers successfully worked as corporate headquarters for such diverse companies as fashion retailer Chico's, medical specialist 21st Century Oncology, and media publisher Source Interlink Companies. If it could work for them, it would work for his small team that provided oversight for the three operating divisions of Multima Corporation.

This will be a significant day, he thought as he opened the door to his car. With a gentle press of the ignition button, the engine started, and he smoothly engaged the transmission of his BMW Z435 convertible.

This splendid sports car was one of his few indulgences and a recent purchase. With sparkling black metallic paint and a seven-speed double clutch transmission, it was eye-catching and fun to drive. Mortimer accelerated quickly and swung the vehicle out from the cobblestone driveway onto Caloosa Drive. Then he turned left onto McGregor Boulevard and cruised toward his office with the top down, his hair blowing freely in the wind.

John George actually enjoyed the brief commute. It always stimulated his senses. He admired the swaying royal palm trees that majestically lined both sides of McGregor Boulevard leading to the city center. He was always in awe of the elegant and graceful motion of the palm leaves swaying in a seemingly permanent breeze wafting from the Gulf of Mexico.

He thought the scene appeared almost choreographed and smiled as he considered the irony of naming Fort Myers the 'City of Palms'. The royal palm tree wasn't indigenous to Florida, and few people realized that Thomas Edison had originally imported them to Fort Myers by barge from nearby Cuba around the beginning of the twentieth century.

Regardless, such regal trees decorated the route towards the center of an evolving city that Mortimer appreciated. Still, Fort Myers' current leaders were working diligently to rejuvenate the core and create a unique municipal persona to compete with several other redeveloped and equally appealing cities along Florida's increasingly popular southwest coast.

He recalled the previous evening's spectacular sunset as he drove. Fiery shades of red and brilliant orange with a soft background of yellow had all formed a colorful mosaic. The sky became a dramatic contrast with the dark and brooding blue of the Caloosahatchee as it journeyed towards the Gulf.

It was another powerful reminder of the many good personal reasons John George had decided to make Fort Myers home. It also served to reinforce his earlier conclusion. It had become time to enjoy more golf, more travel for pleasure, and more Florida sunsets. Of course, full indulgence would need to come later, after this newly diagnosed challenge with cancer achieved the remission stage.

For a few moments, wistful thoughts about his contented private life were overshadowed by a gnawing concern about the upcoming surgery and underlying reasons for the meeting he was about to conduct, but he forced himself to set aside his health to focus on final preparation for the imminent session with his team of direct reports.

He knew this meeting would be crucial, perhaps one of the single most significant in his long career. John George realized it would be paramount to choose his words carefully and manage his body language with care. For his strategy to play out as hoped, the potential CEO candidates must not become aware of either his illness or intention to retire. So, he had planned for this day with his usual attention to detail.

The cancer diagnosis triggered doubts about his ability to continue leading the company. After receiving the dreaded news, Mortimer spent several days evaluating his options before meticulously formulating a strategy. He decided to retire from the company at the end of June. The end of his storied career would coincide with the last day of Multima's fiscal year.

However, he was not ready for the world at large to learn about such a crucial decision. Instead, he wanted to hold all the cards when it came time to name a successor. That might not be possible, should the business media start to speculate openly about potential candidates to succeed him and possibly short-circuit his personal preference.

Even worse, his diagnosis was serious. Should they become aware of this motivation for him to retire, the board of directors might even choose to remove him and appoint interim leadership immediately. Thus, his recent secret disclosure to the board concealed his health concerns and instead focused on a proposal for a covert contest to select his replacement.

Today, he earnestly wanted to avoid giving any signal about the upcoming surgery or the resignation timetable he'd shared with his board. On the other hand, he was anxious to convey the importance of their assignments eloquently. It was crucial that the three division presidents approach their upcoming projects with a collective sense of urgency to make the plan work. It had to work, because Mortimer fully expected one of them to be chosen CEO by the board.

Mortimer usually read the people on his board and their individual quirks quite well. He was confident each would undertake seriously his or her responsibility to choose someone with all the attributes necessary to lead a successful multi-billion dollar corporation.

John George had also incessantly focused the board's attention on Multima's business culture over many years. There was already broad acceptance among directors that his successor should be someone from within the corporation, and everyone accepted his several good reasons an executive with practical experience leading a Multima business unit should become CEO. However, John George knew some board members harbored lingering concerns about the bench strength of supporting management in the operating units.

While he thought all directors clearly recognized the genius of Wendal Randall, some had quietly expressed apprehension about the depth and practical business skills of the technology-obsessed folks reporting to him. Although subordinates might be called 'direct reports' at Multima, the board recognized the nomenclature of second line management mattered little. Rather, it was the team's collective leadership skills that would determine future successes should the board pluck Wendal from their division to head the entire corporation.

While the brilliance of James Fitzgerald in all matters financial was unquestioned, Mortimer knew the board sometimes perceived the style of his direct reports at Multima Financial Services as somewhat methodical and plodding.

Meanwhile, Suzanne Simpson's polished people skills and larger than life personality had become legendary at Multima Supermarkets. As a consequence, some board members quietly wondered if it would be possible to maintain the unit's stellar level of labor harmony and unwavering employee loyalty should Suzanne leave the business.

These insights about the board's concerns were underlying factors in the way John George molded his succession plan. It would be crucial that the three management teams identify outstanding new business initiatives to radically overhaul their business units. It was equally essential for each of them to develop powerful new ideas and present them succinctly to the board of directors for review and approval. Indeed, Mortimer wanted the three division presidents to treat this project as career defining. Creating such urgency would be his mission today.

If the division presidents successfully rose to this challenge and impressed the board with their business acumen, Mortimer had little doubt his preferred candidate would ultimately seize the opportunity and outshine the others. That would make it easier for the board to endorse his choice. It would also make it easier for him to step away from the CEO role and transition to private life as just a major shareholder.

As Mortimer made the left turn from McGregor Boulevard onto Altamont Avenue, he quickly reviewed the division presidents and some characteristics he had observed working with them.

Wendal Randall was clearly the most technology-savvy of the group, and the way he looked, dressed, and acted conjured the commonly held image of a nerd. The MIT graduate lived up to all the advance billing Howard Knight had described before Multima's purchase of Wendal's company. Randall was quick thinking, fast-talking, and always showed an unusually high energy level. John George suppressed a smile as he tried to visualize Randall's brain churning restlessly as it perpetually processed data with lightning speed and spewed out streams of innovative ideas.

Wendal seemed to gush with enthusiasm and passion. Of course, all of the division presidents were smart, but Randall clearly and consistently exhibited the highest intellect. However, he occasionally failed to analyze his ideas with enough depth, causing a failure to assess all possible implications. No doubt that tendency contributed to the earlier financial problems that allowed Multima to take over his company. On the positive side, Wendal seemed aware of this limitation and appeared to have learned much from his previous mistakes.

He had responded positively when Mortimer injected Joseph Kowntz, his hand-picked financial operations leader, to control the purse strings of the newly acquired technology and logistics group. Not only did Wendal accept that requirement, but he also seemed to embrace the new circumstance. Apparently, he now consulted with Kowntz and tested ideas with him before implementing them or making proposals to the board.

Randall would almost certainly be a first choice as a CEO candidate with several directors, and he would respond with enthusiasm to the challenge Mortimer was about to issue. In fact, Randall's sole difficulty might be limiting ideas to just one. He would need to do that first, and then precisely focus his direct reports around a single concept to create enough structure and detail to sell it to the board.

Wendal should be alright with the assignment and would probably welcome an opportunity to demonstrate his considerable creativity and intellect. From a big picture perspective, some on the board might still wonder if he lacked consistently grounded business judgment.

James Fitzgerald might need an extra jolt, John George mused as his thoughts shifted to the president of Multima's Financial Services division. Fitzgerald projected the classic, clean-cut image of a seasoned and highly successful executive. Tall, handsome, fit, and usually dressed in finely tailored suits, he always carried himself with confidence and poise.

James had joined Multima Supermarkets right after graduating near the top of his class at Harvard. During the following few years, he successfully earned his Certified Public Accountant credentials and quickly progressed through the management ranks of Multima Supermarkets, eventually becoming chief financial officer. He had been an extraordinary CFO.

He seemed to grasp all aspects of the financial world. From the subtle intricacies of financial markets through the mundane complexities of accounting and tax regulations, he had consistently demonstrated superior knowledge and almost total recall of minute details. What's more, Fitzgerald had another rare business attribute: vision.

To his credit, the idea to create a financial services company originated with James. He had clearly visualized the long-term value of generating greater customer loyalty by offering a credit card that customers could use to pay for purchases at Multima stores. He had articulated how the cards would become more powerful tools when used to reward customers.

Fitzgerald thought loyalty points should earn discounts or special prices for subsequent purchases, and he intuitively anticipated that many customers would also use their cards at many other merchants, generating attractive transaction fees for Multima with every purchase.

Well ahead of Mortimer, Fitzgerald had foreseen that about seventy percent of customers would pay their full outstanding credit card balance every month. The remaining thirty percent would make the minimum payment required and generate lucrative interest income on their balances. With interest charges calculated at about twenty percent annually, Fitzgerald demonstrated to Mortimer that Multima could almost double its net profits from annual supermarket sales by adding financial services to its business model.

When they all became convinced it could work, John George created an entirely new operating division, Multima Financial Services, and appointed James Fitzgerald to lead it. He had never disappointed. Every year, he and his team generated increasing profits. As forecasted, financial services made almost as much profit for Multima as the original supermarket business.

James Fitzgerald's decisions always seemed well considered. Then, his team intricately planned strategies and almost flawlessly executed them. The one potential board concern was Fitzgerald's direct reports.

John George recalled one director's candid comments over a drink. "They're all unquestionably accomplished, but they're also finance professionals with a little grayness to their style."

"What do you mean by that?" John George remembered inquiring.

"Every decision seems ponderous as key participants debate all identifiable risks, explore multiple execution strategies, and try to mitigate every risk. This approach works well in the financial services industry where loss mitigation is critical to success, but it also can make them appear dithering or indecisive," he said.

Just to be sure James Fitzgerald and his team would attach the requisite urgency to the upcoming assignment, Mortimer knew he must create an unusual twist. It was imperative Fitzgerald and his direct reports not only match but surpass the anticipated brilliance of the Wendal Randall team. He made a mental note to inject an extra jolt for James at the coming meeting.

Suzanne Simpson was the third key player in the drama Mortimer was trying to direct. If he were to describe her in one word, it would be 'extraordinary'. Among the top of her graduating class in the MBA program at Stanford, Suzanne had consistently demonstrated superior intellect and unwavering willingness to tackle any challenge.

She was so beautiful and poised that many wondered if she might have once been a beauty pageant candidate. But she would never have competed to become Miss America as she was from Canada. Actually, she was Québécoise, as she and other women from Quebec prefer to be called. Like many Québécoise, Suzanne exhibited a flair for fashion and elegance that set her apart from her colleagues, male or female.

More importantly, Suzanne displayed people skills that distinguished her from her peers. She consistently demonstrated a remarkable ability to recall instantly the name of almost every person she met. Thousands of them, it seemed. She projected an unusually positive outlook and exuded genuine warmth and enthusiasm in every personal encounter. She embodied the image of a 'people person'.

Mortimer thought she combined an outstanding intellect with an ability to consistently make and execute tough decisions. The result was a business leader who became president of a Canadian supermarket chain before the age of thirty-five, then president of Multima Supermarkets soon after John George Mortimer acquired her company a dozen years earlier.

The board of directors knew Suzanne's direct reports well. Her management style emphasized teamwork, and she always highlighted accomplishments of those reporting to her in presentations to the board. She also invariably invited some member of her management team to join her for board meetings, the only division president to do so.

Mortimer expected that most directors would become comfortable with the bench strength and business acumen of more than one member of Suzanne's team. Nevertheless, an important question lingered. Could the directors picture a woman—even one of her stature—as head of a corporation as large and complex as Multima? Regrettably, as with most other boards in America, he had seen strains of conservative reluctance among a few of his directors.

He had little doubt Suzanne would rise to the challenge and find a superior solution to the project Mortimer was about to demand. She was also sensitive to minute shifts in the economy and would probably tilt intuitively towards the urgency Mortimer would request. He could remain confident that Suzanne Simpson and her team would present formidable competition for the two male division presidents.

All factors considered, he was growing increasingly confident the board of directors would reach a consensus on the candidate he felt most suited to move into the crucial role of chief executive officer.

Adequately reassured, John George arrived at the nondescript four-story building that housed Multima Corporation's headquarters in downtown Fort Myers. He parked in the outdoor lot and paused a moment to gaze out over the slow-moving body of water. As he collected his thoughts, he drew in a deep breath of the clear, refreshing Gulf of Mexico air carried up the Caloosahatchee River on a gentle breeze.

He closed the BMW convertible top, locked the doors, and strode with purpose towards the building. He was off to chair a very interesting meeting.

FIVE

Multima Corporation Headquarters, Fort Myers, Florida.
February 23, 2016

Everyone was standing around informally chatting with each other in the conference room as they waited for him to arrive. Upon entering, he completed his gregarious handshake welcomes and pats on the shoulders with each member of the team in his typically relaxed manner.

As usual, John George Mortimer then sat at the head of the long, polished mahogany conference table and glanced around the spacious and tastefully decorated room. As everyone took a seat, he organized his final thoughts.

A couple years earlier, he had begun using video conferences for these monthly meetings to review each unit's progress. The cost savings were dramatic. His direct reports also gained more time to focus on their individual responsibilities with less time required for travel. Therefore, his request for all participants to attend this meeting in person signaled its importance.

Wendal Randall's home base was closest. That morning, his flight on the Multima Logistics' Learjet 85 took only a bit more than a half hour to travel from Miami to the Page Field private jet port in Fort Myers.

Suzanne Simpson's trip on the Multima Supermarkets' Bombardier Global 5000 jet was a little longer. She needed about two hours from Atlanta.

James Fitzgerald started his day in Chicago with a four a.m. wake-up call. After his morning preparations, he had more than an hour's drive to meet his Multima Financial Services' Bombardier Challenger 300 for a three-hour trip to Fort Myers.

All the other meeting participants were senior operational support executives who helped John George Mortimer oversee his profitable empire, and they worked from this Fort Myers office and lived in the area.

Alberto Ferer, a skillful corporate attorney, served as general counsel at Multima Corporation and was a director on the board. As general counsel, he was the senior legal expert in the corporation and advised both management and the board of directors on legal matters.

Wilma Willingsworth, as Multima Corporation's chief financial officer, also served on the board. Considered among the hundred most influential women in America, she impressed Mortimer every day with her knowledge of the complex financial markets. Her passion for regulatory accounting compliance was an obsession.

Only Alberto and Wilma were already aware of the meeting's purpose and general tone because they were among the directors of the board previously sworn to secrecy about his imminent retirement.

Mortimer noticed that they looked calm, natural, and relaxed. Nothing in their body language projected anything unusual or suggested undercurrents of change, and both appeared to have put on their game faces. He was confident neither would divulge, in either word or action, a single morsel more than Mortimer himself was about to relate.

Edward Hadley was the only other attending executive who reported directly to Mortimer. He was Multima Corporation's vice president of corporate and investor affairs, but not a member of the board of directors. Like the division presidents, this would be his first knowledge of Mortimer's assignments. Managing Edward's natural inquisitiveness would be important.

Mortimer respected Hadley's desire to understand intimately every aspect of the corporation's activities to be sure the information he provided to investors and business media was both accurate and timely, but his tendency to pose persistent questions might inadvertently kindle curiosity among other meeting participants. If Hadley headed down that path today, it might become awkward and complicate the strategy. He would need to be neutralized early in the discussion.

John George Mortimer started his unusual meeting with monthly rituals. First, he asked each of his direct reports to brief the assembled group about results of business activities within their span of control, including an outlook for future performance. He listened intently to their remarks.

Wilma Willingsworth provided her customary thirty-minute overview of the consolidated company financial results for the previous month and fiscal year to date. At the end of her presentation, John George applauded her team's successful efforts to streamline and simplify complex performance charts and graphs.

Alberto Ferer delivered his monthly legal advice to management. This month's focus was potential liabilities related to employee injuries in the workplace. His twenty-minute dissertation reminded all executives of their personal, as well as corporate, obligation to ensure employee workplace safety committees met regularly. "Such importance also means that business unit management teams should seriously consider this feedback," he had drily ended.

Edward Hadley made a short presentation about a video Multima Corporation had recently produced to inform employees about a new payroll deduction program and to encourage them to purchase shares in Multima Corporation.

In turn, each division president made a half-hour PowerPoint presentation highlighting the performance of their respective businesses during the month just completed, comparing actual results with the annual budget plan. They discussed both positive and negative results with specific comments about how they intended to address any weaknesses. None of the three divisions reported any alarming variances to the budget plan or surprises.

Another example of just how proficient this management team has become, Mortimer thought as the regular meeting agenda concluded. All attention immediately shifted towards his usual summary comments.

"No doubt you've been wondering why I asked you all to meet here in Fort Myers today rather than simply by video conference," Mortimer started. "There are three reasons. First, I want to underscore the importance and time-sensitivity of the subject I'm about to discuss with you, and I cannot over-emphasize that urgency as we meet here today.

"Second, I've become increasingly convinced our economy will soon experience a downturn even worse than the great recession we suffered during the financial crisis of 2008. I believe this could have grave consequences for the future of Multima.

"Finally, before we break today, I want to be sure each division is crafting a game-changing strategy to do much more than merely survive this downturn. Rather, I want every unit poised to catapult Multima to an entirely new level of profitability. Let me outline my thoughts.

"You will all remember the information Warren Wrigletts shared with us at the Ritz-Carlton in Naples last month. You'll also recall my introduction when I explained why I respect him so highly. He is more than a Nobel Prize winner. He's one of those rare economists who gets it right most of the time. And, as you all know, I place considerable importance on that valuable quality." He smiled wryly, and paused to let his direct reports make the implied connection between this comment and his well-known expectation that they never make the same mistake twice.

"Since his presentation to us," Mortimer resumed, "I've had three follow-up conversations with Warren. I've examined and challenged every one of his assumptions. He convinced me that we'll see a more than four-percent drop in national economic output next year. That suggests an increase in unemployment of more than two percent and negative growth for six to eight quarters starting next calendar year.

"If we use 2008 as a comparison, this could create a drop in top-line Multima sales revenue of more than twenty percent. Bottom line profits could reduce by double that. And it might take up to five years for us to return to our current levels of sales revenue and profits.

"I hope you'll all agree such a circumstance is simply not acceptable. As I listened to your monthly presentations, it was apparent you've all heeded Wriglett's warnings to some extent, and you've already identified some belt-tightening measures to manage expenses better during the coming downturn. For that, I commend you.

"But we need to go much, much further and far more quickly than any of you have planned. So today will be one of those rare occasions when I vary from our typical consensus-building approach to making decisions. Instead, I'm going to invoke executive privilege to issue a top-down directive." He paused again to allow adequate time for his audience to process his message.

"At this point, Edward, I'd like you to turn off your recording device because I am also going to invoke our prerogative for secrecy related to crucial corporate strategic planning. There will be no public comment on the information we're about to discuss. In fact, Alberto has prepared a standard confidentiality agreement for each of you to sign before you leave. And you'll have all your direct reports sign a similar document before you brief them about your individual projects.

"Take note. Any violation of this confidentiality agreement provides for immediate dismissal from the company. I expect full compliance from you and your direct reports with all of the terms of this legally binding document."

He looked intently around the table, trying to gauge the reaction of the participants. Suzanne Simpson had straightened her back and raised her chin, signaling full concentration and alertness to hear and absorb every word. James Fitzgerald had picked up his pen, prepared to make his usual detailed notes about the message to come. Wendal Randall revealed only a tiny outline of a smile as he leaned forward, tilted his head, and projected a keen interest. Mortimer continued.

"Every economic downturn has winners and losers. During the coming recession, I want Multima to emerge as an absolute winner. I've shared with you the ugly picture of the economy that Warren Wrigletts has painted and the negative impact this could have on the corporation and our individual operating divisions.

"I've discussed that view with our board of directors. I've also imparted my strongly held opinion that we can alter that forecasted trajectory with appropriate action. The board agrees. Let me describe my vision for Multima Corporation as we emerge from an economic downturn two or three years down the road.

"As you know, we are in a flush cash position that's far healthier than our competitors. We're confident that our operating costs in the supermarket division are now the lowest in the business. Our board agrees it's time for us to use this strong financial position to catapult the company to a new level, and the board shares my conviction that each division must make an extraordinary contribution for us to succeed.

"I see a corporation that continues to grow top-line revenue by five to ten percent each year in each unit, despite a potentially brutal recession. I picture annual sales twenty-five percent higher than we currently have. We'll do it by the end of 2019, and we'll do it despite a recession. I see us actually increasing profits during the same period by one or two percent per year, with annual profits six percent higher than we enjoy now by the end of 2019. I see a company with almost one billion in cash, ready to buy competitors who failed to plan and execute as efficiently as Multima.

"With a couple quality strategic acquisitions in 2019 and 2020, we'll be able to double the revenue of Multima within a five-year period, with annual profit levels increasing proportionately within seven years. By the end of 2020, we should be doing business all along the eastern seaboard of the United States and Canada, and rank among the top three supermarket chains in the country. But none of this vision is possible unless we dramatically alter the current direction of our company.

"We won't double our size by doing the same things we've been doing, despite the fact we do those things better than most of our competitors. We can succeed, and we will reach our goals if we develop strategic growth plans for each business unit that are absolute game changers. We'll succeed if we completely re-invent our existing business model and leap-frog ahead of our competitors. Such a fundamental redefinition is what I need each of our units to do. We have to execute these new strategies more quickly than we've ever implemented plans before.

"Today, I'm asking each division president to meet with your teams. Describe the scope and urgency of the task for them and elicit their support to create one single strategic initiative to re-invent their business unit and achieve the ambitious goals I've just described. We're going to move quickly. This project will become your single greatest priority over the next sixty days. Each division will articulate a detailed plan—one that is ready for approval and execution—for us to review at the April twenty-third board meeting.

"We want you to involve all of your key direct reports. I would also like you to include at least three of your senior people to present and sell your plan to the board. As usual, presentations should include full costs and execution timelines and should be limited to thirty minutes. Most important, the strategies must be absolute game changers that will re-define how your unit will do business in the future. One last thing, your plan should be one you can fully implement within sixty days of board approval."

Mortimer paused once again to let his audience absorb this information. He tried to gauge the immediate reaction of the division presidents. Each was apparently already deeply absorbed in thought, processing the message, and seemingly already mentally developing next steps and necessary action. There were no questions.

They appeared to sense that the deliberate generality of the required game changer projects, combined with such an urgent call to action, was a test of his or her team for some purpose. With satisfaction, Mortimer watched facial expressions tighten, postures stiffen slightly, and heads gradually tilt upwards in acceptance of the challenge. Although none should be aware of it, the competition to succeed John George Mortimer was now officially underway.

In closing, he pledged the resources of his team at headquarters to provide any needed financial information or technical support as the business units developed their plans. He reminded all participants that he would conduct the March monthly meeting by video conference and wished each division president success with their assignments. Then he stood, signaling the end of the meeting. Warm parting handshakes followed. With the last brief farewell, he left the conference room, walked purposefully down the corridor, entered an elevator, and left the building.

Within minutes, the three division presidents were sharing a Multima limousine to nearby Page Field to board their respective company jets. At the airport, an informal procession formed as their aircraft taxied towards departure.

In flight, they each mulled over the sixty days ahead.

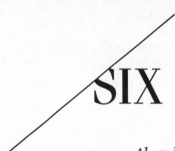

SIX

Aboard a Lear jet between Fort Myers and New York.
February 23, 2016

Wendal Randall knew his first call must be to VCI. Knight had made it clear that he expected regular updates on any communication with John George Mortimer, as well as regular progress reports on Multima Logistics' game changer assignment. To assure relative secrecy while using their cell phones or email, Knight had created a code name for the project: Operation Bright Star.

With no attempt to stifle his satisfaction, Wendal smiled at the irony of this code name as he pressed the speed dial on his smartphone. Almost immediately, he connected with Howard Knight in his New York office.

"The meeting went exactly as you predicted. No surprises," Wendal announced without any formal greeting.

"Thanks, Wendal. Tell me, how are your whiz kids progressing on Operation Bright Star?"

"Alright, but we hit one snag," he responded. "You'll remember the pivotal driver is to get rid of traditional checkouts and cash registers and replace them with electronic devices at the point of sale. The company we intended to buy the new devices from won't work out. We visited them last week and learned they have a severe backlog already, with no ability to ramp up production for at least fifteen months. Too late for us to deliver a solution for Mortimer's deadline."

"How do you fix this?"

"We have another source in Düsseldorf, Germany," Wendal explained. "That company has supplied automated check-outs to a large retailer in Europe, and our sources are confident they'll have adequate capacity to meet our needs. We have a technology team over there right now just to be sure their software is compatible with ours. I'm also planning to visit them in Düsseldorf to meet their management team and negotiate a final contract."

"Is there any reason to expect their software will not be compatible with Multima's?" Knight asked with a slightly anxious tone.

"Only a small chance," Randall responded. "It's a German company with strong connections to PAS Inc., our software provider, and one of the biggest suppliers in the world. Fortunately, the large retailer in Europe who bought their check-outs is using a version of PAS software only two generations earlier than ours. But I thought it best to have our experts complete a thorough assessment before we're too far along this path, just to be sure there are no surprises later."

"Good idea. What time does your speaking engagement end today? I'd like to meet for dinner if possible and hear more about the Mortimer meeting."

"I should finish about five o'clock."

"Let's meet in the lobby of the Waldorf-Astoria at seven. I know a little Italian place nearby where we can have a good meal. I'd like to learn more about Operation Bright Star," Knight said.

Knight hung up without another word, an abrupt end to their conversation. *Curious*, thought Wendal, *how his manner has become so assertive in just a few days*. Wendal made a mental note to approach their dinner conversation with extra caution.

SEVEN

Aboard a Bombardier jet traveling towards Atlanta.
February 23, 2016

It was rare for Suzanne Simpson to be the sole passenger on such a trip, but Mortimer's invitation expressly required that she travel alone. Now, she comfortably curled up in her preferred swiveling and reclining leather chair on the Multima Supermarkets' executive jet.

She would usually take advantage of the two-hour flight to digest what seemed to be a constant stream of reports, summaries, and data prepared by her management team and support staff. She had a voracious appetite for reading and took pride in her awareness of most issues impacting her business. But today she felt compelled to review the meeting with John George Mortimer and the game changer assignments he had mandated.

First, she was perplexed about the meeting dynamics. Why had Mortimer found it necessary to summon the division presidents to Fort Myers? There had been no significant time for discussion or personal interaction with him. In fact, there was little interaction among the division presidents after Mortimer announced his strategy. It seemed the only purpose to meet in person was to underscore the assignment's importance. Such an approach seemed out of character for the CEO.

The news about some deterioration in the economy was not new either. After all, Wrigletts had presented the same data and dispatch of alarm to the division presidents and their teams at the Ritz-Carlton offsite meeting a month earlier.

Finally, and uncharacteristically, Mortimer had not encouraged— in fact, had not even permitted—more discussion about possible alternative solutions. His rationale for a game-changing strategy made plausibly sound business sense. Without a doubt, he considered the forecasted economic malaise a unique opportunity to expand Multima Corporation significantly at the expense of financially weaker competitors.

A fundamental question lingered. Why such urgency to put a vitally crucial plan into place within an almost impossibly compressed sixty-day window? Wouldn't it be more prudent to take whatever time was needed to create, develop, and execute the best possible strategy?

After thinking about it, she decided there simply had to be other issues at play, factors that would probably need more investigation. Regardless of the background for it, the challenge to develop a game changer strategy remained. She would circle back later to devote more time and research to the motivation for Mortimer's assignment with such an urgent call to action.

Instead, she preferred to focus on which game changer project might be appropriate, and how to guide her management team to prepare for it. She was already moderately sure where the team would focus and its preferred path to capture a competitive advantage in the supermarket business.

Over the past three months, several of her direct reports had approached her with discoveries from a book titled *The China Study*. There had already been long, and sometimes animated, internal discussions about the book's conclusions.

The China Study detailed some startling implications for diet, weight loss, and long-term health. Immediately upon release of the book, food industry spokespeople successfully suppressed publicity about the book by marginalizing the author's findings. However, over the past few months, Netflix, PBS, and CNN all broadcasted widely viewed programs about the book. As a result, it had experienced a remarkable resurgence in popularity with renewed awareness about its main messages.

Some of her direct reports were convinced that increased interest in the book had already influenced many Americans to reconsider their lifestyles. They argued such changes could have far more impact on Multima Supermarkets' profits than Warren Wrigletts' prediction of a coming economic downturn.

The findings articulated in *The China Study* were certainly compelling. In fact, since re-reading the book during her recent Christmas vacation, even Suzanne had been re-assessing her diet and lifestyle. It pointed out that people living in the rural regions of China maintain primarily plant-based diets, eating vegetables, fruits, seeds, nuts, and legumes. The author compared foods consumed by rural Chinese with habits in Western countries. His findings established a clear statistical relationship between the consumption of meat, dairy, and related animal fats with exceptionally high rates of cancer and heart disease.

In fact, *The China Study* observed that Chinese living in the countryside usually die from other illnesses. Heart disease and cancers found in America are comparatively rare in the remote regions of China. Even more startling, evidence showed that greater affluence in Chinese cities now has more people drinking milk and eating larger quantities of meat. With this increased consumption of animal fats, researchers found an alarming rise in the incidence of several different cancers and heart disease. Simply stated, the book made a convincing argument for a total change in American diets, a switch to plant-based foods, and the elimination of all meat and dairy products.

Should significantly more consumers change their diets, reducing meat consumption while increasing their intake of vegetables and other plant-based foods, this could have dramatic and negative implications for Multima Supermarkets. Fresh fruit and vegetables represent only about ten percent of total supermarket sales. About twenty-three percent comes from meat, poultry, and fish. Processed foods, including dairy products, generate more than half of total supermarket revenues. *The China Study* tacitly dissuades American consumers from buying products that represent almost three-quarters of Multima Supermarkets' annual sales!

Already, there were early indications of such change. Whole Foods Markets, a competitor targeting health-conscious shoppers, seemed to be opening new stores almost everywhere, diluting Multima's share of the total market in every city it entered.

Further, Asian-American customers were increasingly showing a preference for independent or regional Chinese food stores with their broad selections of more familiar Asian foods. Such stores all seemed to operate with razor-thin gross profits, creating an added threat.

Recent focus group studies with randomly selected Multima customers in three major cities had demonstrated a common trend. They loved the look of Multima stores and liked the quality of service they were getting. However, there was a growing desire to do at least part of their weekly food shopping elsewhere for a better selection of healthier foods.

Several in the focus groups had strongly expressed their disappointment that Multima stores didn't regularly stock less common fresh vegetables like kale, Swiss chard, or bok choy. Affluent respondents, whether recent immigrants or not, had expressed displeasure that prepared foods like fresh sushi, kimchee, and dim sum were not readily available for purchase.

Suzanne processed this information, considered the implications, and concluded the time was right to escalate the level of discussion with her team. They needed to study seriously whether the game changer Mortimer was looking for might include a major reconfiguration of the Multima Supermarkets formula to address this apparent shift to healthier foods and increasing demand for Asian cuisine.

At the very least, they needed to find a strategy to avoid further loss of sales and the resulting erosion of profits to those new competitors apparently meeting customers' shifting preferences. With that conclusion, Suzanne reclined in her comfortable leather seat and extended her legs on the plush footrest. She was pulled back to the still tantalizing question: What was John George Mortimer trying to accomplish?

Perhaps equally important, why was the timeline so unusually short?

EIGHT

Aboard a Bombardier jet traveling towards Chicago.
February 23, 2016

James Fitzgerald was not at all pleased with the meeting or its outcome. First, it had been necessary to delay his Caribbean vacation to attend it. Originally, he had planned to take his family to Barbados that week. Monday was President's Day, and his two sons were home during a short break from college, so Fitzgerald had booked an exquisite villa on the sun-drenched west coast of Barbados, right next to the landmark Sandy Lane Hotel.

When John George Mortimer had asked him to attend the meeting in Fort Myers in person rather than by video conference, Fitzgerald decided his wife and two sons should leave for Barbados anyway. He then planned to use the Multima Financial Services' jet for the two-hour flight from Fort Myers to Bridgetown, Barbados, right after the meeting.

Now he was annoyed on two levels. First, the meeting should have been conducted by video conference. James could have indeed booked a communications facility in Barbados to watch Mortimer's performance. It would have been just as effective as being there in person because Mortimer had autocratically outlined an assignment for each division president without even a single opportunity to clarify objectives or articulate concerns. That alone was bad enough to raise some ire against his old friend.

But to also create such a short and arbitrary deadline for completion of the game changer assignment was completely out of character for Mortimer. Such inconsistencies underscored the reasons he was now heading north towards Chicago rather than south to Barbados. The windy city's weather might be unseasonably warm, but it still wasn't the Caribbean.

As soon as Mortimer used the term 'game changer' in his comments, Fitzgerald fully grasped the significance. In fact, the last time he heard John George use that expression was when James had proposed the creation of a financial services division some twenty-two years ago. He guessed Mortimer intended to inspire some similar stroke of genius from the division presidents. He knew him well enough to realize there must also be a compelling reason to create this sort of competition between them. Cooperation and cross-division teamwork had consistently been the mantra Mortimer emphasized throughout his career.

Why was all this happening right now? Was there some major change brewing within the corporation? Was John George finally starting to consider succession planning? Was the board nudging Mortimer in some new direction?

Regardless of possible answers, Fitzgerald reluctantly recognized that creativity and urgency to respond were not characteristics his team usually displayed. With less than two months to research, develop, and present a major game changer strategy, Fitzgerald knew he could ill afford a few days on the glorious beaches of Barbados with his family. Rather, he expected it to require every hour of every one of the fifty-nine remaining days to prepare for the crucial meeting with Multima's board of directors.

With that chilling thought, Fitzgerald glanced at his watch. He calculated that he would arrive at his office in just over three hours. He reached for the aircraft satellite telephone to call his assistant in Chicago and asked her to summon all his direct reports for a meeting at six o'clock that evening. No exceptions.

As an afterthought, he also requested she order lots of soft drinks, coffee, and sandwiches. The meeting might even last until midnight.

NINE

Howard Knight's dinner with Wendal Randall had been satisfying. The Sicilian veal Marsala with pasta was delicious. The two bottles of young Chianti were delectable. And Wendal had not disappointed with his almost verbatim report on John George Mortimer's soliloquy to describe the new game changer missions.

Wendal was entirely confident his team's Operation Bright Star project would dramatically respond to Mortimer's challenge. The newly identified technology firm in Düsseldorf seemed to have a product adequate for their needs, and it probably was a good idea for Wendal to visit that company to finalize negotiations quickly.

An early decision about a supplier for the new equipment and a confirmation of quick delivery would allow Wendal and his team to focus attention on their presentation to win the support of the board. That should put Wendal into the forefront of the competition to succeed Mortimer as CEO.

From Knight's perspective, Operation Bright Star certainly sounded appealing. As he understood Wendal's explanation, it would convert Multima Supermarkets from the current business model where cashiers processed all items and collected payments from the customer to an entirely automated point-of-sale model.

Using this new concept, customers would scan their purchases at the specially equipped point-of-sale machines. Then they would put all of their purchases in a bag and pay for them with cash, debit, or credit cards. Customers would do all the work! According to Wendal, this was unquestionably the wave of the future. Multima would still need a couple of people for every shift. These workers would help customers who encountered problems and assure all goods passed through an automated point-of-sale device as intended.

Wendal had enthusiastically explained that potential savings in labor costs were astronomical. With automated checkouts, they could eliminate thousands of cashier jobs. With a reduction in the number of employees, Multima would not only have direct savings in salaries, there would also be massive reductions in health insurance premiums, pensions, and other employee benefits.

Once they covered costs, millions of additional dollars would flow directly to bottom-line profits every year. Wendal guessed those savings to be in the hundreds of millions. He would know the precise number in a few days, after his team completed a detailed cost-benefit analysis of actual payroll and benefits data.

Wendal had explained that Multima would be the first American supermarket chain to automate the point-of-sale function completely. In his mind, this first-off-the-line strategy would help the company increase market share as well as profitability. It unquestionably qualified as a game changer.

There were still a couple hurdles to face. There was little doubt Mortimer and Suzanne Simpson would both oppose Operation Bright Star to some extent. Both were passionately loyal to employees of Multima Supermarkets and strenuously resisted the idea of layoffs or terminations to achieve higher profits.

Knight recalled a CBNN interview with Mortimer last November. At that time, national unemployment still hovered around five percent. When asked how many employees got termination slips at Multima during the great recession of 2008, Mortimer had emphatically responded with one word: "None."

Mortimer had gone on to offer his opinion. "Companies that reduce costs by slashing their number of employees are shortsighted. They're victims of a myopic business school dogma that thinks head-count cost reductions are the only sure path to improved profitability." Knight remembered him saying this with disdain.

Such resistance seemed only to be blind stubbornness in Knight's view. Many other companies had already boosted their profits by shedding unnecessary employees; it was not a strategy to ignore. But Mortimer would certainly voice intense resistance. Knight made a mental note to do some lobbying privately with Multima CFO Wilma Willingsworth. Financial people usually had more balanced views on these issues. It would be useful to win Willingsworth as a supporter of Operation Bright Star before Randall made his presentation to the board. Her opinion might become crucial to winning Mortimer over, or at least gaining the support of enough directors to counter his position should they fail to sway him.

The other potential hurdle was still Wendal Randall himself. Knight recognized his genius, particularly in the field of technology. He also was confident Randall's personality would be malleable enough to allow Knight some significant influence over future decisions Randall would make as CEO. Unquestionably, the nasty situation with the college girl still provided adequate leverage.

Knight knew he could use some of that sordid information to influence his behavior should Randall start to waiver. But might he require even more clout? With time running short, was it possible to bolster his control of Wendal Randall? He'd need to think about a way to achieve added assurance in the coming days.

As his chauffeured limousine headed towards his Park Avenue apartment, Knight reclined comfortably in the rear seat to reflect on the intricate steps it had taken to come this far.

Ironically, it had been several years since Knight first thought he had identified an opportunity to penetrate the ownership of Multima Corporation. It surfaced when a well-known supermarket chain in eastern Canada found itself in dire financial straits. The chain was surprisingly successful in the smaller Canadian business community. It enjoyed a high share of the market, had attractive modern stores, and used a sophisticated distribution system that efficiently served about a hundred stores in the provinces of Ontario and Quebec.

An unusual sequence of events had occurred soon after the newly appointed president and CEO concluded a thorough internal audit of the chain's books, using some newly hired financial experts. Those auditors discovered that previous management had been negligently raiding the company's pension funds for several years to prop up weaker than reported operating results.

The new CEO learned there were unfunded pension fund obligations of more than one billion dollars, with little hope of meeting future obligations to retiring employees. Beyond the legal requirements, it seems she felt a strong moral responsibility to long-serving employees. However, her analysis of the situation identified few strategic alternatives. After each possible path came to a dead-end, she reluctantly decided to look for a buyer for the company. She searched for a major corporation with enough financial strength to assume those unfunded pension obligations, one able to honor daunting financial commitments to its employees.

The CEO of the Canadian supermarket chain at that time was Suzanne Simpson, a darling of the Canadian business media, considered by many to be an executive with star potential. She had discreetly engaged investment bankers to identify American companies that might be willing suitors. During this process, an old investment banker friend contacted Howard Knight.

Initially, it had been a challenge to get John George Mortimer interested in the deal. There were dozens of markets more logical for expansion and much closer to Multima's Atlanta base and business roots. However, Knight persisted and eventually brought them together.

Surprisingly, after a single exploratory meeting with Simpson, John George Mortimer developed a keen interest in the Canadian company. Knight didn't immediately understand why. Whatever the reason, it took just a few weeks for Multima to complete the negotiations and take full control.

Knight tried to provide financing for that transaction. However, Mortimer had shown no interest. The Multima balance sheet was strong then, and Mortimer asserted he had no shortage of suitors ready, willing, and able to make acquisition loans with extremely attractive conditions. At that time, Knight was obliged to settle for a modest $10 million fee for Venture Capital Investments' role in finding and arranging the transaction.

Soon after that acquisition, Knight thought he understood Mortimer's dramatic transformation of interest in the Canadian super-market chain. Within just three months of closing the deal, Mortimer had quietly announced the promotion of Suzanne Simpson to president of the entire Multima Supermarkets division.

This rising star of Canadian business had somehow skillfully managed to keep her company virtually intact. More surprisingly, her new promotion made her the head of one of the most successful super-market chains in North America. Now, ironically, she was competing directly with Knight's preferred candidate to run the entire corporation.

As they approached his home, Knight's thoughts darted back to the excite-ment of potential opportunities. Yes, controlling Multima would undeniably create massive benefits. Money laundering would be just the start. What about the ability to require Multima Supermarkets to purchase from com-panies already owned or influenced by The Organization? Or the potential for some service and maintenance contracts with companies it controlled?

Was there also a chance to impose a pliable labor union at Multima Supermarkets, and then collect millions in union dues from employees every month? Such intriguing opportunities didn't scratch the surface of what might be possible in the other divisions. As Howard Knight cheer-fully stepped from the limousine into a brisk New York breeze, he could almost taste the sweet reward of long-awaited success.

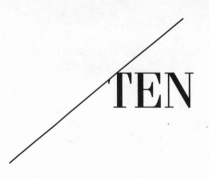

TEN

Suzanne Simpson and her team had just crossed the international dateline aboard the Multima Supermarkets Global 5000 business jet. They were nearing the halfway point in a flight segment between Anchorage, Alaska and the final destination, Haneda Airport in Tokyo, Japan.

The aircraft was cruising smoothly at Mach 0.85, a little less than 600 miles per hour ground speed, and was now about two hours out from Anchorage, where it had briefly landed to refuel. Suzanne had slept comfortably during much of the segment from Atlanta to Anchorage because she had purposefully scheduled the business jet flight for a Saturday evening departure.

Her plan was to sleep for a few hours on the flight, with an arrival in Tokyo early Monday morning. They would check-in at a hotel, then have a quick shower and change of clothes to prepare for a nine o'clock meeting with Japanese government officials. She intended to use every available hour in the country as productively as possible.

Suzanne and her fellow passengers had all enjoyed a tasty breakfast on the ground in Alaska while the aircraft refueled. The dining room décor in the private service area of the airport was sparse but clean, and cheerful staff had quickly prepared nutritious breakfasts. As hoped, within less than an hour they were all back in the air jetting towards Tokyo. Looking back, it seemed a good strategy to get some rest during that first segment of the trip, for the group now appeared cheerful and alert on departure.

Immediately after takeoff from Alaska, they established small discussion groups to finalize objectives and strategies for meetings with the Japanese government and agricultural and business interests. The past couple hours had been productive, but the team now paused for a short break while associates in Atlanta transmitted additional data via satellite.

Back at the business unit headquarters, a large team would work shifts to provide continuous coverage throughout the trip. Suzanne and her team could retrieve data or relay information at any time. Moreover, they could carry out vitally required consumer research within hours.

Now, as Suzanne sipped a second cup of green tea, she had a few moments to relax until the groups reconvened. She started to think about how well circumstances worked out sometimes.

———————

Almost every working day, Suzanne was grateful John George Mortimer had the support of the board to buy this new generation Bombardier Global 5000 business jet. Last year, they debated intensely about the need for a larger aircraft, one with both longer flight ranges and greater passenger capacity. Despite the significantly higher cost, the board eventually acceded to her request because Suzanne convincingly demonstrated her use of the jet as a productive operating strategy, as well as a cost-effective means of travel.

It was one tool to help create and then nurture a carefully considered business culture. In fact, Suzanne assiduously visited every store location, in every city, at least once per year. From the time she first joined the company, she had consistently encouraged not only her direct reports but also buyers and merchandisers to travel with her to visit Multima Supermarkets and competitors' stores. Most weeks found her spending one or two days out in the marketplace with four or five managers in tow.

She gained essential information listening to front-line store employees who deal with customers every day. This practice spawned a passionate loyalty among her employees. They genuinely valued Suzanne's willingness to listen to their comments and then quickly act on their frequent suggestions for improvements.

Suzanne also recognized that her visits to stores stimulated feverish activity for a few preceding days. Clerks labored to stock shelves to the brim. They imaginatively designed and built appealing product displays. Crews cleaned and polished meticulously to ensure their store was sparkling before her arrival. It worked. Suzanne always expressed her appreciation and applauded their efforts.

It turned out to be a good formula for increasing retail sales too. Customers valued those same store attributes in their supermarket shopping experience and bought more.

Suzanne usually learned what was working well in the stores and where there were challenges with operational processes, products, or shifting consumer preferences. Meanwhile, her travel companions would typically interview store employees, inspect merchandise displays, take photographs, and keep pace with how the local marketplace perceived the products they bought and promoted for sale.

Initially, she used a smaller aircraft, but the board gradually came to value the significant contribution these visits made to Multima's success. With the new larger plane, she could accommodate more travel companions. These days, there were often ten to fifteen associates in her entourage, each sharing the enriching experience.

Suzanne used blocks of time before and after such visits to hold meetings with her team. Typically, she would discuss strategies for each store tour, listen to each participant's concerns about that location, and learn particular statistics or trends spotted by her team. They did all this in flight and arrived prepared.

Immediately after visits, they discussed individual observations about the store, shared information, and decided on necessary action, often before they either deplaned for a subsequent store tour or returned to Fulton County Airport. As a result, questions, instructions, and information flowed from her aircraft to the division headquarters in Atlanta. There, Suzanne expected her team to react quickly, and they usually did.

This flight would be an exception, only due to its length. She designated the segment from Atlanta to Anchorage for a well-deserved rest because they had all been working almost non-stop since her meeting with John George Mortimer in Fort Myers three days earlier. Discussions had started as soon as Suzanne arrived at the Atlanta office and continued long into that first night.

She had correctly anticipated the interest of some direct reports in the lifestyle and diet issues raised in *The China Study*. As expected, those subordinates forcefully expressed their desire to develop a Multima Supermarkets strategy to respond to a growing consumer preference for fresh, non-processed, plant-based foods.

Somewhat surprisingly though, she found her team divided about the direction they should take and which project they should embrace to meet Mortimer's game changer challenge. Only half of Suzanne's team argued for a merchandising shift to focus on healthy plant-based foods. The other half was equally vociferous about their concerns with another trend.

That recent phenomenon showed a growing number of consumers buying products from big-box retailers or club warehouses with deep discounts rather than making their purchases at Multima. Such a tendency convinced some associates that low prices were now driving the market.

To keep pace, they argued, Multima needed to shift focus urgently and become an aggressive discounter.

Suzanne saw merit in both positions. She became convinced the trend towards more fresh vegetables, and a corresponding reduced consumption of meat and dairy, was not simply a fad. It was undoubtedly becoming a longer-term consumer shift, one her company would need to address.

However, she was equally mindful that a deep recession might increasingly force many modest wage earners to seek lower-priced foods, regardless of potential health risks, merely to survive financially during a severe economic downturn.

Despite Mortimer's admonishment to choose a single game changer strategy, Suzanne decided her team would pursue both potential options. For now, she'd monitor the evolution of both paths, and then choose the most compelling one for presentation to the board of directors. Nevertheless, both strategies would look to Asia for inspiration, advice, and potential business partnerships.

The day after John George Mortimer's meeting, Suzanne and her team were already arranging this overseas trip and scheduling meetings with business leaders in the Japanese food industry. They included sessions with government officials and private agricultural interests. At the last minute, they also scheduled a meeting with the president of Farefour stores in China.

Just before departure, Suzanne decided to invite six growers with sprawling operations in Florida. Multima Supermarkets enjoyed unusually long and close working relationships with them. With any shift in Multima merchandising focus towards more fresh fruit and vegetables, she would need the local growers to follow. Should such a swing include foods not commonly grown in America, they needed to be involved in this research as part of the solution.

In all, fourteen people accompanied her on this trip to undertake research and develop a strategy to meet Mortimer's directive. There were two representatives from each competing faction. The financial operations leader and store operations leader represented those who wanted deep discounts to compete more efficiently with the big-box retailers. The two other leaders, responsible for marketing and distribution respectively, both favored a shift towards healthier foods.

———————

With about three hours remaining in their flight to Haneda Airport, Suzanne intended to use every possible minute to fine-tune objectives, prepare presentations, and identify issues of concern. As planned, the contingent was gathering again in small groups to process and discuss new data received from the Atlanta headquarters moments earlier. It was time for Suzanne to resume her leadership role and be sure her team was as prepared as possible for the day to come.

She permitted herself one more diversion before continuing those discussions. Concern still lingered about John George Mortimer's motivation to initiate an apparent competition among the Multima divisions. For Suzanne, the whole idea seemed out of character. What had happened to his vaunted and well-liked consensus-building style of making important decisions? He usually insisted on getting things done right rather than fast. Why such a dramatic change now?

Over three days, Suzanne had occasionally revisited these same nagging questions, but she hadn't reached a conclusion that was anything more than pure speculation. Further, her generally reliable sources of information at Multima's office in Fort Myers either didn't know or weren't saying.

Suzanne wasn't sure of John George Mortimer's motivation for the game changer division projects, nor why he had created such an internal competition. However, she remained certain the outcome would be crucial for her team. This dilemma prompted her to ratchet up the intensity to find some truly revolutionary business strategies.

Briefly, she anticipated the delight a successful game changer strategy might bring for her team. Breakout success for Multima Supermarkets—success that doubled growth within five years—would change many things for them.

It would probably translate into tangible career enhancements with job promotions, earnings increases, and greater security for her management team and staff. New career paths would open. Her people should see more money and enjoy more satisfaction from their jobs.

As she convened the next round of discussions, such potential rewards for the team intensified her already high motivation.

ELEVEN

Aboard Lufthansa Flight LH401 to Frankfurt, Germany.
February 28, 2016

As Wendal Randall settled into the sumptuous leather seats of the Lufthansa Airlines first class section, he accepted the offered glass of chilled, quality champagne and ruminated about his current annoyance.

He didn't fly commercial airlines very often. He naturally used the Multima Logistics' Lear jet for most travel, but with every international flight found himself locked in an argument with Joseph Kowntz, his leader of financial operations. This Mortimer appointee protested that flying an aircraft and crew to Europe, then keeping them there for a week, made little economic sense. Further, it precluded use of the plane by other Multima Logistics management, requiring them to use expensive commercial flights while a high-priced jet sat idle on the ground in Europe.

To fly their aircraft to Germany with an immediate return to Miami, followed by a repeat voyage back to Europe five days later, seemed to be uneconomic as well. Wendal compromised by accepting first class tickets instead.

His travel planner had given him the bad news just moments before the speech he delivered in New York. Wendal could spend the full day there Saturday after his speaking engagement, but he would need to leave Sunday afternoon for Germany, with a stop in Frankfurt. It seemed there were no flights available from JFK directly to Düsseldorf, making the trip somewhat less than convenient.

After a brief conversation with this travel planner, they decided she would book him a first class flight to Frankfurt. Then, he would take a high-speed *Deutsche Bahn* ICE train from Frankfurt Airport directly to downtown Düsseldorf. There, a limousine would drive him to either his hotel or to the offices of Technologie Bergmann GmbH.

Wendal planned to shower quickly in the first class lounge at the Frankfurt Airport. Then he would be ready to visit the TBG offices immediately after arrival in Düsseldorf. This timing would let him start negotiations early Monday morning, and hopefully, conclude them before week's end.

In spite of the constant background hum of the engines, he enjoyed his refreshing glass of champagne. The more he sipped, the more reasonable the arguments of the financial guy became. Together, the flight and train tickets cost about sixteen thousand dollars, but this was still apparently much less than the cost to fly the company jet.

Still, it irked him that Mortimer required him to kowtow to his division financial operations leader on such minor expense issues. A little wistfully, he allowed his mind to wander and started to consider how much better he would feel should the moons align to make him CEO of Multima. There was some delight in this anticipation. He would indeed no longer be required to acquiesce to the bean counters. It would be good to dispense with concerns about trifling expenses in the mere thousands of dollars.

However, there seemed to be a new level of oversight by Howard Knight that he would need to assess. The most recent example came just hours before boarding the flight to Frankfurt early Sunday morning when Knight had unexpectedly phoned.

"It might be useful for you to have some help over there," Knight said. He had then sprinkled their conversation with phrases like "language issues", "local knowledge about TBG", and "added comfort". All this apparently justified his decision for a European representative of VCI to join Wendal for the crucial negotiations.

Calmly, Knight said he had no doubt Wendal would want to do everything possible, cover every eventuality so to speak, to ease his promotion into the role of CEO at Multima. Knight left no wiggle room for discussion about the matter. Further, he had concluded their conversation with a casual, almost offhanded comment. "It might be best to keep this extra VCI negotiating assistance just between us," he said.

That made Wendal Randall squirm a little in his plush first class leather seat. It was disconcerting how involved Knight had become over the past few days. Assertiveness at this juncture was curious when John George Mortimer was still supposed to be running Multima. At this stage, Wendal's promotion to the CEO role was far from a done deal. This dichotomy gave him cause to consider what kind of relationship might develop with Knight should he eventually occupy the office of CEO and manage the entire corporation.

Ruefully, his mind darted back to those ugly circumstances surrounding that college girl. It should never have occurred. Sure, he could have treated her better. He hadn't at all intended for their session of sex to become violent, but she also seemed to like it at the time. She hadn't complained at all about his hands tightly gripping her throat, and the marks on her neck were hardly noticeable the next morning.

It had come as a cruel shock to him when her lawyer made contact with Wendal just days after the start of crucial negotiations with John George Mortimer. It became even more devastating when the lawyer's letter and an accompanying video suddenly fell into the possession of Howard Knight.

Knight made it clear such a problem would surely scare off Mortimer should he learn of it. Such a discovery would certainly scuttle a potential deal and likely trigger the collapse of his then-struggling company. It had all been such a horrible mess!

Wendal had no idea the girl surreptitiously recorded a video of their frolic in bed. He had paid her generously for their night of passion. Furthermore, she had not complained any time after their session, not until that demanding letter from her lawyer almost five years later.

It seems the girl was much more clever than Wendal had realized. Apparently, she not only conducted the escort business advertised on Craigslist. She also meticulously retained videos, and then monitored significant developments in the lives of her better-known clients. As Wendal became ever more celebrated in the business and technology communities, she apparently made a connection between their one-night tryst and her video at a most opportune time.

Still, it astonished him the way her lawyer made contact at precisely the point discussions began with Multima. How could she have known the most fortuitous moment to make such a demand? Was it possible she knew that Wendal had started secret negotiations for the sale of his company? Was there some possible connection to Howard Knight? Questions like these whirled in his mind whenever his thoughts reverted to that fateful incident.

At that time, Wendal Randall no longer had enough money to make his problem with the girl go away. There was no way to raise the money her lawyer demanded. In the end, he had no alternative but to let Howard Knight advance the necessary funds to the girl's lawyer in return for a release from further legal action, but Knight had insisted that he retain the legal document, and all the evidence, in exchange for the payment of $100 thousand.

Evidently, Knight was continuing to exert pressure. It also appeared likely he would try to apply even greater influence over time. Wendal needed a workable solution to offset this potentially damaging threat, and that would be no easy challenge.

First, he must find a way to deal with this new spy, brazenly injected into his business affairs by Howard Knight. He would then look for a way to escape Knight's menacing clutch.

TWELVE

Chairman's Suite, Four Seasons Tokyo Hotel at Marunouchi.
February 29, 2016

This trip was Suzanne Simpson's first to Asia, and her initial impressions of Tokyo, with its population numbering near thirty million, were a little overwhelming.

She was glad to be back in her suite in the heart of the city. Her sixth-floor room had a view of a sprawling rail station and the magnificent skyline of the megalopolis where she had spent her first day in Japan.

She felt more than a little unease with the hotel's $5000 per night room rate, but her travel planner adamantly insisted that Japanese businessmen expected executives of her caliber to stay in such luxurious facilities. In fact, they might find it a curiosity should she choose more modest accommodations.

Reluctantly, Suzanne had accepted that advice. Now, enjoying the understated decor of the suite and a spectacular view of towering buildings with millions of lights sparkling in the evening's darkness, she conceded that it all combined to create a certain rare exhilaration.

Furthermore, she still felt remarkably energized even though it had been nineteen hours since those few hours of sleep on the jet. Both the rest periods and meetings during the flights had been good ideas. Suzanne felt satisfied with the in-flight preparation, and she particularly liked the way they all performed that first day. Everyone had remained alert, enthusiastic, and intently focused since arriving in Tokyo that morning.

After whisking through customs and immigration formalities at the private aircraft section of Haneda Airport in downtown Tokyo, the group sought out their waiting limousines. Then, chauffeurs wearing black business suits and spotless white gloves transported them at a snail's pace to the Four Seasons Hotel.

The hotel concierge cheerfully welcomed them just outside the front door of the lobby with a broad smile and a long, deep bow of respect. Then, the concierge hastily summoned a team of bell staff to collect their luggage and follow her, at an energetic pace, to their pre-registered rooms.

Less than an hour later, Suzanne and her team had showered and changed outfits from travel casual to business attire. Some applied fresh makeup while others quickly gulped down the continental breakfasts waiting in their rooms. With military-style precision, they all punctually reconvened in the hotel lobby for the required eight-thirty departure.

The next challenge for their always patient and courteous chauffeurs was to navigate skillfully through the seemingly gridlocked streets of Tokyo to a high-rise tower and functional meeting room provided by Dane Capital's Japanese subsidiary.

Multima Supermarkets occasionally used the services of Dane Capital, so the managing partner they worked with had been delighted to offer the meeting room of their Tokyo offices for Suzanne and her team to conduct discrete meetings.

At Multima board meetings, Howard Knight frequently teased Suzanne about giving some business to one of his venture capital competitors. But it was with precisely this kind of a circumstance in mind that Suzanne steadfastly maintained relations with an alternative, business-savvy partner with global reach.

Out of the eye of business media and competitors, Multima Supermarkets could comfortably conduct meetings with Japanese government agencies, agriculture associations, and food producers. Back home, such encounters would almost certainly start speculation on TV networks or in business publications.

What a first day in Japan it had been! Dane Capital had demonstrated their unique acumen for direct access to high-level contacts in both government and industry. With only a weekend to prepare, they successfully assembled a formidable roster of senior officials, starting with a morning presentation by Hiromi Tenaka, the managing director of Japan's Ministry of Agriculture.

Considered the second most powerful official in the ministry, Tenaka was at the peak of his career. He was broadly respected among elected representatives and throughout the Japanese government bureaucracy. Most people who met him also genuinely admired his encyclopedic knowledge and soft-spoken style.

Tenaka brought one additional and valuable attribute to his meeting with Suzanne and her team. In the late seventies, he had studied business management overseas at Southern California's UCLA. During that time in his education, he developed genuine affection for American people and found their culture fascinating.

Hiromi Tenaka delivered a convincing presentation to the group. For almost an hour, he used humor, charts, graphs, and flawless English to formulate his case for Japan's agriculture industry. He highlighted the movement towards organic farming, resulting in a dramatically reduced reliance on pesticides or artificial fertilizers. He spoke about the increasing efficiency of small Japanese farmers, and he detailed proposal after proposal to entice Multima Supermarkets to consider sourcing more food products from farmers, cooperatives, and processors in his country.

Tenaka explained how Multima might gain a competitive advantage by importing food from Japan. Surprisingly, the thirteen-hour time difference with the east coast of the U.S.A. could work to their advantage. It would permit Multima to deliver fresh food products to its stores all across the southeast U.S. and Canada within only two days of harvest.

He explained the cozy working relationship between Japan Airlines and the government. With a wry smile, he assured them his government had the necessary tools to make it imperative for the airline's management to schedule essential daily shipments to Atlanta and Toronto. He also outlined an incentive program the Japanese government had recently introduced to subsidize prices of exported fresh vegetables and explained how this might reduce Multima's purchasing costs.

Suzanne and her team were impressed with his enticing message. They were equally impressed with the tone of the meeting as they challenged Tenaka and his staff with questions and concerns. For more than five hours after his presentation, her team peppered the Japanese delegation with clarifying questions to be sure they had correctly interpreted the facts.

She observed an unfailing patience and politeness among the Japanese team. She liked the way they always listened intently to the questions asked, never interrupting until the questioner finished entirely. Unfortunately, such decorum was not always the case during meetings or intense negotiations in the rough-and-tumble interaction of the highly competitive food industry back home.

For every potential problem or concern expressed, a Japanese team member had a thoughtful and reasoned response. For a few unanticipated questions, they had assured them they would have an answer as soon as possible. Since some younger Japanese team members exhibited a penchant for using their laptops and smartphones in meetings—like their American counterparts—the information was often delivered just minutes after an issue surfaced.

As a result, when Suzanne returned to the Four Seasons Hotel, she was immediately able to convene a team meeting. In her spacious and comfortable suite, they dissected and discussed the vast amount of useful information received. They tried to reach quick conclusions and take decisive action as they worked through their list of issues.

But the data collected were complicated, so her director of finance decided to assign an additional expert team of cost accountants back at the Atlanta headquarters. Those analysts would dissect the presentation and determine if the economics Tenaka proposed actually could work for Multima Supermarkets.

Because the headquarters office in Atlanta would not officially open for another five hours, the Multima financial analysis team could still have a full working day to complete their study. Then they would summarize findings and report conclusions to the team in Tokyo while the travelers slept.

Suzanne requested an email of their analysis by four o'clock that afternoon, Atlanta time. The information would be ready and waiting for her and her team to read, study, and discuss at a breakfast meeting scheduled for seven o'clock the next morning, Japan time.

There was also an immediate decision to convene new focus groups to talk with current Multima customers. They felt it important to elicit their views on the idea of importing Japanese food products, determine prices they were willing to pay, and identify any potential concerns.

Earlier, Suzanne's team had anticipated a requirement for such intensive market research, readied interview facilities, and recruited participants in Miami, Tampa, Atlanta, and Toronto. The interviewers lacked only guidance about specific questions to ask. Suzanne's team in Tokyo would work to articulate their information needs before midnight, giving the Atlanta marketing team a half-day to prepare for the sessions planned that evening.

Before concluding the meeting in her suite, Suzanne had drawn attention to final planning and preparation for the next leg of this trip, the visit to China starting in two days. She reminded her colleagues they had only a short time to develop their final strategy and begin work on their presentation to the board of directors once they returned to headquarters.

Every hour in Asia was crucial.

THIRTEEN

Düsseldorf, Germany.
February 29, 2016

The morning train segment of Wendal Randall's trip from the busy international airport hub in Frankfurt to Düsseldorf's *Hauptbahnhof* proved surprisingly enjoyable. The functional, high-quality leather seats in first class were very comfortable, the large German breakfast tasty, and the service unexpectedly delightful. Like many Americans, Wendal harbored an image of German people as rather dour, overly serious, and humorless folks. The server in his car on the just-arrived eleven o'clock train that morning had not fit that image at all.

Statuesque, blonde, and appealing, the hostess charmed Wendal with her infectious laugh and cheerful personality throughout the two-hour journey. As he stepped down from the train to the station platform, the young woman waved heartily, flashed her engaging smile, and bid *auf Wiedersehen.*

What a pity there's not more time to explore this gorgeous creature, Wendal thought, as he reciprocated with an equally charming smile and a broad, enthusiastic wave. As he turned, his gaze immediately struck yet another strikingly beautiful woman. She was cradling a small sign with his name in bright, bold letters. *The new spy,* Randall realized with some annoyance as he moved forward to meet her.

"Welcome to Germany, Herr Randall. Your car is the black Mercedes-Benz sedan just across the street. I hope you had a nice flight and train ride," Frau Klaudia Schäffer gushed as she quickly led him to the car.

"Let me get the door for you, then I 'll explain why I took the liberty of modifying your schedule this morning." Closing the car door, she snapped instructions to the driver in German.

"I was quite sure your American travel planner overlooked the need for a briefing with your team before we visit Technologie Bergmann GmbH today, so I went ahead and scheduled a conference at your hotel suite for noon with the team already here.

"Of course, you're already checked into the hotel. No need to be bothered with such details," she continued without waiting for comment.

"Also, I ordered lunch for the team and arranged delivery to your suite for most efficient use of your valuable time during the debriefing discussions. And, I already contacted senior management at TBG to delay our initial meeting until three o'clock this afternoon. Is there anything else that might need my attention during our four to five-minute ride to the hotel?"

Wendal seethed silently. Altogether unaccustomed to taking direction from anyone, and particularly from a woman he hardly knew, Wendal's initial inclination was to give her a good piece of his mind. He had no intention of letting this woman organize his life for even a day, let alone all week!

He paused a few seconds to assess the situation. He realized her actions did make good business sense. Undoubtedly, he had made a rather serious tactical blunder scheduling a meeting with TBG before talking with his team. Of course, he had studied the project's private blog and considered himself up to date with emails. He felt completely in the loop, but it surely would be better to review the latest status of discussions with his people before starting a dialog with the senior management of the supplier.

Then there was Howard Knight to consider. Clearly, Frau Schäffer was the local VCI operative Knight had selected to oversee and report to him about negotiations with TBG. It probably would not be a good idea to alienate the woman before she submitted her first report.

"No, thanks. It seems you've got it covered," Wendal responded with little enthusiasm. "I can't think of anything that needs your immediate attention."

They traveled the remainder of the short trip in silence as Wendal feigned interest in the sights of Düsseldorf. Meanwhile, Frau Schäffer diligently scrutinized and methodically disposed of her smartphone messages. They soon arrived at the entrance of the renowned Steigenberger Park Hotel, a stately and luxurious landmark in the heart of Düsseldorf.

Instantly, Wendal warmed to the magnificent, classic gray stone structure. He found the building exuded a feeling of quality, longevity, elegance, and wealth. The charming park right beside the hotel suggested tranquility, an oasis in the heart of bustling Düsseldorf.

As soon as he stepped through the door held open by a smartly uniformed doorman, Wendal admired an elegantly appointed lobby that appeared recently renovated. It was bright, clean, and tastefully furnished. On the left, he noticed a modern, inviting, and well-lit restaurant that looked functional and comfortable. Polished marble floors and designer touches suggested a quiet and understated refinement. *Okay*, he thought. *Things are starting to look better.*

Without comment, he scurried to catch up with Frau Schäffer and the bell captain, already holding the beeping elevator door ajar and ready to guide him to his suite.

His Multima Logistics team lounged casually on sofas and armchairs around the suite, waiting. Consistent with an entirely informal style and a comfortable familiarity with their leader, they had already devoured most of the sandwiches and refreshments Frau Schäffer had arranged. They had seen no reason to wait for Wendal.

The wisdom to reschedule the meeting with TBG became apparent within minutes when his team leader, Ricky Technori, revealed that talks were not progressing as hoped with the German provider.

"I didn't have time to update the internal blog, but we've now got some serious issues," Technori started. "Initial tests with the Multima Supermarkets accounting software identified four hundred and thirty-two compatibility issues. Either TBG or the software provider PAS will need to re-write extensive amounts of code."

"What's extensive?" Wendal demanded.

"Unfortunately, TBG now estimates three to four months to complete the revisions."

"Are you kidding me?" Wendal asked incredulously. After a moment, "Anything else to make my day?"

"Yeah. TBG's hardware complies with European electrical standards, but no one has made application for the mandatory American UL approval. Who knows how long that might take to resolve?" Technori responded.

"Can there possibly be anything else?" Wendal sputtered in exasperation.

"Early this morning I got a report from Juan Perez, our guy responsible for liaising with the supermarket division," another colleague piped up. "Juan's usual contact at Supermarkets steadfastly refuses to provide the data file we requested. It's the only place we can get the information we need to prepare a credible cost-benefit analysis. The excuses they gave to Juan were privacy and confidentiality concerns."

This disappointing start to his trip was a cause for alarm. Wendal now acutely realized that he would probably need to draw on every one of his creative negotiating skills to extract some level of success from this week in Germany. He also grudgingly acknowledged that he would also need to rely much more on the skills and influence of the highly organized Frau Schäffer than he would have liked.

Neither revelation gave him much comfort or confidence.

FOURTEEN

In a modern Hoffman Estates' building near Chicago.
February 29, 2016

It was a little after seven o'clock Monday morning, and James Fitzgerald was seated comfortably behind his massive, polished, spotlessly clean desk. As usual, there was only a single piece of paper in front of him.

As he liked to tell people, he could only do one thing really well at any given moment. Further, his direct reports had long-ago learned there was no subject too complex to summarize in a well-structured, one-page memo. Therefore, he had developed an unusual practice of keeping only one piece of paper on the desk in front of him at a time.

He would devote his full and undivided attention to that one piece of paper, act on it, and then extract the next piece from the pile located in his desk's top left-hand drawer. At regular intervals throughout each day, his assistant would enter the office, her arms stacked with papers. Each time, she would reorder that cache in the drawer in a priority she deemed appropriate.

By the end of each day, Fitzgerald would typically read and make a decision about one hundred or more documents. Most days he started with one called Business Intelligence. An elite team buried deep within the Multima Financial Services marketing group began its shift at midnight and worked until eight o'clock weekday mornings. They mined the Internet, newspapers from around the world, and other information sources to prepare a daily briefing of information that might impact his business in some way.

Two pieces of information caught Fitzgerald's eye near the top of the page. Wendal Randall was in Germany visiting a technology provider, and Suzanne Simpson was in Tokyo meeting with agricultural interests. Early in his career, Fitzgerald had learned that other executives within Multima Corporation, and particularly other division presidents, could have a direct impact on his financial services group. Thus, his business intelligence team also nurtured sources of information in each of the corporation's divisions to keep Fitzgerald informed about the daily whereabouts and activities of his peers.

There could be little doubt both international visits related to John George Mortimer's game changer dictate. Fitzgerald was curious about the attraction of such global treks when it might be better for his colleagues to stay closer to home, narrowly focused on getting their new strategies and presentations together. His team surely had no need for global travel to complete its assignment. What he did need was a consensus among his direct reports.

Last Thursday's meeting had started immediately after his evening arrival from Fort Myers and stretched well into the early hours of Friday morning. Fortunately, his direct reports had responded to his account of Mortimer's mandate with uncharacteristic enthusiasm. Ideas about possible game-changing strategies for their financial services division flowed continuously for hours. It was like molten lava streaming from an erupting volcano.

New ideas came in wave after wave. A facilitator at one end of the room jotted detailed notes on whiteboards with equations, arrows, and numbers building semi-organized clutter. Frequently, someone electronically captured the jumbled subject matter from the whiteboards. Then the discussion leader would erase the visual aid to start over again. The whiteboards would accumulate yet another mass of information with notes, asterisks, and arrows all competing for attention.

For someone accustomed to dealing with one piece of paper at a time, the experience proved to be slightly unnerving. When Fitzgerald adjourned the meeting just before three o'clock that Friday morning, he had been awake for almost twenty-four hours. He felt physically and mentally drained.

The team reconvened just six hours later. Such an early start was necessary to begin a laborious process of analyzing the suggestions from the previous night and identifying benefits or challenges for each.

They considered the introduction of insurance programs—life insurance, disability insurance, health and dental insurance, extended warranty insurance, and even insurance for pets! They explored brokerage services, mutual funds, and on-line trading services. The team briefly considered automobile leasing and vehicle loans. In the end, it appeared most favored expansion into the business of home mortgages.

A majority of James Fitzgerald's direct reports saw an opportunity to provide financing to Multima customers blocked out of the still-challenging home mortgage market, but advisors in whose business judgment Fitzgerald had complete trust and confidence remained skeptical.

They acknowledged a wide gap in mortgage availability since the real estate bubble suddenly burst eight years earlier. They also understood many current Multima customers still experienced serious difficulty getting mortgages to buy new properties; some perhaps even had challenges renewing mortgages on their homes. Fitzgerald's trusted advisors recognized that traditional mortgage providers remained paralyzed into inactivity by new government regulations, more lawsuits, and risks of further reductions in property values. They even conceded that this created a potential opening for well-funded and savvy new entrants to the home mortgage market.

However, no better-informed authority than economist Warren Wrigletts had just last month cautioned them about another upcoming economic recession. He had forecast dismal economic gloom and related pain for businesses and individuals alike that would make the crippling 2008 financial crisis seem mild in comparison.

The debate was intense. Emotions stirred. Voice levels rose. All were rare occurrences in the sedate executive boardroom attached to Fitzgerald's office. As he ended the meeting, he admonished his direct reports to spend the weekend thinking, calculating, and talking to each other off-line. A decision of this importance required a consensus. He would not move forward until they had one.

As he completed his review of the morning briefing data and business intelligence, James glanced at his watch and realized there remained only thirty minutes to make a few calls. He wanted to explore further just what it was that his colleagues with apparent travel lust were trying to accomplish. Whatever they were doing, it just might impact Multima Financial Services.

After those inquiries, it would be back to the meeting room next door and his quest for a strategy consensus. With only fifty-six days remaining before a presentation to the full board of directors, Fitzgerald preferred to reach a conclusion that day, if at all possible.

FIFTEEN

Technologie Bergmann GmbH office, Düsseldorf, Germany.
February 29, 2016

Wendal Randall and his full entourage finally arrived at the downtown Düsseldorf offices of TBG very late in the afternoon. Frau Schäffer had found it necessary to call twice and further delay their scheduled meeting. Discussions in Randall's hotel suite had been long, animated, and tense as it became apparent they needed to address and overcome significant hurdles before Operation Bright Star could move forward.

Wendal and his team sat on one side of a large, oval, boardroom-style table in the sparsely decorated conference room. Max Bergmann and his team of German colleagues sat opposite them.

The meeting started cordially, with Bergmann politely welcoming Randall to the discussions. Bergmann had met and was now familiar with other members of the Multima Logistics team since they had been working in TBG offices for a week already. So he asked requisite questions about Wendal's trip, his jet lag, and his accommodations.

From Bergmann's perspective, the meeting start was a bit awkward. First, he was unclear about the exact role of Klaudia Schäffer. He knew his team spoke English well and could not think of any language impediment that might harm their dialog. Their meeting issues were highly technical in nature, and from her few opening comments, Frau Schäffer certainly did not appear to be a technologist.

Effective participation required an in-depth understanding of Multima Supermarkets' operating requirements, which he doubted she would have. In fact, he wasn't at all sure what he should make of Frau Schäffer as a new addition to the negotiations. And why was she making her first appearance coincident with Wendal Randall's arrival?

The title *Fachberater* on her business card suggested she was a consultant or technical advisor, but the chemistry between her and Randall appeared a little curious to Bergmann. Despite civility and outwardly cordial communication, nonverbal signals gave him the impression there might be some unusual client-consultant discomfort or tension in their working relationship. His discreet initial inquiry about her role did not extract any specific information from either of them, so Bergmann made a mental note to explore their relationship at a more relaxed and private opportunity.

Once the traditional opening formalities concluded, strong German coffee or soft drinks were offered. Wendal then immediately raised the problematic issues revealed during the hotel meeting with his team.

"Herr Bergmann, I think you know my greatest concern today is the four hundred and thirty-two compatibility variances discovered," he began. "Compatibility between the software for the planned automated checkout counters and Multima Supermarkets' computer systems is far more complex than we expected."

"Make it Max. And you're right, Wendal. A convergence of multiple factors creates a much greater challenge than we all anticipated. But it's not insurmountable," Bergmann replied. "Let me summarize the issues and possible fixes."

Already thoroughly briefed about all the technical matters, for almost an hour Bergmann then patiently and painstakingly detailed the reasons for these compatibility snags. Without any notes, prompting by his colleagues, or presentation tools, he used a soft voice modulation delivered with precise English grammar. He highlighted the critical dilemma: More than two hundred issues related directly to enhancements modified by Multima Supermarkets' technology experts to comply with US regulatory requirements and financial reporting preferences.

PAS had created another one hundred system conflicts with improvements to its base software since the initial installation of automated point-of-sale devices at the European retailer. The remaining one hundred or so glitches were the result of that European retailer making progressive enhancements to its computer systems to better meet its financial needs and European regulatory requirements.

His company, Bergmann insisted, had extensive experience installing the high-performance automated point-of-sale equipment they produced for the European retailer. However, Multima's operating needs seemed fundamentally different. To modify the code and achieve full compatibility, they would need almost one hundred thousand hours of programming!

Then, he led them through the calculations used to reach the conclusion they'd have to assign one hundred and ninety-two software programmers to the project and would require at least three months to write the code. After, they'd also want to test it to assure no further defects lingered.

"I can only divert fifteen people from my staff to such a project," he explained. "Our initial research suggests that we can draw an additional fifty or so from universities across Europe. That means we'll have to find more than one hundred programmers in countries like Russia, China, or India. The task is going to be daunting. Risks will be high. And costs will certainly be in the tens of millions of dollars."

"And how long to complete the project?" Wendal inquired as Bergmann paused.

"We think they'll need about three months for completion. But that timeline can only start after we've recruited the additional programmers. Remember, not only do we need to find these people, we also must train them to make the program modifications.

"My best estimate for final completion, if we should start the process today, would be six to eight months, and that's assuming there are no new surprises," he said.

"And who is expected to incur the costs for these programmers?" Wendal asked.

"Multima Logistics must bear these additional costs. Our original quotation has no provision for such extensive modifications and related outlays of cash," Bergmann responded with a firm tone.

Wendal Randall and his team had listened mainly in silence as Bergmann outlined the dire circumstances and magnitude of the challenge to meet their requirements. As he listened, he didn't know how he could begin to express his frustration.

He was shocked at the enormity of the gap between their initial expectations. Worse, even estimates provided by TBG only a few days earlier had now ballooned in time and cost. He was devoid of ideas to achieve a solution. So, he opted to wait in simmering silence until Bergmann finished his lengthy update, just as Frau Schäffer had counseled earlier.

"UL electrical standards are much less ominous," Bergman resumed, filling the awkward silence. "My team proactively contacted UL in the US and the Canadian Standards Association. Both have confirmed they will recognize existing European certifications as compliance with standards for each country. So we do have some good news."

Bergmann then changed his tack altogether. "May I make a suggestion? Might it be best for both teams to use the remainder of today to digest my rather complex analysis and our current conundrum?

"Wendal, I have tons of respect for the technology acumen of you and your team. I've certainly never met a more qualified group! With the talent you have, we just might find better solutions for some of these challenges.

"Let's have both teams reconvene tomorrow for some more dialog. We'll be completely transparent about all analysis and costs and will truly value your engineering input," he said with his arms open wide in a gesture of welcome and inclusion.

Then, with a wry smile, Bergmann offered another idea. "Maybe Wendal and I should take ourselves out of those discussions. That way, our teams can focus on the grinding details of cost analysis without senior management further muddling up an already complicated predicament," he said with a magnanimous laugh.

"It might be better for us to travel south to the city of Heidelberg and tour the facility where we'll produce the automated point-of-sale equipment," he added. That this would give the leaders a chance to become better acquainted before they tackled some more tough negotiations and equally hard decisions was left unsaid.

Wendal immediately grasped the wisdom of Max's suggestion. He needed some time to think about how he could salvage Operation Bright Star from what appeared to be a developing disaster. What had seemed so comfortably sure only a week ago now looked like a total debacle.

Worse, there was no backup project ready to propose for Mortimer's game changer assignment. His credibility with Knight was probably about to take a major hit, all while this annoying Frau Schäffer appeared to be enjoying her front-row seat as the spectacle unwound.

A trip to Heidelberg would provide temporary relief from the extremely messy situation that had evolved and suppress tensions while both sides regrouped. He agreed they should meet in the Steigenberger Park Hotel lobby at nine o'clock the next morning.

By now, Wendal had no doubt he would need most of the next sixteen or so hours to develop a strategy to salvage Operation Bright Star. It was still too early for him to concede defeat. However, perhaps even within the next few days, it might become necessary to abort and create a whole new game plan, and then try to justify it to Howard Knight. He did not at all look forward to such a possibility.

SIXTEEN

Chairman's Suite, Four Seasons Tokyo Hotel at Marunouchi.
February 29, 2016

Alone after a long day of travel and discussions, Suzanne Simpson shifted her thoughts back to the meeting with Hiromi Tenaka. The managing director of Japan's Agriculture Ministry had made a strong impression as he led their meeting with confidence, charm, and conviction.

He had also arranged to get a few minutes apart from the teams when he pleasantly surprised her with an invitation to join him that evening for dinner. The idea was tempting. The chemistry between the two seemed electric when they made eye contact, and who knew when she last had time for a real date.

But her business intuition prevailed. It wouldn't be appropriate to accept his invitation while the meeting was still underway. Instead, she drew a solid line between personal and business interest and agreed to let him know after they finished the discussions. With a smile she found hard to resist, he gracefully accepted her delay.

A couple hours later, he discretely glanced her way with eyebrows slightly arched. Since the meeting had advanced so favorably, she actually had decided to join him for dinner. But before she could nod her assent, life got in the way again. Her smartphone beeped to signal a message highlighted with an 'urgent' icon.

Suzanne. See note below from Multima Logistics requesting release of payroll data files for all cashiers and front-end staff, system-wide, including benefits, for FY 2014/15. For use in cost-benefit study for board presentation. See my denial of such request pending your authorization—due to privacy and confidentiality issues. Pls provide further guidance. Sharif

What possible mischief might Wendal Randall be up to with such a bizarre request? Suzanne immediately became more than a little suspicious. Payroll information was the most sensitive of all data. Everyone in senior management knew that. The corporate office had repeatedly stressed the imperative of guarding privacy and maintaining the confidentiality of all employee records to an absolute need-to-know basis.

With a sigh of resignation, she realized this issue must take priority. Further, John George Mortimer's game changer strategy assignment was so crucial that she felt pressure to make optimum use of every waking hour. After all, she was spending thousands of her company's dollars for this research trip. Tenaka's non-verbal signals suggested that he was hoping their dinner might be more than a business meeting, and this would be a dalliance that could potentially leave her with more guilt than satisfaction. As their discussions ended, she declined his invitation with as much charm as possible.

The past several hours focused on business back home, studiously reading reports and briefing information about Japan and China prepared by her staff. Periodically, her thoughts would drift back to the curious email message until, eventually, she knew it was time to reach a conclusion and provide the requested guidance.

Most requests for inter-division information were quite mundane. Certainly, it was also normal for Wendal Randall to use a subordinate to seek information from another Multima business. In fact, John George Mortimer encouraged complete cooperation and open communication among his three divisions, and Suzanne's business unit was Multima Logistics' largest customer as well.

However, like other executives of major corporations, Multima leaders often used subordinates to make sensitive inquiries and maintain a degree of separation. It was always useful to be able to deny knowledge of, or responsibility for, requests that might be considered too intrusive. If such extremely sensitive payroll information was genuinely needed by Multima Logistics to prepare for the game changer assignment, it might not bode well for Multima Supermarkets.

Suzanne tried to recall indications of what Wendal Randall might have in mind. A seemingly casual inquiry from him during the Naples off-site meeting in December came to mind.

"Wouldn't it be easier to manage automated point-of-sale devices with a single computer server than continue to manage a few thousand cashiers who all want wage increases every year?" he had asked light-heartedly as they engaged in casual conversation at the cocktail reception.

Suzanne felt a surge of blood flowing to her brain and a quickening of her heart rate. Her anxiety was increasing rapidly. Her face felt hot and flushed. She deployed her simple stress reduction method before starting her reply. Three times she inhaled and exhaled deeply. Then she slowly counted to ten. Just to be sure, she counted to ten once more before typing into her smartphone.

Sharif: Agree with your decision. No release of files including human resources data under any circumstances. S.

After a moment's hesitation and one last quick review, she pushed the 'send' button.

By drawing this line in the sand, Suzanne realized a confrontation with Multima Logistics would almost certainly follow. There might even be a conflict with Wendal Randall. However, she didn't intend for Logistics to build some game changer strategy that in any way involved her people without direct and detailed discussion with her personally. Randall would only be able to win her support if the project under consideration created a real win-win outcome for both divisions.

As she prepared for sleep, she thought again about the email and recalled an earlier observation she made during one of Wendal's presentations. Logistics' perpetual love affair with everything related to technology often seemed to overlook the roles and vital contributions of people in the success of Multima's business model. They usually appeared to be concerned only with technological innovation, productivity improvements, and rapid increases in bottom-line profits. People seemed almost incidental to the process.

She would not allow this latest request for information to feed that tendency.

SEVENTEEN

It was not at all out of character for John George Mortimer to take a vacation. Despite his passion for successfully building the Multima empire, he enjoyed frequent mini vacations to relax and refresh. Short breaks usually occurred around statutory holidays, when some of the businesses might close for at least one day. He would then escape to some location outside the country.

Before such absences, he advised Alberto Ferer, the general counsel of Multima. As the senior legal advisor to the company and secretary of the board of directors, Ferer would implement Multima's temporary succession plan in the event any tragedy should befall. Therefore, it was normal for him to advise Ferer he would not be reachable for a few days. Alberto discretely respected Mortimer's need for an occasional pause from the continuous stress and hectic pace of managing a Fortune 500 company.

Because Multima Corporation was a publicly traded company, Mortimer was indeed expected to notify the entire board of directors about the upcoming surgery to remove his left breast. However, Mortimer had feared such a disclosure just might put his carefully crafted succession strategy in jeopardy.

So, late Friday afternoon Mortimer had invited Alberto Ferer to walk over to his office where they discussed a couple of routine business issues that Alberto wanted to resolve before the weekend. At the end of the conversation, Mortimer casually told him that he would be unavailable for a few days. What had been a little unusual was his further request that he not be disturbed, for any reason, until the seventh of March. That was almost twice as long as his usual breaks.

With a conspiratorial wink and a carefree, broader than usual smile, Mortimer implied there might be some new lady who deserved his undivided attention in a secluded location for a few days. Mortimer had carefully observed Ferer's reaction to discern if there were any signs of doubt or concern.

He saw none. For certainty, Mortimer added that there might not be email available, and he probably wouldn't respond by smartphone immediately. Ferer assured him that he would treat this information with care, then wished him a good weekend and fabulous trip. Ferer had mimicked Mortimer's mischievous smile, confirming his full understanding.

The only other person with whom Mortimer shared information about his planned absence was his long-serving and highly respected executive assistant, Sally-Ann Bureau. He had complete trust in her. She had faithfully performed her duties for more than thirty-five years and always responded to his business demands with unwavering loyalty and absolute prudence. People around Multima liked to use an old analogy about trying to squeeze water from a stone when they referred to Sally-Ann's discretion.

Mortimer had advised Sally-Ann about the breast cancer. "Think of it as a bump in the road of life," he told her with a brief overview of the planned surgery, hospital contact details, and expected prognosis. He let her know about his conversation with Ferer and suggested a story she might relate to others while he was away. Then, Mortimer sought and received her solemn promise that she would not share information about this circumstance with anyone.

Now, patiently waiting for the next steps in preparation for surgery, and with his tracks reasonably covered, Mortimer permitted his thoughts to drift. He wasn't concerned about what was to come that morning, nor was he remorseful or embittered. Still, he couldn't resist thinking about how he found himself lying on this gurney, about to be cut and prodded.

It had all started a few days after his sixty-ninth birthday. He had just discussed results of a thorough medical check-up with his doctor. John George felt fine, but the insurance company Multima used for executive health and life coverage required physical examinations every year. They usually involved extensive testing and screening, and previous results had always been routine and uneventful.

Despite his age, Mortimer exhibited better health than many. His cholesterol readings remained well within ranges deemed to be safe. Blood pressure was normal, and his blood sugar count was consistently well under control. Mortimer had always taken meticulous care of his body with regular exercise and a reasonable diet.

Early on, he assumed there was a direct relationship between a healthy body and a well-performing brain. To maintain an edge over his aggressive competitors, he consistently strove to be mentally acute and well-tuned physically. His extraordinarily successful career appeared to have had virtually no negative impact on his health. So, the small, hard lump his doctor had discovered on his left breast became a reason for genuine concern.

"To possibly err on the side of abundant caution," the doctor explained as he ordered a mammogram for further investigation. A mammogram of all things!

"Although breast cancer is a disease usually associated with women," the doctor added, "about two thousand American men are diagnosed with it every year. It wouldn't be wise to take unnecessary chances. You're already here. I strongly recommend you visit the screening section for a mammogram today."

John George followed his advice. The next morning the doctor phoned. He notified Mortimer the discovered lump was a tumor and possibly malignant. Immediate intervention was required.

Another visit to the medical office followed. Right after, an oncologist undertook a further extensive examination. Within moments, the specialist confirmed there was cancer, then sought and received permission to schedule early surgery to remove the invasive lump.

John George made these decisions in a dense fog of shock and a feeling of unease that immediately enveloped him. Powerful yet confusing feelings surged. Despite all the knowledge and sophisticated tools, might this diagnosis be wrong? Should he demand a second opinion? Could this really be happening, or was it instead a nightmare?

Gradually, logic prevailed and his doubts subsided. The computer screens clearly displayed the culprit tumor, he reasoned. The oncologist was among the best in America and had treated thousands of patients. He'd welcomed questions, encouraged them in fact. His manner was confident and left no doubt his recommendations were the best solution.

John George's emotions ranged from total surprise to outright bewilderment. He was feeling as fit as he had any time in his life. There had been no pain or discomfort. *How does cancer get started in a specimen of good health*, he wondered. What could he have done differently? Might he have prevented it?

Anger briefly surfaced. Why should this be happening to him? Why now? A transition from anger to sadness followed, then reluctant acceptance.

The oncologist provided information about surgery and possible follow-up treatments. He mentioned the high rates of survival the medical community now expected with breast cancer.

However, to Mortimer's considerable concern, the oncologist also conceded they were together wading into less charted waters. "To be candid, we have much better data and treatment guidance available for women than men," he confessed. "Because of the comparatively smaller numbers of men diagnosed with breast cancer, we just can't predict the outcome with the same certainty."

At home, Mortimer devoured all the information he could find on the Internet, spent several hours scouring medical articles, checked terminology, cross-referenced studies, and scanned dozens of comments from survivors. In the early hours of the following day, he finished his research, stoically resigned to do everything possible to treat this cancer.

His survival and potential physical limitations were now uncomfortably unclear. For the first time, John George Mortimer acknowledged this to be the catalyst for his retirement from Multima Corporation. He found himself confronting the haunting question of his own mortality. While death may not be an immediate concern, he started to focus more intently on its inevitability. The cancer might not kill him, but something eventually would.

Succession planning never seemed urgent, for whatever reason. Of course, Multima Corporation had contingency plans in the event of a health emergency or his sudden incapacity. However, the substance of those discussions was always about temporarily filling a leadership gap until the board of directors grappled with a longer-term solution.

Mortimer now directly faced an immediate requirement for a permanent successor. Addressing this disease would certainly require more of his time and focus in the near term. Once the cancer was under control, it would probably be better to reduce his demanding workload to allow more time to relax and enjoy some of the pleasures he hadn't previously allowed.

First, he needed someone to fill his shoes. There were no family heirs to the business. His parents had both died many years earlier, and Mortimer was an only child. There were no close relatives. He had never found time to marry. Although there had been lots of short-term liaisons, and even several long relationships over the years, John George had never committed to a sustained relationship. Instead, throughout his adult life, he had been devoted exclusively to nurturing Multima.

Now, at the pinnacle of this phenomenal business success, this self-made man was jolted into an uncomfortable reality. His leadership must soon end. Somewhat earlier than he would have preferred, it was now time to move on.

He reached another conclusion. When they started the process to find a successor, he would be much more than passive. Who better than he to fathom the strength of character and leadership qualities needed to lead such a sprawling and complex corporation?

In those days immediately after diagnosis, naming an appropriate successor grew increasingly important. As he methodically worked through the challenges of selecting a new CEO, he also became determined to do everything possible to convince the board to support his preferred choice.

Mortimer already knew his ideal candidate for chief executive officer. After years of observation and recent days of thoughtful analysis, he harbored no doubts at all. One executive above all the others was the right one. But such a crucial business decision could certainly not be his alone. Any appointment of his successor would need the approval of the board. He was also mindful that no other director would be more influential in that process than Howard Knight, who represented the interests of the company's other major shareholder, Venture Capital Investments.

He expected Knight would have a preferred candidate, quite possibly a different one. Consequently, he recognized a need for some serious advance preparation to manage the succession process and thought about several possible approaches.

Time was limited. In fact, most avenues he considered required more than he could permit. Several ideas he initially thought innovative or creative ultimately proved fruitless as he thought them through to logical conclusions. Nevertheless, after several days of careful reflection, he came upon a workable idea to sway the majority of the board towards his choice.

A few days earlier, he had unleashed that plan with the secret disclosure of his intention to retire. Now, looking back on that crucial meeting with the board, execution of his strategy seemed flawless. He found broad acceptance and support for his scheme. Subsequently, his address to key management as he launched their pursuit of game changing assignments had gone equally well.

Mortimer assured himself things would be alright as he patiently waited for transfer to a cold and sterile hospital operating theater. He watched the hovering and masked form above him adjust the flow of the intravenous. Then, he hazily switched his focus to the immediate future. He had few concerns about the surgery. He understood the objectives and had complete confidence in his doctor.

The specialist had thoroughly explained the process earlier. First, there would be a full mastectomy to remove his left breast and all the cancerous tumors. Then, they would take a biopsy of the area to determine if any additional cancer cells had spread to the lymph nodes. The surgeon estimated this procedure might take an hour or so and confidently informed Mortimer his recovery should start by late morning.

It would probably be one or two days before he could leave the hospital, and then he should plan a week at home to recover. No meetings or travel for at least ten days and limited work activities for about two or three weeks, the specialist advised.

John George intended to follow the first suggestion and totally disregard the rest. He fully expected to be back at his desk, completely in charge of Multima's businesses, on March seven as he had arranged with Alberto Ferer.

A drug-induced sense of calm enveloped him despite the underlying churn of conflicting emotions and lingering unease. Between the treatments for cancer and his transition from CEO to retirement, the coming days promised to be interesting. John George Mortimer had no idea just how gripping they would become.

EIGHTEEN

In a modern Hoffman Estates' office building, near Chicago.
February 29, 2016

It was after nine o'clock in the evening. James Fitzgerald had just signed the last remaining piece of paper from the pile his assistant had deposited into the top left-hand drawer of his desk before she left the office. This action brought him to the stage of his highly structured day when he could review his day's accomplishments. And what a day it had been!

His early morning meeting to discuss the Mortimer assignment with his direct reports had been fruitful beyond his expectations. There was no doubt; his team had made extraordinary efforts to build the consensus that eluded them before the weekend.

Although all his direct reports arrived for the meeting freshly shaved, showered, and impeccably dressed, Fitzgerald detected dark circles below their eyes and slight slowness in their speech. Both indicated the team probably slept little over the weekend. Initial exchanges among the participants also displayed tinges of tension or irritation.

Just at the point he had mentally resigned himself to the probability of a long, arduous, and challenging session, the chemistry in the room seemed to change. Douglas Whitfield, senior vice president for credit card operations, emerged as a spokesperson for the group and his body language showed that he came prepared.

"We propose to expand our business charter to include an innovative home mortgage business," he said. "This strategy will allow us to benefit from our millions of Multima Supermarkets' customer relationships and our highly successful credit card operations. It's a genuine game changer, and we'll leverage these valuable assets to introduce home mortgages that will disrupt the lending industry.

"First, let's remember that we already connect Supermarkets' customers with our credit card operations. Our Multima One card awards loyalty points for every dollar they charge and generates points equal to about one-half of one percent of their purchases. Remember too that we reward cardholders with more points for paying on time, special promotions in stores, and for the monthly volume of dollars processed on their credit cards.

"Our customers remain extremely loyal because they can redeem their accumulated points for cash, gifts, or travel. We know most of our clients estimate the value of using their Multima One credit card at thousands of dollars every year. This brings us to the most significant benefit. Our cardholders are excellent credit risks." He waited to see if there were any challenges.

With no opposition offered, he enthusiastically carried on. "Because the value of their card is tangible, you all know the default rate we experience is far below the industry average. Without taking anything away from our risk management efforts, I think we can all agree that our success managing losses relates directly to the compelling value we have created with our cardholders.

"A consensus started to evolve when our team identified a possible link between mortgages and the credit card. Here's our thought process. There are three main risks in the mortgage business: Failure to pay the mortgage, reduction of value in the financed home, and administration costs. We decided all of these risks can be managed adequately by expanding the fundamental principles we use to manage the Multima One credit card program successfully.

"Home mortgages will be offered to current and future Multima One cardholders only. To further minimize risk, we'll target only those customers with credit scores rated between 'good' and 'excellent'. Moreover, we'll approve mortgage loans only for customers willing to accept a stringent requirement for a significant cash down payment on their financed home. And as a last pre-condition, we'll require customers to repay their mortgages by authorizing weekly charges to their credit card account rather than monthly from their bank accounts."

Whitfield paused to be sure Fitzgerald fully absorbed the significance of this radical new payment approach. When no concerns surfaced, he expanded on their intentions with even more passion.

"History shows us that customers with higher levels of equity in their homes tend to default less often, even when the value of their home decreases. So, we'll demand a down payment of at least twenty percent.

"We'll divide annual mortgage repayments by fifty-two to establish weekly schedules. Then, each week we'll debit that amount to our customers' credit cards. Charging on a weekly basis will help customers build more equity in their homes faster, further reducing our risk. We'll also digitize the processing of those weekly debits to drive down administration costs," he added.

"With our lower costs, we can afford to reward clients with Multima One loyalty points for each weekly charge, giving them another incentive to finance their homes with us. A bonus for our customers: Their overall financing costs will reduce substantially over the term of the mortgage.

"Our team believes all these factors will encourage customers to become more loyal, doing everything possible to pay Multima first, even if they encounter income disruption or payment challenges," he said.

Whitfield then highlighted one last significant advantage that he considered compelling, should customers became delinquent on their credit card payments. "We'll collect delinquency interest at the rate of about twenty percent on the outstanding balance, compared with about four percent at current mortgage rates. With five times the revenue, we can manage delinquent accounts very profitably. Ultimately, we also think it can allow a much smaller balance sheet reserve for risk.

"Moreover, the legal team believes we can make a default on a credit card account also become a default on the mortgage and begin foreclosure processes more quickly. Again, both our administration and risk costs should be reduced."

Whitfield followed with the preliminary business plan his team had developed, projecting Multima Financial Services revenues would double within three years and annual profits increase even faster over the same period.

Fitzgerald was impressed. Truly, this proposal was a game changer that could position them among the largest lenders in North America. Almost certainly, it would also make their business unit the biggest operating division within Multima Corporation.

For the next few hours, he peppered Whitfield and the other team members with questions. He challenged their assumptions and relentlessly probed minute details. When sandwiches and drinks arrived around noon, the discussion had already moved from the 'Should we do it?' stage to the 'How do we do it?' implementation phase.

Fitzgerald was gratified to see everyone support the proposal. Skeptics of the previous week had shifted their positions to become enthusiastic proponents. Even the most reluctant and conservative members of his team expressed confidence in the quality of the research, analysis, and conclusions. When the meeting concluded in the late afternoon, there was a multi-page to-do list.

First, they needed to find a way to deal with corporate bond rating agencies. Since widespread embarrassing failures to predict the 2008 global financial crisis, rating agencies had become far more conservative with their evaluations. To make the new plan work, Multima Financial Services would issue attractive low-cost bonds for periods matching the lending term of mortgages. Delicate negotiations with those influential agencies would surely be necessary, and Whitfield had volunteered to lead that effort.

To get the most favorable bond ratings, a guarantee of performance from Multima Corporation for the obligations of their division would also be required. Fitzgerald himself had been drafted to negotiate such a guarantee with John George Mortimer.

Legal experts were assigned responsibility to develop new agreements for customers to sign and prepare the documentation necessary to modify the company charter and bank licenses.

As James Fitzgerald looked back on that day, he took great satisfaction from different perspectives. Most apparent, his decision five years earlier to appoint a dedicated product development unit to consider, research, and create new ways of doing business now appeared validated.

Those exceptionally bright young people selected to work in relative anonymity, in a secret off-site location, had already percolated ideas that more than justified the investment. This new proposal had extraordinary potential and reflected the bold characteristics of the people on his product development team. When he made Douglas Whitfield their leader, it was in addition to his regular day job, and he did it with an expectation that one day Whitfield would assume a mantle of leadership exactly as he had today.

James also took more than a small measure of satisfaction from a recommendation he had made to John George Mortimer ten years earlier. At that time, James recommended Mortimer allocate to Multima Financial Services the surplus money that Multima received from Venture Capital Investments.

VCI's investment to acquire a fifteen percent equity position in Multima had been an integral part of the capital needed to buy Wendal Randall's company, but it totaled more than a billion dollars—ten times the amount they paid for the tiny logistics company. Mortimer immediately recognized the wisdom of parking the remaining nine hundred million dollars cash at Fitzgerald's business unit.

Regulators and bond rating agencies took great comfort from Multima's reduced need to borrow. They considered this responsible balance sheet management. That massive cash horde, combined with the confidence they built with the bond rating agencies over a decade, would surely help their game changer business expansion.

Fitzgerald leaned back in his comfortable leather chair and thought, *I like the symmetry. It's all coming together at the right time.*

He would be able to demonstrate to John George Mortimer and the board of directors that Douglas Whitfield and the rest of his management team could carry on very well without him. Because, feeling tired and spent at the age of fifty-five, James Fitzgerald wanted out.

With diligence over the past thirty years, he'd saved and invested wisely and still held all of his purchased or awarded Multima Corporation shares. He was the largest single shareholder behind John George Mortimer and VCI, owning about four percent of the company's total equity, with no debts. The last of his children would graduate from college next year, and he had a nice cabin in Wisconsin. Of course, it was a five thousand square foot, fully winterized, elegantly decorated and landscaped house on Little Silver Lake. It also had a spacious five-car garage for his cars, trucks, ATVs, boats, and snowmobiles.

Once they completed this game changer project and clearly established Whitfield as his rightful successor, Fitzgerald would be able to discuss an exit strategy with his old friend John George Mortimer.

NINETEEN

MPH Hospital, Fort Myers.
Monday, February 29, 2016

John George Mortimer tried to wake fully from his drug-induced sleep and noticed her standing at the end of his bed. It seemed he had been sleeping for some time, as he vaguely recalled seeing the same face earlier that day or night, whatever time it was.

Her gentle face reminded him of his grandmother when he was a little boy, with her rimless eyeglasses resting partway down her nose. Her sympathetic smile was warming, even in his current condition. She had asked if he needed some water. As she helped him fill a small plastic glass from a larger container, she said that it looked like he had slept well and asked if he was in pain.

Mortimer slowly sipped the water, which immediately delivered welcome relief to his parched throat. He nodded, for the sharp pain in his chest became quite intense right then. She said that his surgery seemed entirely satisfactory.

She also instructed him to use the morphine dispenser when he needed it and pointed out a button to trigger the release of the drug. She assured him it was completely safe. "It will automatically limit the amount."

The nurse also promised to return soon to give him different medications to ease the pain. A physiotherapist would help him up from the bed and start him moving around. "We like to do that as quickly as possible now," she said. "But first, I need to remove that catheter."

"Are you starting to feel more comfortable?" she asked as she finished the procedure. However, she was apparently not expecting a reply as she fussed with the bed's pillow and sheets. "I'm leaving now, but the call button is right there should you need help. I'll be back soon."

As she walked away from the bed and almost reached the door, she seemed to think of something else and stopped abruptly. Turning to face Mortimer she said, "By the way, your registration records don't indicate a religion. Would you like to have someone from the clergy visit?"

"Thank you. That won't be necessary," Mortimer responded politely and softly, with a voice still hoarse from the powerful drugs and the breathing tube used during surgery. Religion was not a factor in his life. He didn't oppose it per se. In fact, when he was younger he devoted considerable time and thought to philosophical questions. However, these days he rarely thought about it, an afterlife, or even the question of a deity.

He had become completely comfortable with his views. As long as those people who choose to follow a religion don't try to impose either their beliefs or their values on him, he would be content just to live and let live.

The soothing effects of a morphine hit started to induce sleep again, and his eyelids suddenly felt heavy. Before dozing off, his last thoughts reflected calm confidence and determination. He would enjoy this life and accomplish as much as possible every day. One day he would die, and it would naturally all come to an end.

John George Mortimer was the only child of Gavin and Mary Mortimer. Gavin was a respected professor of American history at Kennesaw State University in the small Georgia town of the same name. Mary was a typical American mother of that time, moderately content to be at home caring for her family.

Gavin Mortimer kindled his son's passion for reading at a young age. As early as four years old, John George liked to read about an hour every day. As his son matured, Gavin encouraged him to explore a broad range of books and challenged him to develop an open and inquiring mind. Critical thinking, Gavin often repeated, was crucial to understanding people, events, and life itself. He inspired John George to investigate, question, and explore everything possible.

Did an author's logic seem reasonable? Were data offered accurate? Was a described event plausible? Could there be other explanations for an occurrence? Is there an alternative possibility? Is it a logical conclusion? Usually, dinnertime discussions overflowed with such penetrating questions and challenges as Gavin tried to impart a powerful desire to think independently from an early age.

Gavin wanted his son to consider carefully all perspectives to arrive at his own conclusions, not necessarily those a teacher, the clergy, or a government leader might want people to reach. Most importantly, he encouraged him to nourish a deep-seated passion for continuous learning to feed the insatiable hunger of an inquisitive mind.

When Gavin and Mary tragically died in a head-on automobile crash, John George was a freshman at Kennesaw University. Although

Gavin had patiently and thoughtfully devoted almost twenty years developing his son's critical thinking skills, it turned out that he'd been far less adept at his own financial and estate planning.

John George found himself entirely alone after his parents' tragic deaths. He learned there was inadequate life insurance. They had failed to plan for such an unfortunate eventuality, and the insurance amount left behind covered only the remaining balance of the mortgage on their home.

He suddenly found himself the sole owner of a fully paid house, but with no financial means to support his college education or even meet his daily living expenses. There was no extended family to offer help, and friends of the Mortimers either felt no compelling obligation to see John George through the difficult transition or themselves lacked a means to help.

He could have sold the house or borrowed to finance his education and living expenses, but he reasoned such a course might require him to begin a future career deeply in debt. Instead, he decided to abandon college. He would find a job and start the next phase in his life. He did so with both calm resignation and firm determination.

Of course, he had been deeply saddened to lose his mother and father. They had been affectionate and loving parents. John George knew he would miss their continuous support and encouragement terribly, but the independence imparted by his father served John George well in the difficult time after their deaths and for many years to follow.

With only a high-school diploma, career options seemed limited, but a neighborhood supermarket had advertised for full-time employees, and he immediately responded. After applying and completing the requisite interviews, he was hired as a clerk in the grocery department with a modest hourly wage.

He quickly adapted to the routine of working in a supermarket and enjoyed the camaraderie. He learned the nuances of retailing as he charmed shopping homemakers with his humor and good cheer. Soon, he decided that he would try to become manager of a supermarket and set out to be the best he could be. Eventually, he achieved success far beyond his wildest dreams.

Today, US business media liked to tease him good-naturedly about being a billionaire college dropout. In reality, few people realized that he had pursued post-secondary school knowledge and continuous personal development with passion, ever since those first days working in a supermarket in Alpharetta.

First, he signed up for a course in food distribution, completed by correspondence from Cornell University. Then, he enrolled in business management, again studying in the privacy of his home with mail-in lessons. In subsequent years, he completed college programs in business law, economics, and accounting.

Through all of his twenties and thirties, John George arose most days about four o'clock in the morning to study for two or more hours. He also devoted most weekends to study, spending one day and sometimes more with relevant subject matter. Evenings ended with reading again for an hour or more. In fact, he read about one book a week, year after year after year.

In his forties and fifties, Mortimer discovered he had an aptitude for languages. He expanded his quest for knowledge beyond business studies to become fluent in French, German, and Spanish. At the same time, he also studied philosophy, religions, and several categories of history.

This was all undertaken using correspondence courses until the Internet became popular as a learning tool. His studies usually took place in the privacy of his home and mainly in early morning hours. Over the years, his academic achievements accumulated while he continued to build a successful business that ranked among America's finest.

Now, well into his sixties, he continued his life-long search for knowledge and still started most days with two or more hours of learning.

———————

While Mortimer fitfully slept with help from drugs, nurses in the intensive care unit of MPH Hospital frequently monitored his progress. Of course, no family or friends visited, and Mortimer's smartphone was safely tucked away in a drawer. With the aid of morphine, a quiet environment, and respectful staff, he spent most of the twenty-four hours immediately following surgery in a deep sleep.

During those tranquil hours, he was completely unaware of how many people were desperately trying to reach him.

TWENTY

Chairman's Suite, Four Seasons Tokyo Hotel at Marunouchi.
March 1, 2016

It was late in the evening, a time for Suzanne Simpson to collect her thoughts and review the day while she sipped from a glass of fine French wine. An ever polite and friendly room service attendant had delivered a vintage Bordeaux moments earlier. She noted and appreciated that every employee in the hotel courteously and cheerfully greeted her as Mrs. Simpson, all the while making an effort to pronounce her name with precision.

She couldn't recall feeling this tired before. Suzanne opened the heavy window drapes, closed earlier that day by cleaning staff to reduce energy consumption in the room. Once again, she marveled at the urban beauty of the Tokyo skyline with its hyperactive neon lights, multiple colors, and continuously metamorphosing appearance. Even at night, the financial district exuded frenetic energy.

Her day was good, though not nearly as productive as she had hoped. It started well enough with a seven o'clock breakfast meeting in her suite. For more than an hour, her team reviewed and discussed preliminary feedback from their colleagues in Atlanta.

Most critical in the analysis were some problems with Hiromi Tenaka's assumptions and projections for shipping fresh food from Japan. But the headquarters team had consulted some third-party shipping experts who thought there might be ways to modify the Japanese Agriculture Department's assumptions to address those concerns and still represent good value for Multima Supermarkets. A conclusion was likely by the end of the week.

They tackled the remaining issues with patience and careful deliberation. Before the breakfast meeting concluded, the team again compiled a list of assignments for the folks back in Atlanta. Suzanne's insistence on a deeper analysis of potential radiation issues associated with the Fukushima disaster and possible contamination in the Japanese food chain was at the top of the page.

She directed staff to include questions about customer perceptions or concerns about radiation in their next series of focus groups. Even though it was now five years since the nuclear disaster, it was important for Suzanne to know exactly how customers perceived the safety of food grown in Japan.

Immediately after their review and discussion, and before Suzanne concluded the breakfast meeting, she asked her team travel planner, Jennifer Wong, to outline the day's agenda. The perky assistant cheerfully explained they would divide into three groups crisscrossing Japan to achieve as much as possible in one day. Her concise overview of their group arrival and departure schedules took more than fifteen minutes to deliver and included excursions by jet, bus, and limousine. Looking back, Suzanne smiled as she recalled how she already felt a little fatigued just listening to their program for the day.

The wine was making her slightly drowsy, and her jet lag was more evident after their long first day in Japan. Nevertheless, she maintained her discipline to review and candidly assess results of the day's events before sleeping.

———————

"Udon noodles continue to be a staple of the Japanese diet," Gordon Goodfellow, her enthusiastic marketing leader, asserted as they began their in-flight briefing right after takeoff. Suzanne silently chuckled, but realized Goodfellow was doing the right thing to bring everyone in the entourage up to speed. They all needed to understand the background and objectives for their first meeting of the day with Samato Corporation, a manufacturer of udon noodle making equipment.

Late last year, Suzanne had authorized a visit to Japan to attend the Samato Noodle School at their training facilities in the Kagawa Prefecture. The Multima Supermarkets marketing team had conducted exhaustive research about udon and persuaded Suzanne it could be a healthy and convenient food that harried American consumers might take home from supermarkets as part of a prepared nutritious meal.

They pointed out that Japanese people in all strata of society eat large quantities and broad varieties of noodles. Kiosks for noodles peek out from seemingly every nook in Japanese cities. Additionally, noodle meals are quick to prepare, inexpensive, and healthy. Udon is one of the most nutritious of the Japanese noodles, especially when made from rice, making them gluten free.

The marketing team had studied an introduction of udon kiosks in Multima stores as one possible response to growing consumer demand for nutritious Asian foods. They were excited about the potential for cross-merchandising udon kiosks near fresh vegetable counters and displays of seasoning choices to spice up servings.

The combination of market research and experience at the noodle-making school eventually led to some exploratory negotiations with Samato for a joint venture that would launch those kiosks within Multima Supermarkets.

As expected, Gordon Goodfellow provided a comprehensive briefing on the company background, history, and financial strength. He updated the team on the status of negotiations and summarized unresolved points in the discussions. His thorough research and preparation provided real answers and sound rationale for each of the questions posed by Suzanne or his other colleagues. After about fifty minutes of discussion, Suzanne felt comfortable with the information and preparation.

Their meeting with the Samato chairman and twelve of his senior executives was to resolve all of the outstanding issues possible, and it had not disappointed. From the formal greeting and welcome at the grand front entrance, chairman Hiromi Akiyama had directed the proceedings with almost military precision. Initially, Suzanne was surprised to learn neither Akiyama nor his executives were comfortable speaking English. For the first time in her career, she found it necessary to conduct an entire meeting using an interpreter provided by Dane Capital and was grateful for Jennifer Wong's foresight to arrange one.

After some initial discomfort, she learned to speak directly to her hosts using short, precise sentences, avoiding common slang or expressions, and relying heavily on body language and non-verbal communication. She was relieved to see how quickly good conversational chemistry could develop, even with the filter of an interpreter.

She also recalled her initial discomfort with the absence of women among the Japanese management team. She thought it curious there was not a single woman among the executives. In fact, the only women present were virtually servers, pouring tea and running errands at the beck and call of the Japanese businessmen. However, these young women, who all appeared younger than twenty, seemed perfectly satisfied and cheerful about their roles. In such an environment, Suzanne was taken aback but pleased with the courtesy and underlying respect each manager demonstrated.

They all toured the Samato facilities. Akiyama beamed with pride as he led her through spotlessly clean buildings and patiently answered questions about their extensive use of robots and other advanced processing technologies. Suzanne was impressed with the good cheer of the workers. She noted their attention to immaculate sanitation practices, their broad smiles, and deep, welcoming bows from the waist whenever Suzanne's team approached individual workstations.

Remaining details to resolve before signing a joint venture contract proved to be a little more complicated. Discussions proceeded more slowly than expected. Although there appeared to be broad agreement among the parties, the Samato team seemed concerned with each minute detail of the draft accord. Language was an issue, as it became apparent there were variances between the English version that Suzanne and her team worked from and the Japanese translation prepared by Dane Capital.

Several times the interpreters from Dane became flustered and found it necessary to apologize in both Japanese and English, explaining that there might be a slightly different meaning in the Japanese version. After almost an hour of discussion, Suzanne confronted her host.

"We Westerners are always in a hurry to get a deal," she started with a smile. "So, I must ask you a question directly, Akiyama-san. Is your team ready to reach an agreement with Multima Supermarkets?"

Akiyama immediately responded in Japanese with much animation. The Dane Capital interpreter explained, "Samato certainly would like to work with Multima in America. But he also protested that his team would not be rushed to sign an agreement with which they were not entirely comfortable."

Satisfied with both his passion and body language, Suzanne suggested, "Let's form a small working group made up of Dane Capital and one or two representatives from each of our companies. We'll have this group massage the final details and translate a document they can all agree upon, then submit a revised version for both of us to sign within a few weeks." Akiyama accepted this elegant proposal with a warm smile of appreciation and promptly suggested they move to the company dining room for lunch.

The meal turned into a bonding experience. Akiyama and Suzanne truly came to know each other better with the help of the Dane Capital interpreter. She was relieved that both companies shared fundamental business values in the crucial areas of quality, integrity, and superior customer service.

After the lunch discussions, she was convinced this relationship should become a component of the game changer proposal to the board of directors. She also thought it could be ready to move forward immediately after the meeting with the board and thought they'd sort out and sign an agreement within weeks.

Once again aboard the company jet, flying towards Kyoto, Suzanne verified her impressions with her companions. They agreed the session's results were promising. The team also prepared for the next meeting with Kyomeshi Corporation, one of Japan's largest distributors of rice and tea. The objective was to establish a private label arrangement in which Kyomeshi would produce and package a range of Japanese products using formulations exclusive to Multima Supermarkets. Packaging would also feature Multima's brand name and logos.

Such a relationship could dramatically reduce purchasing costs and make it possible to sell unique selections of rice and tea at reasonable prices in America. Compared with well-known brands, privately branded products usually earned more profit for every package sold, despite a lower retail price.

Her marketing team briefed Suzanne on those issues remaining to resolve, possible impediments to an agreement, and their recommended strategy to accommodate Kyomeshi management. They warned her the company culture was different from the highly professional business environment at Samato.

"Even though the management team at Kyomeshi speaks English more fluently and trade more internationally, its executives seem to be less polished and professional in their approach to customers," Goodfellow had cautioned. "Despite possible appearances to the contrary, everyone should remember that Kyomeshi is the largest distributor of rice and tea products in the world. They have an incredibly powerful influence on both growers and global prices."

Suzanne was grateful for the heads up. From the time the Kyomeshi management team greeted them at the front door of their nondescript office building and throughout the meeting that followed, she was uncomfortable. Of particular concern was a tendency for Kyomeshi managers to treat her as almost invisible.

When she posed questions during the meeting, the Japanese hosts usually made eye contact with her male colleagues as they responded. Suzanne initially attributed this annoying tendency to greater familiarity with the men from when they had visited during their trip to Japan last year.

However, over the course of the meeting, she became firmly convinced their behavior was purely sexist. Her annoyance turned to displeasure. She displayed her irritation by asking increasingly difficult questions, more deeply examining proposed pricing structures, and firmly insisting on more favorable transaction terms.

Her team noticed her uncharacteristic resistance and eventually suggested a break. "Maybe it would be helpful to tour the office, warehouse, and packing facilities first, and then return to negotiations after our tour," Gordon Goodfellow had diplomatically suggested.

Suzanne reluctantly agreed. During their walk through the factory, she noted a hushed conversation between Gordon and the Dane Capital interpreter. Moments later, the interpreter discretely whispered something to the Kyomeshi chairman. Over the following few minutes of the tour, she noticed him huddle for a brief talk in Japanese with a colleague. Then, she watched that individual quickly circulate among the rest of the Kyomeshi management team, quietly communicating some unknown message.

Upon their return to the negotiations, Suzanne detected an immediate and profound change in the tone of the meeting. Eye contact focused on her. Questions were answered directly, patiently, and completely. Their manner became noticeably deferential, and concessions she had requested earlier were accepted. She made a mental note to check with Gordon to confirm what transpired to evoke such a dramatic change.

After the meeting, they all climbed into a mini-bus and traveled to an upscale and traditional Japanese restaurant. There, the group was warmly welcomed by serving staff with deep bows, big smiles, and a stream of cheerful greetings as a hostess led the way to a private tatami dining room.

After multiple opening toasts with sake, the Kyomeshi chairman announced that dinner would start. Moments later, a massive whole salmon arrived on a long wooden plank carried by two young women. The plank was about one inch thick and more than four feet long. The fish on it was just spectacular and naturally beautiful.

She guessed it measured more than three feet with mounds of clear chipped ice tightly packed all around. Decorations included lemon slices, a parsley garnish, and a colorful assortment of Japanese vegetables. To Suzanne, presentation of the brilliantly colored salmon was a work of art.

The servers gracefully and respectfully lowered the large cedar plank into the center of the table. As they ceremoniously positioned the salmon, a hush fell over the room. Then, as one, all of the participants breathlessly rushed to comment on the impressive majesty of the fish. For a brief moment, there was a cacophony of sound in English and Japanese.

In the midst of this spurt of enthusiasm, to Suzanne's astonishment, the majestic salmon suddenly twitched! She looked again. Another gentle quiver. Her Japanese hosts joyfully explained this fish was so fresh the body was still releasing its last remnants of life. Amazingly, this quivering was occurring even after the salmon had been cleaned and filleted into bite-sized sections using precise incisions that appeared almost invisible.

Her Japanese hosts exhorted Suzanne to select the first portion of the still moving and uncooked salmon. Hesitant, Suzanne tried to find excuses to delay the process. She asked trivial questions about the fish, its preparation, its probable origins, and other morsels of non-essential information that bought her a little time to think.

Her hosts noticed the hesitation and commented that eating fresh salmon would be just like eating sushi back home. That helpful clarification was not a terribly reassuring message. "But sushi is usually served wrapped in rice, Japanese seaweed, and wasabi mustard," she pointed out. "This magnificent specimen that you are urging me to sample is completely raw." *Raw, uncooked food. Salmon without the benefit of any smoking, heating, spices, or other preparation*, she thought.

Her unpleasant memory of a sushi experience from her college days distressingly resurfaced. She understood why the first US President Bush had embarrassingly thrown up his dinner on Japanese hosts years earlier during a meal in a similar environment. Still, she was determined to avoid such an occurrence. She also resolved not to display any further signs of trepidation to her hosts.

With a dramatic flair, Suzanne raised the large white cloth napkin from her lap for all of her hosts to see. Then, after leaning forward to hold her outstretched napkin directly above the salmon, with a gesture of elegance and style, she gently covered its head with her napkin.

"I simply can't eat the poor thing while it's still looking at me!" she said.

With chopsticks delicately cradled in her hand, Suzanne reached forward and deftly gripped a cubed fillet. Cautiously, she raised it to her mouth. Then, to the delight and applause of her Japanese hosts, she chewed and tentatively swallowed the chilled fish.

To her surprise, it was very appetizing. The texture was velvety smooth, the flavor satisfyingly mild, and there had been no unpleasant odor. She served herself several additional portions and also enjoyed a variety of soups, salads, and noodles that followed. She could describe the rest of that dinner as uneventful, even enjoyable.

As dinner and discussion came to a conclusion, Gordon Goodfellow unexpectedly announced that he and his other male colleagues would stay in Kyoto for a few hours more to do some relationship building with the Kyomeshi executives. Since there were no further meetings planned until eight o'clock the next morning, he assumed Suzanne would not mind traveling back to Tokyo with the Dane Capital interpreter. The male colleagues would catch the last train to Tokyo after some 'off-line' discussions with the Kyomeshi team, he explained.

Suzanne took note of the partially suppressed giggles from their Japanese hosts as Goodfellow outlined their intentions. She assured her colleagues she would be fine, and they would discuss today's meeting in more detail at the scheduled session the next morning in her suite.

Jokingly, she expressed hope the intended relationship building exercise would result in a further five or even ten percent discount from the prices they had discussed that afternoon. With all participants laughing, bowing, and shaking hands, their dinner meeting concluded without any formal agreement. Suzanne remained not entirely comfortable with either the business culture of Kyomeshi or the proposed private-branding deal.

On the mini-bus to the Kyoto airport, the Dane Capital interpreter suggested that her male colleagues were likely going to visit a hostess bar or *kyabakura*. That would probably explain why they had not invited her to join.

With Suzanne's prompting, the interpreter explained that visits to kyabakura were a traditional practice for Japanese businessmen to build relationships with both customers and colleagues. Most kyabakura bars are upscale drinking establishments. They earn their name 'hostess bars' because patrons are warmly greeted and guided to an area away from other customers. Once seated, attractive women who work as hostesses join the guests. The establishment often offers an individual hostess for each patron.

They are typically young, charming, and very friendly. Their job is to make their guests feel welcome, engage in conversation, and encourage them to drink. Consumption of large amounts of alcohol might be the single most important objective. In fact, bar owners usually pay hostesses a generous commission based on the size of the total bar bill.

These servers seem to encourage the consumption of the maximum possible without a customer becoming intoxicated. They urge their assigned companions to eat different kinds of freshly prepared snacks as they drink, sing karaoke, and engage in playful flirtation. It's all relatively harmless fun.

The Dane Capital interpreter assured Suzanne that her male colleagues might have a little too much to drink and suffer from nasty hangovers the next morning, but that would probably be the extent of the damage. Further, they might find their relationship with Kyomeshi managers even better because of the experience.

As she poured a second glass of red wine and relaxed in her suite, Suzanne doubted her colleagues' visit to a *kyabakura* would do much to modify the sexist attitudes of the Kyomeshi management team. Still, she decided to withhold final judgment until she had an opportunity for a frank conversation with her marketing leader.

Then she had another quick inspiration. Earlier, the Dane Capital interpreter finished her *kyabakura* explanation with a light-hearted suggestion that Suzanne should treat herself to a massage in her room. This practice was another long tradition of Japanese businesspeople, she explained. She added that it would be much more relaxing than her male colleagues' experience and leave Suzanne pleasantly refreshed in the morning.

Although the tall, antique grandfather clock in her suite indicated that midnight was rapidly approaching, she decided she would act on the interpreter's playful suggestion. She picked up the phone in her room, called the concierge assigned to her suite, and asked to arrange a massage in her room as quickly as possible.

"And let's make that masseur male," Suzanne had instructed, almost as an afterthought.

TWENTY-ONE

On the German Autobahn A-61, to Düsseldorf.
Afternoon, March 1, 2016

Max Bergmann excused himself from a pleasant conversation with Wendal to link into an important video conference. He listened intently through a professional-quality headset connected to his latest generation tablet. Focused with equal intensity on the device's screen, he studied the body language and mannerisms of the current speaker carefully.

During this trip, Bergmann had frequently checked the Internet for information or clarification while they chatted. Now, he was using Skype for a video conference. Because Max was using a headset, there was no sound coming from the tablet and Wendal heard only an occasional comment or question in German. Otherwise, the vehicle was silent.

Wendal focused first on his smartphone messages. Meanwhile, Frau Schäffer, seated in front next to the chauffeur, also seemed to be busily absorbed with her emails. Wendal was still silently seething with her insistence that she join them for this trip to Heidelberg. He sensed that Bergmann wanted to discuss something privately, but there had been no dissuading Howard Knight's informant. As a result, while the plant tour had been informative, it was also uneventful. There had simply been no opportunity for Wendal and the president of TBG to get to know each other better.

Max's BMW 750i limousine seemed to glide the Autobahn with only a smooth purr from its finely tuned, high-performance engine humming in the background. Incredibly, the vehicle speedometer indicated they were currently traveling well over two hundred kilometers per hour—more than double limits back home.

Traffic flowed smoothly at similarly high speeds as they swept past large exit signs indicating the city of Koblenz to the right. They would probably arrive at the Steigenberger Park Hotel in Düsseldorf "within the next ninety minutes, depending traffic," the chauffeur had stiffly responded to Wendal's query a few moments earlier.

The gentle, pulsating motion of a luxury automobile, combined with Wendal's short sleep the previous night, had initially tempted him to close his eyes and nap for a few minutes. He fought off this urge to relax because he urgently needed to process events of the past twenty-four hours. He also wanted to prepare for an evening telephone call with Howard Knight.

He had slept little the previous night for one simple reason: stress. Immediately after meeting with Max Bergmann at TBG, Wendal and his team returned to the Steigenberger Park Hotel. But there had been no time to explore the gracious ambiance of the well-known landmark. Instead, the team convened in the huge dining area of Wendal's sprawling suite. Frau Schäffer ordered sandwiches with soft drinks and snacks as the group reviewed and debated the challenges with TBG's fulfillment schedule and the crisis with software compatibility. The situation seemed to worsen with each passing hour, despite Frau Schäffer's repeated assurances that the challenges really were all manageable.

"It's common for German businesspeople to overestimate costs as part of their negotiation strategy," she explained. "Should they get an agreement with those higher expenses baked into the price, they then aggressively seek ways to economize when they start to produce goods or deliver services. Any savings they can make then flow directly to the bottom line as added profits."

She was also sure the same principle applied to delivery schedules. "Often they propose much longer than necessary delivery timetables to give themselves a chance to speed up the pace of completion and further reduce their costs."

To further allay concerns, Frau Schäffer repeatedly reminded the team that VCI had associates in Russia who could find and deliver all the computer software programmers TBG might need to make the necessary software modifications.

But to Wendal, Frau Schäffer's optimistic efforts to convince the team that circumstances were manageable seemed like arguing whether a glass of water was half full or half empty. It was what it was. From his perspective, the constant stream of bad news and challenges seemed to grow with each passing hour.

First, there had been one more call from a TBG executive to the technology leader of Wendal's team. He had just concluded a follow-up conversation with the software developer, PAS. In that conversation, he discovered PAS planned another new software release within a few days that would create even more compatibility issues.

The previously estimated one hundred modifications had now grown by more than half. Further, PAS would not be able to free up any software engineers to work on Multima's required changes until the release of that new version launched in mid-March. This new complication would require an astounding five thousand additional programming hours and further delay modification of the software code by at least two weeks.

A few minutes later, Frau Schäffer gingerly reported receipt of an additional email from her colleagues at VCI. "They now imply it might take longer than first thought to round up one hundred or so needed resources from Russia. Apparently, they'll have to direct some additional cash to the right people to complete the difficult task in such a short time." Certainly, more discussion would be necessary.

Finally, just before concluding the meeting at two o'clock that morning, there was an email from Suzanne Simpson's surrogate in Atlanta. Forwarded by his assistant in Miami, it notified Wendal that Suzanne was not prepared to release the crucial payroll data needed for a cost-benefit analysis. Without substantial evidence of the project's benefits, the board of directors would almost certainly withhold approval of Operation Bright Star. They might even scoff at such a radical proposal.

Wendal weighed all of these circumstances and tried to identify alternatives well into the wee hours of the morning. He had finally concluded there was no other immediate game changer strategy he could propose to the board in such a short time. He saw no alternative but to press forward with Operation Bright Star and somehow pull it all together—regardless of costs.

He also decided that he could not appeal directly to Suzanne Simpson at this stage. She would almost certainly oppose it. Of that, he was quite sure.

With this rather gloomy background, Wendal desperately sought some brilliant new inspiration to allay the anticipated concerns of Howard Knight and counterbalance the presumably negative information he would surely get from Frau Schäffer. So far, in the brilliant new inspiration department, Wendal was drawing a blank.

As the streaking BMW 750i approached Düsseldorf, Max Bergmann concluded his video conference. He turned slightly in his seat to more directly face his companion. Then, ignoring Frau Schäffer in front, Max started to bombard Wendal with a series of questions about his personal activities and interests outside of work.

In what part of Miami did Wendal live? Did he have a significant other? What kinds of exercise did he like? What about recreation? Had Wendal traveled outside the U.S.A. often? Where did he enjoy visiting? One question cascaded into another as Max Bergmann quickly and efficiently accomplished his objective to learn as much as possible about the life and personal interests of Wendal Randall.

Wendal felt surprisingly relaxed and open with his responses and comments. For whatever reasons, he liked Max Bergmann and felt entirely comfortable relating information to him, fully expecting that Frau Schäffer was absorbing every word.

As the chauffeur exited from the Autobahn and dramatically decelerated to speeds appropriate within the city, Bergmann leaned towards Wendal and asked quietly, "Ever been to Amsterdam?"

Wendal shook his head one time in response. Even more softly, Bergmann whispered, "No matter how it ends this week, care to join me for a couple enjoyable nights in Amsterdam?"

Intrigued, Wendal smiled conspiratorially and nodded. Sitting up front, Frau Schäffer could not see the head gesture or hear the full conversation. But she did discern a name, "Amsterdam".

She knew she should follow her intuition. It was seldom wrong. Combined with her impressions about both passengers in the rear seat and her intimate knowledge of the Netherlands, she had heard enough to develop the embryo of a unique opportunity. Her resources in Amsterdam were extensive. The idea just might work.

However, a little more planning was necessary before she'd be ready to reveal her evolving scheme to Howard Knight.

TWENTY-TWO

James Fitzgerald became a little perplexed after he telephoned John George Mortimer's office earlier that morning. Mortimer's assistant informed him her boss would not be available for almost another week. March seven was the date she expected him back in the office. This concerned Fitzgerald more than a little, because Mortimer had not previously mentioned anything about a vacation.

Of course, Mortimer had no obligation to alert Fitzgerald to his plans, holiday or otherwise. Nevertheless, John George usually signaled such intended time away in deference to their long friendship. Usually, it would be one email sentence, an assurance he would be immediately accessible by phone should Fitzgerald urgently need to discuss something. Of course, he rarely acted on such invitations.

This time, though, John George had not given any notice at all. Further, Sally-Ann had also told him not to bother trying the smartphone because Mortimer would not have access to Wi-Fi, voice communication, or email. He was probably somewhere outside the country, possibly in a remote area. It made Fitzgerald curious and altered his long-held impression that Mortimer always would let him know when he'd be outside the country, just in case.

Mortimer's housekeeper came in each day, so Fitzgerald tried to reach her at John George's home number. Unfortunately, a recorded voice message greeted him, informing him that Mortimer was not available and requesting the caller to leave a message. Fitzgerald decided to try his smartphone number regardless. Same recorded message, with no particulars. At that juncture, James finally left a message requesting a return call at Mortimer's convenience.

Throughout the morning, as Fitzgerald finished his scheduled meetings and processed correspondence in an order determined by his assistant, his inability to reach Mortimer continued to resurface, causing a gnawing sense of discomfort. This intensifying unease finally prompted

Fitzgerald to call his favorite and most trusted resource in Multima Financial Services' business intelligence group, Natalia Tenaz.

He asked her to make a couple completely confidential and discreet inquiries to determine the current whereabouts of John George Mortimer. That incredibly bright young woman in business intelligence quickly got back to him with startling news. Mortimer was currently in a critical care bed of the cancer treatment section at MPH Hospital in South Fort Myers, Florida, hidden away from official records.

"According to my informant, his hospital archive is sketchy. Not even a date of admission," Natalia said. "Everything related to his stay has a secret classification that's impossible to access in the MPH computer system. I can't divulge the identity of my source, but I'm one hundred percent confident about the reliability and accuracy of the info I got. There's no question Mortimer had surgery yesterday, is recovering well, and is expected to remain there another few days. That's all the news I could get so far, but I'll dig for more if you need it."

"Keep digging," James Fitzgerald directed. "I want to know as much as possible, as soon as possible. I know it's not necessary to say this, but all inquiries need to be completely discreet, entirely confidential. Share it with me only."

James Fitzgerald silently processed this unsettling new information. Things were starting to add up. This news would certainly explain why John George had not alerted him to the planned time away. It might also explain why Mortimer expected to be incommunicado until the seventh of March. Perhaps more importantly, it might suggest an underlying motivation for Mortimer's uncharacteristic behavior at the February management meeting.

In addition to being a subtext for his unusual autocratic management style that day, Mortimer's announcement of the game changer projects, which at first seemed bizarre, now made sense. It was all starting to trace an outline of his real intentions. He likely had a process underway to name a successor.

That development did not fit at all well with Fitzgerald's personal succession plans. Typically, boards of directors at major corporations wanted to avoid departures of key senior leaders at the same time. A gradual transition was the usual axiom. This collision of timing would certainly require some careful thought over the next few days. At that moment, however, increasingly louder alarm bells penetrated his vigilant political subconscious.

THREE WEEKS LESS A DAY

It was the parting comment the young woman in business intelligence shared just as she was ending her call. "My source gave me one
more important piece of information," Natalia Tenaz relayed in a tone
that seemed perplexed. "It seems Howard Knight is also trying urgently
to find Mortimer, but my source didn't give any info to him."

This was most curious. Why would this secret informant apparently be willing to share such information with Natalia, then specifically
mention that she had not shared the same discovery with Knight? It all
seemed peculiar.

TWENTY-THREE

In an office tower near Wall Street, New York.
Early afternoon, March 1, 2016

Howard Knight answered the telephone at his desk on its first ring with his usual brusque greeting. "Knight here."

"Checking in for our agreed conversation, Howard," Wendal Randall started tentatively. "Is now still a convenient time for you?"

"Absolutely. Tell me how your discussions in Germany are progressing," Knight demanded, jumping in without any opening pleasantries.

Wendal swallowed hard and cleared his throat to be sure his voice remained strong and confident. The news he was about to impart was not ideal, and he needed to choose his words carefully. He also expected that Frau Schäffer had probably already shared her detached perspective on the situation with Knight. It was important that Wendal's version of the facts not vary significantly. His only latitude would be the spin on these bits of information, and he planned to give the best possible appearance to a perilous situation.

"The issues are much more complicated than I was initially led to believe," he started. "And it's unquestionably opportune that I made the trip over here. We've got one fundamental hurdle to navigate, but it's a big one. For multiple reasons, the PAS software needs to be re-written and updated to meet our needs. It's a bigger job than anyone expected.

"Fortunately, the CEO at Technologie Bergmann GmbH is ready to work with us to get the revisions done as soon as possible. And your German colleague Frau Schäffer has been very helpful in her efforts to find software coding resources in Russia. In my view, we'll still be able to get the job completed within the original sixty-day window, but it's going to cost us a lot of money."

"Will the added expense still produce a favorable cost to benefit?" Knight probed.

"Not sure yet," Wendal replied. "We're still trying to get payroll information from Suzanne's team. So far, they've been reluctant to share it."

"Do you need to get Mortimer involved?" Knight asked.

"Not yet," Wendal responded. "He might not be helpful. With his reluctance to shed headcount, I don't think he'll help. I wouldn't expect him to make any contribution to building an opposing value proposition. So I've set another channel in motion."

Counterintuitively, Wendal decided to divulge a hint of the plan. "With the technical capabilities of the guys on my team, we'll get that info one way or another, and I've made sure we won't leave any trail that can be traced back to me."

"Tell me more," Knight insisted with an edge of annoyance.

"Before I called you today, I arranged for a long-time and completely reliable colleague to take a leave of absence for the next few weeks. Willy Fernandez is a former classmate from MIT who joined me right at the beginning, and I trust him implicitly. There's nobody who can penetrate a computer system better. There isn't a firewall he can't break. He'll retrieve the info we need."

"I hope no one can trace a path to anyone at Multima Logistics or to VCI for that matter," Knight said.

"Right," Randall responded. "Willy's from Colombia. He's buying a new laptop in Miami before he leaves for Bogotá tonight. He'll do his thing from an Internet café there, then disappear for a few weeks to visit his family's small village. I'll destroy the new laptop right after he sends me the file. I've assured him I'll personally take care of all his expenses, pay him while he is away, and give him a nice five-figure bonus to keep it all confidential. We can trust him, and any attempt to trace will end with an Internet café in Bogotá. There will be no paper or electronic trail. Full stop."

"Okay," Knight replied. "But don't pay Willy yourself. Somebody might eventually connect the dots. Let me know how much you owe and how to reach the guy. I'll have someone in VCI's Bogotá office give him what you've promised in cash. You can settle up with me later."

"Right, that does sound better," Wendal conceded.

"Now, back to that value proposition you mentioned. You're right. You'll need to convince a skeptical board of directors that the benefits of Operation Bright Star exceed the costs of implementation by a wide margin. What'll you do if the numbers don't work?"

"Once we know the projected costs of the software revisions and get our hands on the supermarket division's labor cost file, we'll know the delta we need to achieve. Frau Schäffer also said there may be some price flexibility with the Russian sources if we put some cash in the right hands," Wendal said tentatively.

"Yeah. I know about that," Knight acknowledged. "But you need to remember that we'll owe for more than the incentive money you have to pay. While our source may be able to influence the price you're charged, the people doing the work still need to be paid the going rate. Somebody will have to cover that cost.

"Maybe," he continued, "we could get them to submit a low price in their proposal and have a side agreement for their actual invoices to reflect real costs. Maybe they could delay those invoices until Multima's new fiscal year."

"I get it," Wendal acknowledged. "Is that something VCI can take care of or do I need to get involved?"

"Schäffer will handle it," Knight replied. "We'll make the incentive payment. You'll need to settle up with us for that expense plus some compensation to the provider for delaying his invoices. Together, that will be about twenty percent of the full contract amount. Are you okay with that?"

Wendal had no idea how much that twenty percent would be. However, he saw little alternative under the circumstances.

"Yeah," he murmured with little enthusiasm.

There was no goodbye to conclude the call. As the grating buzz of the dial tone continued, Wendal felt what seemed like the weight of an anvil press down heavily on his shoulders.

He realized that rather than escaping from Howard Knight's clutches, he was gradually becoming more indebted. He sensed that his growing desire to become CEO at Multima had started to outweigh his trepidation about potential circumstances. He believed there would still be time to correct all that.

He reached for a bottle of premium Russian vodka sitting on the desk. He filled a tall glass to the brim and then gulped the entire contents without the bother of a mixer. Then he put on his winter coat, left his suite, walked the length of the corridor, pushed the elevator call button, and descended to the hotel lobby without a word to anyone.

It was time to find another pay phone. He needed to talk to Willy Fernandez again.

TWENTY-FOUR

Cancer section, MPH Hospital, Fort Myers.
Late afternoon, March 1, 2016

It was sharp, throbbing, and continuous. Periodic morphine hits dulled the pain temporarily, and oral medication provided some further relief. Still, the surgery to remove his breast created an intensely sensitive area with excruciating discomfort. John George Mortimer found it increasingly difficult to manage.

He tried to read, but even the slightest movements of his arm caused him to cringe. Earlier, he had checked his messages, learning that James Fitzgerald and Howard Knight were both trying to reach him. Both were apparently ignoring the excuses Alberto Ferer or Sally-Ann Bureau would have given them. Other emails also continued to accumulate in his inbox, but Mortimer lacked the energy to read them.

His surgeon had visited again that morning and said all appeared to be progressing well. There were no apparent infections. The wound area looked as expected, and the surgeon took evident pride in pointing out the remaining trace of an incredibly small incision. He had used a hand mirror to show the mark to John George, all the while assuring him any remaining scar would be minuscule.

More important, the surgeon emphasized his conviction that he had removed all the cancerous cells. The biopsy apparently confirmed no cancer had spread to the lymph nodes. To complete his good news, the surgeon suggested that Mortimer could probably continue recovery at home if all continued to go well for the next twenty-four hours. This suggestion required a commitment from Mortimer in return. He could not start to work, either at home or his office, for another two weeks.

Then there was some less welcome news. The oncologist was recommending four weeks of chemotherapy and six weeks of radiation treatments. Even though the surgeon was confident he had removed all the cancer, to be entirely safe, the oncologist wanted to take extra treatment steps to minimize the risk of any recurrence. Preventative medicine, the surgeon had added.

Because Mortimer was otherwise fit and healthy, the medical team was confident his body could withstand the rigors and terrible side effects of those treatments. The added precautionary steps would help put his mind at ease that any return of cancer would be dramatically less likely.

The surgeon assured him there was no need to decide right now. He should take a few days to think about it before he made a final decision, but the medical team was strongly recommending chemotherapy, then radiation treatments, with the process to start in about two weeks. John George agreed to let them know his decision early the following week, sometime after the seventh of March.

In those hours since the surgeon's visit, Mortimer had reworked the timeline repeatedly in his mind. Two weeks forward would be the middle of March. Assuming he could start chemotherapy then, he would complete the treatments by mid-April. That would be only a few days before the scheduled meeting of the board of directors to review and approve the division presidents' game changer assignments.

Everything he had read about cancer treatments suggested to him that chemotherapy would be a most debilitating, uncomfortable, and telling experience on his body. He would lose his hair and probably experience some degree of nausea. He would look drawn and as pale as chalk. Who could know what other side effects might occur?

It was also unlikely that he would look much better before the meeting with the board on April 23. Everyone who saw him would certainly know there was something awry. A denial wouldn't work, and there would be no practical way to camouflage the physical damage or hide the ravages of the cancer treatments.

He definitively concluded that chemotherapy couldn't start until sometime after the meeting of the board of directors. He would not risk a possible diversion or an effort to displace him by divulging his cancer treatments. The medical team would just have to develop an alternate plan.

At that critical juncture in his career, there was now nothing more important for him than oversight of the process to choose his successor as CEO. He vowed to do everything within his power to assure the successor would be his preferred candidate. Should it become necessary to do so, he was prepared to put his health at some risk to achieve that goal.

With that matter settled in his mind, John George pressed a button to produce another hit of morphine. He leaned his head back, sinking deep into a fluffy pillow, and breathed deeply to welcome the warm glow. A gradual easing of pain and sleep would follow soon.

TWENTY-FIVE

Fitness room, Four Seasons Tokyo Hotel at Marunouchi.
March 2, 2016

It had been four days since Suzanne Simpson made time for some vigorous exercise, an extremely unusual occurrence. She understood the role of fitness in the delicate preservation of her trim and attractive appearance. She also completely embraced the notion of a correlation between physical exercise and brain function and wanted to ensure no diminution of her mental capacity, especially during this period of hectic schedules and jet lag.

She asked the concierge to wake her at five that morning. By five-fifteen, dressed in workout clothes, she was running on the treadmill in the Four Seasons Tokyo's small, functional fitness room. The only hotel guest working out at that hour, she welcomed the tranquility as she gazed out the panoramic floor-to-ceiling windows offering another spectacular view of the Tokyo business district skyline.

As she gradually increased her pace to a steady run, Suzanne's mind started to wander, as was usual when she worked out. She always enjoyed this private time to exercise and liked to let her mind roam, without the intense focus and discipline she continuously imposed on herself throughout her workday.

She realized this practice had served her well over the years. In fact, some of her most creative ideas were both seeded and nurtured during thirty-minute runs uphill on a treadmill. Not surprisingly, that morning her mind veered down a path that was unquestionably more personal. Suzanne felt a pleasant warming sensation return as her attention drifted back to the amazing massage in the privacy of her suite only a few hours earlier.

The male masseur Suzanne requested from the hotel concierge arrived within thirty minutes of her call, precisely as promised.

During the wait, Suzanne had enjoyed a soothing hot bath, after which she slipped on a complimentary plush cotton robe provided by the hotel. She responded promptly to the doorbell ring and cheerfully greeted the concierge, who accompanied a rather short, elderly Japanese man lugging a folded, portable massage table.

After she performed quick introductions, this energetic and versatile woman immediately helped the masseur assemble his massage table in the spacious living room. As Suzanne watched, she sensed that the masseur might be blind.

Speaking Japanese, the concierge issued brief instructions to the man, to which the masseur promptly reacted with confidence and surprising physical grace. As the concierge back-stepped her way towards the door, stopping to bow every few feet, she encouraged Suzanne to feel comfortable about removing the cotton robe. It allowed the masseur to deliver a much better massage, she explained. Then she helpfully confirmed the masseur was, unfortunately, blind.

Closing the door, the concierge motioned Suzanne to lie on her stomach on the massage table. Without hesitation, she completely disrobed. Having had several lovers, she was at ease being nude and equally relaxed about the masseur touching much of her body. After she had shed her robe and tossed it casually on a nearby leather sofa, Suzanne approached the massage table. She gracefully slid onto the table with her stomach down as instructed and murmured to the masseur that he should begin whenever he was ready. The masseur seemed to understand. He acknowledged with a heavily accented, "We start now, okay," in English. However, his comment sounded more like a question than a statement, so she confirmed her readiness.

Within minutes, she became more relaxed than she could ever recall. The blind masseur quickly achieved an exquisite balance as he massaged her back. He combined firmness with slow and deliberate movements. His deft hands were strong and muscular, but his touch remained surprisingly gentle. The fragrant oils he applied became almost hypnotic.

He carefully kneaded the muscles in her shoulders and upper back. As he patiently and methodically moved his hands in an organized pattern from her neck to lower back, she could feel stress, jet lag, and fatigue flow from her body. Then, he repeated his magic on each of her legs, from the tips of her toes slowly upward towards her thighs. She could gradually feel a release of tension from her tired muscles that was both subtle and soothing. She was so completely relaxed she almost fell asleep.

A few minutes later, the masseur asked her to roll over onto her back. He massaged each of her toes and methodically worked his way up her legs. As he was kneading her left inner thigh, he gently roused the dozing Suzanne and queried in a quiet and soothing voice if she might like an "extra special massage."

His Japanese accent so distorted his pronunciation that Suzanne had difficulty understanding and asked him to repeat his question. He repeated himself a little more clearly.

Suzanne had already agreed to pay a fee of fifteen thousand yen, which she calculated to be about one hundred and fifty dollars. She assumed she was already receiving the best available one-hour massage. To clarify, she asked the masseur what he meant.

To her surprise, she felt the masseur ever so lightly touch her pubic region, where he applied gentle pressure for just an instant. Her body immediately responded. As a reflex, her legs relaxed and parted slightly, and her heart rate accelerated in anticipation. The masseur's other hand gently brushed the nipple of her left breast, before he cupped her breast in his wonderfully soft hands and squeezed with mild pressure.

He asked again. With these subtle touches of her sensitive sexual areas, it dawned on the somewhat groggy Suzanne exactly what the masseur was proposing. She did not reject the idea outright. As he patiently continued to massage the inside of her upper thigh, just inches from her vagina, she inquired how much more an extra special massage might cost. Quite clearly and precisely, the masseur responded the cost would be five thousand yen.

Suzanne had never before encountered such an offer. She had never previously paid anyone for any form of sexual activity, knowing well that she could attract virtually any man, at almost any time. But there in Tokyo, in the middle of the night, in the privacy of her suite, and in the hands of this gentle blind Japanese masseur, the idea was not at all repulsive. Rather, it seemed intriguing.

Yes, she finally whispered. At the same time, she slowly and deliberately gave way to the mounting tension and allowed her legs to spread, almost imperceptibly, more open and relaxed.

The masseur and his extra special massage did not disappoint. For several minutes, he continued to lightly stroke her inner thigh with fleeting diversions to her pubic patch, where he would apply increasing pressure with each visit. Then, he focused higher on her body as Suzanne lay on the massage table with her arms at her side and her legs still slightly apart.

Soon, his hands were slowly and softly stroking her breasts, skillfully taking her nipples between his fingers as he pressed in a slow circular motion. Suzanne could feel her nipples harden with arousal, her breathing shorter and deeper.

After several minutes, the masseur started to massage her pubic region gently, with both hands. Suddenly, he probed inside her moist vagina with his long index finger and immediately reached her most sensitive spot. This touch caused Suzanne to twitch slightly in reflex, moan softly with delight, and spread her legs more invitingly apart.

Knowingly, the masseur focused on her most sensitive sexual nerves, and his hands seemed more energized. First, he applied varying amounts of pressure as he lubricated her vaginal opening with the warm liquid already secreting from her aroused sexual organs. He altered the pace of the massage, with one hand gently stroking her clitoris and the other alternately rubbing her pelvic region, then deeply probing inside her vagina.

It took only a few minutes for Suzanne to experience an orgasm and only another short time to experience an even stronger, prolonged rush of delicious satisfaction.

A stream of intensifying orgasms erupted, one quickly after the other. Each left her wanting more as the intensity grew and her glow of pleasure amplified. It was all she could do to suppress her desire to scream as she often did during intensely pleasurable intercourse with a lover.

Unbelievably, using only his masterful and gentle fingers, this blind elderly Japanese masseur had given her satisfaction almost as intense as her best sexual experiences. After several minutes, he stopped and whispered in her ear softly, inquiring if it was okay for him to leave.

Suzanne sat upright on the massage table. She took a moment to regain her physical balance and perspective, and then dismounted from the table, covering her very relaxed and satisfied body with the plush hotel robe. As she wrapped it around her, the masseur presented a small paper invoice with Japanese characters confirming his fee for the massage.

She noted that either the concierge or the masseur had excellent foresight. Printed in neat English characters was the word 'Extra' with ¥ 5000 displayed beside it. Suzanne smiled as she signed the chit authorizing the charge to her hotel suite billing. She fully realized that someone had expected her to enjoy the extra special massage option, even before the masseur had ventured into her room.

As Suzanne continued to run on the treadmill, she suddenly realized she'd spent almost as much time reliving this wonderful event in her memory as it had taken in the first place. With one somewhat wistful wish it could all occur again, Suzanne jolted her thoughts back to the present and the issues demanding her immediate attention for the day ahead.

There would be just enough time to shower, dress, and pack her luggage before a planned eight o'clock breakfast meeting with her team. Before that, she needed to read the several emails on her smartphone. With a towel wrapped loosely around her neck to absorb a surprising amount of perspiration from her workout, she started reading those messages as she waited for the elevator.

An exclamation mark highlighted the first one. To her immediate dismay, the subject line announced a shocking discovery. Just minutes earlier, Multima Supermarkets' mainframe computer system had been mysteriously compromised. They'd been hacked!

Valuable, sensitive, and highly confidential databases containing information about both employees and customers had been copied and stolen according to her executive responsible for information technology.

He could only speculate that perhaps thieves were looking for customer credit card information and advised that Multima should immediately consider announcing this security breach to the public so customers would be alert to possible identity theft.

Suzanne grimaced as implications of this disastrous news set in, and she considered what such an announcement might mean. Security breaches were very, very bad for business. Like other retailers recently, Multima Supermarkets could lose crucial customer confidence. She needed to be more than careful as she plotted a strategy to contain any damage.

Intuitively, she also wondered if the theft might be intended as a distraction from another target. That ultra-sensitive employee payroll information she had earlier refused to share with her colleagues at Multima Logistics immediately popped to mind.

Without hesitation, Suzanne typed a brief response. She told her information technology leader, Dieter Lehren, that he should convene a conference call right away with their media relations specialist and Alberto Ferer, general counsel at Multima headquarters. She instructed them to draft a media release to announce the theft as quickly as possible and email a draft version to her for approval before distribution.

She went back and added John George Mortimer's name to the email heading so he too would be aware of her instructions. With a shudder of apprehension, she worried that this less than auspicious start to the day just might be an omen of a very long and challenging one to come.

TWENTY-SIX

In Düsseldorf's Steigenberger Park Hotel.
Afternoon, March 2, 2016

Wendal Randall's team had just left his aptly named Deluxe Suite. Frau Schäffer had ordered a lunch of spicy German sausages, fries, and green salads for the group. She abruptly canceled the intended beers after Wendal's intervention. "Only soft drinks and coffee. We need one hundred percent focus from everyone," he brusquely admonished when he overheard the German word '*biere*' in Frau Schäffer's telephone conversation with room service.

As they washed down their food with room temperature soft drinks, the team dissected their impressions of that morning's meeting at Technologie Bergmann GmbH. The mood then was somber as the technology specialists from TBG methodically reviewed hundreds of pages of data accumulated from their discussions and analysis.

Conclusions were clear. Modification of the PAS software—changes required to accomplish Operation Bright Star's automation of the checkout process at Multima Supermarkets—would now cost five million dollars more than originally forecast. That amount might escalate further should there be more unforeseen glitches.

During the lunch discussions, Wendal dissected every individual section of the analysis to determine if they might identify additional savings or ascertain if TBG analysts had made errors in assumptions or calculations. He found none.

With the meeting over and his privacy returned, Wendal wandered over to the fully stocked minibar. He poured a large glass of vodka and filled it to the brim. Without adding ice or a mixer, he swallowed a large gulp and enjoyed the instant warming sensation. Then, he decided to sit on the tiny balcony outside his suite. Overlooking an adjacent park, he would process the mountain of new information, assess the dire circumstances, and decide what his next steps might be.

———————

Shortly after yesterday evening's telephone conversation with Howard Knight, Wendal called a pay phone in Bogotá, Columbia. Willy Fernandez answered.

Willy confirmed his successful capture of the targeted Multima Supermarkets data files. It had taken less than thirty minutes, and he had downloaded all data to his new personal computer without complications. All he needed were instructions about what he should do next. Wendal gave Willy a freshly created email address on an obscure Internet domain in Romania.

The files transferred within minutes. Successfully received, they were then saved to a brand new computer at an Internet café in Düsseldorf. The stolen, highly confidential Multima Supermarkets' employee payroll information now resided on a laptop computer purchased by Frau Schäffer from an unknown source the day before. She paid cash, of course.

Within an hour, those files were copied to a USB memory stick and then copied to yet another newly purchased personal computer. Before midnight, a hammer was used to smash both the first new computer and the memory stick. Bits and pieces of each were scattered along one hundred feet or so of the Rhine River where it lapped up against a cement retaining wall. Both would eventually become hundreds of tiny particles settled among other debris accumulating on the silt-laden river bottom.

Shortly after midnight, three analysts Wendal had entrusted to determine the cost/savings benefit of Operation Bright Star started their task. These folks would forego sleep and communication with the rest of the team. They were prepared to struggle through the captured data to determine the financial benefits of converting Multima Supermarkets from cashier-attended check-outs to fully automated devices at the point of sale. They needed concrete evidence that benefits to Multima would significantly outweigh the costs of making this business model conversion.

He had instructed them to come back to him when their analysis confirmed an advantage of at least one hundred million dollars over the coming three years. They should continue their investigation until they could show benefits of at least that amount, regardless of how much time it might take.

———

It now concerned him that more than twelve hours had already passed with no communication from them. This information vacuum intensified his growing fears. Might his team find it harder to quantify financial benefits than he had expected? Was such a potentially catastrophic development occurring even without knowledge the project's costs had increased yet another five million dollars during that morning's meetings? How had things gone so awry so quickly? Why did it now feel like he was losing sight of the CEO office rather than closing his grip on this coveted position? More importantly, how could he get things back on track?

Technology, he thought. Technology had always been his comfort zone and strength. If Operation Bright Star was in peril due to costs and questionable financial benefit, how could he use other technology to modify the mission? Was there some way he might expand the operation to include not only automating the point-of-sale function but maybe also to widen the scope of the project with an additional game changer idea?

All factors considered, only Howard Knight knew about Operation Bright Star. Only he knew what the project entailed. Surely, Knight would be more concerned with their eventual success before the board of directors than with such minor details as the project's scope, Wendal reasoned.

Newly inspired, he dialed Frau Schäffer and instructed her to schedule a meeting with the team back in his Deluxe Suite at five o'clock. Even those closeted resources working on the cost/benefits analysis should take a break, get some sleep, and join the meeting. It would be okay to order some beer, he added.

TWENTY-SEVEN

The morning meeting with his team was both satisfying and productive. James Fitzgerald could certainly justify taking time for a lunch hour workout in the company fitness center. He had authorized renovations to accommodate a gym five years ago because an internal satisfaction survey clearly indicated employees wanted an opportunity to exercise conveniently before or after work or during their lunch breaks.

At this time of the day, fewer people frequented the facility. Nevertheless, several folks were using state-of-the-art equipment in a brightly lit room with a thirty-foot ceiling. Creating this extra height was the most expensive part of the renovation, but he believed any fitness center needed to be appealing to users, and his personal experience suggested an open and comfortable space to exercise was just as important as the quality of the equipment available. He personally authorized the multi-million-dollar expense.

To his delight, the investment proved its worth many times over. Annual surveys of employees heralded an improvement in satisfaction every year since the gym opened. Absenteeism dropped significantly. Many employees lost weight. Health insurance claims reduced dramatically. Furthermore, Multima Financial Services' contributions to employee insurance plans had increased less than the rate of inflation for the past two years. Such a trend was truly a rare occurrence among most American businesses, and James took personal pride in it.

As he walked through the gym, he briefly greeted employees who were working out. He shook hands with some, patted others on the back, and shared warm, enthusiastic words of encouragement. He enjoyed watching their faces brighten with such small rituals of personal recognition and thought he even detected a little more intensity in their workouts after these brief interactions. High employee morale was an essential ingredient to the long-term success of his business.

As he adjusted the seat of a stationary bicycle to his tall frame, Fitzgerald made a mental note to meet with human resources. They should identify potential employee satisfaction issues to expect during the planned transition into a mortgage provider.

New people would bring different types of lending skills to the company, and they would surely need to integrate those new recruits. A subtle transition in business culture for existing employees would also take place. Both would require careful planning and execution, Fitzgerald thought as he mounted the bicycle for a thirty-minute, high-intensity stationary ride that would leave his heart pumping hard and his spirits soaring. In the meantime, he revisited that morning's meeting with his team to determine if more action might be needed.

James was pleased with the consistency demonstrated by his colleagues. The first part of their meeting dissected results of various test case scenarios. His risk management people had examined the possible pitfalls and rewards of the proposed home mortgage business from broad and varied perspectives.

What might happen if the economy declined? What should they expect if it plunged even more dramatically than forecast? What if it improved, but unemployment rates didn't? What if residential home prices dropped even further, or if the default rate on mortgages increased?

All of these questions addressed possible scenarios the new business might realistically face. The team had developed a numeric conclusion for how each factor might impact the proposed profitability for the home mortgage business as well as overall business results in the financial services division.

Fitzgerald was impressed with the depth of analysis in the short time since their last meeting. He was also satisfied with computer modeling created to identify possible alternative strategies to cope with such scenarios, should they occur. After the risk team had finished their two-hour presentation with a short question and discussion period, they outlined a timeline for further scrutiny during those crucial days remaining until the board of directors meeting.

The timing looked comfortable. There was little doubt his risk experts would be ready to respond to any question or concern about this game changer strategy or implementation plans. Satisfied, he then guided the discussion towards delivery of the presentation to the board on April 23. Fifty-three days remained for preparation, and James wanted to ensure his team would use every moment prudently.

They would have thirty minutes to explain their plans to the board of directors, followed by a question and answer period. Fitzgerald counseled that thirty minutes was a sacred length of time. John George Mortimer had no patience with submissions that exceeded the limit and would probably cut the speaker short when the time expired, finished or not.

This tendency underscored the importance of a presentation that was polished, carefully timed, and expertly delivered. James thought it critical for the emerging team leader, Douglas Whitfield, to enlist experts' help with the submission delivery.

Several months earlier, Multima Financial Services' senior executives participated in an advanced communications development program. Fitzgerald had been impressed with the dramatic results his people demonstrated after the tutelage. They exuded confidence. Oral presentations became crisp. Their body language projected more warmth, passion, and empathy in meetings or interviews. Now might be an ideal time for a refresher.

To underscore his conviction, James took a few moments to recount his personal successes after multiple sessions with communication specialists. He thought such openness about his experiences might encourage these executives to buy-in most positively to further skill development. It worked. The group responded with enthusiasm.

After some further discussion, they concluded that Fitzgerald's role in the presentation to the board of directors would be limited. He would use four minutes at the start to introduce each of the participants and highlight their responsibilities, background, and experience. Then, each team member would have about six minutes to describe the proposed business strategy, explain their background research and data, provide an overview of risks and rewards, and outline the implementation strategy and timing.

He would serve as a traffic cop during the question and answer period. Using this tactic, James could direct a query to the executive best qualified to respond. Just as he knew the thirty-minute presentation time was sacrosanct, he also understood time consumed by questions and answers often exceeded that of the original presentation.

James was also well aware some members of the board liked to phrase their questions in a way that would telegraph their concerns and probable voting position. He welcomed this clever communication tactic. It would give him warning of potential unplanned hurdles and permit him to handle any question that might become an inadvertent pitfall.

With seven weeks remaining until the meeting, Fitzgerald was confident his team could be ready to impress. With expert coaching added to his intimate working knowledge of the board, he could confidently devote his attention to other issues.

He glanced down at the electronic indicators on the stationary bicycle. He noted the session and time for reflection were almost complete. Now was his chance to peruse other pressing concerns before the end of his day.

First among those issues to consider was the troubling news about John George Mortimer's hospitalization with breast cancer. It continued to be a major worry on a few levels. Of course, he was saddened and deeply concerned his friend and colleague of many years might suffer a fate far worse than hospitalization with such a potentially deadly and insidious disease. He remained troubled that Mortimer had not shared information about this circumstance with him.

Of most immediate concern, Mortimer had still not responded to the message James had left two days earlier. The first task after a shower must be a call to Natalia Tenaz in business intelligence. He was now more than a little curious about what additional information this remarkable, well-connected young woman might have discovered.

TWENTY-EIGHT

Grand Hyatt Hotel, Hong Kong.
Early morning, March 3, 2016

After that run on the treadmill back in Japan, Suzanne showered, dressed, and prepared for an eight o'clock breakfast meeting with the team in her suite. But she didn't make it to that meeting. Rather, her colleagues discussed, reviewed, and prepared without any input from her at all. That's because things started to go completely awry very early that day.

First, as she toweled dry from the shower, the flashing red light on her smartphone alerted Suzanne to a waiting message. She rushed to finish preparation and once fully dressed and ready for work, dialed her voicemail number.

There was one new message and Suzanne listened intently to the clearly distressed voice of her media relations specialist. With short, rapid phrases, the woman explained that cable business network CBNN had already learned of the Multima hacking incident, and a New York news producer had called seeking comment. The exasperation of Suzanne's media relations specialist was evident as she briefly grumbled her incomprehension that such news leaked to CBNN even before Multima Supermarkets could prepare a draft press release for Suzanne's review.

Since the unfortunate event transpired only a few hours earlier, the media relations specialist wondered if someone within Multima might have fed this information to the business network. At any rate, she was desperate for Suzanne to call her as soon as possible.

First, Suzanne called Gordon Goodfellow in his nearby room to request he chair the planned morning get-together in the living area of her suite. To her annoyance, it seemed she was waking him from a sound sleep, even though their meeting would start in just minutes. Her executive gave assurances he would be there on time to lead the discussions. Ruefully, she mused that an obligation for him to chair an important meeting after a long night of 'relationship building' with the executives of Kyomeshi Corporation might represent some form of appropriate justice.

She worked from the bedroom of her spacious suite. She chose a comfortable chair, kicked off her shoes, and called her media relations specialist at the office in Atlanta. A receptionist informed Suzanne that instead, she would link her to a teleconference already underway. Seconds later, she joined that conversation.

For the next fifteen minutes or so, she patiently and intently listened to vigorous interactions between Dieter Lehren, her information technology leader; Judy Smith, the media relations specialist; and Alberto Ferer, general counsel of Multima Corporation.

The IT leader outlined the scope of the incident. He explained the mainframe systems had been breached to steal information about all American employees of Multima Supermarkets. Hackers had stolen information ranging from extremely sensitive social security numbers to weekly payroll details. They had copied and pilfered individual health insurance claims and reimbursements for the past three years. They also got personal addresses and telephone numbers of US employees.

It was clear whoever had hacked this data was primarily interested in learning everything possible about American employees of Multima Supermarkets and not necessarily those located in Canada. The thief curiously appeared less interested in their customers, Lehren explained. The only other database accessed was a summary of clients' current balances of Multima loyalty points. There was no apparent attempt to hack debit and credit card details.

Alberto Ferer carefully explained the potential legal intricacies and strongly counseled against any admission of guilt in any media release. Instead, Ferer advised that Multima Supermarkets should only acknowledge a breach had occurred, an investigation was underway, and more details would follow later. He suggested a media release of not more than two or three sentences and recommended no expressions of apology or regret. Either might weaken their legal position and should be avoided.

Equally strongly, Judy Smith advocated an alternative approach. She recommended communication that summarized what they already knew and what still was under investigation. The media relations specialist bravely insisted any communiqué should include an apology to both Multima customers and employees for any inconvenience this breach might cause them.

Suzanne listened to the debate among her advisors for several minutes as she processed the information, weighed the divergent options, and reflected back on her personal experiences and training. The advice of Judy Smith seemed similar to her intuition about the right thing to do and was consistent with information she had received from experts in disaster management.

Those professionals claimed the best way to contain damage was for a CEO to adopt a prominent and open media position. They also underscored there could be no substitute for the truth in such circumstances.

After listening patiently and carefully to each of the perspectives, Suzanne revealed her decision.

"We'll do the right thing," she said. "Prepare a media release right away for my approval. Explain the scope of the breach and reassure our customers that hackers stole only limited data. Highlight that credit and debit card data appear to be completely untouched and safe.

"Draft a separate message for internal distribution. Using my email account, communicate with all Multima Supermarkets employees letting them know about this theft. Let them know we'll work with individual state governments and federal authorities to monitor their tax accounts for any suspicious activity. Be sure the tone of the email assures employees that we'll do everything possible to minimize damage," she directed.

Despite Alberto Ferer's objections, she said, "Both announcements should include expressions of concern and sincere apologies for any inconvenience either customers or employees might encounter as a result of the security breach. Both messages should inform readers that Multima Supermarkets would immediately work to prevent any future violation."

She concluded by gently prodding Dieter Lehren for his concurrence with such an undertaking, and he agreed without hesitation. Alberto Ferer made one final attempt to delay the announcements, tactfully reminding her that such a sensitive issue really should include John George Mortimer's input, insisting that Multima's CEO should have the last word on such an important and delicate subject.

"Agreed. Ideally, we should draw him into the discussion. Unfortunately, he hasn't responded to an email I sent him earlier to make him aware of the breach," she countered.

"John George Mortimer is unavailable for a few more days, until March seven," Ferer said. "You probably should wait those five days until he is available."

She understood both the recommendation and the implications of the warning and quickly weighed the alternatives before she restated her final position. "We'll draft releases immediately. Alberto, please review them to minimize potential legal issues. I'll sign off on the final versions.

All of this should be to me within the next hour. I'd like it done before I leave the hotel for my flight to Hong Kong."

Suzanne took another minute or so to thank the participants for their input, perspectives, and opinions. "Alberto, I have no doubt these actions might weaken our legal position, and I'll accept all responsibility," she added with conviction.

Immediately after the call, she was a little less confident. Nevertheless, she reminded herself that her first obligation was to Multima customers and the second was to the employees. Third in her ranking was a desire to minimize potential legal exposure. She would live with whatever fallout might occur.

Hurriedly, Suzanne then packed her luggage and responded to a few other pressing emails while she waited for the media releases. Within minutes, she received both documents and made minor edits. With a final brief cover message, she instructed Judy Smith to release and distribute the approved communiqués within fifteen minutes.

At that point, she joined the meeting in the living area of her suite and noted they were already past the departure hour her efficient trip planner had established to meet the limousines. Nevertheless, Suzanne insisted on a recap of the session.

Before their discussion resumed, she told her team about the theft of their personal information and empathetically voiced her concern, including the apology included in the approved communiqués. She carefully observed their individual body language and assessed their reactions.

She was relieved to see their expressions uniformly conveyed minor concern, but she could detect no overt anger or other negative reaction. Within seconds of this announcement to the team, Suzanne started to hear a sequence of multiple smartphone beeps that announced her team members were probably already receiving the formal communication about the hacking incident.

One advantage of a corporate jet is the ability to change departure times as necessary. That morning they required flexibility because Suzanne was not entirely comfortable with the recap she received from her team.

Her somewhat groggy, and probably a little hung-over, marketing leader had conducted the meeting without Suzanne's trademark attention to detail and accuracy. As a result, there were several gaps in their preparation for the meetings in China, and conclusions from the previous day's meetings in Japan were less than precise.

Suzanne drew Jennifer Wong, her travel planner, aside for a hushed conversation. She asked her to delay departure from the hotel for a further hour and to arrange an additional limousine for a private discussion with Gordon Goodfellow during their short trip to Haneda. Back with the full group, she insisted on a much more intensive review and discussion while everyone's memories of the previous day were still fresh.

After the additional hour, Suzanne was more or less satisfied with their conclusions. Subsequently, she divided the team into three working groups for the four-hour flight from Haneda to Hong Kong, provided guidance on some of the remaining issues to be communicated to the team in Atlanta, and then isolated specific concerns to research for the meetings in China.

Finished, they all rushed back to their individual rooms to collect personal effects for immediate departure from the hotel lobby. During the ride to Haneda, her private conversation with her marketing leader started out a little tenuously.

"I'm curious about the change in plans at Kyomeshi. What prompted that sudden need for relationship building?" Suzanne asked directly.

"It was certainly impulsive, and I apologize for not giving you a heads-up earlier, and also for my less-than-splendid physical condition this morning. There's no doubt consumption of unusually large amounts of alcohol formed part of our relationship building activities. In fact, I just got to sleep when you called."

With his two male colleagues, Gordon Goodfellow spent the better part of the night with the executives from Kyomeshi. In fact, the Kyomeshi chairman had made arrangements for the party to continue at the *kyabakura* long after its official closing. Their night finally concluded about three o'clock that morning, with the Japanese hostesses in various stages of undress, and with the male guests in varied degrees of inebriation. Of course, Gordon judiciously highlighted only the most necessary facts and prudently omitted those last details in his brief summary to Suzanne.

"At the end of our evening festivities, the chairman of Kyomeshi graciously arranged for his limousine driver to bring us back to the hotel. But there was virtually no alternative. All trains had stopped running for the night well before the party finally ended.

"The good news is," he pronounced with a rueful smile "our strategy worked out rather well. Do you recall the significant discount you lightheartedly suggested as you were leaving yesterday? Believe it or not, Kyomeshi agreed to grant it.

"Plus, they decided to provide a new healthy variety of tea to us exclusively. They also consented to split the costs of promoting this new tea in North America with print *and* television advertising.

"My back-of-the-napkin estimate of profits from this new development is in the tens of millions of dollars. Furthermore, we'll gain a strategic advantage over our competitors in the tea segment for the next five years."

"A satisfactory outcome," Suzanne conceded.

Before their conversation could wrap-up, a vibration from her smartphone alerted her to an incoming call. A quick check of the screen indicated that Judy Smith, her media relations specialist, was calling. At once, she again became entangled in the latest developments in the hacking saga.

"CBNN aren't satisfied with the press release we just sent them. Instead, they're insisting on an interview with you for more detailed comment," she said.

"What do you recommend?" Suzanne asked.

"I'd really encourage you to do it in a studio rather than by telephone. You project so well and are so engaging with interviewers. It would definitely assuage viewer concerns, and I know they have facilities in both Tokyo and Hong Kong."

"OK. We're on the way to the airport here, so let's try for Hong Kong," Suzanne instructed.

Just before their departure from Haneda Airport, Judy Smith called again. "CBNN welcomes you for an on-air interview in Hong Kong. I'll email the exact address and confirm the time.

"By the way, their iconic on-air personality, Liara Furtamo, is visiting Hong Kong. This week she's making one of her periodic visits for meetings and interviews with foreign business leaders. They do that to better position her and the network as legitimate sources for international business news," the media specialist continued.

"During such trips, I hear she typically sleeps at irregular local hours to keep her body clock as close as possible to New York time to remain alert for her regular late afternoon time-slot. Her production assistant has agreed to wake her a couple hours before the interview to allow her time to dress, apply make-up, and prepare to meet with you. Apparently, Liara cheerfully agreed."

"I'm honored," Suzanne replied, sensing more than gossip with this heads-up.

"I'm guessing her extraordinary intuition about newsworthy stories leads her to believe our hacking incident has the potential to become a major news event, and she always likes to be at the forefront of a breaking story," Judy pointed out as a less than subtle caution.

While the three teams worked on their assignments, Suzanne devoted the first three hours of the flight to preparation for her interview. She spent most of that time speaking by satellite telephone with her IT leader to refresh her knowledge about, and understanding of, Multima Supermarkets' computer systems. She wanted to be absolutely sure she had all of the facts straight before visiting the CBNN studio.

She then devoted the last hour to changing into a business outfit more suitable for television, styling her hair to be camera-ready, and applying fresh makeup to highlight her best features for the camera.

On arrival in Hong Kong, she traveled directly to the CBNN studio for her live interview with Liara Furtamo. Only Jennifer Wong accompanied her. The rest of the team waited for separate limousines, and then found their way to the Grand Hyatt Hotel for more discussions in preparation for the next day's schedule of activities.

As a parting gesture, Suzanne established that Gordon Goodfellow would once again chair the meetings. His enthusiastic body language in response reaffirmed her confidence the coming sessions at the Grand Hyatt would be more productive. She left her team comfortable that they would be ready for their next day's discussions. She could focus exclusively on the crucial CBNN interview.

The interview went well from Suzanne's perspective. Liara Furtamo's questions were good ones, posed with standard professional decorum, and Suzanne responded well to the inquiries about privacy, confidentiality, and security.

Suzanne's measured responses reassured Multima Supermarkets' customers. Her demeanor clearly established that she understood the gravity of the breach, and she displayed a genuine empathy about possible privacy worries. Her calm tone exuded a quiet assurance. Her grasp of those details studied on route from Japan projected astute management awareness, sensitivity, and a genuine desire to investigate and correct the breach to avoid a recurrence.

Liara Furtamo challenged Suzanne's comments in a respectful and reasonable way that allowed her to project journalistic neutrality without hostility or confrontation. A good interview, Suzanne was thinking, as Liara proceeded towards the wrap-up.

"One last question," she said casually. "Can you share any perspective about news circulating today in New York that your CEO, John

George Mortimer, is undergoing treatment for breast cancer in a Fort Myers hospital?"

Suzanne audibly gasped at the completely unexpected question. In a fraction of a second, the television camera dramatically captured her total shock. Despite her valiant efforts to resume a neutral expression during the instant it took her to process this alarming news, it became apparent to any viewer that she was totally unaware of Mortimer's situation. The unerring eye of the camera captured concern as well as bewilderment.

Gordon Goodfellow greeted her as she stepped out of the limousine at the Grand Hyatt Hotel. With a sympathetic grimace, he suggested she might want to check out the CBNN broadcasts when she reached her room. They had replayed her flash of shock frequently, he warned.

She promptly followed his advice and turned on the television as soon as she entered her suite. She saw the latest replay of her reaction. Intuitively, she sensed she was now at the heart of a crisis far more perilous than the hacking situation that she had handled so deftly during the earlier part of the interview.

In fact, during the five-minute segment Suzanne watched, there was only a brief reference to the interview's purpose. Instead, Liara Furtamo and New York-based program moderators speculated openly about John George Mortimer's health and the implications of his illness on Multima Corporation's future. Their furtive tones suggested Mortimer's death might be imminent. Multima might undergo dramatic management changes. Perhaps even an extensive corporate makeover would result.

Suzanne watched the segment in silence and disbelief. How could they speculate this way about John George Mortimer? Where were official comments from the corporation or Mortimer himself? Who could provide balance to this breaking news story? It was all more than a little puzzling.

Despite the gravity of the media speculation, there was little time for reflection. The preparation meetings with her team beckoned urgently. She also needed to prepare for a dinner meeting scheduled at seven-thirty that evening with her old friend from Stanford.

Before those activities, she made a series of attempts to get information. She tried to reach John George Mortimer at his home, on his cell phone, and by email. While he was usually accessible this early, today all efforts proved futile.

Next, she woke General Counsel Alberto Ferer at his home number. He knew nothing about Mortimer's whereabouts and claimed to have no knowledge about possible treatments for cancer. Given his surprised reaction, Suzanne believed him. She also alerted him to check out the morning CBNN newscasts. It was better to be candid about her unexpected shock than have Ferer discover the media capture of her momentary bewildered expression later.

Suzanne also reached James Fitzgerald on his cell phone as he drove to work in the early Chicago morning. He had already seen the CBNN interview. His distress was as great as Suzanne's, and he voiced complete surprise with the news about John George's health. He also sympathized with her unseemly ambush by Liara Furtamo during her interview. "Those media people will do absolutely anything for a dramatic breaking news story," he complained.

Although he was saying all the right things, something struck Suzanne as a bit odd in the tone of his response. She wasn't entirely sure why she had this feeling, but she found herself wondering if her CBNN interview truly was Fitzgerald's first indication of John George's illness.

Her longest telephone conversation was with Edward Hadley, Multima Corporation's vice president of corporate and investor affairs. Hadley was also at a loss for words. He could add nothing about the facts behind the rumors and wasn't even aware Mortimer was unreachable.

He had seen the CBNN broadcasts, though, and expressed outrage at the interviewing scruples of both Liara Furtamo and her superiors at CBNN. Nonetheless, the damage was done. He was already getting calls and emails from other media people. Even at this early hour, the Twitter universe was speculating about John George Mortimer and his breast cancer.

Hadley promised to investigate what was going on with John George, see what concrete information he might be able to learn, and circle back to Suzanne with information and guidance as quickly as possible. In closing, he congratulated Suzanne for her handling of a nasty situation. Her responses to the hacking incident questions were expert, polished, and reassuring, he said.

Suzanne was not fully able to participate in her team's meetings to prepare for the next day's discussions in Hong Kong. However, she shifted from telephone calls made from her bedroom to the team discussions in her living room suite, as necessary. Each time she returned to the sessions, Gordon Goodfellow paused and quickly brought her up to date with developments since her last departure.

Her ability to listen intently, grasp minute details, and process information with computer-like speed permitted her to be both informed and helpful with the discussions. While more tiring and stressful than Suzanne would have preferred, her skill to compartmentalize the crises contributed to an aura of calm professionalism in the suite.

She would have also preferred to delay the planned dinner meeting with Michelle Sauvignon, but she knew her friend from her Stanford days was already in transit from an office in Shenzhen, China. More than a good friend, she was also president of Farefour Stores China, a subsidiary of the mammoth French supermarket chain. Suzanne knew a personal conversation with her might be as important as any other on her trip to Asia.

Michelle had offered to travel to Hong Kong to meet with Suzanne, thinking it might be safer. Though not extensively publicized in the West, affluent women were apparently attractive targets for Chinese criminals. According to Michelle, there was a risk of theft, rape, kidnapping, and even murder for women traveling by car in some areas of China. She would come from Shenzhen in an armored limousine and a security detail of three armed guards. That was her usual mode of travel in China.

With her friend taking such measures to visit with her, Suzanne felt a special obligation to maintain their dinner plans, regardless of the whirlwind of crisis and activity around her. It turned out her judgment was again good. Michelle proved to be extremely helpful. Her knowledge of the supermarket business globally allowed her to hone in on fundamental issues of price sensitivity, business operations with extremely small gross margins, and a market with ruthless competitors.

These were all matters Suzanne wanted to address as part of her game changer strategy to compete with the big-box retailers in North America. Michelle immediately sensed the importance of this project and openly discussed ideas, experiences, and opinions without relaying any information proprietary to Farefour.

They talked continuously for more than three hours while they nibbled at an excellent meal in the Grand Hyatt dining room. Regrettably, there were few moments for any conversation about memories of their carefree days together at Stanford University or recent events in their personal lives.

Michelle raised the John George Mortimer cancer issue only as they parted. She understood what Suzanne was going through, she whispered in support as they hugged goodbye. Then, with a cheerful good

luck wish and a smile, she swept out the door with her security entourage in tow.

As soon as she was back in her Grand Hyatt Hotel suite, Suzanne
received a call from Edward Hadley, vice-president of corporate and
investor affairs. He was traveling with Alberto Ferer in Alberto's sports
car, his smartphone on speaker mode.

They explained that Sally-Ann Bureau finally realized the serious-
ness of the media issue and the impact it might have on the company
after some rather intense questioning by Ferer and Hadley together.
Tearfully, she confessed that Mortimer had sworn her to secrecy. She
then confirmed he had cancer and was recovering from surgery at MPH
Hospital. They tried to reach John George there, but the staff steadfastly
continued to deny that Mortimer was a patient.

Sally-Ann Bureau provided the number of the hospital room
where they would find him, and they were racing there as they spoke
to Suzanne. They planned to locate and then meet with him in person.
They promised to update her when they had more information and again
requested she try to avoid media responses until they could circle back
with her to formulate a strategy and message.

Suzanne had relayed this information to James Fitzgerald and left
a message on Wendal Randall's voice mail requesting that he call her as
soon as possible. She again instructed her unit's media relations team to
continue to withhold any information until she directed otherwise. Then,
she returned to the myriad other daily issues clamoring for her attention.

As Suzanne concluded an insufferably long conference call with
her team back in Atlanta, she glanced at her watch and realized that it
was just past three o'clock that Thursday morning and Suzanne had still
only partially settled in at the Grand Hyatt Hotel overlooking Hong
Kong's spectacular Victoria Harbor. It occurred to her that she had
already been there for several hours, unable to enjoy either the extraordinary view from her living room window or the luxurious comfort of
the wood-paneled decor in her Garden View Suite.

Her clothes remained in her luggage, except for the one business
suit hung in the closet immediately on arrival to ensure it would be wrin-
kle-free for Thursday's meetings. She noticed dozens of soiled dishes,
glasses, and cups littered the furniture of her suite. All were remnants of
a series of meetings underway almost continuously since her arrival at
the five-star luxury hotel several hours earlier. She felt exhausted.

Her stimulating early-morning treadmill run in Tokyo was now a
distant memory. Although she enjoyed the exercise, it seemed more like

days than hours had elapsed. Her head ached. Her feet were swollen and sore. Fatigue permeated every pore of her body. Even her emotions caused some rather intense discomfort.

Ruefully, as she changed from her business suit to comfortable loungewear, she smiled and thought there would certainly not be any massage on this busy night, extra special or otherwise. Instead, she would nap for a few minutes while she waited for a response from those colleagues who were desperately trying to locate and talk with John George Mortimer.

TWENTY-NINE

In an office tower near Wall Street, New York.
March 2, 2016

It was late in the business day, a good time to reassess the entire Multima project. Howard Knight was starting to have real doubts about Wendal Randall's ability to win the board of directors' approval for Operation Bright Star. Randall assured him, with similar assertions from Klaudia Schäffer, they could still complete the project on time with some dramatic additional costs. However, it was becoming increasingly apparent that Randall's plan had several critical flaws.

Those defects were so potentially grave that Randall's ascension to the role of CEO at Multima was now in jeopardy, a circumstance Knight wanted to avoid. It also reinforced that his preferred candidate to run Multima Corporation had poor business judgment as well as a tendency to make questionable decisions in his personal life.

Those significant shortcomings apparently had not improved with maturity or experience. Mortimer's decision to install his own financial controller at Multima Logistics was looking more prescient all the time. It was evident Wendal required a healthy counterbalance to keep him on the right path.

Over the previous few days, it had become equally clear to Knight that great, perhaps blind, ambition drove Randall. A diligent student of human behavior, Knight understood well that this combination of poor judgment and unbridled passion to advance were precisely the best characteristics to serve his purposes and those of The Organization. Over time, Wendal should become even easier to manipulate.

Knight was also aware the game changer projects of the other Multima division presidents were far more developed. His information source within the supermarkets unit secured updates about Suzanne Simpson's meetings in Japan and the resulting flurry of research and analysis underway. His source in the financial services division reported that a mortgage lending project was in the works. Fitzgerald's team was so advanced it had already drafted its presentation to the board.

Knight was beginning to fear that Randall's Operation Bright Star was developing so poorly it might eventually become impossible for him to exert enough influence over the board to win the required number of votes. In the final analysis, the board of directors would be genuinely concerned about the future of Multima Corporation. Any leverage he might exert would be limited in comparison.

He leaned back in his plush leather chair, feet on the edge of his desk, and thoughtfully gazed out the office window. This had become his usual posture when he needed to calculate the next steps. He remained lost in thought until he received a most timely phone call from Janet Weissel.

A public relations specialist on Edward Hadley's investor relations team at Multima Corporation headquarters in Fort Myers, Weissel had first come to the attention of The Organization while she was a student at Columbia College in New York. Vivacious, beautiful, sexy, and enterprising, she put herself through college by advertising her availability for casual sexual liaisons. She used an assumed name, of course. For the right price, she was prepared to do almost anything, with almost anyone, at almost any time.

Despite her sexual adventures, she maintained consistently high grades and graduated near the top of her Columbia College class with a degree in political science. Of course, it proved little more than a formality for her to apply successfully for a job at Multima Corporation. The Organization helpfully suggested this might be a good opportunity, so she promptly completed an application. With her academic qualifications, personality, and charm, she easily secured the position.

The only snag was the fifty-thousand dollar per year salary. While competitive with starting wages paid by other businesses in the Fort Myers area, Ms. Weissel found it woefully inadequate for a woman with her talents.

Eventually, they reached an agreement. The Organization would pay her one hundred and fifty thousand dollars on her first day of employment and again on the anniversary date of her hiring every year. Naturally, this was in addition to the modest salary from Multima. Ms. Weissel graciously accepted.

The transfer of funds took place only after the execution of a secret document clarifying that all amounts from The Organization would be transferred electronically to a numbered account in the Cayman Islands. This agreement assured there would be no troublesome income tax receipts or other evidence of payments. The Organization expected useful intelligence about the inner workings of Multima Corporation in return. Ms. Weissel understood and was fully prepared to do whatever was necessary to get it.

Logically, she first tried to attract the attentions of John George Mortimer. She started wearing increasingly revealing outfits around the office, shamelessly flirting whenever she was with him. However, she detected no interest at all from Mortimer, despite his well-established reputation for frequent liaisons with younger women. Maybe he was one of those few corporate titans who practiced that old-fashioned concept of not dipping his pen in company ink. To her complete astonishment, she could not attract any attention at all from Mortimer, despite multiple overt attempts over several months.

Howard Knight then suggested she try to draw the attention of Alberto Ferer. He spent one delightful night with her after a company recreation event and was a very satisfactory sexual partner. However, he had shown little inclination for subsequent interaction. Despite repeated efforts, Ferer ignored her messages. His demeanor was polite but aloof.

Ferer was an unattached bachelor, so she didn't have much leverage, though she kept the video of their sexual encounter in a safety deposit box, just in case. She guessed that should she ever reveal that video, Mortimer and the board of directors would probably view their sexual dalliance as an isolated lapse in judgment. Ferer might get a reprimand for the indiscretion, but it was hardly a career-threatening impropriety that she could use to pry useful information from him.

Her efforts were not without some successes, though. In fact, one board director always traveled to Fort Myers the day before a scheduled meeting and stayed on for a few days to enjoy sexual romps with her at a Sanibel Island hideaway.

A mid-level manager on the Multima financial team also regularly provided sensitive information, expressly identified by Knight, in direct exchange for Weissel's favors. She also initiated a few useful relationships among Wall Street financial analysts.

Howard Knight remembered she first appeared a little reticent when he asked her to cultivate and nurture a sexual relationship with the quiet, unassuming sixty-year-old husband of Sally-Ann Bureau, John George Mortimer's long-serving executive assistant. Weissel eventually followed Knight's prompting with her customary enthusiasm and considerable charm. She successfully achieved an ongoing relationship in which they had sex with increasing frequency.

However, she had not learned a single piece of information that might be useful to Howard Knight or The Organization. Until yesterday.

———————

Janet was succinct in her report.

"Yes, I was hesitant to follow your guidance in this matter. Initially, I thought it would be a waste of time. Bureau and her husband are both born-again, practicing fundamentalist Christians. Frankly, I thought those people didn't engage in that sort of thing," she started, while Knight listened without interruption.

"However, Mr. Bureau was undeniably receptive to some altered notions. His response to my initial approach was quick and dramatic. Within days of my first contact, we had already spent several secret hours in a hotel room off Interstate 75, out near the airport.

"His sexual appetite was insatiable. Our meetings became more frequent and passionate, at least for Mr. Bureau. However, after our last session in bed, he appeared despondent. When I probed about the reason for his sadness, I was more than a little surprised to learn that I was the cause!"

"Let me get this straight," Knight interrupted. "You're having great sex with this guy, and he becomes 'despondent'?"

"Yeah. Mr. Bureau complained that it would now be a little longer before I could have him full-time. When I inquired why this might be so, he explained that he thought he had finally found a way to leave and quickly divorce his wife so he could become my exclusive lover. His idea hadn't worked out, and that's why he was unhappy."

Weissel was clearly repressing her amusement as she explained the next part to Knight with a mischievous giggle.

"It seems he entered their home unnoticed a few days ago and discovered his wife alone in their bedroom, her back to the door. Apparently, she was kneeling on the floor in a position of intense prayer, talking to God as though He was right there in the room with her. As Mr. Bureau silently eavesdropped on his wife's private conversation with God, he heard her use John George Mortimer's name.

"His wife passionately sobbed as she prayed, and Mr. Bureau claimed he distinctly heard his wife tell God she would do anything for Him, if only He would let her have Mortimer back. Mr. Bureau heard her tell God how she loved John George Mortimer and how much she needed him. This led Mr. Bureau to conclude his wife must be having an affair with her boss."

"So he thinks his wife is cheating on him with Mortimer?" Knight asked.

"Yeah. He immediately pounced on that apparent superb new opportunity. He hired a private investigator to collect proof of her infidelity. He figured with concrete evidence, he could establish grounds for a divorce and leave his wife. Then, he could become my lover on a full-time basis!" she chortled.

"So this guy has fallen for you head over heels, it seems."

"Completely over the top. So, he's completely dejected because his scheme ultimately fell apart. The private investigator reported he couldn't find any evidence of adultery. He had shadowed Sally-Ann Bureau the entire previous day, just as they agreed.

"Here's what happened. After finishing work at Multima, she visited a nearby florist and bought a small arrangement of flowers. The private investigator then followed Sally-Ann Bureau to MPH Hospital, where she went in the main entrance. She walked directly to a patient's room, and gently placed the flowers on a side table. Then, she came back out of the hospital room so quickly the investigator had to duck into a nearby restroom to avoid detection. She then traveled directly home with no further stops."

"Is there an ending to this story?" Knight asked with impatience surfacing.

"I think so. After the private investigator followed Mrs. Bureau home, he revisited MPH Hospital and charmed a nurse after she looked in on the patient in the room Sally-Ann had visited earlier. The private investigator captivated the nurse and engaged her in conversation until she eventually divulged that John George Mortimer was her patient."

"Mortimer?" he clarified.

"Yeah. John George. The nurse also helpfully added that Mortimer was recovering from surgery for breast cancer."

With no more than a thank-you-and-good job ending, Knight immediately knew he had the perfect solution for his angst. He pressed a speed dial number of a private cell phone.

The Organization's usual and covert contact in the production department of CBNN immediately recognized the tremendous news value of the hacking incident and John George Mortimer's cancer. She agreed to act quickly. This time, there was no need to prod her into action with veiled threats about some disgusting personal photos that might become public, as was the case at least once previously.

Within a few minutes of Knight's call, she assigned a junior writer on the team at CBNN to draft the breaking news story about a theft of data from Multima Supermarkets' computer system.

After she had Judy Smith's agreement that Suzanne Simpson would do an interview, she called Liara Furtamo's producer in Hong Kong. At the end of their call, in a casual manner implying that she was sharing information as an afterthought, the production assistant delivered the bombshell news about John George Mortimer and his treatments for cancer.

———————

That was yesterday. Today, he could bask in this moment of initial success and think once more about both the incongruity of Weissel's story and his remarkable good fortune with the idea hatched as he listened to her improbable story.

It seemed a perfect recipe to hijack Mortimer's little succession planning game. Start with a less-than-enchanted board of directors freshly exposed to a negative media barrage. Mix that gingerly with a weakened CEO and add some subtle encouragement in the background. Perhaps the board would ultimately abandon Mortimer's game changer projects. They might even shove him to the sidelines as an observer while Knight maneuvered Wendal Randall into the CEO position.

Unwittingly, Furtamo had compounded the impact of his achievement with her masterful ambush of Suzanne Simpson during those closing moments of her interview.

As the hours passed, other media repeated the story on radio and television. Simpson's momentary expression of shock on CBNN circulated widely in the mainstream media, YouTube, and blogs. Speculation was rife about Mortimer's cancer treatments. Naturally, conjecture about reasons he and Multima might want to keep such information secret followed.

Mortimer's inability to respond immediately, together with Multima Corporation media specialists' failure to mount a counter-attack, had already started to yield the results Knight hoped to achieve. Already that day, three members of Multima Corporation's board of directors called to discuss the media coverage and Mortimer's health.

With satisfaction, Knight listened as conversations with each director started out as expressions of concern about such serious, even tragic, news. Then, the dialog gradually shifted to unease because they found themselves in the dark about his illness. Discussions eventually evolved to speculation about John George's ability to lead the company going forward. This was exactly the thought process Knight had hoped to create. The quickness with which such dialog started gave him added satisfaction.

A broad smile crossed his face as he realized his plan was unfolding flawlessly. He took a few moments to admire just how elegantly it had all come together. This comedic tragedy, which he had neither foreseen nor expected, had produced a mine of valuable information.

Mortimer's bout with cancer became the nucleus of his scheme to derail succession plans that might otherwise prove problematic for Wendal Randall. That misfortune might also permit Knight to advance another step closer to full control of the lucrative business operations at Multima Corporation.

It was time to make a few more calls, this time to some of those members of the board who remained loyal to Mortimer. He would commiserate with them about the misfortune that seemed to have struck John George and inquire if they had any prior inkling of the tragic circumstance. Some somber news would provide the opportunity to plant a few seeds of doubt. Then, he would feed and nurture them as diligently as possible in the coming weeks.

THIRTY

MPH Hospital, Fort Myers, Florida.
Late morning, March 2, 2016

The beautiful floral arrangement first caught John George Mortimer's eye when he awoke the morning after his surgery. Two days later, colorful petals were fully bloomed with bright, cheerful hues. He inquired, but the nurse couldn't tell him who brought the flowers. There was just a scrawl on the card, she explained.

He was out of bed for the second time that morning and moving around with great effort. With a physiotherapist's help, he made his way towards the floral arrangement and opened the attached envelope. Just as the nurse reported, there was a scrawl, but he recognized the scribble as a large, looping "S". He had little doubt it was a discreet abbreviation for his loyal Sally-Ann.

He smiled as he considered that perhaps his assistant might be just a little too thoughtful. She probably could not accept the idea of not doing something for him in such a difficult time. She likely assumed her gift of flowers with an ambiguous signature on the card would comply with his request for total confidentiality about his illness and whereabouts. The flowers' pleasing scent wafted throughout the room, and Mortimer basked in the intended warmth of the gesture.

Moments later, his good humor evaporated when he turned on the television. He switched the channel to CBNN and had just set the remote down when his name suddenly flickered in a little banner creeping across the bottom of the screen. Talking heads were actively speculating about his cancer, his health, and his future!

Aghast, he watched the entire segment. Anger and annoyance gradually increased as clips of Suzanne Simpson's moment of shock interspersed the narrative. All the while, commentators spewed entirely speculative conjecture and opinions for their viewing audience, with voices so loud they seemed almost to be shouting.

They ambushed her, he thought. Why was Suzanne even asked that question? Moreover, why was CBNN interviewing her in the first place? A lot was going on, and he was out of the loop. He turned on his smartphone and watched as a flood of data rapidly populated the small screen.

Notification beeps steadily streamed for several seconds, creating a sound that resembled a musical arrangement. When the blur of data stopped and the symphony of beeps receded, Mortimer observed that almost one hundred emails demanded his attention with 'urgent' icons and another two hundred were of lower priority. He decided to sort the emails by the name of the sender and started with Suzanne Simpson.

Within seconds, it all became clearer to him. He read Suzanne's messages about the hacking incident. He saw her repeated attempts to reach him about the cancer rumors and read her candid heads up about the CBNN interview, including a straightforward explanation for her momentary shock. He felt it was entirely understandable.

Suddenly, he felt a whole different sensation, one he didn't immediately recognize. As he read her warm wishes for a complete and early recovery should those nasty rumors of cancer be accurate, he felt his eyes moisten for a moment. Fleetingly, he felt a strange awareness as he absorbed the intensity of Suzanne's warmth and good wishes. "It must be the drugs," he murmured.

Next, he sorted messages from Alberto Ferer, who appeared equally desperate to make contact, and got his first indication of the tsunami of media inquiries. *A shame they all have to deal with this*, Mortimer silently lamented. Nevertheless, he felt no pressing inclination to react to the appeals of Suzanne and Alberto Ferer for him to reply as quickly as possible.

James Fitzgerald's emails came next. His messages started with a request for the best time to talk about a corporate guarantee for a bond issuance. Inquiries about John George's health followed. There were also several differently worded requests, but all shared the theme that he should make contact soon.

The tone of one email prompted Mortimer to think Fitzgerald might have taken some offense that he had not let him know earlier about his situation and absence. *That's justified*, he thought. Still, he didn't feel enough remorse to respond immediately to the admonitions.

For the next couple hours, despite multiple interruptions from well-meaning healthcare providers, John George Mortimer quickly and methodically worked his way through dozens of emails. He absorbed the content, but still made no effort to respond to a single message.

Later, he sorted through his voicemail messages with the same methodical approach. In fact, he had just finished listening to the last one when Alberto Ferer and Edward Hadley awkwardly barged through the doorway, with two protesting nurses in tow. With a nod, a grin, and a casual wave to the nurses, Mortimer signaled his willingness to receive them.

He drew a deep breath to ease the pain that just started to intensify. He thought it necessary to mask the discomfort for the next few minutes. Certainly, this wasn't the right time to push the morphine dispenser button, so he cleared his throat to add strength to his voice, then greeted his guests.

"Good morning, Alberto, Ed. It's very nice of both of you to come." He smiled at the sheepish and uncomfortable executives standing at the foot of his hospital bed. They looked like over-sized schoolboys suddenly caught out.

Alberto Ferer broke the silence. "I don't pretend to know what motivation you had to keep us all in the dark about this, but you must know we are all very concerned about your well-being. First and foremost, how are you doing?"

"As well as can be expected in the wake of a procedure to remove a breast tainted with cancer," Mortimer responded. Then, to ease the tension, he acknowledged his acute understanding of the current adverse situation. He wryly conceded with characteristic understatement, "It appears my strategy to maintain a low profile with this issue has not played out as hoped."

"No, John George. It hasn't. We're in a precarious position. But more important, was the surgery successful?" Hadley asked.

"Everything is fine," Mortimer replied without hesitation. "You're going to have me around to harass you for a good while yet. The surgeon is confident he removed all cancer with the breast. The biopsy indicates none has spread to the lymph nodes. We'll see later if further treatments are needed. I plan to be out of the hospital tomorrow and start working from home on Friday."

"I'm sorry to heighten the urgency," Ferer began apologetically, "but we may not be able to wait as long as Friday to deal with this."

"I've never seen anything quite like it," said Edward, nodding to the television. "We're inundated with media inquiries from all over North America. We're trying to mitigate genuine public concern about the Multima Supermarkets hacking incident that I imagine you've heard about, in addition to all the speculation about your health."

"And it's not only the media calling," Ferer added. "This morning I've already had calls from concerned directors. The Multima

Supermarkets unions are grumbling publicly. Even some employees have called with concerns about their job security and future. It's rather bewildering how much momentum this is developing, particularly on the heels of the hacking theft."

"I think I understand the magnitude of the issue," Mortimer replied. "And I'm sorry you guys and your teams have to deal with all this. What do you recommend we do to contain it?"

Hadley paused before asking, "Are you feeling well enough to handle a video interview we can release to the media and employees?"

Mortimer shook his head. "The hospital would probably permit video equipment in here, but I'm still feeling a lot of pain and side effects from the drugs. I'd rather shoot for a brief statement from home on Friday if you think that might help. I doubt I'll be up for any interviews, though."

"What about your surgeon?" Edward asked. "Could we ask him to make a prepared statement and field questions about your condition?"

"He might cooperate with you, and I think he'd be okay on television with a little coaching," Mortimer replied. "Would you like me to have a word with him?"

"That would be great. Here's what I propose, if you concur. First, let me get the team to draft a media release. I'll get them to email it back to me for our review and sign-off. They can have it on the wire services within the hour.

"In the meantime, if you can, speak with your surgeon and get his support to meet with us for a few minutes. We'll arrange a media conference for this afternoon. We'll need to coach him before we let the media at him. "Let's try to schedule the press conference about three o'clock. That will leave enough time for the business stations to carry the story before the dinner hour, and major networks can feature it on their evening newscasts.

"This will go a long way towards cooling media interest and assure the reporters and public you're recovering well. They need to hear from a credible source that you'll be back at the helm of Multima soon and for a long time to come."

With Hadley's last comment, Ferer cast a knowing and concerned glance at Mortimer. John George's disclosure to the board of directors about his intention to retire made that last part glaringly inaccurate. Ferer realized Hadley would soon need to learn the truth before he built an incorrect impression with the media.

Mortimer immediately read Ferer's concern and understood the implications. "Let's start with the communiqué, Ed. Get your people started. I'll call the surgeon and ask for his support. Let me have a word with Alberto while you coach your team. Then we can reconvene for a chat."

Hadley dashed off to the parking lot. He sought the privacy of Alberto's car for a telephone conference with his colleagues back at headquarters.

Mortimer called for the surgeon, explained the general background, and got his agreement to prepare for a media conference. He understood his mission to be one of reassurance to calm jittery Multima customers, employees, and shareholders.

Mortimer and Ferer then huddled in the hospital room, the door firmly closed, to discuss several sensitivities about the current dilemma. They knew they had only one chance to get the message right and that the battle they were about to wage might be the most challenging of Mortimer's long career.

John George wished he might have a little more control over the timing, but characteristically he didn't dwell on the negatives. It was what it was.

Even though his colleagues occasionally rolled their eyes when he used this old cliché, he felt it important to remind folks that life is akin to playing a game of cards. There's no certain way of knowing which cards will come, so we have to play the cards life deals us.

That was exactly what he planned to do.

THIRTY-ONE

Wendal took the first few minutes to reassure his team Operation Bright Star would go ahead even if the cost-benefit relationship was not as attractive as desired. Their efforts over the past few weeks were not in vain, and he reassured them their hard work and research would still contribute to the game changer strategy.

Next, he candidly revealed that hoped-for benefits of the automated point of sale alone might not be enough to offset the escalating costs of installation. Accordingly, the team must devise an additional technological enhancement to strengthen and complement the automation of checking out in their supermarkets. They desperately needed some new and valuable bells and whistles.

When he asked for ideas, suggestions gushed. As expected, his team had thought extensively about their customer. They had looked at ways technology could change its business model and discussed operating challenges and opportunities at length with their counterparts at Multima Supermarkets. Clearly, over the days, weeks, and months before they had occasionally even let their imaginations run a little wild.

Ricky Technori, Operation Bright Star's team leader, guided discussions and served as meeting facilitator. He hurriedly scratched brief descriptions of ideas on a flip chart and could barely keep pace with the deluge.

Wendal sat silently in a corner of the suite. There, he listened intently and weighed the benefits of the suggestions. After about an hour, he heard an idea that immediately resonated. It was simple yet brilliant, and it absolutely had the potential to revolutionize the way Multima Supermarkets did business.

A young, newly recruited systems engineer talked about a recent meeting with Multima Supermarkets to discuss shrinkage—the unexplained disappearance of inventory by theft, damage, or accounting errors. Managers in the supermarket group had voiced great concern about the massive and growing losses from shrinkage and asked the technical wizards at Multima Logistics to consider solutions.

The young engineer on Wendal's team had thought about ways to eliminate the issue, and she might have a solution for at least part of the problem. However, she needed affirmation from her colleagues that her idea made sense.

"When I was working on my masters," the engineer started, "I participated in a study group that used employee ID cards to capture information. We embedded a tiny microphone and GPS-based motion detection device in every person's card. Everyone wore the badge around their neck on a lanyard. The microphone recorded every conversation. The motion detection device captured every movement of an employee anywhere near the base. Compilation of both data allowed us to reconstruct every activity of every employee for an entire shift digitally."

The room fell silent as the young engineer's colleagues started to absorb the implications and imagine the potential.

"I'm not sure exactly how we should use such info, but I think there may be several possibilities that require only limited programming," she added with growing confidence.

"For example, should an employee steal merchandise, the motion detector could capture the movement of any goods leaving the store with that person. If someone is passing stolen goods to an accomplice outside the building, it will detect that. And, if we require suppliers to affix that same tiny microchip transponder we use for other customers, Multima Supermarkets could also precisely identify individual stolen goods."

The idea was brilliant. They all saw the potential immediately. They could apply technology for which Multima Logistics was already famous to virtually eliminate employee theft.

"Your idea could do even more," said a colleague. "The motion detector could track any productivity lapses. If employees take unauthorized breaks or spend too much time talking, Multima Supermarkets could take remedial action."

"It would also be a great way to weed out disgruntled employees," another teammate added.

"Perhaps the computer system could compare all employee productivity and output to create higher performance standards," another speculated.

"If all suppliers affixed the microchip barcode, receiving goods could become entirely digital. Multima could eliminate all manual processing, and accounting discrepancies could virtually disappear." They were tripping over themselves to add their thoughts.

As soon as he first heard the idea articulated, Wendal realized he had the magic solution he so desperately sought. Wafer thin barcode technology was already in place. Multima Logistics already used it to help the supermarkets manage inventories more efficiently. GPS motion sensor technology was there as well. Logistics had installed similar technology in vehicles to permit car rental customers to check out and return a vehicle without ever visiting a sales counter. All that remained was a system to capture and analyze the data.

Wendal gestured to Technori, indicating his desire to explore more deeply the young engineer's idea. Their discussions should immediately focus on that single, far-reaching solution with so much potential.

In the following five hours, the team tackled this idea with enthusiasm and determination. Frau Schäffer ordered more beer, chicken wings, and sandwiches. Later in the evening, she ordered beer again, as the ideas percolated, technical challenges surfaced, and the lively group debated potential snags.

Despite a couple quickly dismissed concerns about employee acceptance of intrusive levels of monitoring, this new idea seemed to fit perfectly with Operation Bright Star. Regardless of their challenges building a cost-benefit case to eliminate cashiers, this concept to reduce shrinkage would provide lots to discuss with the board.

By the time Wendal Randall released them for a few hours of relaxation, the young engineer and her idea were the toast of the team. In the wee morning hours, they visited several busy bars in Düsseldorf's renowned *Altstadt*, or old city, where they sampled from a multitude of beers offered in trendy microbreweries. With each glass, their mood became more raucous.

The team continued to churn out ideas, suggestions, and good-humored observations about their latest twist to Operation Bright Star. By the time they had returned to their rooms at the Steigenberger Park Hotel, bars were closing and revelers were unsteadily wending their way through the streets. Wendal's team blended seamlessly into the celebratory atmosphere.

No one had bothered to check news coverage on CBNN because they had little interest in the stock markets or finance. As a result, they remained oblivious to the hacking crisis at Multima Supermarkets, their sister company and largest customer.

Wendal Randall awoke with bright sunlight streaming into his room, all because he forgot to close the drapes before he went to sleep. He felt just a touch of a hangover and a slightly cloudy mental residue from inadequate sleep. By his best estimate, he had slept for about three hours. Still, he felt remarkably energized as he swung out of his bed to start morning preparations and continued to experience the after-glow of their highly productive brainstorming session.

He prepared for breakfast in his suite and chose to ignore both an email and voice communication from his nemesis, the financial controller, Joseph Kowntz. Both messages had arrived during those few short hours of sleep and implored Wendal to contact him immediately about a sensitive corporate issue.

He had no desire to lose his newfound sense of euphoria. He was quite sure any response would result in yet another depressing conversation with his bean counter. After all, Kowntz was probably only contacting him to complain about their mounting expenses.

He pressed the red icon on his smartphone screen and shut down the device. No more email or voice messages would intrude. Still, Wendal conceded that he really should call his financial controller once the offices in Miami opened for business. That gave him five or six uninterrupted hours to focus on the implementation of this latest brilliant idea.

Later, he would bring to a close those complicated and costly discussions with Technologie Bergmann.

THIRTY-TWO

Fort Myers, Florida.
Late morning, March 4, 2016

John George Mortimer gingerly shuffled his way towards the bedroom of his home using a cane. He had been discharged from MPH Hospital early that morning after demonstrating to physiotherapists his ability to move about adequately. He could walk comfortably enough to navigate stairs and avoid injury. The cane was just a temporary precaution until he fully regained his strength and balance.

Alberto Ferer had insisted he meet him at the hospital to bring him home safely and comfortably. It also provided an excellent opportunity to compare impressions about the surgeon's performance during the press conference and deliver other news during their short drive to Mortimer's home.

Ferer had discussed the media conference in detail the previous evening with Edward Hadley. Both felt the surgeon handled questions well, despite his lack of media experience and extremely compressed preparation time. They agreed there was only one possible shortcoming: There was no definitive statement from the doctor that Mortimer would be fine, with no further treatments necessary.

Mortimer listened dispassionately. He didn't yet care to reveal the actual reasons for the surgeon's qualified responses. John George had been well aware the doctor would not make a definitive statement. In fact, he had already recommended extensive additional treatments and was expecting John George's acceptance of the plan during the next few days.

Sensing little likelihood of further clarification during this conversation, Alberto related one other piece of good news from Hadley. Their media conference had served its purpose, and the flood of inquiries had reduced to a trickle after the press conference.

"Perhaps the media feeding frenzy has been temporarily sated," Ferer suggested. He then alerted John George to a different pod of sharks now circling.

"Every independent director of the board has contacted me to voice concern that you withheld significant information about your health during the February board meeting," he reported. "A few expressed frustrations. With two of them, it approached anger. Because they were completely unaware of your health issues when the media barrage began, they felt completely exposed.

"Directors were also genuinely concerned about the hacking incident at Multima Supermarkets. Some made clear their annoyance that Suzanne Simpson was in Japan, or China, or somewhere else far away. They wanted to know why was she working on Mortimer's game changer project instead of being close to the crisis in Atlanta.

"During a call from Howard Knight, he speculated that the board might need to get together to discuss the current dilemma. I didn't directly respond to his implied request. Instead, I suggested a meeting might be premature until you could personally make a statement and hinted a media appearance might occur next week.

"Knight conceded a few additional days wouldn't make a dramatic difference, but he warned action may be required if your media appearance doesn't quell concerns of the shareholders," Ferer said.

John George Mortimer was a good listener. From Ferer's choice of words and subtle tone, he detected that he shared some of the sentiments voiced by directors. In retrospect, those poorly planned tactics used earlier to notify Ferer about his absence were terribly flawed.

To think he could ever hope to keep such an issue secret in today's instant news climate was entirely misguided. He would have to heal some badly bruised relationships in the coming days, he realized.

Ferer condensed all his information into the short ride to Mortimer's home and took his leave as soon as he saw John George was able to move about comfortably. Mortimer guessed that he'd adequately camouflaged the intense pain experienced during their ride. Although throbbing had flared up in that acutely sensitive surgical area where his breast once was, he faked coughs to camouflage his grimaces. He also gathered that Ferer was satisfied he'd be secure with his loyal and doting housekeeper taking over responsibility for his care.

At that moment, all Mortimer wanted was sleep. Weak, tired, and uncomfortable, he slowly lowered himself onto the high king-sized bed. He then asked his housekeeper to let him sleep for a few hours without interruptions. Perhaps she could silence the phones to be sure. With that, he fell into a fitful slumber, oblivious to a gathering storm in New York.

THIRTY-THREE

Hyatt Grand Hotel, Hong Kong.
Early morning, March 5, 2016

Suzanne Simpson was on the treadmill again. It was five-thirty in the morning in Hong Kong, and her muscles protested as she gradually increased her pace. Her whole body had voiced similar objections when the concierge phoned cheerfully announcing it was time to wake.

She had only turned out the lights a couple hours earlier, and the prior day had been stressful, demanding, and exhausting with no time for her usual review of the day's activities. She was just too tired. Within only moments of lying on a bed covered by a spongy cotton duvet, she'd fallen fast asleep. It was now time to revisit the myriad details flooding back into her mind. It seemed crucial to regroup, organize dozens of separate thoughts, and develop a strategy to deal with several concurrent challenges. "Just another day in the life of a company president," she mumbled aloud.

When she arrived that morning, she found a companion in the Grand Hyatt hotel gym. Gordon Goodfellow, her marketing leader, was already perspiring profusely, pedaling hard on a stationary bike and well into his second thirty-minute segment.

She touched his shoulder lightly and warmly thanked him for his excellent work leading the planning sessions over the past couple hectic days. She let him know she was both grateful for his support and impressed with his leadership skills before she moved to a treadmill on the other side of the room.

Gordon Goodfellow knew this routine, for they often traveled together. Suzanne needed the next thirty minutes to recharge her energy, clear her head, and prepare for the day. If this were to be a typical one, she would probably accomplish as much today as two or three ordinary people.

So far, the Hong Kong visit was proving far less productive than the team's earlier two days in Japan. While Wednesday evening's dinner with her friend Michelle Sauvignon of Farefour Stores was fruitful, meetings with suppliers were not. It had started badly when the minister

147

of economic development for China decided he wouldn't attend their scheduled meeting. Instead, he dispatched a junior associate who was obviously both ill-prepared and inexperienced.

It seems the Chinese minister took offense to a request from Multima's travel planner to change the meeting venue from Beijing to Hong Kong. While staff in the minister's office had not indicated any dissatisfaction during their planning calls, apparently the minister found the excuse for the change to be inadequate.

There had been a question about getting a visa to enter China from Hong Kong on such short notice, so Jennifer Wong recommended they avoid going to the mainland. Instead, they would ask contacts to come to them. This approach would be much less risky, she assured, and pointed out the Chinese invitees would only require flights of two or three hours. Suzanne had some discomfort with this recommendation but deferred to the counsel of her travel planner.

Apparently, it was all too much for the Chinese minister. He concluded that if Suzanne and her team did not have enough time to visit Beijing, her delegation was not important enough to merit his time to fly to Hong Kong. A junior official would suffice.

Suzanne had done her best to make the nervous junior official at ease, but language became a real handicap. The Dane Capital interpreter spoke some Mandarin but admittedly was not as comfortable as with Cantonese. As a result, there were awkward delays for clarification and re-translation. It became frustrating for all.

After about an hour, Suzanne and her team had decided they'd learned all that would be possible from the junior official and asked their interpreter to find a tactful way to conclude the discussions. About all they could take away from that first meeting was a glossy brochure extolling the general benefits of investing in China.

The next four sessions were marginally better. Suzanne's finance leader and her head of retail operations had worked with Dane Capital to organize presentations from leaders in the Chinese food processing industry. Each performance was polished and detailed. Each extolled their low-cost processing capability, with promises to offer such attractive prices that Multima Supermarkets would be able to compete favorably with any big-box retailer in North America.

However, each presentation seemed to follow a basic template. Presenters focused on the low wages they paid, the exceptionally good relationships they enjoyed with officials of the Chinese government, and their longstanding experience preparing foods for major retailers around the world. Advocates on Suzanne's team seemed thrilled with the unbe-lievably low prices and genuinely impressed with their government con-nections and experience. Suzanne, however, harbored some doubts.

None of the pitches included specifics about sanitation or quality control in their facilities. There were few references to health or nutri-tion with the processed foods. Disturbingly, she heard only scant details on the farms or methods used there. All four companies seemed to focus almost exclusively on costs and prices.

When her team broke for lunch, Suzanne huddled with her leaders of finance and retail operations to voice her concerns. In the privacy of her suite, she asked them to consider how an obsession with costs and prices would mesh with Multima Supermarkets' overall strategy. She reminded them that they had long portrayed an image of impressive stores selling high-quality products at reasonable prices.

Her executives questioned the wisdom of maintaining such posi-tioning in current market conditions, particularly with a severe reces-sion looming. Wouldn't it be better to shift focus to the lowest prices? Weren't consumers prepared to sacrifice a little quality if they might save significant amounts on their weekly shopping bills? If the quality of these producers was adequate for the big-box retailers, was it not good enough for Multima?

Suzanne believed such outlooks might not bode well for her company and questioned the wisdom of 'me too' product positioning. She feared excessive price orientation might make it more difficult for Multima Supermarkets to differentiate itself from competitors. Most of all, she worried what impact such thinking might ultimately have on their employees.

Logically, a proposal to cut all costs to the bone and offer the best prices possible led to slashed employee wages and benefits. More impor-tantly, it would ultimately result in a reduction in the actual number of workers. Labor is the single greatest expense for any supermarket chain. Significant cost reductions must necessarily include employees, and result in far fewer of them.

During that short intermission, Suzanne urged them to be mindful of such sensitive people issues as they worked through the remainder of their schedule in Asia. "Once we're back in Atlanta," she cautioned, "we need to get everyone on the same page. People issues are fundamental components of our game changer strategy. They could become divisive."

When they reconvened, there were five more sessions until they concluded the last just after eight-thirty that evening. To her chagrin, afternoon presentations mirrored those of the morning. Low costs, low prices, and excellent relationships with the Chinese government officials remained the dominant theme.

However, she noted both her finance leader and the head of retail operations had posed questions about product quality, sanitation standards, and working conditions for employees. All presenters replied with polished, carefully designed responses to reflect respect for all Chinese regulations. For Suzanne, there still was a certain hollowness towards these critical components. Her doubts lingered.

After a day of these meetings, Suzanne's team divided into separate groups to discuss impressions and review strategies. They ordered in pizza, snacks, and refreshments as they lounged around different areas of the spacious living area furnished with several comfortable chairs, sofas, and recliners.

Just before midnight, they finished their recap and were in their rooms for a few hours of sleep before it started all over again in the morning. Friday would be their last day in Asia.

Meanwhile, rather than working with her team, Suzanne was ensconced in the luxurious bedroom. She worked at a large desk with lots of space for her laptop, tablet, and speakerphone. The laptop connected to a printer that Suzanne used to download several dozen documents requiring her signature. She had hastily signed, scanned, and emailed the stack back to her assistant in Atlanta.

With mundane paperwork out of the way, Suzanne dealt with issues back at headquarters until almost three o'clock in the morning. She had several conversations with her media relations team about questions and concerns related to the hacking incident because inquiries continued to surface from both curious reporters and anxious customers.

She spent two hours with the Information Technology team and Multima corporate security representatives discussing discoveries related to the data theft, listening intently to the theories they had developed and evidence collected as both teams provided updates about next steps. She was intrigued to learn her IT team was sure the theft was the work of an inside perpetrator, or at least someone inside Multima who facilitated an illegal entry. They were scanning all secure accesses to the system with sophisticated tracking devices. Several indicators pointed towards a Multima employee or contractor.

"When we find the hacker," said IT leader Dieter Lehren, "we'll be able to determine guilt conclusively. We'll also know precisely how many times the hackers subsequently transferred our data. There's a hidden tool embedded in the software that will make an absolute determination. We'll see everything!"

Suzanne, the IT team, and the corporate security people spent more than an hour discussing possible measures to prevent another attack. She reminded everyone that future prevention was more critical than finding proof of guilt. Simply stated, there should be no recurrence of such an incident.

Because it was mid-afternoon back home, she received a few telephone calls interspersed among the outgoing ones. One came from Edward Hadley, who complimented Suzanne and her team for their excellent work to assuage media concerns related to the data theft. He understood how difficult it was to handle a crisis from afar. He made a point of telling her she could not have handled it better, even if she were in her Atlanta office. She caught the implied suggestion that not everyone shared his opinion.

She also received a call from James Fitzgerald. He seemed genuinely concerned about John George's health. In the few hours since Suzanne had last spoken with him, Fitzgerald had apparently done extensive research on breast cancer. He relayed some of his discoveries, including one that suggested success rates with male cases of breast cancer were considerably lower than with females. One article even claimed most oncologists lacked experience treating men and highlighted the scarcity of available treatment data compared to the trove of information for women.

Fitzgerald was aware John George was resting comfortably at home. He still didn't know when it might be possible to talk with him. Before concluding their call, they compared impressions of these issues, followed by promises to keep each other informed.

Finally, there was Wendal Randall's return call. They had played phone tag for a while. First, he left a voice message on Suzanne's smartphone while she talked with Fitzgerald, then she called him, only to reach his voice mail. On Randall's second attempt they finally connected. Suzanne glanced at her watch just as the telephone rang. It was two-thirty in the morning in Hong Kong, but a reasonable eight-thirty in the evening in Germany.

When Suzanne queried him about all the recent developments with Multima, Wendal didn't know about anything new and asked Suzanne to explain. Once she completely recounted news of the hacking problem and John George Mortimer's cancer, Wendal professed not to know about either. He'd been swamped with some delicate negotiations in Germany. Didn't even have a moment to turn on a TV, he claimed.

Suzanne quickly did the calculations. Her interview with Liara Furtamo first aired about four in the afternoon Hong Kong time on Wednesday. More than thirty hours had passed. Was it truly possible for someone as well connected as Wendal to be unaware of such major company developments for that long?

Suzanne's revelation about her moment of shock in the Liara Furtamo interview also appeared to be a genuine surprise to Wendal and lent some credence to his denial of any knowledge of the hacking incident.

He seemed sympathetic to the misery the theft of data created and offered any resources she might need to help solve the mystery. If she desired, he'd leave Germany immediately and personally contribute whatever technology expertise he could. She should count on him to help in any way possible.

Suzanne thanked him for the concern and offer of aid, but politely declined. After the call, she continued to mull his curious unawareness of the crises until she fell asleep.

When the timer on the treadmill indicated almost thirty minutes had elapsed, her damp top provided ample evidence of a good workout as she digested information gleaned over the past few hours.

She thought again about Wendal and his role in the hacking incident, if there was any at all. She had no more evidence of any involvement than an intuitive inkling he might just have both the technical expertise and a possible motive.

For the Asia meetings and game changer process, Suzanne felt further from a conclusion than she had when they set out a week earlier. Positions within her team were becoming increasingly entrenched and more divergent. Moreover, Suzanne did not feel entirely comfortable with either the health-conscious focus voiced by one faction or the cost-cutting, discount-pricing direction of the other.

Monday, they would all meet back in Atlanta to draw conclusions and build a consensus. It was clear she needed a way to bridge differences, unify her team, and rally the group around a common strategy.

In the meantime, she needed to prepare for another twenty-hour day of meetings and telephone conferences. With a final deep breath, Suzanne slowed the treadmill to a stop. She then set off with her usual energetic and determined bearing as Gordon Goodfellow still pedaled feverishly on his stationary bicycle.

THIRTY-FOUR

Deluxe Suite, Steigenberger Park Hotel, Düsseldorf.
Late night, March 4, 2016

His telephone conversation with Suzanne Simpson had been illuminating. While the news about Multima Supermarkets' hacking incident was no surprise, information about John George Mortimer's cancer was a revelation that commanded more thought.

Seconds after finishing his call with Suzanne, Wendal hurriedly called the financial controller he'd ignored all day. "I left those email and voice messages so you would call to get a heads-up on both issues," Joseph Kowntz complained, before saying hello.

Wendal apologized for his slow response. "Just so much going on in the negotiations with TBG," he offered.

"Right," Kowntz replied. "Are you aware of John George Mortimer's health issues?"

"Yeah! I hear he's been diagnosed with breast cancer and just had surgery. Is he doing OK?" Wendal asked, knowing Kowntz had a long and trusted relationship with Mortimer and might know more than Suzanne.

"Nobody seems to know. Apparently everything is hush-hush, and even the corporate guys aren't talking."

"Well, I sure hope he recovers soon. We need his leadership, and such a great guy shouldn't have to deal with this kind of challenge. It just doesn't seem right," Wendal said, trying to touch all the appropriate bases.

Changing the subject, Kowntz asked, "Have you heard about the hacking crisis at Supermarkets?"

"I just got a high-level heads-up from Suzanne Simpson. Not much detail. What should I know?"

"It looks like they've got real problems over there. It seems the hackers got a lot of employee data and some consumer info, too. Corporate security thinks it may be an inside job, and they've called in the FBI. I hear there are agents all over the Atlanta offices interviewing staff."

GARY D. McGUGAN

Wendal flashed back to his conversation with Suzanne Simpson. Did he detect any nuance or suspicion from her? None jumped out immediately. Nevertheless, he should keep a close eye on her activities and behavior, just in case.

"Is everything OK in our shop?" Wendal asked.

"Yeah. Everything's fine here. Nothing out of the ordinary," Kowntz replied, before adding, "Are you folks almost finished over there? The dollar just dropped against the euro again today. Anything you're planning to buy just got more expensive."

After talking with his financial controller, Wendal tried to reach Howard Knight for information and guidance. When he tried his smartphone, the call went immediately to voice mail, suggesting Knight had shut off his phone. Wendal tried the office number, but Mr. Knight was not immediately available, according to an executive assistant. In fact, there was none of the charm and good humor he usually observed when he called Knight's office. With no reply to his messages, Wendal sent an email.

So far, there was no response. He needed Knight's read on John George Mortimer's cancer. He also wanted to give notice of his intention to sign a contract with TBG the following morning with those new and higher costs included. He also felt a need to assure Knight that his team had found additional enhancements to Operation Bright Star, and one of them could be an even bigger game changer that might revolutionize virtually all retail businesses in America.

Even though he was operating in an information vacuum, Wendal's intuition and keen political sense alerted him to the possibility the CEO succession issue might be at a delicate new inflection point. He needed to be entirely sure he still had Knight's crucial support.

Wendal wondered if these new circumstances might create a different initiative from the board of directors, and speculated whether the Mortimer game changer directive might shift in some way.

All evening, Wendal left his team to continue working on the final revisions to the draft agreement TBG delivered earlier in the day. He knew they would have patience he didn't have to deal with all the minutiae of multi-page documents. Instead, he'd be satisfied with a brief oral summary at breakfast the next morning, just before they went to the offices of TBG to discuss and sign a final contract.

As he sipped a final vodka nightcap, it suddenly occurred to him that he should also connect with James Fitzgerald. It would be the right team-player thing to do, he supposed. Besides, James had a special relationship with Mortimer and might just have some juicy new details.

Fitzgerald was in his office and picked up the call on the first ring because his executive assistant had left for the day. He was his usual calm, reasoned, and rather predictable self as the two reviewed the two major pieces of news in the Multima world. However, Wendal didn't learn anything new.

As their conversation wound down, Fitzgerald light-heartedly said, "Düsseldorf is probably a good place to be during this whirling media storm." Wendal realized he hadn't mentioned anything about Germany and was using a smartphone that would display a Miami area code. How did Fitzgerald know he was out of the country?

Immediately on guard, Wendal responded with some equally light-hearted comments. When he thought it appropriate, he switched the conversation to the hacking incident. "Have you had any similar security issues at Multima Financial Services?" he asked.

Fitzgerald seemed measured in his response. "No unusual activity has been detected anywhere in our division. Still, the FBI wants to determine whether someone here may have compromised the computers over at Supermarkets. Has the same investigation started at Logistics?"

With a realization the investigation was expanding, Wendal was panic-stricken for a moment. Then, he responded, "None that I'm aware. Any FBI investigation of my team would surely find no involvement. Our people all require government security clearance for their assignments. That might be the reason we haven't heard from them." Then, with mutual good wishes for patience and perseverance during the current turbulent times, their call ended.

Wendal had already consumed more than one drink. Alcohol typically gave his face a twinge of red. However, as he stepped away from the phone and gazed into a large wall-mounted mirror in his suite's living area, he was completely ashen. He realized that his hands were trembling too.

THIRTY-FIVE

In an office tower near Wall Street, New York.
Early evening, March 4, 2016

Howard Knight decided to take a well-deserved break. He was able to look back on forty-eight highly productive hours with satisfaction. His calls to each of the independent board members had borne fruit. It had taken only a few minutes with each to evoke expressions of unease, frustration, and even scattered anger. There was apparently widespread discomfort about the way Mortimer had outlined his plans to retire in a few months but failed to disclose his cancer.

All independent directors seemed to agree that an unscheduled meeting of the board should take place soon. With a little gentle prodding from Knight, a couple even suggested the board might need to accelerate the CEO succession timing given the new developments. In just a few more days, Howard Knight would make precisely such a proposal. Within weeks, a change in the senior management of Multima Corporation might very well be completed.

Moments earlier, there had been an unexpected bonus. Frau Schäffer had called from Germany. She had coyly started their conversation with news that she had hatched a scheme to achieve their goal in Düsseldorf. Knight listened with growing enthusiasm as she outlined her intentions.

"Wendal appears ready to sign an agreement with TBG tomorrow," she reported. "They're requesting only minor changes to TBG's draft contract, and I expect their management will eagerly accept them."

"What's the deal?" Knight asked.

"Multima Logistics will pay millions of dollars over the original budget to get the automated point-of-sale equipment and software modifications. Completion within three to six months is still possible. Of course, TBG will make a huge profit on the transaction, but Wendal Randall can get his project completed. Just in case he can't sell the idea to Multima Supermarkets and the board, there's an escape provision—with a multi-million-dollar penalty."

"What's in it for us?" he queried.

"VCI will become the general contractor and provide all the resources needed to write the modified software code. I insisted that

TBG becomes legally bound to use us and pay a minimum guaranteed fee," she pointed out as Knight listened.

"My contacts in Russia confirm they are now certain we can complete the job for about three million less than TBG's guaranteed fee. That's three million dollars for us after paying all expenses, including bribes. They'll agree to it all by noon tomorrow."

"Good job. What about your other idea?"

"That plan is coming together," she explained. "Max Bergmann of TBG and Wendal Randall plan to leave Düsseldorf almost immediately after they sign the contract. According to my new source in TBG, they'll travel by car to Overveen. That's a small village just outside Amsterdam.

"I've learned that Bergmann made some discrete arrangements there for them to spend the weekend in a house where they'll sample all the temptations the Netherlands has to offer. They plan to resurface sometime on Sunday so Wendal can catch a flight home from Amsterdam and Bergmann find his way back to Düsseldorf."

"Sounds interesting," Knight responded with a smile. "Anything else I should know?"

"Yes. They'll be the only guests in that house for the entire weekend. The only other people present will be the usual willing residents, delivering all services requested. Max Bergmann has already paid the substantial fee from his personal bank account. I understand the regular participants received their reward in advance with an expectation they would perform spectacularly and often."

"And your part?" Knight demanded.

"Yes, I was successful. I was able to recruit one who quite nicely meets our needs. The owners of the house will pay the standard fee. Our petty cash account in Amsterdam will take care of the bonus. She's prepared to cooperate in every way."

For the next fifteen minutes, Frau Schäffer outlined the remainder of her scheme. Knight posed questions every few minutes to clarify his understanding. He made only one suggestion to make her plan even more impactful and ended their call by warmly congratulating her on her creativity and thorough planning. Then, he slowly replaced the handset in its cradle and smiled.

Knight decided he could allow himself to take the rest of the day off, and there would be no return call to Wendal Randall that night. It was time Randall started to learn some new lessons. Although he might eventually become CEO of Multima, he would play by different rules and answer to Knight alone. Now was a good time to start that practice.

THIRTY-SIX

Overlooking the Caloosahatchee River, Fort Myers.
Early evening, March 4, 2016

He awoke about five o'clock that morning still feeling exhausted. His housekeeper arrived well before and had hot coffee and cold cereal waiting for him. After eating, he performed his morning rituals, albeit more slowly, deliberately, and laboriously than usual.

Within an hour, he sat at a huge glass table that served as a desk in the large and comfortable study he used as an office at home, determined he could manage through the pain and fatigue. His first call was to Suzanne Simpson. He knew she was still in Hong Kong, where he supposed she would be just finishing standard business hours. Chances were good they would connect, so he was not at all surprised when she answered on the first ring.

He thought he detected relief in her voice as he explained his current condition and reassured her about the prognosis for his future. They spoke for only a few minutes about his health and Suzanne's moment of shock during the Liara Furtamo interview.

"By the way," he added. "I want to compliment you for the outstanding recovery you made with that ambush. With all of your attention focused on the hacking incident, I can only imagine how shocked you might be to hear about my news. Your quick thinking and professionalism really helped with damage control.

"And, speaking of the data theft, bring me up to date with what's happening on that front," he said, quickly changing the subject.

Mortimer listened attentively for more than an hour, asking questions when appropriate. Suzanne thoroughly briefed him on what they knew, what they didn't yet know, and what they were doing to fix the problem.

He was pleased to see she focused on how the theft occurred and ways to prevent such occurrences in the future rather than waste energy on finding the culprit. The FBI and corporate security could worry about crime and punishment. Suzanne needed to keep her eye on the business issues related to the theft, and Mortimer was gratified to learn that seemed to be her focus.

He didn't enquire about her trip to Asia, but Suzanne volunteered why she was there.

"You may find it curious to learn that I'm in Asia, but it's been very fruitful so far. We had two very productive days in Japan where we got a great proposal from the Japanese government. And, it looks like we're going to be able to introduce both udon kiosks and an exclusive private label tea. Both deals will be joint ventures, and both come with substantial promotion funds to launch them. Hong Kong's been less successful, but we've sure learned a lot about sourcing goods here. I think the team looks ready to start crystallizing a lot of ideas into our game changer project.

"We'll leave Hong Kong tomorrow. That puts us in the Atlanta office Monday morning. Let me know when you're back in your office. I'd like to chat more about our progress on the game changer," she ended.

The telephone conversation with Suzanne was informative but tiring. He finished their conversation with wishes for safe travel and warm thanks for all she was doing on the game changer project and the hacking crisis. He cheerfully encouraged her to get some sleep on the flight home; the coming week would be another busy one for them all.

After his conversation with Suzanne, he needed some time to regroup. The pain was intense again. He gratefully accepted a cup of green tea offered by his sympathetic housekeeper and relaxed for about an hour.

His next call was to Wendal Randall because he found something rather curious. Among those three hundred or so voice and email messages that he reviewed a couple days earlier, why were there none from him?

John George dialed Wendal's smartphone. He answered and requested a moment to leave a meeting to find a more private area to talk. When they resumed the conversation, Wendal immediately focused on Mortimer's health, surgery, and recovery. He repeated good wishes for a quick recuperation several times and apologized profusely that his schedule in Germany precluded a call. John George was a little surprised to learn that Wendal, too, was currently out of the country.

When Mortimer inquired about his trip, Wendal provided general, high-level explanations about software and technology they were considering for a possible game changer project. "It's still early stages," he said. "However, we're actively exploring projects with the potential to improve productivity dramatically using some far-reaching new technology. We're investigating concepts some European companies have developed to see if they might have ideas we haven't considered or cost savings we might realize by cooperating with a European producer.

"There appear to be several real possibilities. We'll need to review and more carefully analyze costs and benefits before we're ready to make a recommendation. But I have no doubt they'll be ready for the board of directors meeting in April."

John George listened carefully to Wendal's update without interruption or comment, his antenna always alert to overly general messages, dialogs that lack specifics, or updates that quickly gloss over issues. Usually, little good resulted from such conversations and Wendal's just-finished monolog raised warning flags on all three.

However, Mortimer decided not to pursue his concerns right then. Maybe Wendal's thoughts were just a little disorganized because of the interruption. Perhaps he was suffering a little jet lag. On the other hand, maybe he was just reading too much into the narrative.

After a few more pleasantries about Düsseldorf, the weather there, and some final good wishes from Wendal, Mortimer concluded their conversation. It was much shorter than the call with Suzanne. He was a little grateful for the brevity as pain persisted and another short break was most welcome. Once he drank another cup of green tea, accompanied by a small bowl of sweet red grapes, he was refreshed and ready to speak with James Fitzgerald.

James was on another call when his phone buzzed. He asked John George to hold while he quickly finished the other call. Within seconds, he returned to the line with multiple, rapid-fire questions about John George, his surgery, recovery, and prognosis. As quickly as he provided one answer, Fitzgerald posed another question. It seemed he was genuinely interested in Mortimer's physical condition and how he was coping.

When questions started to abate, Mortimer subtly shifted their discussion to the email request from Fitzgerald, the one about a guarantee for bond issues. Mortimer pointed out that Multima Financial Services already benefited greatly from the extraordinary amount of cash sitting on its balance sheet. Why should they issue new bonds?

Fitzgerald knew any request for a corporate guarantee would require full disclosure of their game changer project plans. After he had confirmed John George might be comfortable taking a few minutes for an explanation, Fitzgerald detailed their intentions for the home mortgage business. It actually took more than half an hour.

He reviewed the path they followed to recommend diversification into home mortgages and highlighted reasons they became convinced it was the right strategy. He provided a synopsis of profit and loss projections and explained the various sensitivity tests used to assess risks. Finally, he asked John George to support the issuance of Multima Financial Services bonds to match borrowing and lending costs to the mortgage term as precisely as possible.

John George listened carefully to the summary of the project. Initially, he was pleasantly surprised and impressed. The one team he originally expected might be slowest to respond to the challenge was currently far ahead of the others.

His response, however, was neutral, conveying neither admiration nor his overwhelmingly positive impression. Instead, he thanked James for the update and told him he needed a couple of days to think about it. He also asked whether Fitzgerald's team was far enough along to send him a one-page summary of the information just discussed. Of course, it would be for his eyes only. Fitzgerald immediately confirmed that he would send it by email before the end of the day.

Their call ended with more good wishes for John George's quick recovery, and the relief in James Fitzgerald's voice was palpable.

John George rested for a while and then resumed his telephone calls to catch up on corporate information and activities. He conducted brief conversations with each of his direct reports in the Fort Myers office—all nine of them.

He devoted more time for discussions with Alberto Ferer than the others because he wanted to alert Mortimer about the simmering unease among the board of directors. Another call included the director of corporate security, who was personally leading the investigation into the theft of data at Multima Supermarkets. Both conversations provided Mortimer with valuable information and new insights. He mined the information presented in minute detail and made extensive notes.

Throughout the day, Mortimer repeated this pattern. He made a call, and then took a break. Slowly, patiently, and methodically, he worked through a process designed to accomplish two goals. First, he needed to re-engage in the business and quickly catch up on all he had missed during an eventful week. More importantly, he needed all his direct reports to know he was firmly back at the helm and ready to navigate the storm.

Finally, John George Mortimer sat on the screened lanai of his Fort Myers home taking in a spectacular sunset as he gazed out over the wide and slow-moving Caloosahatchee River. His housekeeper had agreed to work a few hours longer and had just served a delicious spicy vegetable soup guaranteed to make him healthy in no time.

Pain was starting to subside because he had swallowed his first medication of the day a few moments earlier. As promised, John George was back at work that day. Discomfort or not, he had been determined to avoid medication until the workday was complete. It was important to be alert, his judgment unimpaired to perform essential tasks.

As the sun disappeared in a blaze of color, the sky formed jagged, otherworldly patterns with the lower-than-usual cloud cover and receding light. The contrasting hues of the sunset blended to create a mysterious new tapestry that lasted little more than a few moments. Still, John George Mortimer never tired of this daily performance. If he had any say in the matter, he would continue to enjoy these magnificent shows in the skies of southwest Florida for a long time to come.

Satisfied that he had executed his corporate responsibilities and duties well that day, he shifted to his next most important constituency, the board of directors. He was developing more than a little unease with his board. Clearly, he'd miscalculated the intensity of their backlash. Of course, he had never intended for news of his cancer to become public, nor had he expected such a revelation on the heels of another serious, unforeseen crisis. He also hadn't expected the directors to be embarrassed. However, that had all occurred. That was the hand he had been dealt. He must now play it out.

After a quick assessment, he decided it would be better to wait until the following day to start calls to the individual directors. Those conversations would probably prove even more taxing and would require more energy than he could currently muster. The medication began to do its work. He needed only to lie back in the reclining chair and let sleep gently envelop him. For sleep was always an essential way to prepare for life's great challenges.

THIRTY-SEVEN

In heavy traffic towards downtown Chicago.
Early evening, March 4, 2016

James Fitzgerald was becoming more irritated and impatient with the Chicago-bound traffic congestion. Although he was going opposite the main flow out of the city, he had twice been obliged to call his waiting associates alerting them to his delay.

During the most recent call, he detected a little good-natured impatience in tone, for he understood well that both men valued their private time. The associates waiting for him at the Hyatt Regency Chicago were influential members of the board of directors of Multima Corporation and crucial allies whose support he needed to maintain. Chuck Jones and Cliff Williams were attending this get-together at his request.

———————

John George Mortimer had resisted each of James Fitzgerald's several requests to become a director of Multima. Reasons varied each time, but it eventually became apparent that Mortimer preferred to limit the number of Multima Corporation executive officers on the board and seemed to prefer directors who were independent of management. It was equally clear that his will would prevail.

Fitzgerald, on the other hand, felt exposed because he was not privy to board discussions, only the decisions. A few years earlier, when he knew Mortimer was planning to replace two retiring directors, he had suggested he consider these two well-known leaders of influential Chicago-based corporations.

Chuck Jones was the founder and CEO of a successful printing company. A brilliant entrepreneur, he was a billionaire before the age of forty and claimed to print one of every ten advertising flyers distributed in the country. Cliff Williams was CEO of Greatmass Insurance, one of the largest property insurance providers in the world. Williams was an actuarial expert who had patiently climbed the corporate ladder until he reached the summit, then grew Greatmass by more than double.

It would be beneficial for Multima to have such respected names on the board, he had pointed out, and would project favorably on the company if a couple directors lived and worked in the Midwest. Since it was apparent Mortimer wouldn't appoint James to the board, perhaps he would consider those candidates.

Though Mortimer made no comment, James was sure he immediately recognized the self-serving motivation behind such a proposal. Surprisingly, within less than a month both Jones and Williams were elected to the board. As a result, for the past several years, James Fitzgerald had been privy to virtually every formal discussion at the board level. Well aware of Fitzgerald's intended proposal to Mortimer beforehand, each had implicitly agreed to keep James informed about board deliberations before he put their names forward.

Coincidentally, he was on the phone with Chuck Jones when John George Mortimer made his anxiously awaited call. Immediately after concluding the call, Fitzgerald resumed his original phone conversation. What followed led directly to the upcoming meeting.

An unanticipated and negative tone used by Jones had shocked him. For several minutes, James listened as his associate vented about Mortimer's lack of communication, foresight, and respect for the board. Of course, the director also expressed concern about John George's health, but it seemed he was more concerned about the possible damage to Multima's image among investors and customers.

Fitzgerald listened patiently. When he heard a reference to a proposed emergency meeting of the board of directors, he realized there might be more going on than some temporarily damaged relationships. After several further questions to ferret out details, Fitzgerald eventually concluded that Howard Knight might covertly be scheming to engineer the ouster of John George Mortimer from his position as CEO. According to Jones, the board had already achieved a consensus on the need for a meeting. The only remaining questions were when and where it would take place.

At that point, Fitzgerald requested they meet urgently. Chuck Jones agreed. When James suggested that they also include Cliff Williams in their discussion, Jones concurred without hesitation and offered to extend an invitation. He needed to talk to Williams about another issue anyway.

As the Chicago Hyatt Regency finally came into view, James Fitzgerald drew a deep breath. He sensed the coming few minutes might have a dramatic impact on the future of Multima Corporation and perhaps directly affect the future of John George Mortimer. Even more worrisome to Fitzgerald, it could drastically alter his own succession strategy. It might be time to call in some favors.

After parking, Fitzgerald quickly made his way to the Hyatt's Stetson Lounge where his associates seemed already comfortably engrossed in conversation, with untouched frosted steins of beer sitting in the center of a round cocktail table. They appeared to be having a serious talk. With shoulders hunched forward, their conversation was subdued as James approached the table.

When they noticed his arrival, both men immediately sprang up to shake his hand. They used exaggerated energy to clasp his hand firmly and express how delighted they were to see him again. It had been far too long, Williams said. Chuck Jones complained that Jim must have been working too hard. He needed to come downtown more often for friendly chats. It's not necessary to wait for a crisis, he'd said with an easy grin of friendship.

The conversation immediately got underway with the predictable and almost ritual opening, a dialog about professional sports. First, they commiserated on another disappointing season for the Chicago Bulls, agreeing that things just hadn't been the same since the days of Michael Jordan. A brief comment or two about the just-completed Bears season followed, with some helpful suggestions about changes 'da Bears' must make off-season to contend for a title next year, like a new coach and a better quarterback.

Next, some usual expressions of gloom were voiced about the seemingly perpetual disappointments of the Chicago Cubs, despite their flirtation with the playoffs last year. In Arizona, spring training had just started for the coming baseball season. A favorite exercise among these three was wagering by what margin the Cubs could disappoint their fans in the coming year. Their light-hearted predictions were usually remarkably accurate.

Their conversation then ambled its way to its real purpose. James started by asking his associates to explain what the emergency meeting of the board was all about. For the next several minutes, each director took turns expressing both frustration and disappointment with John George Mortimer's reckless disregard for his board.

Both men were CEOs of well-known, publicly traded companies. They knew the rules of good corporate governance. They understood accepted protocol between a CEO and his board. They valued good communication between a board and corporate management, and they made clear their disappointment with Mortimer's behavior related to all of these issues.

James listened intently for several tense minutes. He knew it was crucial to let both directors vent their frustrations. It was equally important to measure the intensity of their disappointment before proposing a course of action they might reasonably accept. Eventually, there was a pause in the conversation, and Cliff Williams asked James for his opinion. James sensed that moment might be a pivotal point in the discussion. It would be necessary to choose every word carefully. This was the time to call for their support.

For a few moments, James voiced his personal disappointment. He empathized with the position in which the directors found themselves due to Mortimer's error in judgment and pointed out that John George had also not made him aware of his situation. He shared the initial angst this caused him, reminding the directors he had spent his entire career working with the guy. Then he asked the executives if he could walk them through his thought process to see if they might concur with the current situation. Both nodded, and James started to make his case.

"First, John George Mortimer is suffering from breast cancer, a disease not common among men. After his diagnosis, there may have been many conflicting emotions that led him to decide it was better not to make his condition public immediately," Fitzgerald ventured. "Let's keep this in mind too. Although breast cancer is a terrible disease that causes significant pain and hardship, the statistics on survival rates are impressive, even among men.

"Let's also remember there is nothing about breast cancer that affects John George Mortimer's brain function or considerable cognitive powers. He called me this morning, and we spoke at length. We talked about his cancer, his current condition, and several important business issues. He was articulate, reasonable, and energetically engaged at all times. And this only a few days after major surgery.

"He told me he's still experiencing some pain but is mobile and active. He said he had already been on the phone for a few hours before we spoke. There was nothing I could detect in his manner, thought process, or comments that would suggest he was other than fully in control of his faculties ... and his company."

James paused to let the directors absorb his implication, then made and held eye contact briefly as they pondered his comments.

"You know we all feel badly for John George. This isn't about his cancer," Jones said after a moment.

James continued to make his case. "As I listened to you, I heard your frustrations. In many ways, I share them, but I must question what an unscheduled meeting of the board will achieve. You suggested that Howard Knight seems to be leading a movement to hold a special session. If I heard you correctly, you also indicated that he planned to invite only independent members of the board. No company management. Is that because he expects there will be objections to such a meeting from management representatives, or is Howard Knight trying to hasten the departure of John George for other reasons?"

Fitzgerald detected tiny signals of surprise with both men. Williams tightened his smile slightly. Jones averted his eyes for just an instant. Perhaps this possible motivation had not occurred to them. On the other hand, maybe they were surprised James had somehow separately surmised Mortimer's secret and confidential disclosure of retirement in June. They probably had already confirmed that neither had divulged any details, consistent with Mortimer's requirement for secrecy.

"I expect you have both signed enforceable confidentiality agreements," James continued. "And I understand this legal obligation is one reason you couldn't share Mortimer's underlying objectives for the game changer projects. I understand your quandary, and I bear no hard feelings that neither of you informed me as you usually would. I suppose John George had you sign those agreements to keep his real intention from me, as well as my colleagues. I'm okay with that.

"What I am not okay with is any idea that Multima's board of directors would convene a meeting to discuss the future of the man who created and built the company, just because he became ill and may have made an error in judgment that caused some embarrassment and unease. How would you both feel if your boards of directors took similar action with your companies? Would you not expect the opportunity to explain or defend your actions at the very least?"

"I get what you're saying," Chuck Jones interjected. "However, you know the board has an obligation to take some action under the circumstances."

"I know the Multima corporate bylaws intimately," James replied. "The board of directors can only legally meet if two-thirds of the board attends, and at least one of those directors represents company management. The only other time the board can legally convene a meeting is with the unanimous agreement of all independent directors, and then only to discuss grave issues such as succession in response to a life-threatening emergency or alleged criminal offense.

"I understand the reasons you may want to get a pound of flesh from John George Mortimer. I only have one request. I need one of you to contact Knight to let him know you will only attend the meeting he has planned if John George and the other directors representing management are all invited."

"If your suspicion is right, and Knight has some ulterior motive scheduling this meeting, will it truly help to have Mortimer attend?" Cliff Williams wondered.

"Knight probably knows the corporate bylaws better than I do. He'll recognize that he'll have to issue invitations to the entire board because neither Alberto Ferer nor Wilma Willingsworth will attend a meeting to discuss their CEO if John George isn't there. Have your session with him. Make your own first-hand analysis of Mortimer's capability to manage and lead the company for the coming five or so months. Discuss his preferred succession planning strategy, if you like, but make your judgments after you see for yourself his current condition and listen to the explanations of the man who has devoted his entire business life to the growth and success of Multima."

There was a brief silence as the two directors weighed his arguments. Several minutes of discussion followed to reconfirm James' impressions of the CEO's health, the corporate bylaws, and Mortimer's potential inability to travel to attend a meeting in New York. Fitzgerald answered their questions and suggested they leave a meeting location and timing to eventual discussions between Mortimer and Knight. Within a few minutes, Chuck Jones offered to call Howard Knight from his car to abort the planned emergency meeting of the board.

James thanked him and suggested they all have another beer for the road. Discussion reverted briefly to sports, things their spouses and children were doing, and plans for the coming weekend. Within a half hour, they warmly shook hands, this time in farewell. James held each handshake and made direct eye contact just a moment longer than necessary to convey his profound gratitude.

THIRTY-EIGHT

Suzanne Simpson decided to give her team a break. Moments before, the Multima Supermarkets corporate jet had crossed the international dateline on their return trip. They'd been meeting in small groups continuously since departure from Hong Kong about nine hours earlier. Their only previous reprieve from discussions was a required few minutes on the ground in Seoul to refuel the company jet.

After their Friday appointments, Suzanne declared that evening to be free time and some immediately dashed to Hong Kong's vaunted markets for bargain hunting. Others set out to explore the city's dining and nightlife, and the remainder signed up for an evening cruise of the harbor. Suzanne remained behind to work.

It also turned out that she would have an extensive debriefing with John George Mortimer. After that conversation, she had resumed her series of phone conferences with the IT team in Atlanta and corporate security in Fort Myers. It appeared they might be closing in on the mystery of the hacking incident.

Knowing most of her team would probably return to the hotel late and craving a little extra sleep for herself, she scheduled departure from the Grand Hyatt Hotel for nine-thirty Saturday morning. They were wheels up by ten o'clock.

Before departure, Jennifer Wong informed them the flight to Atlanta would stop in Korea and Anchorage. Their return flight from Hong Kong was a few miles longer than the inbound trip. That longer distance, combined with prevailing wind conditions, generated computer calculations suggesting they might run low on fuel over the Pacific should they not refuel somewhere in Asia.

The company pilots always avoided risks, so they had selected Seoul as the most convenient stop, a location almost directly below the most desirable flight path. Accordingly, Jennifer apologized that their flight home would take a little longer. With a cheerful smile, she reminded the team they were picking up that day lost going to Asia and should arrive in Atlanta mid-afternoon Saturday.

Suzanne planned for meetings on the flight to begin bridging the rather wide gaps in game changer project preferences shown by her team. She left it to the team members to choose whether they worked for the first half of the trip or the second. She was gratified when the majority elected to work immediately after departure.

Discussions over the past several hours were fruitful. Now, she needed to pause and organize some of the many thoughts and ideas still churning in her mind from the last day or so. She pressed the recline button on her leather swivel seat, leaned back, and started thinking about the informative dinner meeting with her old friend Michelle.

She gained much from Michelle Sauvignon during their few pleasant hours discussing retailing in China, and Suzanne also learned there were significant gaps in her level of knowledge. A wise mentor often counseled her to be wary of information she might be missing. "What you don't know might actually be far more crucial than what you do know," she remembered him saying often.

During their conversation, Michelle Sauvignon mentioned her intention to remain in Hong Kong for a couple of days to meet with investors and local bankers. She invited Suzanne to call should any additional time free up to meet for coffee or another meal.

After the meetings with the potential Chinese food-processing providers arranged by Dane Capital, Suzanne had called her friend. There was no time to meet for coffee, she explained, but could she impose upon their friendship and ask Michelle to meet with her team for an hour Friday morning?

Suzanne then outlined her hope that Michelle might make an hour in her schedule to explain—without giving away confidential information—some of the challenges encountered when dealing with Chinese suppliers. There was so much they needed to learn. More importantly, Suzanne thought learning from Michelle might carry tremendous weight with her team.

With only a short hesitation to weigh risks and benefits, Michelle agreed to one hour at eight o'clock Friday morning. She was just down the road at the Four Seasons Hotel and could come to the Hyatt—but for only one hour, she emphasized, and there would be no proprietary information discussed.

Michelle's talk proved valuable beyond Suzanne's expectations. Her talented friend made a thirty-minute presentation to the team. No prepared script. No PowerPoint slides. Her only speaking aid appeared to be one small index card with four bullet points neatly printed in large block letters.

"China is a fascinating place to do business," she started. "Chinese people can certainly be excellent partners, but it's not always easy. First, there is the elusive issue of quality control. I think it's possible for most Chinese companies to achieve whatever level of quality a buyer desires— if a purchaser of goods is prepared to be patient, invest adequately, and recognize such patience often can translate into lots of money too."

She highlighted the core issues. Neither the concept of quality control standards nor the processes of quality management is embedded in Chinese culture to the same extent as Western or Japanese cultures. Until recently, few Chinese businesses invested in process management and control to meet world-class expectations. Instead, the primary focus had been continuous and dramatic cost reductions.

In Michelle's view, "Western companies working with Chinese providers only achieve consistent and acceptable levels of quality if they are prepared to insert their own resources. They're essential at all stages of the processes and should become embedded within those manufacturing facilities. Again, such investments involve significant amounts of time and money.

"Third-party inspection companies or the producers' quality control teams usually prove to be inadequate," she maintained. "For reasons ranging from sub-standard training and education to outright corruption, most Chinese producers do not deliver reliably high-quality products if left only to their habitual devices.

"Such factors force experienced Western buyers to build into prices the full costs of housing their own people in China. Usually, those inspectors are inside a supplier's plant or factory campus, and that requirement is especially critical with food products. As we all know, any lapse in food preparation or quality could prove fatal."

She explained that even with products like toothpaste, grooming products, or cosmetics, quality could vary widely from day to day on a given assembly line of a particular facility. "Farefour employs several hundred people devoted to quality control in China. More than one hundred of those are highly paid expatriate workers from Western countries."

Michelle's next topic was government relations. With her arrival in China, she had been appalled to learn that corruption, particularly bribery of bureaucrats, was relatively routine. During her first two years in China, she devoted much of her time and energy to sorting through and removing such tendencies at Farefour. She focused primarily on dependable supplier relationships and steadfastly resisted an inclination for government officials to request illicit payments for almost every activity they undertook.

"Farefour Stores' corporate policy forbids payments of bribes," she explained. "So, I did everything in my power to adhere to that policy. But I would be only kidding myself to think we had eradicated bad behavior from all activities our company undertakes in China."

It remained a great concern for her because corruption can be punished very severely in China—should the government choose to enforce the law. The current maximum penalty for corruption is death. "Every year, a few dozen people among millions of government officials and business executives in China are executed after highly publicized trials that are closed to the public," she said.

After a quick glance at her watch, Michelle quickly summarized her remaining two points.

"Communication is still a formidable challenge," she said. "Many Western companies arrive in China through the gateway of Hong Kong. That city only reverted to Chinese control from the British in the mid-nineties. Customs and values in Hong Kong are more Westernized and feel more familiar to newly arriving managers of many foreign companies. Almost all business people also speak English, making it easier to do business.

"Consequently, many Western companies tend to hire Hong Kong representatives. This can sometimes be a mistake. Cantonese spoken in Hong Kong is different from Mandarin, the official language spoken throughout mainland China. Some people compare the relationship between Cantonese and Mandarin to that of Spanish and Italian. While there are many similarities, there are also significant differences. Language gaps, misunderstandings, and miscommunication often occur as a result."

This point forced Suzanne's team members to avoid glancing at the Dane Capital interpreters in the room. Of course, they could all clearly recall the uncomfortable challenges they had recently encountered with these issues.

Summing up, Michelle pointed out that Western business people often do not take enough time to learn about China. "It's a vast nation with a huge population, but it's also bewildering how complex this country is," she cautioned. "More complicated than any other culture I've ever experienced. It's like peeling away layers of an onion.

"Discover one facet of Chinese life, and a new, slightly different aspect of behavior is apparent," she said with a laugh. "It seems the more one learns about China, the more one learns how much more there is yet to learn!"

Impressed with Michelle's words of experience, the Multima Supermarkets team broke into spontaneous and sustained applause when she finished. Michelle responded to a flood of questions and answered patiently until she reached her one-hour limit. Then, she abruptly bid good-bye to the group without further explanation.

As she swept out the door of the meeting room, her entourage immediately surrounded her. Under the watchful eye of this security detail, Suzanne quickly embraced her friend once more and whispered that she owed her big time. Michelle only smiled as their eyes said farewell.

After her flamboyant departure, Suzanne's team resumed their schedule of appointments organized by Dane Capital. Throughout that day, the team listened to a stream of polished presentations from Chinese food processors. To no one's surprise, the prepared performances seemed to mirror those of the previous sessions.

However, she was pleased to see her colleagues more discerning in their scrutiny of the information they received. What exactly did good relations with government officials mean? How did they achieve such low prices? They admonished several to describe quality control processes in more detail.

Some answers were good ones. Others served to underscore the cautions Michelle Sauvignon had raised. By the end of the day, Suzanne was starting to feel less confident about her company's preparedness for sourcing products from China, even if the cost savings were truly dramatic.

In a brief wrap-up before releasing her colleagues for their night on the town in Hong Kong, Suzanne alluded to these lingering concerns. She asked her team to start thinking about the discussions they would have on the plane the next day. She reminded them time would be precious during their flight to Atlanta, and it would be in even shorter supply once they arrived.

On the way to Alaska, follow-up discussions among her team had surpassed her expectations. Initially, she had divided them into three working units. Each group sat around a solid table with adequate space for laptops and tablets. The comfortable leather seats swiveled, so teams could each create three circles with enough separation to have independent conversations without disturbing others.

The Florida-based growers huddled around a table closest to the toilet in the rear of the aircraft, where the noise was loudest. Suzanne decided to begin her participation with that team. She started their conversation by asking if they had learned enough to propose any new offerings she might consider game changers.

She was astounded as one grower after the other responded with outlines of new products he or she felt their farms could start to produce. Their input was concrete and detailed. They also seemed realistic about when they could begin such production based on planting seasons, fallow land capacity, harvesting issues, and labor availability.

She shouldn't have been surprised. These growers bore no resemblance to the image many Americans conjured about farmers. In fact, the small family-owned farms many people visualize now cultivate only limited, specialized foods.

Instead, the bulk of America's grains, fruits, and vegetables comes from large, well-capitalized corporations like those where these delegates worked. They used complex computer models, financial analysis tools, and sophisticated business plans to manage far-flung operations that generated mountains of food for supermarkets like Multima.

Suzanne was also taken aback to learn expected price ranges of the proposed new food varieties would compare favorably with the prices offered by the Japanese government official, Hiromi Tenaka.

Further, she was pleased to note that more than one of those growers had already given considerable thought to promoting the new products with Multima Supermarkets. In fact, they already had a rudimentary advertising strategy to create adequate consumer demand for new foods and attain profitability.

By the time she left that table of producers and moved on to the next group, Suzanne had prepared some detailed notes on her tablet. She organized this data for her team back in Atlanta in the same order she would ask them to perform analysis from several perspectives over the next few hours.

Before joining the next table, Suzanne prepared a cover memo for the team in Atlanta explaining the types of information she required, the comparisons she sought, and the level of detail needed. Moments later, fresh employees in Atlanta would begin their midnight work shift to process the requests. Similar eight-hour rotations of the staff were scheduled throughout the coming weekend to assure analysis and support as needed. She had every confidence the information she needed would arrive by the wee hours of Monday morning.

As she unbuckled her belt and gingerly stood up from a leather swivel seat to join the second group, she noticed something had changed. Instead of two other working groups as initially planned, there was now just a giant circle with nine participants sitting around the tables. She watched the interaction for a moment before advancing. Gordon Goodfellow was writing on an easel-mounted flip chart, and the group appeared to be brainstorming ideas.

When Suzanne joined and stood just outside the perimeter of the circle, her financial operations leader, Heather Strong offered an explanation. "We folks who were focused on waging war on the big box retailers quickly reached a new consensus. We're no longer comfortable recommending a shift from our current quality supermarket format to one designed to attract bargain-seekers."

Strong was not known for shifting her position, once established. Suzanne was intrigued with not only the decision but the dynamics of reaching that conclusion, too. She kept her response as simple as possible. "Why?"

"Our thought process evolved with the China meetings. We agree it would be preferable to acquire a regional, well-established warehouse-style retailer who already has expertise dealing in a low-cost environment, including purchases from offshore providers. We thought it would be much safer to buy a company that already had experience sourcing products from foreign countries," Strong replied.

"Interesting," Suzanne responded with her eyebrows arched in curiosity.

"Actually, we have a target in mind. In fact, we already compiled a significant dossier of data about a potential company before setting out for Asia. We thought it prudent to have a backup plan," Strong confessed.

"We formed an acquisition team back in Atlanta, and they've been working all week on a detailed purchase proposal. It'll be ready for you to consider Monday morning. So we thought we could add the most value during this flight by helping our colleagues focused on the healthy food orientation. For the current supermarket model, we completely agree with this direction."

More than a little astonished, Suzanne was also pleased. They had apparently averted an anticipated showdown, and there was no need to choose one strategy over the other. She also expected the new acquisition strategy might be a more comfortable direction for her. Her conviction about the wisdom of the healthy food path had grown stronger over the past several days as she weighed the strategic benefits.

A question remained about how best to deal with John George Mortimer's explicit directive for each division to propose only one game changer strategy. Was it better to focus all her team's efforts exclusively on a healthy foods option? Assuming the acquisition opportunity her team had identified was a good one, would it be better to build on that idea, or should she disregard those instructions and deliver a game changer concept with two principal components?

As these alternatives churned in her mind, she concluded that she first needed another short nap before reaching Alaska. About two and half hours remained in that flight segment—almost equal to the amount of time she had slept both nights in Hong Kong.

With a touch of her seat's recline button, a footrest automatically raised, while lumbar support adjusted to her preferred settings. Suzanne wrapped herself in a comfortable wool blanket and snuggled against the padded armrests. Then, she plugged a Bose headset into her tablet and selected a classical music file.

Within moments, she was sleeping soundly, a soothing symphony playing on.

THIRTY-NINE

A house in Overveen, the Netherlands.
About noon, Saturday, March 5, 2016

They left the offices of Technologie Bergmann GmbH late Friday afternoon. When they stepped out of the elevator one level below ground,
Max Bergmann pointed to a magnificent Porsche in the first parking
space. They put Wendal's overnight bag in the tiny storage compartment
and set off for the Netherlands.

From that point, their drive to the town of Overveen took about
two hours because a few minutes after they passed Angermund, Max
left narrow, well-maintained two-lane roads and blasted onto a multi-
lane *autobahn* with a phenomenal burst of speed. Wendal didn't notice
the number because he was so distracted by Max's sudden and powerful
acceleration. A thrilling sensation, something Wendal had never before
experienced, developed as incredible engine torque thrust the Porsche to
more than a hundred kilometers per hour in just a couple seconds.

They engaged in jocular banter as they made a short drive north
through Düsseldorf to connect with regional road number eight.
Then, they whisked along this lightly traveled roadway for about
fifteen minutes until Max Bergmann pointed out the village where he
lived, Angermund.

Wendal's head and shoulders snapped back against the passenger
seat head restraint, momentarily locked there by the force of the sports
car's powerful torque until Max reached a cruising speed at more than
two hundred kilometers per hour.

He laughed good-naturedly at Wendal's startled expressions.
Max could see his vehicle's performance surprised and genuinely
impressed him.

"It's a pity we aren't making this trip early on a Sunday morning,"
he said. "That's when traffic is light enough we Porsche drivers can
finally experience speeds close to the maximum. For my 911, that would
be something more than three hundred kilometers per hour. You see
how well German drivers usually keep to the right lanes on *autobahns*,"
he pointed out with a broad grin. "But such high speeds can be lethal

because the roads are congested. Sunday mornings are great because there are typically few other cars on the road. Drivers watch our Porsches streak past them in a fleeting blur—but only for a few seconds!" He laughed heartily.

Max's Porsche intrigued Wendal, particularly the incredible acceleration. Such interest was unusual for him. Up to now, cars of any kind had no appeal. He hadn't even bothered to get a driving permit until prodded to do so by taunting roommates during his sophomore year at college. Unlike most young American men, Wendal had always regarded cars as merely a means of transportation. It mattered little to him what vehicle he was in, or even who might be driving, as long as the ride was comfortable.

For the following hour, Wendal savored exhilaration from the sound, torque, and motion of the Porsche, and chatted about all of the appealing characteristics of the magnificent machine. Max detailed the vehicle's features with the same care and passion he might use to describe a beautiful woman. Wendal listened in a state of rapture as he discovered a previously unknown world.

As they passed a roadside sign indicating their arrival in the Netherlands, Max took his foot off the accelerator entirely, and their speed abruptly dropped to about one hundred and twenty kilometers per hour. Although they had reverted to about the same rate most vehicles travel on American freeways, it now seemed they were creeping in comparison.

"Photo radar," Max grimaced. "The Dutch have installed cameras all along their expressways. On this stretch of the highway coming from Germany, there seem to be even more. Dutch government officials like to collect lots of money from German drivers. They must still be seeking restitution!" Wendal noted the less than subtle reference to lingering resentments still harbored by the Dutch since World War II.

With the slower traffic flow, Wendal noticed his euphoria about the Porsche waned somewhat. For the rest of the drive, their conversations shifted to more mundane topics. He remained curious about their destination but thought it better not to ask too much.

Max made or received an almost constant stream of phone calls once they arrived inside Dutch territory. Speaking German and occasionally Dutch, he seemed to be confirming various details. Wendal couldn't understand any of the conversations. Curiously, Max never once offered to explain who called or why. Like many language-challenged Americans, Wendal found that a little impolite.

When they arrived in the village of Overveen, Wendal's first impressions were very positive. Stately old homes built with brick or stone lined narrow cobblestone streets in straight, neat rows. People walked on sidewalks carrying bags and parcels. Others shared the streets with cars, riding bicycles laden with sacks of groceries or other goods from local shopping trips. It seemed almost a society of a different era.

Once stopped in front of the highly anticipated house, he noticed the front window drapes were drawn closed. This small detail caught his attention because window curtains for every other home they passed were completely open. In fact, as they had slowly progressed down that tranquil street, he found it curious to look directly into living room windows only a few feet from the road. He could clearly see the occupants inside and watch what they were doing.

The front door opened before Max could ring the doorbell. A tall, dark-haired, and stunningly beautiful woman greeted him with a short, quick embrace. Max kissed her briefly on each cheek, then a second time on the left cheek, apparently for good measure. She guided him through the doorway and Wendal followed.

The woman closed and locked the door. Max introduced Wendal to Nicole. She murmured a welcome with a short, quick embrace and offered her cheek for Wendal to kiss. Wendal kissed both cheeks, only to find the woman was again offering the left one. "It's a tradition!" she explained, laughing. "The Dutch seem always to seek just a little more pleasure than the rest of Europe." She flashed a charming and conspiratorial smile.

For the next few minutes, Nicole casually busied herself making sure Wendal and Max relaxed and became comfortable. She served drinks and snacks, which she carried from a kitchen behind the living room and down a short corridor. Each time she returned to the living room, Nicole brought another new woman and Wendal and Max were both introduced. Each new woman seamlessly joined into friendly, meaningless chatter.

Over the following hour or so, Nicole gradually introduced Yvonne, Sonia, Emerald, Karina, Helina, and Waan. Individually they might be taller or shorter, well developed or petite, outgoing or shy, but they were all incredibly beautiful, enticing women, with infectious laughter and lilting voices.

Wendal and Max were the only men. During an hour or so, their strong drinks were replenished a couple of times. Their conversation became increasingly animated. Laughter was boisterous. The background music developed deeper and more pulsating beats with rich bass tones. The atmosphere in the room felt energetic, with a particular edge.

Wendal found himself seated next to each of the women at one time or another. They circulated casually around the living room, making conversation with each other or their guests, laughing easily and growing more familiar. They all invariably seemed to make a point of touching Wendal whenever they were close.

One time there might be a simple tap on his arm. Later, perhaps it was a playful squeeze of his knee or a gentle brush against his shoulder. Then, he noticed, such touches became longer and more intimate. All the while, Nicole or one of the other women took turns serving food to the group.

Mounds of delicious Russian caviar came before large quantities of tiny shrimp served with a spicy sauce. At one point, a little dripped onto Wendal's shirt, and one of the women helpfully removed the stain. To his delight, she playfully eliminated the small errant spot using her tongue.

Over the next couple hours, the food service continued. At some point, Wendal was no longer making any effort at all to feed himself. Instead, the lovely women took turns delicately selecting bite-sized fruits and vegetables, meat-laden skewers, or pastries from a platter, and then feeding him before taking some for themselves.

After a while, they playfully insisted on some kisses before they would serve more food. Not the formal kisses of greeting they all used earlier. Instead, these involved their tongues, which probed increasingly deeper and with passion. After a while, their time spent kissing surpassed eating time by a considerable margin.

He started to lose track of names. They all became *Cherie*. That was Nicole's suggestion. Wendal became increasingly less aware of which *Cherie* he was actually kissing or fondling. They all became much more intimate. It was about then he saw Max go up the staircase with the women who looked more Asian than the others.

The remaining women stayed in the living room with Wendal. It seemed the drinks gradually slowed. Then, they all switched to marijuana. By the time the smoking stopped, he had made what to him seemed an important observation. It was as though he was looking at himself from outside his body, from the perspective of an entirely separate person.

He was wearing no clothes at all. He saw that none of the remaining women wore any either. With a full, somewhat inhibited grin, he gazed down to admire his most magnificent erection. There, two women were seductively stroking his member and the surrounding highly sensual areas.

At least two women, maybe more, accompanied him to a third-floor bedroom, and he experienced sex with those women at the same time. Never before had he enjoyed two lustful sexual partners simultaneously. Perhaps it didn't meet the strict definition of an orgy, but it surely seemed like one to him.

He now remembered doing the same sorts of exquisite things with other women later, but he couldn't remember which ones. Those sexual romps were long. He didn't know how long, but he recalled that his pleasure seemed to go on for hours at a time. After one particularly exhausting session, he took a break in the toilet just off the bedroom, where he saw two of the women, still nude, as he peered down the stairwell. They looked up and waved with warm, sensual smiles as they entered a door on the level below. He guessed they were visiting Max.

When he returned to the large bedroom, someone suggested a line of cocaine. They all joined in. That high provided another gigantic surge in energy. The sex that followed was again passionate and intense, until he lost consciousness.

Now, through the fog of a massive hangover characterized by a dull throbbing and persistent pounding inside his head and a memory best described as fuzzy, Wendal was trying to make a recovery. Someone handed him a ghastly liquid concoction. Its color was odd, much like the putrid green and yellow tinges of a still-water pool devoid of vegetation or life. The odor was noxious. At first, Wendal instinctively jerked his head away from the glass.

Eventually, he changed his mind and forced himself to swallow for two reasons. First, a nude, shapely, and exquisitely attractive tall blonde handed him the drink with an assurance it would soon cure his hangover. Plus, she confided, the beverage contained a generous squirt of vodka.

There was an added incentive: a promise from this statuesque beauty to administer another massage with the assistance of an equally gorgeous, entirely nude companion. Smiling and without any apparent inhibition, both stood before his craving gaze until he gulped down the entire concoction.

Wendal subsequently found himself lying comfortably on his stomach with his arms relaxed at his side. Two gentle hands kneaded away any tension in his shoulders. Simultaneously, two more hands lightly stroked his temples in a gentle, repetitive, and circular motion. Within minutes, Wendal started to feel considerably better.

Hung over or not, he was still basking in that lingering glow of sexual satisfaction as though it had just occurred. Then, he suddenly realized the new massage, administered by two lovely ladies named *Cherie*, had now moved again to increasingly sensitive areas of his body. Once more, his male member was rising to a new call for action. One *Cherie* whispered in his ear that they should all move over to the massive bed where it would be much more comfortable to continue their gentle strokes.

FORTY

Anchorage Airport.
Early morning, Saturday, March 5, 2016

They had dozed off or slept for the past couple hours and now woke as they arrived at the private jet section of Anchorage's international airport. It was about eight o'clock, so travel planner Jennifer Wong suggested they all disembark to have breakfast while a crew refueled the corporate jet.

Suzanne turned on her smartphone as she walked to the terminal in brutally frigid air, and watched as a rush of accumulated messages loaded onto her handset. After ordering a simple breakfast of cold cereal and fruit from a surprisingly cheerful server, she started to review the message summary. She noted several attempts to reach her during the hours she had shut off her phone to sleep. One was from Eileen Lee, her executive assistant, and the others were all from the same number in Quebec, one she didn't recognize. There was also one voice mail message.

She checked her voice mail first, thinking perhaps the unknown caller had left details there. A recording prompted her for her password, as usual. Then, she heard the strained voice of Eileen Lee asking Suzanne to call her urgently at home. Her tone projected stress as she emphasized that Suzanne should call her as soon as possible after receipt of the message. It was a family matter.

A shroud of dread and concern immediately enveloped her because something serious must have occurred. Her executive assistant usually had a calm and controlled demeanor and wasn't one to create urgency where none existed. She called her back right away. There was virtually no small talk. Instead, Eileen immediately thanked Suzanne for the quick response and explained her earlier message.

Suzanne felt her brain grow numb as she listened to the shocking news. She needed to call a Monsieur LaMontagne in Quebec City as soon as possible. Suzanne's mother had suffered a major heart attack and currently was under intensive care at Hôpital Laval.

Eileen apologized that she could not provide more details, but Monsieur LaMontagne had not been willing to provide any. He wanted to speak with Suzanne directly. The executive assistant also explained that she found the hospital telephone number on the Internet and called. Staff there confirmed Suzanne's mother was in their care. They would not provide more details except to a family member.

Suzanne made note of the numbers and immediately dialed Monsieur LaMontagne at the number Eileen Lee had provided, the same number she saw listed multiple times in her call record. He answered on the first ring.

"Good day, Madame. I am the *notaire* for your mother, Louise Marcotte," he began. "She was in my office yesterday evening when it happened. After Madame Marcotte had climbed the three flights of stairs, she appeared to be experiencing some difficulty breathing. My secretary offered her a chair to rest and a glass of water. Initially, this seemed to help her breathing normalize. We started our meeting a few minutes later, exactly according to schedule.

"However, shortly after our discussions started, I realized your mother appeared to be suffering some anxiety. When I inquired, she admitted to feeling some discomfort. Her chest felt tight. She was having difficulty to breathe, and there was an intense, sharp pain penetrating deep into her chest. At that point, she suddenly fainted in her chair and slumped awkwardly to the floor of my office."

"What happened?" Suzanne asked, anxiously.

"I immediately shouted out to my secretary to call 911." Monsieur LaMontagne said. "Then I helped Madame Marcotte lie flat on the floor. I checked to be sure nothing blocked her throat and started to apply pressure to her chest, just as I learned during CPR training."

"I understand," she acknowledged.

"I continued those efforts while my secretary ran three flights of stairs to find the building defibrillator. When she returned, also breathing with some difficulty, we both tried to remember exactly how to use the device," he added.

Suzanne was desperately anxious to know the current condition of her mother, but she patiently allowed the *notaire* to continue his wandering narrative without interruption.

"We were just starting to read the instruction manual," he explained, "when three emergency workers rushed into my office and took over. They used a defibrillator several times, all the while consulting with someone by telephone. I realized the situation was extremely grave. As the rescuers carried your mother from the room on a stretcher, one of the emergency responders confided that things did not look good.

"He asked me if I knew how to notify Madame's family. He said they would transport her to Hôpital Laval for treatment, but the patient's condition appeared grave," his voice lowered respectfully.

"My secretary looked inside the handbag of Madame Marcotte, but she couldn't find any names or emergency contact telephone numbers. Then, she thought to check your mother's last will and testament. We had one copy on file in the office. It was in that document she found telephone numbers for you, Madame Simpson.

"We tried both numbers, again to no avail. We left messages with both numbers requesting an immediate return call, but only this morning we heard back from your assistant. I'm terribly sorry for such a long explanation, but I want you to be aware of all of the circumstances surrounding your mother's unfortunate illness," he concluded.

Suzanne then calmly posed the obvious question. "Where is my mother now and what is her current condition?"

"Her situation remains perilous," Monsieur LaMontagne replied. "I am right now at Hôpital Laval. I spoke with her cardiologist an hour or so ago. He recommends that you come to the hospital as quickly as possible. Madame Marcotte experienced a massive attack with extensive damage to her heart. The prognosis does not look good.

"Your mother is receiving excellent treatment and care. Hôpital Laval is well known as one of the best hospitals in all Canada for cardiac issues. They will certainly do everything possible." He again lowered his voice to underscore the gravity of the situation.

Suzanne calmly told him she would come as quickly as possible, though it would still take several hours. She explained that she was in Alaska and outlined the likely travel time necessary to arrive in Quebec City. She thanked him for his information and all the help he and his secretary had provided to her mother when she was in such distress. She also begged him to keep her informed of any developments.

She then asked to speak with someone from the hospital. Monsieur LaMontagne passed his phone to a nearby nurse, who confirmed her mother's status. She obtained the necessary contact details for updates and again extracted a promise they would alert her to any change in her mother's condition. Once more, Suzanne affirmed she would come to the hospital as soon as possible.

These conversations left her feeling both extreme shock and intense unease. Jennifer Wong had overheard Suzanne's side of the conversations and realized she was dealing with a serious emergency.

"Should we adjust the flight plan?" the travel planner inquired. Suzanne only nodded in the affirmative, then quickly added that she'd like to meet with her team first, just to get their support for this change to their return. Running, Jennifer fled from the building to the aircraft. She briefed the pilots on the new situation and asked them to file a modified flight plan for Quebec City immediately. There was no doubt the team would support Suzanne's intention to alter their route.

Meanwhile, Suzanne gathered her team in the airport cafeteria and explained her crisis. Tears welled up, but she was determined to maintain her composure. Before she could complete her explanation, Gordon Goodfellow interrupted.

"Of course, let's change the plan. Don't worry about us. It's an emergency, and we'll adapt," he said. Choruses of similar assurances followed as the marketing leader further suggested everyone bring their breakfasts and return to the aircraft so they might quickly be on their way.

Jennifer Wong shepherded her charges back into the business aircraft. Within minutes, the pilots confirmed clearance from air traffic control for departure, and the jet taxied down the runway for takeoff. As they picked up speed, Suzanne still fretted about the inconvenience this change in schedule would cause the group traveling with her. All would be delayed returning to their families. Everyone would be further disrupted preparing for the game changer project. Further, she also doubted how effectively she could lead over the coming days.

As tears welled up again, Suzanne felt this awful experience was testing her. She knew she must find a way to balance and compartmentalize her personal crisis with the demands of her role as a division president. That was a signature requirement of her position, and she would find a way to fulfill her responsibility.

Instead of taking the rest originally planned for this second flight, she asked her team to modify plans one more time. They should revert immediately to game changer discussions and preparation. Just in case she couldn't fully participate when they arrived back in Atlanta, they could accomplish a lot during the long flight to Quebec City.

"We're ahead of you on that one," Gordon Goodfellow replied. "We already decided to use this segment productively, just as soon as we reach cruising altitude."

FORTY-ONE

The discomfort from surgery had subsided somewhat when John George awoke about five o'clock that morning. He remembered that his house-keeper had graciously agreed to stay the previous night. Now, as he awoke in his upper-level bedroom, Mortimer breathed in the delicious aroma of freshly brewed coffee wafting up the stairwell from the kitchen on the lower level.

After dispensing with his morning habits, he slowly navigated his way down the staircase towards a comfortable wicker rocking chair on the outdoor lanai. It was there he enjoyed a cup of strong black coffee offered by his housekeeper. He sat for some time, thinking about the dis-concerting news Alberto Ferer had shared in their telephone conversa-tion the morning before.

Alberto was alarmed. Apparently, several company directors had confided a desire to convene an emergency meeting of the board. John George didn't understand the real motivations behind it. He was pre-pared to declare *mea culpa* for his failure to notify the board about his diagnosis and surgery for breast cancer, but surely the directors knew him well enough to anticipate that.

He understood the discomfort and embarrassment he had caused the board when they were unprepared to respond to inquiries from the media and others. He also understood some directors might have ques-tions about his ability to lead the corporation for the long term. He got all that. But he had already advised the board of his intention to retire in less than five months. Why should there be such urgency to discuss his future? What other factors might be in play?

His thoughts drifted back to a private conversation with one of the titans of American business before finalizing his decision to make Multima Corporation publicly traded. He sought advice about the pros and cons of leading a corporation with many diverse, individ-ual shareholders.

He clearly recalled the advice. "Manage your board of directors the same way a general prepares for battle. Assume every director has the potential to be either an ally or an enemy depending on the issue at hand. Remember to make an objective assessment of each director's probable position every time. Then, try to ascertain a motivation for such a likely preference before every discussion."

Mortimer grasped the wisdom of that advice and had followed his mentor's counsel rigorously. Today would be no exception. So, what were the most frequent and potent motivators he had encountered over his long career? Fear came to mind first. Fear of the unknown. Of change. Of possible consequences, like lawsuits. Maybe add fears of criticism, fear of omission, or a failure to act. Yes, it was possible one or two of the directors might seek an emergency meeting because of fear.

Self-interest was also a strong motivator. Was it possible one director, or more, might hope to become Mortimer's replacement as CEO and use the current circumstances to seize control? He dismissed that scenario as unlikely. Most of the independent directors were themselves chief executive officers of large and successful businesses. He doubted Alberto Ferer or Wilma Willingsworth harbored secret ambitions either.

Greed was the remaining tendency on Mortimer's short list of common motivators. He faced greed regularly, and he found it to be an insidious enemy. There had often been occasions when directors voiced positions that to him appeared to originate with deep-seated greed.

John George recalled some of the comments. "Profits must increase using any means necessary." "Management's sole role is to optimize shareholder returns." "Slash expenses to maximize profits." Such thoughts surfaced at various times during board discussions, and he fundamentally disagreed with them. He considered such comments to be greed driving a discussion. Instead, he preferred a thought process soundly based on reason and logic. In his view, the primary role of any company management is to build a corporation that will consistently generate profits over an extended period, for years and even generations. Short term, quarterly achievements were of only passing interest.

He rhymed off again the real priorities. Satisfy customers. Keep employees. Be socially responsible in communities where Multima does business. Contain costs perpetually. These were the key contributors to ongoing, viable business success and profit—in that order.

He made it a point to defend those four missions in every interaction with his board and came to identify the directors more tainted by greed. There were a few on the board who interpreted a business school mantra of 'optimizing shareholder value' to mean companies should always generate the greatest profit possible in the shortest possible time.

Some, like Howard Knight, representing VCI on the board, made no secret of their desire to get an immediate return on investment, regardless of long-term consequences. "We can always deal with new problems later," some liked to say.

Alberto Ferer thought Howard Knight was spearheading this movement to hold an emergency meeting of the board. Might there be some reason to believe Knight could have some other and less obvious motivation? Maybe.

Mortimer had never become entirely comfortable with VCI's ownership position in Multima. Although he had initially questioned what motivated VCI to make such a massive investment in his company, he finally decided it was just greed. Greed he felt he could manage by generating reliable, consistent profits over time.

In fact, over those past ten years, Knight had never promoted his views unreasonably during board meetings. From his arguments or tone in those discussions, there was never evidence of a VCI agenda other than the interests of a substantial shareholder.

However, VCI might view the current circumstance as an opportunity to thwart Mortimer's plan to elect a Multima executive to the CEO position. Perhaps VCI might prefer to win approval for an outsider to lead the company. Alternatively, Knight might anticipate one probable winner and actually prefer another.

John George recalled a passing reference Wilma Willingsworth made during their conversation yesterday. His CFO mentioned that Howard Knight had recently called. Not, apparently, to discuss a possible emergency meeting of the board, as was the case during his call to Alberto Ferer. Rather, the call seemed more to explore her receptiveness towards a concept Wendal Randall was apparently incubating. Something about automating Multima processes to save millions in overhead.

John George had not attached significance to Wilma's comment at the time. He'd always encouraged directors to communicate freely with his direct reports. He genuinely wanted the board to benefit from the vaunted Multima culture of open communication and expected his management team to be comfortable sharing sensitive information with them. It wasn't out of the ordinary for Wendal Randall to bounce an idea off Howard Knight, or for Knight to seek insight into the game changer direction of the Multima Logistics team.

What seemed a little strange was Knight's apparent effort to assess the level of support Wendal's project might garner from Wilma Willingsworth. Knight would surely be aware that Wilma's financial assessment of any idea carried weight with the board, indeed with Mortimer himself. Could Knight be favoring Randall to become CEO? Was he anxious to assess Randall's probability of success? Or was Knight anticipating the probable victory of Wendal Randall while instead preferring someone else? From what little he knew, no clear-cut conclusion was possible.

That analysis of possible motivations, combined with consideration of alternatives to manage his currently tenuous relationship with the board, led John George to conclude the best course of action was to take no action at all. That would be rare for the usually decisive business leader. However, he remained unclear about the motivations and agenda of some on his board. Because he was equally uncertain about their real goals, it just might be better to wait until the board made its next move.

He knew there would be legal obstacles to calling an emergency meeting. He also knew that Knight, or whomever was behind this initiative, would ultimately be required to make clear its purpose. What he could not know was how the board might interpret overtures to mend fences or to apologize for the rough ride they experienced due to the leaked news of his cancer.

Usually, it's better to take the lead and influence an agenda, but this time he decided a more prudent tactic would be to wait for members of the board to show their hand. Once he knew more precisely which cards they would play, he could better formulate the best countering strategies.

It might also be a good idea to connect again with his executive responsible for corporate security, Dan Ramirez. In addition to the investigation into the Multima Supermarkets hacking incident, Mortimer intended to add a new assignment. He would ask the security team to make some discreet inquiries to explore whether the relationship between Knight and Randall might be more complicated than it appeared.

FORTY-TWO

Haarlem, the Netherlands.
Sometime at night, Saturday, March 5, 2016

He was groggy and his head ached terribly. As he slowly opened his eyes, Wendal Randall jolted upright with a dreadful realization that he was in a minuscule closed room with a high ceiling and bare walls painted a dark shade of green. There were no windows. He was alone, and the temperature was very chilly.

There were only a few pieces of furniture—the single firm cot he was sitting on and a small table with two chairs, one on either side. In the corner, he saw a toilet and porcelain washbasin.

Wendal realized he was naked. On the small table, he noticed a neat pile of clothes and two bottles of water. He looked down at his wrist and noticed his Rolex was missing. He had no idea what time it might be or any sense of how long he'd been there. Fully awake, he felt disoriented and isolated. He was slowly starting to retrieve fragmented memories of his last conscious moments when he heard the click of a lock release.

"We see you've recovered," the tallest of the uniformed men said dryly. "You may want to put on those clothes."

"Where am I? And what am I doing here?" Wendal asked quietly.

"You are in the holding cell of police office number fifteen in Haarlem. Later this morning you will be charged with attempted murder," the slightly shorter uniformed man advised. "Get dressed as my colleague suggested. We'll bring some food. Then we'll talk."

With that admonition, the two uniformed men left the room and Wendal heard the firm click of a lock bolting the door. As he moved towards the table and pile of clothes, he glanced around the room again. There in one corner, right where the ceiling meets the wall, he spotted a miniature camera well out of his reach. That must be how they knew he was awake. A closed-circuit camera was probably recording his every movement.

As he started to dress, memories of his last conscious moments began to resurface. With a sense of horror, he remembered two large armed men bursting through a door. One pointed a weapon that looked like a gun. His body experienced a violent spasm and suddenly everything went black.

More memories surfaced as Wendal quickly pieced together those final few minutes at that house in Overveen as a full realization gradually set in. He was in very serious trouble.

––––––––––––

It had all started sometime that afternoon. Sex, drugs, and vodka again. Probably too much of all three, and his judgment became impaired. He seemed to fall under some form of a spell with the one named Karina, the one who said she was Russian. She had shown an unusual interest in him throughout the night. She seemed unlike every other woman he had ever known.

He had always paid to have sex. This time, with Karina, appeared to be unique. He was not paying anything for the experience, although Max Bergmann had arranged the house party and presumably compensated the women.

Karina seemed different from the others. Her touches were always gentle caresses. She whispered softly and smiled often. She gazed at Wendal with wide, brown eyes that suggested both love and intrigue. She also had a voracious appetite for sex.

She repeatedly suggested new and different sexual positions. Several times, she lowered her head to his erection and created sexual ecstasy. Her lips and tongue had deftly teased his penis and testicles until he experienced seemingly ever-greater pleasure. With total abandon, she welcomed more and more into her mouth until Wendal exploded with a sexual release that seemed more powerful each time.

She suggested they try to be more adventurous. She'd like to do something special. "What gives you erotic enjoyment? Is there a position you've never experienced before, but would like to try? Is there something you've been afraid to ask other women to do?" Such were the questions she posed with an alluring and seductive smile.

Their sex started gently, almost lovingly. He kissed her tenderly all over her body in a way he had watched porn stars prepare their partners. Then, he asked her to kiss and fondle him the same way. She responded without hesitation and with apparent enthusiasm.

Gradually, their sex became more heated and much more passionate as they urgently touched, stroked, and explored every intimate orifice of each other's bodies. The tempo of their sex also became more

192

violent as Wendal thrust his member further inside with increasing urgency. He grasped her more tightly with each deep penetration.

Just as he reached the pinnacle of his sexual tension, he squeezed her throat tightly and made one last desperate lunge before releasing. When he looked down at her, she did not seem to be either moving or breathing. In a panic, he let go of Karina's neck and jumped awkwardly from the bed.

It was at that moment two armed men burst through the door. One pointed a Taser gun and fired a single shot.

———————

Wendal finished dressing just as the men with weapons returned to his isolated room. One carried a bowl of cold cereal and a tiny container of yogurt. The shorter one brought a plastic spoon, banana, and cluster of red grapes. They unceremoniously placed this food on the table and told him to enjoy his dinner. They also affirmed they'd be back for some discussion in a few minutes.

He felt tears well up and despair beyond any he had ever experienced enveloped him. He felt utterly alone. He had no means of communicating with anyone.

Food was the last thing he wanted.

FORTY-THREE

Traveling towards Quebec.
Afternoon, Saturday, March 5, 2016

It was already almost noon Eastern Standard Time when the Multima Supermarkets' Global 5000 business jet departed from Alaska. Suzanne was still absorbing the unsettling news of her mother's heart attack, and it was evident her mother was not yet out of danger. She felt helpless in the corporate aircraft as she listened to the jet engines whine loudly during their climb to cruising altitude.

The wonderful woman she felt so attached to was facing her greatest crisis and Suzanne could do nothing to help. There was not even a chance to fluff her pillow to make her comfortable or hold her hand to help to ease the excruciating pain.

She thought about her mother. An unremarkable woman in many ways, Louise Marcotte still personified a generation of radical change in her city. Torn between traditional values of the church and the rapidly changing preferences of young people in Quebec, she always asserted her independence.

She never married. She enjoyed occasional lovers, but always without a long-term commitment. She worked hard at her job and progressed at a snail's pace, without complaint or bitterness, in an environment still dominated by male thinking and an old boys' network. All the while, Louise Marcotte unfailingly encouraged her daughter to study hard, get the very best education, and expect to succeed in a man's world by striving to make everyone she interacted with feel valuable and important.

Her mother's positive passion for making people around her feel better about themselves became one of Suzanne's ballasts in life and continually inspired her to achieve ever greater successes. She could visualize her mother now, telling doctors and nurses what a wonderful job they were doing, even as they helped her deal with pain and personal crisis in a hospital bed.

She also came to realize her current train of thought probably wasn't very helpful and concluded nothing could be gained sitting there wallowing in self-pity, worrying about a circumstance over which she had no control. Instead, she resolved to make the best possible use of the long flight to Quebec City. As soon as they reached cruising altitude, she plunged into work by assembling the three work teams again, spending about fifteen minutes with each to prioritize efforts.

First, she met with the group who had previously advocated remaking Multima Supermarkets into a discount operation to compete with the big-box retailers. They were now recommending acquisition of an established discount competitor to complement the existing supermarket model. Briefly, she outlined her intention to discuss everything they had on the proposed acquisition target on this flight rather than waiting until they were back in Atlanta. They no longer had the luxury of time.

Instead, the support team back at headquarters should upload all available data, using a satellite link if necessary. In thirty minutes, they should all be prepared to start a review. Suzanne intended to spend half the flight sifting through the intricate details of that proposal.

For another fifteen minutes, she focused attention on the healthy choice faction. They would have three hours to prepare final recommendations for review. She wanted to discuss specific product offerings, projected profit and loss contributions for the next three years, and the outline of a launch strategy, complete with timing and budgeted costs. They should make use of their Atlanta resources to the greatest extent possible and prepare for an hour of discussion as soon as she completed her meeting about the acquisition.

Last, she met in the corner with the growers. "I was genuinely impressed with the way you guys were prepared for our last discussions. You were way ahead of my expectations, and I can easily understand why our buyers are so loyal to you!

"But, as you would expect, I want more," she continued with passion. "I need you to bring together all those great ideas we discussed. During the next few hours, I need you to create concrete, workable plans that fit our game changer strategy.

"Let's be very specific about new product introductions you can manage for the coming twenty-four months. Give me all the projected costs, timelines you can live with, and launch ideas that get us off to a phenomenal start. As before, I strongly urge you to draw on all our resources back in Atlanta to help you in anyway necessary, because I also need you to be ready for a discussion in the final hour of our flight."

A flurry of activity erupted immediately after briefing each team. By the time she had visited them all, there was a hum of conversation competing with the background drone of the jet engines. Fingers rapidly tapped computer keyboards, printers spewed out pages of graphs and charts in a monotonous flow, while coffee fueled ever-increasing output.

Thoughts of Suzanne's emergency and the fate of her mother were set aside as all energy focused towards their assignments, for all participants sensed her need for this diversion. They seemed equally motivated to achieve the most possible in those few hours, as though they too felt uncertain about how much could be accomplished in the days to come.

Suzanne was able to compartmentalize her emotions and focus attention better than most. Moments after she had received the distressing news about her mother, she was already thinking, communicating, and structuring decisions more quickly than many business executives perform under normal circumstances.

Given the gravity of the situation, each team drew inspiration from her leadership. In fact, their first few hours produced results beyond expectations. Now, being able to rejoin the teams in Atlanta immediately was less crucial. Each team had advanced to such a degree that attention could shift to polishing and refining rather than the tough slogging to reach a consensus.

In fact, they finished most of the arduous work during their six-hour flight. With satisfaction, Suzanne completed her conversations with the last group—the producers and growers—and settled back to relax in her comfortable reclining seat. A sense of dread struck her as soon as she heard her smartphone. Reluctantly, she pressed an icon to respond, and the aircraft became deathly quiet.

She listened in silent, hopeless horror as Monsieur LaMontagne told her he must deliver some awful news. Her mother experienced another massive heart attack at the hospital. The doctors had done everything they possibly could but... His soft, trembling voice trailed off as he fought to maintain control of his own emotions.

Suzanne whispered her thanks to Monsieur LaMontagne for letting her know and ended the call. As tears started to stream down her cheeks, most on the team were looking at her. Through a never before experienced fog, she could hear scattered sobs and sniffles around her. All she remembered for some time after were brief, mumbled expressions of condolences and heartfelt hugs as her team shared the shock and grief of their leader with uncomfortable emotions for the rest of the flight.

FORTY-FOUR

New York.
Saturday evening, March 5, 2016

Howard Knight pressed the icon on his smartphone to end his conversation with Frau Klaudia Schäffer. She had called to advise that Wendal Randall had performed exactly as expected and was now under the control of Dutch authorities.

By email, Knight had earlier cautioned her to avoid any specific references during her call. There was always a slim possibility someone could intercept their communication. She had chosen her words carefully and conveyed her message with an ambiguity that became crystal clear to Knight as they spoke.

"Our subject has misbehaved badly and is now in confinement with the appropriate local authorities. There is video evidence of his misdeed, and a copy has fallen into the hands of the authorities, who are now having discussions with him.

"Our girl fed a story to the business associate about his need to leave suddenly to deal with a major company crisis. There's no cause for any concern, as all key participants are cooperating fully. I expect it will be two or three days before any conclusions, but I'll stay close to the situation and update you as necessary."

Knight could now return to his evening dinner, comfortable Frau Schäffer's scheme for Wendal Randall was unfolding as planned. That comment about the cooperation of key participants was the assurance he needed most.

That ambiguous reference to the Dutch local authorities, the Haarlem *politie,* reaffirmed Randall was now in the custody of pliable police officers friendly to The Organization. The regular payments these key participants received would assure Wendal would remain hidden in an isolated cell somewhere in Haarlem.

There would be no record of Randall's 'arrest' or any contact permitted with either the American embassy or legal counsel. Rather, he would be subjected to intense interrogation and psychological pressure until he agreed to sign a full confession. At that point, their plan called

197

for Randall's release into the care of Frau Schäffer, who would bring him back to the United States.

With a signed confession and video of Randall's attack on the prostitute in Overveen, Wendal would become wholly subservient to Howard Knight's bidding until he was no longer useful. It was all costing more than Knight would have preferred, but The Organization had seemed comfortable advancing a few hundred thousand dollars more. Of course, they had arranged the rogue *politie* key participants who made the whole charade possible.

Still, his reliance on them was a growing concern, for he now understood their style uncomfortably well. It started with a little help when needed. In return, they expected an equally small favor. As requests for help increased, the requirement to reciprocate grew larger. Over the years, his obligations had grown dramatically, and his ability to gain control of Multima had become increasingly critical. He knew it would take such a massive reward to even the balance.

Earlier that day, The Organization had also reminded Knight that it was solely his responsibility to exert pressure on John George Mortimer, to get the required emergency board meeting, and to execute the expected change in Multima company management. A familiar voice intoned that they would be watching with interest.

Howard Knight took a final gulp of an aged Italian Chianti and swallowed hard. His elaborate designs to seize control of Multima Corporation were all converging nicely, and he certainly did not need another reminder that there was no margin for error. The consequences of failure were simply too horrible to consider.

FORTY-FIVE

Home on the Caloosahatchee River, Fort Myers.
Saturday evening, March 5, 2016

John George Mortimer finished dinner and retired to his home's comfortable outdoor lanai to watch another Southwest Florida sunset. He was also enjoying the first glass of wine since surgery, a delightful young Californian Pinot Noir with just enough fruity taste to be refreshing.

The mellowing combination of a spectacular sunset and pleasant wine nudged him to contemplate a day that had been relaxing but also adequately productive. He was still completely at ease with his early-morning decision to delay any immediate action to repair damage to the bruised egos of his board. No doubt, he would hear more within a few days and would then map out his tactics.

Rosetta Stone language CDs refreshed both his Spanish vocabulary and pronunciation for a few hours. He also walked outdoors for the first time. Accompanied by his housekeeper (just to be safe), he had circled the wide driveway from the gated entrance to the garage three times. The sun was brilliant, the temperature warm, and the fresh air invigorating.

He used a cane to steady himself. As he exercised, he spoke Spanish with his housekeeper to hone his skills. They discussed a broad range of subjects, forcing John George both to listen carefully and to test his vocabulary. He was able to practice words and expressions that had been dormant the past few months.

As their time together ended, he silently marveled at the depth of knowledge his Latino housekeeper retained about stories in the news, both in America and in her home country of El Salvador. Her grasp of issues surpassed many he encountered in the business world.

Outdoor walking and Spanish conversation were minor achievements in the scheme of things, but he knew recovery from major surgery is a process of making incremental improvements in everyday activities until it all becomes routine again. That day, he could look back to the resumption of two regular activities—his passion for learning and physical exercise.

As his housekeeper wished him well for the evening, continuing in Spanish just as he had requested, she promised to return early the next morning to make coffee and breakfast. He cheerfully answered her goodbye with his customary expression of thanks and appreciation. Mortimer genuinely valued both her kindness and diligent care of his home. He made sure he told her that regularly.

A few moments later, his attention wandered to long clouds stretching across the horizon, partially hiding the radiant red sheen of the slowly disappearing sun. From this idyllic mood, he was jolted back to reality with the buzz of his smartphone. The small screen indicated it was his assistant, Sally-Ann Bureau. He was surprised to hear from her at six-thirty on a Saturday evening, but pressed the green telephone icon to respond.

Sally-Ann made an initial polite inquiry about his current condition. They had already talked about his surgery and recovery at length the previous day, so there was no need for prolonged discussion. Instead, she shifted to her purpose for calling and prepared John George for the information. She had just received some bad news she thought he would want to know.

Suzanne Simpson's executive assistant in Atlanta had just called to advise that Suzanne's mother had suddenly died of a heart attack a few hours before in a Quebec City hospital. Suzanne was there now. She had tried to visit her mother after receiving word of the emergency in Anchorage, but her flight had arrived too late. Sally-Ann thought John George would want to know about this as soon as possible.

Feeling a sudden and unexpected sense of sadness as he processed this news, Mortimer quietly acknowledged the information. He thanked Sally-Ann for notifying him so promptly and added that he'd call Suzanne to express his condolences. As he ended the call, John George paused and sighed deeply, inhaling a large breath of Gulf sea air to calm his emotions.

With dread and deliberation, he made a call to Suzanne that he truly wished wasn't necessary.

FORTY-SIX

Haarlem, the Netherlands.
Early morning, Sunday, March 6, 2016

Several hours had passed since Wendal Randall awoke in the windowless, locked room of a police station somewhere in the Dutch city of Haarlem. Food provided earlier remained on the table. The intervening hours had been too stressful for him even to think about eating. He drank lots of water, thinking that might help diffuse his elevated stress. He felt nauseous, depressed, tired, and utterly helpless.

The uniformed men had repeatedly shown him the damning video on a tablet. Conveniently, the cleverly edited video started only with their torrid sexual intercourse. There was no record of the alluring and seductive whore encouraging him to be more adventurous. The video revealed none of her sensuous smiles and repeated requests for him to try new and exciting sex. Most crucially, there was no mention of her consent, willingness, and desire to engage in the high-risk passion.

With each showing of the video, the uniformed men repeated their intention to charge him with attempted murder. They also implied that Dutch courts would be more lenient towards him if he would just confess to his crime. It wasn't right to cause a terribly overworked police force and justice department to incur both the time and expense of an unnecessary trial.

They had summarily refused his requests for an attorney and increasingly urgent demands to meet with a representative of the American embassy. "You are not in the United States," they reminded him each time. "We have our own laws and rules." Every refusal produced another suggestion that Dutch magistrates would consider his circumstance much more favorably with a full confession.

They ignored Wendal's requests to make a phone call to let someone know of his whereabouts. Phone calls were not part of their protocol, they replied. They had no idea where his smartphone or other possessions might be. Not their responsibility, they scoffed. Once more, they demanded a full confession for this violent crime committed against a defenseless young Dutch citizen.

He desperately wanted to sleep, but he was sure they would barge into the room just as soon as he closed his eyes. That seemed to be their pattern. He found it increasingly difficult to stay alert when they repeatedly and loudly woke him to resume their incessant questions. He concluded it would be better to avoid sleep altogether. It seemed the men came less often when he was awake and better prepared for their clever questions designed to lull him into an admission of guilt.

Instead, he morosely reviewed his dire circumstances. Attempted murder seemed like a rather extreme charge. After all, she must be okay at this stage, he reasoned, or the charge would instead be murder. Further, she had not only consented to autoerotic asphyxiation, she had welcomed it. While Wendal understood such sexual adventure is as dangerous as erotic, no lasting harm seemed to occur. With that college girl and with this latest exploit in Overveen, both women stopped breathing for a moment. Both also experienced wild orgasms as their bodies shuddered with uncontrolled sexual passion just before passing out.

It seemed unlikely police in the Netherlands could make a charge of attempted murder stick. Still, he had no knowledge of their laws and no way of contacting an attorney to help. Regardless of his rights, he might be destined to spend considerable time there unless he could find some way to either escape or get help from the American embassy. Howard Knight might be able to help, if only he could find a way to communicate with him. But would Knight even be willing to assist at this stage? Wendal dourly recalled there had been no return call from messages left on his voicemail and with his office staff several days earlier.

Would Frau Schäffer be able to help? She seemed to have useful connections. As far as he knew, she was still in Düsseldorf. That was only a two-hour drive away if he could find a way to reach her.

Might technology save him as it usually did when he found himself in a tight spot? Maybe, but he had no access to it. They had taken everything. Then an idea struck him.

Might there be a way to trick these guards into leaving behind the tablet they used to show him the videos, even for just a moment or two? It would only take a few seconds to get messages of distress to Frau Schäffer or Knight by email. He knew he could wipe clean any traces of his messages. It took only a couple minutes.

He desperately needed a plan that could work. With newfound energy and buoyancy of spirit, Wendal Randall unleashed his imagination to develop a plausible scheme.

FORTY-SEVEN

Suzanne was staying at a Hilton Hotel right next to the parliament buildings overlooking a historical, well-preserved section of Quebec City. For the past number of hours—she didn't know how many—she had wept almost continuously in the lonely solitude of her room.

Saying good-bye to her team, Suzanne had maintained her composure very well. She controlled her emotions as Monsieur LaMontagne led her to his waiting vehicle, his arm draped around her shoulders in a universal gesture of consolation. She remained calm and composed while he drove her to Hôpital Laval.

There, she was ushered into a small room where a sympathetic nurse gently pulled back the white sheet from her mother's lifeless body to allow Suzanne closure and a final confirmation of her mother's passing. They were there for only a few moments. Suzanne said a short prayer as her years of training in Catholic schools taught her was proper. Then, someone asked her to sign several pages of documents. She did so without taking the time to read them because Monsieur LaMontagne assured her they were all quite standard and necessary for the hospital to release her mother's body to a funeral home.

As they returned to his car, Suzanne received a call from John George Mortimer. He had just heard the sad news, he said with somber gentleness. He was calling to express his sincere condolences and wanted to be sure Suzanne knew his thoughts, and those of all her friends at Multima, were with her at such a difficult moment.

In uncharacteristic hushed and resigned tones, he offered his help in any way possible. He encouraged her to take as much time as she required to grieve and deal with her loss. He assured her this was a time to put her own needs first. She shouldn't worry about the demands of her position. His final expression of sympathy suggested that everyone who had met Louise Marcotte throughout her lifetime shared a little of what she was feeling. Suzanne appreciated the touching sentiment.

Some time later, it occurred to her slightly odd for John George to use her mother's name. She couldn't immediately remember ever mentioning it to him.

During the call, Suzanne had remained composed, with her emotions in check. She had not even noticed the bitter sub-zero temperatures or falling snow as she stood outside the hospital in an alcove.

When she rejoined Monsieur LaMontagne at his vehicle, she learned her travel planner had reserved a room at the Hilton Hotel and had relayed that information to him while Suzanne was speaking with John George Mortimer.

They drove a short distance from Hôpital Laval, less than ten minutes. As they carefully navigated the snow-covered streets, Monsieur LaMontagne suggested that Suzanne should call him the next day. He would accompany her to the funeral home where morticians would prepare her mother's body. He also asked her to consider what funeral arrangements she might prefer, as the will gave no instructions.

He said they would need to meet again later, whenever Suzanne was ready, to discuss her mother's last wishes and finalize other arrangements to satisfy insurance and legal requirements.

During their short ride and the check-in formalities, Suzanne looked like a tired and subdued business traveler. With effort, she managed to keep her emotions in check and address issues as they arose. An observer might think she was just a little preoccupied with her thoughts.

Even as she bade goodnight to Monsieur LaMontagne, who kissed her gently on both cheeks and provided a fatherly hug of support as he left, Suzanne managed to avoid tears or any open expressions of grief. It started when she entered her room at the Quebec Hilton, walked over to the windows high above the old city, opened the drapes, and took in the magnificent view.

Rooftops were laden with fresh white snow. Lights sparkled in an enchanted montage on the horizon. The dark and ice-laden St. Lawrence River brooded sullenly in the background. It was a picture she remembered from her youngest days living in this captivating city so graced with unmatched beauty from the past.

Hundreds of childhood memories seemed to flood back and overwhelm her. Within seconds, tears and deep sobs expressed her immense grief and penetrating loneliness as a stark realization set in. For the first time in her life, she was completely on her own. Her doting mother was gone. She had never known her father. There had never been brothers or sisters. There were no cousins. Her marriage had broken apart years earlier.

The thought of being without any remaining family caused Suzanne to throw herself face down on the king-sized bed and let her tears flow freely. There was no stopping them once they started. The pillows and duvet became damp, and she felt a total exhaustion. An oppressive feeling that she had become completely alone failed to subside for some time.

Later, her emotions shifted to regret. Guilt set in as she considered the meager amount of time she had spent with her mother recently as she built her career in faraway cities. During the past several years, their time spent together could be measured only in scattered days. Usually, they squeezed short weekly phone calls or Skype conversations into Suzanne's relentless schedule of meetings and business demands.

Her mother never complained. Every conversation had been positive and encouraging, almost motivational, with a focus on Suzanne's continuing progression among the business titans of North America. Suzanne understood well the many sacrifices her mother had made to provide a loving and comfortable life during her youth. She thought too about her outstanding Stanford education. With the modest sums her mother earned, it must have drained her financially for years.

Suzanne had always been grateful for all the support and had even tried to repay her in small ways over the past few years, but Louise Marcotte refused to accept the house Suzanne wanted to buy her or a car. After considerable urging, she agreed only to a few brief winter vacations together on exotic Caribbean islands. Otherwise, she always maintained that she had all she needed, and Suzanne should save her money for a less-than-certain future.

Their love was strong, even if they had spent much of the past thirty or so years some distance apart. Suzanne had always welcomed her mother's sage advice, even her helpful suggestions about personal style and fashion. She already felt a massive void that seemed impossible to fill. Intense grief and deep-seated melancholy gripped Suzanne as she processed, and then reluctantly accepted, the reality. Her mother had departed forever.

Eventually, sporadic sleep came. Still fully dressed, entirely spent, and completely on her own, she gratefully welcomed some relief from flowing tears and profound sadness, even if such an escape was only temporary.

FORTY-EIGHT

An office tower in New York.
Sunday afternoon, March 6, 2016

His telephone conversation with John George Mortimer did not please Howard Knight at all. Their conversation had started well enough. Knight positioned the call as an inquiry into Mortimer's well being. "I thought it best to wait a few days to call, John George," he started. "I know it's important to rest and recuperate without the intrusion of business associates."

"Thank you for the thoughtfulness, Howard. But I've been up and around for a few days now. Feeling fairly well, actually."

"Good to hear, John George. I've never known anyone who has experienced breast cancer surgery. Are you in much pain?"

"It was severe for a few days, but the medication manages it to acceptable levels, and I've already cut back the dosage to only one pill before I go to sleep. During the day it's manageable."

"What about therapy? Is there anything special you do to help the recovery?"

"Not really, Howard. They want me moving around as much as possible. Very light exercise, with no workouts. The incision is healing nicely, with no special care required. It just needs a little time."

For a few minutes, their conversation followed such general patterns with Knight probing for potential weaknesses, and Mortimer providing little information that might be used against him later. Knight thought he took care to project empathy and interest. He even added words of encouragement at appropriate places. It seemed to be going well until he broached the subject of concerns some directors had expressed about John George's ability to lead the company in the near term. Knight intentionally introduced the subject as they neared the end of their conversation.

"There's another matter I'd like to discuss with you, John George. We've worked together a long time, and I like to think we're more friends than associates. So, I thought that I should let you know about some recent rumblings of discontent I've been hearing."

"What kind of discontent, Howard?"

"Well, it seems that some on your board of directors think you were a little less than forthright about the cancer when you announced your retirement schedule. Some apparently think you should have let us know about it and let us help decide the best way to manage the issue from a corporation perspective," Knight gingerly suggested.

"More open communication was certainly an option, Howard. But that's not the course I chose. I think that I provided the board all the information needed to approve my game changer initiative to help the board identify a successor. With respect to my illness, I'm guessing some directors might have made exactly the same choice if our roles were reversed," Mortimer coolly responded.

"Fair enough, John George. I get it. But I'm not sure all directors will be quite as understanding. What do you think about calling an unscheduled meeting of the board? Maybe a chance to assuage a few bruised egos and mitigate lingering concerns about your health?"

"There are no plans to meet again before the regularly scheduled date in late March," Mortimer replied coldly. "At that time, I'll oblige any unhappy directors by addressing any questions about my health."

He left little room for further discussion on the matter. Knight patiently approached the issue from another angle. "OK, John George. May I suggest one more thing to consider? I've noticed some pressure on the price of Multima shares with all the recent negative news and speculation. Maybe an earlier meeting could lead to a strong statement of board support and calm those investor jitters," Knight offered.

"We both know the stock price will ebb and flow with all kinds of factors in the marketplace, Howard. Downward pressure might be as much the result of macroeconomic concerns as any worries about my health.

"Frankly, I have no intention to hold unscheduled meetings of the board every time there's some volatility in the price of Multima stock. I'm just not prepared to burden my successor with that kind of precedent," Mortimer replied with a touch of impatience in his tone. Knight retreated with a light-hearted comment that it appeared Mortimer had thoroughly thought the matter through and could count on his continued support. He just hoped other investors would also understand.

Howard Knight had anticipated that Mortimer might react negatively. As always, he had a backup plan. There were two more calls to make. John George Mortimer would soon regret his cavalier rejection of a reasonable business proposal. Of this, Knight had no doubts.

FORTY-NINE

Hilton Hotel, Quebec City.
Sunday, March 6, 2016

When Suzanne opened her eyes that Sunday morning, the clock in her room showed nine twenty-seven, much later than she usually woke up. She blamed the jet lag.

Then the intense grief and tears of the previous night flooded back. She remembered the overwhelming gloom, but just as quickly firmly shut it down. There was nothing more she could do. There was no more sadness to feel. It was time to accept the cruel circumstance, live with it, and cherish fond memories of her loving mother's life. This day was the start of a new chapter in her life, and she would make the best of it.

With that solid conviction, she left her bed and called room service to order a large, healthy breakfast. Before it arrived, she squeezed in a call to Monsieur LaMontagne, just as he had requested. He would meet her at the front door at precisely one o'clock.

As promised, Monsieur LaMontagne arrived at the hotel and drove her to the funeral home. Suzanne recalled how she trembled when he first mentioned transporting her mother's body from the hospital to this place. Once again, she fought back her emotions and refused to let sadness resurface.

Her meeting with the funeral director was short, courteous, and businesslike. Suzanne graciously accepted condolences. She confirmed her intention to respect her mother's wishes for cremation. They discussed fees for services provided by the funeral home and selected a spot in their facilities to permanently inter the urn holding her mother's ashes.

Suzanne paid with a credit card and confirmed her intention to return for a final farewell, post-cremation. With those necessary arrangements behind them, Monsieur LaMontagne drove her to his nearby third-floor office to review the remaining legal details.

Most of their conversation dealt with subjects Suzanne might expect in such a circumstance. The first formality was a certificate of her mother's death, and she'd found it necessary to swallow hard before she reacted to his prompting because a large lump had suddenly formed deep in her throat.

They reviewed several documents required by government agencies. Rather than reading each in detail, Suzanne skimmed through the papers, for they all appeared to be standard certifications with individual details about her mother inserted in the applicable spaces. They discussed the sale of her mother's home. Of course, Monsieur LaMontagne would be prepared to handle this for a reasonable fee.

He presented Suzanne with the original copy of her mother's will, adding that she was the sole beneficiary of the estate and the executor. Because the value of her assets appeared relatively modest, there would not be a requirement to pay any probate fee to the Government of Quebec. Estate taxes would not apply either.

He offered Suzanne an opportunity to read the entire document and said he would answer any questions or concerns that might arise. Within an hour, they finished all of the necessary steps required to wind up her mother's legal affairs. He then proposed to drive her to her mother's home. There, Suzanne decided almost immediately to donate the contents to a local charity. The *notaire* agreed his office could make all necessary arrangements and added that he would not charge any additional fee, given her very generous gesture.

Suzanne collected a few items from her mother's apartment to take with her. There were several albums of photos. She carefully packed them all into one of the boxes Monsieur LaMontagne had thoughtfully brought along in the trunk of his car. There were a few pieces of inexpensive jewelry in a small padded chest. Suzanne didn't see any pieces she would actually wear, but placed the entire collection in her backpack for sentimental reasons.

In another box, she packed all files and records left by her mother. Neatly organized as expected, it appeared all bills were up to date and fully paid. She remarked how few documents and records her mother had, compared to the several dozen boxes stored in a fireproof safe at her Atlanta home.

Almost everything Suzanne discovered was much as she expected it would be, but she supposed a thorough review of the files and records would be advisable when she had more time. That day, there were only two items that caught her attention.

Although her mother's savings account with a local bank reflected a modest balance in a range Suzanne might have expected, the checking account included an automatic electronic deposit of three thousand dollars per month. However, the bank statements listed no details about the depositor. Such an amount stood out quite clearly because the only other deposits were modest pensions from the governments of Canada and Quebec, and they were only a fraction as much.

One other anomaly caught her attention. It appeared her mother had a single investment in addition to her small savings account, a stock certificate for seventy-two thousand preferred shares in a numbered company identified as 136742 (Ontario) Corporation.

Suzanne previously had no idea her mother was receiving a regular source of income, and it was a significant amount. She was also unaware her mother held shares in a numbered company. Preferred shares at that. This bit of information made her smile as she felt some odd sense of satisfaction. Her mother somehow had enough investing acumen to hold the type of equity that was normally more secure. Suzanne made a mental note to investigate both the company and certificates more thoroughly as soon as time permitted.

With legal formalities completed, Suzanne returned to the hotel and checked her messages. A massive file of data from her team was the first item in her email: the briefing for tomorrow's conference call, she sighed. While a review of the information was critical before she slept, a good workout in the Hilton exercise facility would take priority.

There, she found a panoramic view of old Quebec City that provided unexpected stimulation in contrast to the deep sadness she felt when she opened the drapes of her hotel room on arrival Saturday evening. Her long hours of anguished crying that night had been therapeutic, she recognized, as her running pace quickened and heart rate increased. There was still a lingering sense of sorrow. The finality of her mother's death still pervaded her thoughts, but she genuinely accepted the stark reality and had started the process of moving on.

As she ran, Suzanne's thoughts shifted to the pressing game changer challenge, John George Mortimer's bout with cancer, and the media whirlwind created by the hacking incident. It seemed impossible that within just a week she had dealt with all of those crises *and* her mother's death. But rather than feeling overwhelmed by the confluence of activities, she felt stimulated.

She felt added strength and satisfaction from her ability to lead in such a dynamic environment and was coming to realize her leadership and management skills drew close to the best in her field. John George Mortimer was aging. Now he was recovering from cancer surgery. Could it be that Multima's board of directors was using the game changer challenge to identify his replacement? Should she start to assess their objectives differently? Could this be her time? She allowed her mind to dream.

As warning beeps sounded to notify Suzanne her thirty-minute workout program was ending, reality returned.

Those two financial anomalies in her mother's estate resurfaced, and both piqued her curiosity. However, she realized there surely would be little time to investigate either during the coming weeks, particularly if the stakes in the game changers contest had increased.

It would be better to use the services of Monsieur LaMontagne. He seemed conscientious. He certainly had her mother's confidence, and his fees appeared reasonable. The small investment of time and money might be worth it, she decided. One never knows if there might be something important concealed in those mysterious shares and unexpected source of income.

Tomorrow promised to be a busy day, beginning with a conference call at eight o'clock with the team that went with her to Asia. When she finished that, there would be a brief visit to the crematorium for the internment of her mother's ashes.

There would be no funeral service, no memorial, nor any formal ceremony to mark her mother's passing. Rather, Suzanne planned to spend just a few moments alone with the urn to close this important chapter of her life. Then she'd go to the Quebec City airport to meet the Multima Supermarkets' business jet for her return trip to Atlanta. By about seven o'clock that night, she expected to be on the ground again in a limousine traveling home.

After wrapping a hand towel around her perspiring neck, she jumped off the treadmill as it came to a full stop, and then left the exercise room. If she hurried, there would be time to connect with Monsieur LaMontagne again before she started to wade through that briefing document.

FIFTY

James Fitzgerald was startled when his smartphone rang while he was watching television with his wife. It was almost eleven o'clock in the evening, and it was rare for him to get any calls on a Sunday, particularly at this hour. The voice of his favorite resource in the business intelligence group greeted him. Natalia Tenaz apologized for such a late call and hoped she was not disturbing anything important. She thought it urgent to respond to him after his request to get more information.

He assured her the call was not an inconvenience at all as he retreated from the family theater center to his study a few doors down the hallway. He closed the door to block out noise from the television, but he also preferred that even his wife not hear their conversation.

The bright young researcher started to recount her story. She was calling on her cell phone because she had just arrived from Fort Myers and was driving home. She wanted to reach Fitzgerald because she urgently needed his help.

After their last conversation, when James Fitzgerald asked her to dig a little deeper into VCI and its current activities, she had a sudden inspiration and then acted somewhat impulsively. Her roommate from college was the source of the information about John George Mortimer's cancer. Naturally, she could still not divulge this woman's name, but she worked at Multima headquarters, and she wondered if her friend might reveal more information if they met face to face.

Natalia checked with her former roommate to see if it would be okay to visit for the weekend and she agreed. The researcher booked a late evening flight to Fort Myers, and they had spent the last two days together. Sure enough, once they had consumed two bottles of cheap white wine in her condo, information started to flow.

Natalia wanted to determine how her friend discovered the information about John George Mortimer's cancer. She probed in a rather mischievous and conspiratorial way and was stunned by her friend's response. The college roommate got her information not only by subterfuge but also by entirely illegal means.

The girl explained how she had taken to heart a moral dilemma raised by a somewhat radical thinking college professor whose lectures they both remembered. She reminded her friend of a particular talk that professor delivered on the subject of business intelligence. He suggested that business corporations should actually operate more like the Central Intelligence Agency.

"Ninety-five percent of all information the CIA uncovers comes by entirely legal means, using resources available to the general public," he had told them. "To capture the remaining crucial five percent needed to complete a picture, they occasionally and covertly cross the line. How could corporations adequately assess their competitive landscape if they did not do the same?"

Confronted with some activities taking place in her Multima work area, it seems her college roommate recalled that lecture. Apparently, she occupied a cubicle just a few feet away from a communications specialist in the corporate office, Janet Weissel. Since her arrival, she had become increasingly suspicious about Ms. Weissel and her unusual activities.

It started when Ms. Weissel tried so transparently (and unsuccessfully it seems) to attract the attentions of John George Mortimer. Over time, unease continued to build, as she appeared to spend much of her time and energy poking around for sensitive information about the company that had no direct relevance to her job. The final straw had been a conversation she accidentally overheard while they were both taking a smoking break outside the building. She was around the corner from Ms. Weissel and out of her view.

She established that Ms. Weissel was having a cellphone conversation with Howard Knight from the board of directors and found it unusual for a member of the board to be speaking privately with such a junior employee. So she continued listening and heard references to VCI, confidential financial information, and something called The Organization.

Her college roommate was a bit of a computer nerd who apparently didn't get out a lot, Natalia related. It seems she spent many evenings over several weeks looking into both VCI and The Organization.

As her friend dug deeper into the information available on the Internet and public databases, she grew increasingly concerned. A succession of numbered companies appeared to own Venture Capital

Investments. She found more than twenty such firms in the public records. These companies had many corporate officers, but a few surnames were shared by most.

She then shifted her attention to the blogosphere. She tried to find references to VCI or The Organization, but there was little information available. However, buried deep within the content of an investment newsletter, she discovered a caution from an anonymous blogger. Potential investors in VCI should be careful because it might have links to The Organization.

More research revealed another anonymous blog that suggested The Organization generated all of its investment capital illegally, mainly through illicit drug distribution and prostitution in the United States and Western Europe. At this point, her college roommate rationalized that she should cross the line.

She managed to intercept telephone calls on Ms. Weissel's mobile phone by hacking into the provider's system. There, she installed illicit software much like that used by the CIA. All calls were recorded using this sophisticated software, but only those using specific pre-programmed words or expressions triggered a signal to retain and download the call to her college roommate's personal computer.

The secret information about John George Mortimer's cancer came directly from Janet Weissel's telephone conversation with Knight. For that reason, her college roommate had earlier emphasized that she hadn't provided any information to the director. She already feared someone else might have discovered her illegal activities.

Now, her apprehension was even greater. It seems VCI had some direct connection to organized crime, and more crucially, it seemed Multima Corporation might be involved with The Organization in some way. At the very least, Multima appeared to be of keen interest to a company reportedly connected with dangerous and brutal crimes.

James Fitzgerald sensed the emotion and fear in Natalia's voice. He could only imagine the angst of her college roommate at Multima headquarters in Fort Myers. Hairs on the back of his neck started to bristle. His usually reliable intuition was suggesting that little good could come from this startling new information.

Fitzgerald's response to the researcher was calm, measured, and reasonable. "The information you learned was valuable," he said softly. "But let's be careful not to draw conclusions prematurely. Sometimes these things look a little different after we gather all the facts."

In conclusion, he suggested Natalia prepare an expense report that included receipts for her weekend travel and meal expenses, including the bottles of cheap wine. She should submit it tomorrow, directly to his executive assistant. She'd handle it. With further congratulations for her initiative and dedication, Fitzgerald completed the late-night call.

He reluctantly returned to the family media center to inform his wife he wouldn't be joining her in their bedroom anytime soon. With such a tale of conspiracy and intrigue, it would probably take several hours to dissect methodically all of the valuable information received. Then, he would weigh each potential scenario and decide how he should best use such revealing information.

There would be little time for sleep that night.

FIFTY-ONE

An office near Wall Street, New York.
Monday morning, March 7, 2016

Howard Knight had just turned on the wide-screen television mounted on the wall opposite his desk. The on-air personality teased that right after the break there would be an interview with an analyst holding strong views about the morass at Multima Corporation.

Knight shifted his attention to his laptop, opened the CBNN website, and typed MC into a space just right of the logo. Then he hit the enter button. New York Stock Exchange prices for Multima Corporation popped on the screen with current trading values, bid-ask prices, and other data about the stock's current trading activity.

This screen held Knight's attention as he listened to the interview with a little-known analyst, from an even less known brokerage, located in a small town in New Jersey. He was gaining instant notoriety as he recommended, in the strongest terms possible, that shareholders of Multima Corporation head for the exits.

"A critically ill chief executive officer. A board of directors in apparent revolt. And sensitive data missing from an important subsidiary!" he shouted with increasing momentum. "Any one of these would be a reason to recommend selling. With all three occurring at the same time in the same firm, current holders of Multima shares should get rid of them right now, at whatever price they might fetch!"

Knight watched his screen with satisfaction as the prices of Multima stocks started to drop. A computer-generated trading program his colleagues launched at the same time the analyst began to speak probably accelerated this fall. The software would gradually work down the price of the shares, with thousands of high-speed trades in small amounts, until market panic and powerful trading forces took over.

He noted the decrease in price from the previous day was already more than five percent. He expected stock prices would drop dramatically more throughout the day as he listened to the little-known analyst berate John George Mortimer. "An incompetent leader who seems more focused on cancer treatments than his vital responsibilities as head of a

216

THREE WEEKS LESS A DAY

major American corporation!" he roared as his contorted face projected extreme anger, or perhaps disgust.

A five percent decline in the price of Multima shares was exceedingly rare. Sure enough, panic started to set in. By the time that three-minute interview ended, the price had plunged almost eight percent, and the volume of trades was accelerating rapidly.

Permitting himself a tiny smile of satisfaction, Knight clicked off the television. He reached for a sheet of paper on his desk, tore it into smaller pieces, and inserted the shreds into an envelope ready for the mail. The envelope carried the address of a little-known analyst, from an even less known brokerage, located in a small town in New Jersey.

The shredded document was the original copy of a promissory note for one hundred thousand dollars. It related to a loan The Organization had made to cover some gambling debts of the addicted analyst. Knight licked the back of the envelope, sealed the flap, and dropped it in a plastic tray. His assistant would collect it with the outgoing mail later that evening.

Now, Knight would just wait for a call from John George Mortimer, whose personal net worth was about to decrease significantly before the end of that day. He had little doubt that Mortimer would call as soon as he realized about a billion dollars of his fortune had just evaporated.

He now felt quite sure there would be an emergency meeting of the board of directors, and it would take place within days.

FIFTY-TWO

Multima Corporation headquarters, Fort Myers.
Monday, March 7, 2016

One week after his surgery, John George Mortimer was back in his office for a rough first day. Sunday evening, he had decided it might be prudent to make an appearance at the headquarters office, just to allay lingering concerns about his ability to lead the corporation.

He'd already stopped all pain medications to avoid any negative impact on his mental acuity. That decision was not without consequences. He slept poorly Sunday night because the slightest movement created pain and caused him to wake abruptly. Throbbing did not abate throughout the day. In fact, he thought it might have intensified, though it could also just be the fatigue.

John George was working at his desk when the negative CBNN segment about Multima first aired. He wasn't watching the television in his office at the time, but Edward Hadley was. In obvious distress, Hadley called moments after the broadcast. His vice president of corporate and investor affairs was livid. With his animated and disjointed speech, Mortimer did not immediately understand what his colleague was trying to say, and was taken aback by Hadley's vindictive tone, rapid-fire delivery, and a stream of profanities. He included phrases like 'hack job', 'totally unprofessional', 'outright lies', and 'disastrous consequences' to make his point. None of these were characteristic of the usually calm and articulate executive.

Once John George understood both the issue and its implications for Multima, he hastily summoned Hadley, Chief Financial Officer Wilma Willingsworth, and the corporation's general counsel, Alberto Ferer, to an immediate meeting in his office.

While he waited for them to arrive, John George switched his laptop to the CBNN website. In dismay, he watched the recorded video interview. At the same time, he checked the trading activity of Multima stock. He then watched in disbelief as the price of his corporation's shares continued to decline at a rate he had never seen.

The meeting with his three colleagues was instructive and productive. Within an hour, they developed an action plan for each of
the participants.

"I'll get the information I need to do battle with our targeted
editors at some influential newspapers, television, and radio networks ...
the top ten for sure," Hadley confirmed. "I'll try to add some influential
bloggers, too. One way or another I'll generate some immediate, positive
media coverage to counter this malicious attack."

"I'll get with Dan Ramirez for a couple corporate security
resources," Alberto Ferer piped in. "We'll ask them to find as much as
possible on this analyst. No one seems to know his credentials or background. Within a few days, we'll be able to determine if we should launch
some form of legal action."

Wilma Willingsworth said she would contact their top ten investors by shareholding size. "I'll speak with my financial counterparts, try
to allay concerns, and encourage them to resist selling their shares."

"My job is to phone the guys we call our 'three amigos' hedge
funds," John George concluded. "I like your idea, Wilma. Because they
have all previously owned Multima shares from time to time, we know
they follow us and are reasonably familiar with our business model. I
should be able to convince them that neither my health nor leadership
should be issues of concern."

"Most importantly," Wilma emphasized, "we need you to use your
persuasive skills to win their support to maintain a floor level for the
price of our shares."

John George had to persuade the managers of their potential to
earn profits in the millions, quickly, should their funds intervene to buy
shares now at the artificially depressed prices created by the panic. In
short, his task was to stop the bleeding of precious capital value from the
ailing corporation.

More meetings followed. Alberto Ferer asked for an additional few
minutes after lunch to express his concerns about potential legal actions
by shareholders unhappy with the dramatic loss of value with their
Multima shares. He was convinced of a real possibility for lawsuits alleg-
ing negligence and liability for the board of directors should his CEO
continue to resist calls for an emergency meeting of the board.

Wilma Willingsworth also requested a second conversation to express
her private concerns about Mortimer's reluctance to convene an immediate emergency meeting. Such a refusal might compromise her fiduciary
responsibilities. That it might also tarnish her reputation was implied but

left unsaid. She assured John George she would loyally continue to support his judgment. However, she also made it abundantly clear that he should factor her personal concerns into his decision-making process.

When he finished his afternoon calls and meetings, John George again visited the CBNN website for an update on the closing prices for that day's trading. To his astonishment, the value of his company's shares was down more than twenty-one percent at the close of trading. More than one-fifth of his personal net worth—accumulated over fifty years of hard work and diligent management—was wiped away in a single day.

Equally important, the value of shares owned by all of Multima's investors had plummeted just as far. Mutual funds, corporate investors, and individual employees alike had all suffered. He realized this might well impact retirements or cause financial pain for some. There appeared to be no alternative but to capitulate to an emergency board of directors meeting. Howard Knight would win that round.

Without delay, John George dialed the number for his New York office. Knight had been waiting for the call and answered immediately. This time, there was no pretension of friendship, and there was a total absence of familiar jocularity. Politely and civilly, John George inquired what Knight might know about the CBNN segment with the little-known analyst from New Jersey.

With equal coolness, Knight responded, "I can tell you only what I heard during that TV segment, John George. It's certainly unfortunate some people aren't accepting official explanations about your health and the hacking incident at Multima Supermarkets.

"I must also let you know that five members of the board called today, letting me know that they too will join public demands for an emergency meeting if we don't schedule one immediately. They feel they have no other alternative. There are already rumblings of legal actions and potential director-negligence suits from shareholders."

Mortimer had already accepted that the emergency meeting issue was no longer a battle he could win. "I'll get a meeting organized, Howard, but with three conditions. First, any unscheduled meeting should take place at the corporate headquarters in Fort Myers, with an invitation to all members of the board of directors.

"Second, if the board plans to talk about my future, I insist that any discussion about me take place *after* the division presidents deliver their game changer presentations. It's only reasonable. Directors must have an opportunity to assess potential successor candidates before making any decision or voting on my future.

"Last, any meeting should be scheduled Monday, March 12 or later. The division presidents should have at least one week more to prepare their projects and presentations."

Knight considered those positions as quickly as John George articulated them. He knew corporate bylaws required him to accept the first. No management change could be approved without two-thirds of the board consenting and Fort Myers was a logical location for such a meeting.

He didn't like the second condition, but he knew he would probably need to accept it as well. It was an argument most directors of the board would find reasonable. It would be hard to provide a good counterargument, and it should not dramatically change the result. He already had pledges of support from five directors to replace the aging Mortimer with young superstar Wendal Randall. As a matter of negotiating principle, he was not prepared to let Mortimer win all three conditions. He would not agree with the timing.

"I see the wisdom of your first two requests, John George," he responded. "However, it's impossible for us to delay such a crucial issue for a week. Shareholder value could plummet even more in seven days. It's impossible to know what other negative narratives might surface. The meeting must take place in Fort Myers this Wednesday morning. The division presidents can have one more day to prepare."

Mortimer accepted what appeared to be inevitable. They would all need to manage as adeptly as possible in the single day remaining. Like John George himself, the unit leaders would play the cards they had been dealt and make the best of it.

John George then dialed Alberto Ferer and asked him to create a formal notice to directors, announcing the unscheduled meeting by email. Alberto should then personally call each of the division presidents to let them know about the timing and agenda. He must instruct them to arrive at Fort Myers headquarters by nine o'clock Wednesday morning, ready to deliver their game changer presentations.

Alberto Ferer accepted the direction without question or comment. He agreed to have all completed within the next hour or so. There was just one additional issue about which John George should be aware. Wendal Randall was unreachable. Dan Ramirez in corporate security had just advised Ferer they had been trying, unsuccessfully, to contact Wendal since late Friday. He explained that Dan reported the rest of Wendal's team arrived from Germany then, and he was not with them.

Someone from the group thought he might be enjoying a weekend in Amsterdam with the president of the technology company they had been negotiating with in Germany. Nevertheless, repeated messages left on his phone had gone unanswered for almost three days.

After a long pause, Ferer reported that his news got worse. It seems someone finally reached Max Bergmann, the German businessperson with whom Wendal last had contact. He had no idea where to find him. Apparently, they were together at some house party in the Netherlands on Friday night. However, it seems that Wendal disappeared to handle an urgent business issue and had not been heard from since.

Without warning, the sharp pain from surgery in Mortimer's chest suddenly intensified as he tried to absorb and process such sobering news. Thanking Ferer for his valuable update and his efforts to get the board meeting arranged for Wednesday, John George abruptly ended their conversation.

He decided one more call would be necessary before he could seek relief from the surging discomfort and extreme, unexpected fatigue that was starting to set in. He needed to know what additional information corporate security might be able to provide.

Yes, there had been developments, Dan Ramirez responded. The FBI was almost sure the theft of data was an inside job. Their attention had shifted and now focused on Multima Logistics. Considerable evidence pointed in the direction of someone in that part of the company.

Ramirez further explained that a scan of the mainframe computer and company servers at Logistics had not discovered any trace of the missing files. Instead, forensic technologists from the FBI were screening personal computers of employees. All personnel, except Wendal Randall, had surrendered their company-issued laptops for inspection. They became aware Randall was missing only because the FBI wanted to scour his computer as well as those of all other employees.

The FBI still had several hundred computers to check, but teams were working around the clock and expected to complete electronic scans of all available equipment by the end of the following day. The corporate security chief believed they were closing in on the mystery. He expected an outcome with conclusive proof within days.

John George Mortimer needed a little time to process all this startling new information and possible implications. He decided an appropriate place to pursue his thoughts would be on his comfortable lanai at home. There, he'd prepare for the anticipated showdown with Howard Knight, enjoy a good quality Burgundy, and take in another spectacular Southwest Florida sunset at the same time. If he hurried, he might make it.

FIFTY-THREE

An office tower near Wall Street, New York.
Monday afternoon, March 7, 2016

Howard Knight set down the telephone to end John George Mortimer's call conceding defeat. Then, in one fluid motion, he picked up a cheap disposable mobile phone and dialed the international number for Frau Klaudia Schäffer. When she answered after the first ring, Knight barked out his instructions with few words.

"Here's what we're going to do. Get him back here immediately," Knight started. "Take a note to him in Haarlem. Keep it brief. Have it say he has one, and only one, option. He must sign a confession. No discussion. No negotiation. He signs the confession, and you'll have him on a plane home within an hour. No criminal charges. As long as he cooperates in the future, no one needs to know." Frau Schäffer busily took notes as he continued.

"A VCI jet from London will arrive in Amsterdam within the hour. Bring Randall and a signed confession with you. Meet me in New York tomorrow morning. I'll be at whichever airport the pilots select. Let him sleep for a few hours because he'll have a busy day when he arrives. We'll take care of you after you're here. Everything clear?" he asked, with a full expectation there would be no questions.

"Got it," she said.

Howard Knight realized his pulse had quickened. His blood pressure had probably spiked as well. He found himself a little excited. His patient efforts of the past decade were about to bear fruit. After investing so many painstaking hours researching, planning, maneuvering, modifying, cajoling, persuading, and coddling during this monumental task to seize control of Multima Corporation, a satisfactory conclusion now looked imminent.

There was no doubt Wendal Randall would sign a confession. By now, he would be terrified of the possible consequences he faced in a criminal court of the Netherlands. For two full days and nights, the pliant *politie* of Haarlem had interrogated him with unusual aggressiveness, and he had also been sleep-deprived the whole time. After hearing a promise of liberation by jet within an hour, the odds of him refusing to sign a confession were so small they didn't merit consideration.

With a confession in hand, Knight knew his influence over him would become absolute. The young technology genius would meekly follow future instructions. Of that, Knight was entirely sure.

He was equally confident the board of directors would remove John George Mortimer within the next few days. Although he had significant leverage over only two board members, four additional directors had already pledged support. With Knight's personal vote, the total opposed to Mortimer would be seven, a majority.

Mortimer's charade to select a successor would become irrelevant. Let them all deliver their little game changer presentations. Assuming he would be able to stand before the board of directors and speak coherently for thirty minutes, before the end of Wednesday, Wendal Randall would become the new CEO of Multima Corporation.

Howard Knight could take the rest of the evening off. The world was unfolding as it should, and he needn't take further action before a planned early morning pep talk with Randall. He reached for his smartphone and pressed a number on speed-dial. All this excitement was causing more than a little sexual arousal. He knew the perfect solution.

FIFTY-FOUR

Aboard Multima Supermarkets' jet towards Atlanta.
Evening, March 7, 2016

As scheduled, the Global 5000 business jet was waiting on the tarmac of Quebec City's International Airport when Monsieur LaMontagne arrived with Suzanne just before the dinner hour. Initially, she had not intended to either meet or travel to the airport with him. Plans abruptly changed when she called the *notaire* early that morning, just moments before the scheduled conference call with her team.

She had asked if he had an interest in researching the deposits to her mother's bank account and curious share certificates from a numbered company in Ontario. He agreed to perform this service and, astonishingly, also claimed to have all of the answers she was seeking. However, the information was so sensitive he would prefer not to discuss it on the telephone. Perhaps they could meet later, he suggested.

After a brief comparison of schedules, they concluded the most efficient way to meet and discuss this secret information would be for Monsieur LaMontagne to drive her first to the crematorium and then to the airport. While they traveled, he could explain all of the research he had conducted plus some rather surprising discoveries.

Suzanne then held a productive conference via Skype with her team assembled in a meeting room at the Atlanta headquarters. This capability was vital because she preferred to observe body language whenever possible. It made communication so much more clear and useful.

As expected, that morning they achieved demonstrable success over five or so hours because meeting participants had worked doggedly to develop a final strategy for their game changer project. First, they determined that they would defy John George Mortimer's directive to limit the project to a single concept.

Discussions began with the potential acquisition of a regional big-box retailer. They reviewed a draft business plan page by page and line by line. The group modeled various scenarios of possible purchase terms, comparing the relative advantages and disadvantages of an all-cash offer, a Multima shares offer, or a combination of both. The team also debated intricate recommendations received from investment bank advisors they met with all day on Sunday. Throughout that session, designated resources also communicated separately and frequently with their liaison for Supermarkets in CFO Wilma Willingsworth's office. Suzanne wanted to ensure they first gained, and then maintained, support of Multima's chief financial officer and her team as their project developed.

Their healthy food initiative evolved the same way. First, there was an exhaustive review of the financial forecasts. Detailed scrutiny of the strategy, timing, and product launches followed. Suzanne sought assurances of commitment at every stage, effectively underscoring with every member of her team personal accountability for the accuracy of projections and success of execution.

Her team knew she usually managed with a consensus-building style, and she did so in a comfortable and highly personable way. Once they reached a decision, they also knew every member of the team was expected to achieve or exceed the desired results. Lest they forget, she sprinkled a few reminders into their conversations.

With the teleconference completed, Suzanne quickly checked out of the Hilton Hotel, met Monsieur LaMontagne as planned, and made a short trip to the crematorium for a final farewell to the ashes of her mother.

Suzanne's visit for a final goodbye would probably have been much more emotional had she visited alone. Instead, because she needed to maintain full control for her upcoming conversation with Monsieur LaMontagne, she contained her continuing grief. She'd simply need to deal with it later. As was often necessary to do in her role, she subtly shifted sentiment to another compartment of her brain and stored it there. She stoically willed herself to set aside all feelings until another day.

As a result, her visit to the crematorium was somewhat shorter than planned. With a few minutes to spare, Monsieur LaMontagne suggested they stop at a Starbucks on the way to the airport. It might be easier to explain everything if he was not driving at the same time. For a few minutes, they sipped their steaming hot cups of coffee while he recounted his story and filled Suzanne with new intrigue.

"It seems your mother started to receive monthly deposits to her bank account, each in an amount of three thousand dollars, several years before she came to seek my counsel," he began. "In fact, deposits started to appear mysteriously on the thirtieth day of June in 1997."

This date struck Suzanne as significant. However, she was unable to recall immediately just why it should be noteworthy.

"Sometime around the year 2005, Madame Louise Marcotte contacted me to prepare her will," he continued. "During those discussions, your mother explained that she had been receiving these monthly deposits to her bank account for several years. She told me her bank manager had initially made several inquiries on her behalf using bank channels. Unfortunately, his efforts to discover the source of the deposits proved unsuccessful.

"Your mother also explained that for six subsequent years she made the same request of three successive bank managers. After several months' investigation, each reported they also were unable to determine who was making the deposits. One suggested it might be you. After all, you are a successful woman of considerable financial means. He had theorized that perhaps you wanted to share some of that success with your mother secretly," he said with a smile.

"When Madame Marcotte first met me, she asked if I could find the mysterious source of the deposits. Unfortunately, time had been an enemy. I fully intended to help her, but the matter suffered from continual delays."

Suzanne listened without interruption. "Finally, your mother became exasperated and gave me an ultimatum. Either I must discover information about the source of those payments during that year, or she would take her legal affairs to another *notaire*."

She couldn't completely suppress a smile as Monsieur LaMontagne mimicked her mother's customary wagging of her forefinger to express anger or impatience.

"Such a threat was a trigger for me to address her concerns with newfound urgency. I'd spent considerable time investigating during these past several months, much more than I could ever consider billing your mother. Finally, with the help of a lawyer in Toronto, I learned some details about both the mysterious bank deposits and the shares of that numbered company in Ontario.

"They seemed related. Deposits to Madame Marcotte's bank account came from 136742 (Ontario) Corporation, yet another separate legal entity that incorporated on the thirtieth day of June in 1997. Such information was relatively easy to get.

"It was harder to determine who ultimately owned the numbered company. Many legal barriers appeared, apparently to prevent easy identification. Finally, after months of queries, we identified the owner as Countrywide Stores Incorporated, a Canadian entity. Interestingly, that particular business was acquired on June 30, 1997, by Multima

Corporation." His eyebrows arched and he waited for Suzanne's reaction. There was only shock apparent on her face, so he continued.

"I discovered this information only a few weeks ago. Sadly, it was to discuss this recent discovery that I invited Madame Marcotte to my office that unfortunate day she suffered her heart attack. Because of her health crisis, I wasn't able to share the information your mother so patiently sought."

Suzanne was speechless and her mouth gaped open. Countrywide Stores Incorporated was the Canadian supermarket company she previously managed as president and CEO. It was the same company she had arranged for Multima Corporation to buy. Those share certificates had been issued precisely the day of that acquisition. Bewilderingly, all of this had occurred without her knowledge.

Monsieur LaMontagne clearly understood the implications, and patiently waited without further comment. He watched intently as she visibly struggled to process and make sense of it.

She was ill at ease under his penetrating gaze and made a great effort to assert control over her body language. It was almost identical to the horror she felt, and projected, during her momentary reaction to the shock of learning about John George Mortimer's cancer during that dreadful CBNN interview. She recovered with self-deprecating humor.

"The overused excuse that a CEO cannot possibly know everything certainly applies here," she offered with a nervous laugh and her most disarming smile.

Monsieur LaMontagne realized he would likely gain little additional information to satisfy his curiosity that day. He graciously expressed a willingness to seek any further details she might require later, and helpfully added that Suzanne should not worry. He would not charge the estate of Madame Marcotte any more fees than those already billed for his exhaustive research to solve the mystery.

They returned to his car and set off for the airport. He drove the remaining couple miles, deposited her at the ramp of the Multima business aircraft, and wished her farewell with a parting kiss on both cheeks. Then, he gave her a warm hug of affection as he wished her continued success in all her pursuits. Parting, he expressed hope their paths would cross again sometime soon.

Minutes after takeoff, she made a mental note to discuss this whole matter of secret companies and unusual bank deposits with John George Mortimer, privately and at the earliest opportunity. It was then her smartphone vibrated to announce an incoming call. Alberto Ferer, she noted as she answered.

Ferer started the call with an expression of condolences for the loss of her mother. That call was the first occasion for them to speak since Suzanne had received the unfortunate news, and he was clearly a little uncomfortable as he tried to express his sympathy. As soon as politely possible, he switched to the actual purpose of his call.

Suzanne listened without interruption as the general counsel of Multima Corporation explained that John George Mortimer was in some far-reaching difficulty with his board of directors. He provided a brief background of the reasons for the emergency meeting and explained the requirement that she attend. He provided the time, date, and location.

After covering the meeting details, he casually mentioned the bombshell news that Suzanne must also be prepared to pitch Supermarkets' game changer project to the board at that same meeting. He realized this gave her little remaining time to prepare. Before she could object, he also acknowledged the change in plans had shortened the original sixty days for preparation to less than three weeks, and everyone conceded it was not entirely reasonable.

However, she must also understand this directive came from none other than John George Mortimer. Their leader was apparently operating in crisis mode and would be counting on her to do the best possible with her team presentation, despite the unreasonably short remaining time.

Suzanne tersely replied that he could rely on her team's support. They'd do their best to help his cause. With a deep sigh of resignation, she called Eileen Lee's home number. For the next few minutes, she outlined her request.

Her executive assistant must immediately contact all Suzanne's direct reports and those team members who accompanied her to Asia. Ask them to return to the office in Atlanta this evening for urgent discussions. They had a major crisis on their hands. She would explain all the details during the meeting. They would start with her arrival at the office in about two hours. Participants should expect to be on the job for the following twenty-four to thirty-six hours continuously and should prepare accordingly.

Her final comment to Eileen included an unseen but apologetic smile. She was sorry to inform her that she too would need to add her name to the list. They'd certainly rely on all of her valuable support.

That call concluded, Suzanne glanced at her watch. Only about ninety minutes remained before landing. She turned off her overhead light, reclined her leather seat and closed her eyes. To be at her best for the next couple days, it was essential she catch a little sleep whenever possible. A nap now would be an excellent start.

FIFTY-FIVE

The Netherlands.
About midnight, March 7, 2016

Continuously, the uniformed men had prevented him from sleeping for any extended period. It seemed as soon as he fell into the start of a restful sleep, they burst through the door loudly demanding he get up for more interrogation about the pending charges for attempted murder.

They took turns haranguing him about what went on at that private party in Overveen. Every few moments they would demand that he sign a confession. It was the only practical course of action for him. The prosecutor would not want to waste any of his valuable time seeing Randall until there was a full confession, they said repeatedly. Again and again, they denied his increasingly plaintive and fearful requests to speak with an attorney, a representative of the American embassy, or even a friend in Germany. No, there could be no such contact.

All had changed just an hour or so earlier. To his amazement, the uniformed guard suddenly escorted Frau Schäffer into his cell, firmly closed the door, and then locked it again. Stern, she approached him, warning that he must say nothing. He must sit on the chair at the small table. She would give him a note to read. After reading it, he would either nod his head in an affirmative response or shake his head sideways if he would not agree. There would be no further discussion. The matter would resolve within the next five minutes, or she would leave, and there would be no conclusion.

Numb from fatigue, disoriented from sleep deprivation, stress, and confinement, Wendal sat at the table and slowly read the note.

> *Howard Knight sent me. He learned of your confinement and has intervened to help you. When you read this message, make no comments. Say nothing. There is a video camera in the room that records everything.*
>
> *Howard Knight has arranged for your immediate release with one condition. You will read and sign the document I provide you. It is a confession about your activities the night of*

March 3 at the house in Overveen. When you sign the document, you will be released by the Dutch politie. There will be no charges laid. You will suffer no punishment.

You will come with me to Schiphol Airport. We will meet a business jet and travel to New York. This matter will be over if you sign the confession. Continue to cooperate with Howard Knight in the future, and no one will ever know about this sordid incident.

There will be no discussion. There will be no negotiation. Simply nod your head if you are prepared to sign the confession. If you choose not to sign, I will leave. You will be completely alone to resolve your predicament.

When Wendal finished reading, bitter tears welled in his eyes. He felt the greatest despair one could imagine. At that moment, he felt drained of all energy, utterly weak, and helpless. His hands were shaking. His brain seemed to function like a slow-motion dream. He slowly raised his eyes from the paper and looked into the ice-cold eyes of Klaudia Schäffer, which were completely devoid of emotion.

She looked at him for a moment. Wendal could not detect any empathy. After a moment, she turned away and started towards the doorway without a backward glance. In panic, he cried out for her to wait.

Frau Schäffer paused and turned her head slightly to detect his nod of agreement. Wordlessly, she returned to the table, removed a typed document from her handbag, and placed it on the small table. She took a pen from her bag, set it on the table, and pointed where he should sign.

Appearing to carry a burden so heavy it bowed his entire frame, he slowly slouched in the chair. His body language projected total defeat and absolute dejection. He read the document with sleep-deprived eyes. His vision was blurred and tears continued to well, just waiting to erupt.

The document included no information about the girl's suggestions to try new sexual adventures. There was no mention of her willingness to explore erotic asphyxiation. Of course, descriptions of her loss of consciousness, deep welts on her neck, and a need for emergency resuscitation were described in minute detail. But he could see no alternative. He signed the paper.

As Frau Schäffer retrieved the signed confession, she swept another object from her pocket and seemed to compare it with the signature on the document. Satisfied, she stashed the paper and pen in her bag.

The door to his cell opened as though on cue, held in that position by one of the uniformed guards. Without a further word or gesture, Wendal followed Frau Schäffer out the door. At a service counter near the exit, the other guard wordlessly handed him his passport, then pressed a button under the counter that audibly released a lock on the station's front door.

A car was waiting outside, and they quickly got in. No words were spoken, even when they reached the private jet section of Schiphol airport fifteen minutes later. Wendal exited the door on his side of the car, and then followed Klaudia Schäffer up the stairs through an already open aircraft door. Immediately after they had embarked, a co-pilot wordlessly closed and locked the door behind them. Seconds later, a short taxi for takeoff began, and they were underway.

Wendal knew the jet was leaving Amsterdam's Schiphol International Airport and was still climbing steeply to cruising altitude. He also knew the aircraft was owned by VCI only because Frau Schäffer had reluctantly provided that morsel of information. The aircraft itself carried no identification other than a number on its white tail. He was still not sure of the exact time. He knew it was after midnight and the day was Tuesday. She had also shared that meager information, but little more.

She only instructed him to get some sleep and be ready for a discussion with Howard Knight in a few hours. Wendal understood there would be some meeting at an airport in New York before he could continue to his home in Miami. He was terrified by the thought of that get-together.

In his bewilderment, he realized that his Rolex, along with other valuables like his wallet, cash, smartphone, and carry-on luggage had not been returned by the uniformed *politie* in Haarlem.

Wendal felt despondent and perplexed by the bizarre events of the past few days. The house party in Overveen seemed like an out of body experience with alcohol, drugs, and women. His sexual experience with the one who caused his incarceration felt like some vague fantasy that rapidly evolved into a horrifying nightmare. The grueling hours of confinement and interrogation had drained him of every remaining ounce of energy and will.

His final submission—to sign a confession under duress—left him in a void. He could make no sense of the situation. There seemed no logic to it at all. He couldn't imagine what his future might hold, and it was impossible to assess the scope of damage to his reputation and career.

There was no way to measure the leverage Howard Knight would have over him. As he submitted to sleep, he felt only the angst of desperation, without even a glimmer of hope to lift his spirit. He was so depressed that he was no longer certain he even wanted the position of CEO at Multima, though such an offer indeed seemed very unlikely after this fiasco in the Netherlands.

FIFTY-SIX

John George Mortimer decided there was no compelling reason to travel to his office that Tuesday morning. Instead, preparation for the emergency meeting of the board of directors was paramount.

He knew some on the board were seeking his head. Others might prefer only to vent. Few would be silent. None would be neutral. He needed time to think, calculate, and strategize. He knew he could shape a plan to deal with this crisis most effectively if he could remove distractions, ponder his opponents' tactics, and steel himself for the criticism.

He started that process with two calls, both to set the stage for his day. About six-thirty, he called Sally-Ann Bureau at her home. He thought she'd be preparing to leave for her ever-predictable seven o'clock start at the office. He shared his intentions and without further prompting, she knew which issues she should bring to his attention. She'd only disrupt his thinking and planning for subjects that mattered.

The second call was to Alberto Ferer, already at work in his office. Mortimer's purpose for calling was to remind him they should stop generating payments from that special purpose company in Ontario. Mortimer asked him to close it down and convert the shares as required by the bylaws of the numbered company.

Ferer immediately recalled the deal. A few years earlier, he had created the elaborate labyrinth of overlapping companies to conceal the ultimate source of funding. He assured John George that he'd handle the issue that day and would conclude it quickly.

Then, he alerted Mortimer to new information. "Dan Ramirez from corporate security called me at home very early this morning. There's a significant new development in the hacking incident at Supermarkets.

"Ramirez has been keeping close to the FBI technologists pursuing the perpetrator, and they've apparently uncovered some dramatic evidence conclusively connecting the hacker directly to Multima Logistics."

Mortimer listened intently without interruption, engrossed with every detail of the vital new information.

"Some time ago, the technology team at Supermarkets apparently created and embedded into their system a novel new security tool developed to track any movement of the highly sensitive personnel file should it ever be copied.

"Ramirez tells me this capability was designed to send a signal to headquarters every time any stolen software was transferred from one computer to another. Then, it automatically deleted a single digit from each column in its field of data with every transfer from one computer to another. Automatically, an entry of one hundred would drop a zero and become ten, rendering the data inaccurate and useless to anyone who did not know how it worked.

"So the information was automatically altered to make the data worthless to whoever stole it?" John George confirmed.

"Yeah. That's the good news," Alberto continued. "Unfortunately, the outcome doesn't look good. It seems that Supermarkets' technology team has successfully tracked the software through four successive download transactions. Moreover, they can tell the FBI precisely which digits in the software changed, and even tell the FBI what the new values are now.

"During the FBI's overnight scan of company computers, they discovered files on a laptop computer used by a Multima Logistics employee that matched those new values. The FBI are questioning that person right now to determine a possible motive and learn what other information he might have about the hacking incident."

When John George Mortimer became confident he had accurately absorbed all of the disconcerting information, together with its repugnant implications, he suggested Ferer should leave immediately for Miami. There, he could assess the situation first-hand. Mortimer finished the call feeling both profound sadness and disappointment.

He felt a sense of foreboding as Wendal Randall's mysterious disappearance came to mind. This devastating new information implied someone in his Logistics division stole from the Supermarkets group. Such mischief created havoc and now threatened to unravel his game changer succession strategy. However, as usual, he would play the cards he had been dealt. John George's keen intuition sensed this latest unexpected twist might eventually become a critical component of his strategy for survival at the next day's board meeting.

FIFTY-SEVEN

On the tarmac of Teterboro Airport, New Jersey.
Early morning, March 8, 2016

That morning, Howard Knight traveled in a VCI limousine to Teterboro Airport, a general aviation airport in Bergen County, New Jersey. Popular with owners of private and corporate jets due to a convenient proximity to midtown Manhattan, it handles aircraft traffic for both domestic and global flights. And, it was the airport selected by the VCI pilots before takeoff from Amsterdam. Ironically, it took him longer to get there than he planned to spend in actual discussions.

A moment or two after eight o'clock Tuesday morning, he boarded the VCI corporate jet just after it landed with Wendal Randall and Klaudia Schäffer aboard. One of his contacts with The Organization had arranged entry into the highly secure area without the bother of documentation or supervision. There was no verification of the aircraft crew or passengers either. Someone had persuaded someone else in a position of authority that neither inspections or clearances were necessary for the short meeting.

In fact, the encounter took less than fifteen minutes. There was minimal discussion. As Knight's head peered around the corner of the aircraft, he saw Klaudia Schäffer lift her bulky sweater and remove a small leather pouch strapped securely to her body, just below her breasts. Without a word, she handed it to Knight, who issued a polite cursory greeting and welcome to the United States of America. Without waiting for a response, he immediately focused on Wendal. Knight spoke calmly, directly, and with a penetrating stare that never shifted from Wendal's dejected eyes.

"You are probably feeling a lot like you look right now, I expect," he started. "And, if I may be candid, right now you look like shit. But none of us has any time for you to feel sorry for yourself. None of us has any time to commiserate. We cannot afford for you to waste valuable time trying to fit together pieces of the puzzle, nor will we have time for you to try to understand my motivations. Just let it go.

"Despite all your incredibly immature behavior and carelessness, I still intend to make you CEO of Multima Corporation. That should happen sometime tomorrow afternoon. But I cannot allow you to make any more stupid mistakes that might endanger our project.

"Effective immediately, the beautiful and charming Klaudia Schäffer will become your new life companion. She'll be with you day and night until further notice. I think a story that you unexpectedly fell in love during your trip to Europe would be most plausible, but I'll leave it to you to work out the details. Understand this well. I expect you to be inseparable until I determine otherwise."

Knight paused to gauge their body language. He paid particular attention to Wendal. He noted apparent resignation and acceptance as Wendal lowered his eyes with shoulders slumped forward. The woman's face was impassive and her posture neutral. Satisfied, Knight continued.

"As I said, I expect you to be elected CEO of Multima tomorrow at an emergency meeting of the board of directors. However, it is imperative to make a favorable impression on the board. You'll need to call your team in Miami as soon as we finish this little chat and you can use my phone.

"Instruct them to prepare a final presentation for Operation Bright Star to deliver tomorrow morning. Keep your role in that performance limited. Then, make sure you and your team are in Fort Myers for the start of the nine o'clock meeting. Again, I want both of you at the meeting. For the benefit of the board, you can be a new executive assistant," Knight gestured towards Frau Schäffer.

"Get some sleep before the meeting," he continued, addressing Wendal again. "Let your team do the preparation, arrive refreshed, and keep a low profile during the meeting. By mid-afternoon, you should be making about three times more a year in salary, and I'll make sure you earn bonuses of ten times that amount every year. All I need is your continued cooperation. You'll be able to live in outstanding style for the rest of your life. Any questions?" Wendal said nothing.

"Make the call," he instructed before he moved to the back of the aircraft, motioning for Frau Schäffer to join him. They sat at the rear of the plane and huddled in deep but whispered conversation while Wendal spoke briefly with his project team leader, Ricky Technori.

Their conversation was short. Wendal dismissed Technori's inquiry about his current whereabouts and unplanned absence curtly. "We'll talk about that later," he said, delivering an unmistakable signal that further questions or follow-up would not be welcome.

"Here's why I'm calling. There's been a change in timing for the game changer project. We have to deliver it to the board of directors tomorrow. Yeah, tomorrow.

"You'll need to get Margot, Juan, and Mitsi together to create a presentation. All four of you should plan to deliver it. Equal parts. Include all the conclusions from our last meeting in Düsseldorf. Focus on the technology story and don't worry too much about the cost-benefit stuff. Throw in some schematics and flow charts. Use lots of tech speak and benefits of first-launch advantage."

"How are we supposed to create a value proposition? Technori asked.

"Any more luck making the numbers work?" Wendal asked.

"No. They just don't compute with all the other data we have."

"Forget the value story then. Just tell them it brings enormous savings. Focus on the technology. I'll be there in a few hours. We can fill in any blanks then," Wendal replied, dismissing both the concern and their conversation. The call had taken less than five minutes before he shifted his attention to Howard Knight and Klaudia Schäffer, still hunched in animated conversation at the rear of the aircraft.

As soon as Knight noticed the call had finished, he immediately broke his dialog with Frau Schäffer, passed her a brown envelope, and returned to the front of the aircraft. There, he retrieved his smartphone from Wendal and turned to face both of them again. Like a teacher admonishing his students to study for an upcoming exam, he made one parting comment.

"We'll only get one chance to execute this strategy that I've worked many years to develop. There can be no mistakes or surprises. Is there any additional info you need to assure flawless execution of your roles tomorrow?" It was a formality. He expected no problems.

His last pause focused mainly on Frau Schäffer. His penetrating gaze met hers for several seconds before he issued a curt goodbye. His dramatic departure left no doubt in Wendal's mind that Frau Schäffer's role had changed from spy to controller. He squirmed with unease.

Howard Knight bounded down the steps of the aircraft. The ramp to the plane immediately lifted with a hum and folded towards the fuselage. A new co-pilot closed and locked the door. Freshly refueled, the VCI jet was in the air moments later with an expected arrival in Miami before noon.

Somewhat rested from five or six hours sleep on the previous flight, Wendal planned to use every minute of this leg for some serious re-assessment. He desperately needed to find a way to deal with this ever expanding, menacing, and encircling disaster. He felt as though it was smothering him.

FIFTY-EIGHT

In a modern building, near Chicago.
Afternoon, March 8, 2016

James Fitzgerald finished his workout in the exercise facility and stopped briefly to pick up lunch at the employee cafeteria. Juggling a salad encased in a slippery plastic container, a banana, and two bottles of water, he ambled back towards his office. As usual, he stopped for brief greetings with colleagues along his route and chatted during a short elevator ride to the fourth floor. His expansive office suite covered the entire southwest quarter.

He took a quick shower in his luxurious private bathroom just off the alcove behind the elevators and became very relaxed. This calm pervaded despite the storm swirling around the emergency meeting of the board of directors and the urgent message from Alberto Ferer bringing forward delivery of the game changer presentation.

As he took a seat on a comfortable padded leather chair in a cluster of furniture tastefully arranged in one corner of his office, he carefully organized his lunch for orderly consumption. Then, he gulped the food and drinks quickly and without ceremony. Moments later, James touched a paper napkin to his lips as he finished his lunch, then carefully gathered up the empty plastic bottles and salad container to deposit them neatly in the blue recycling box under his desk.

Then, he gathered his tablet and walked next door to meet with his assembled team. Fitzgerald had relayed news of the surprising corporate developments and sudden change of schedule for their game changer with an email from his assistant right after his conversation with Alberto Ferer. All came prepared.

They had polished off the hard work last week, Douglas Whitfield confidently declared as he glanced around the assembled group. Heads nodded, and discussion moved to travel logistics and final touches to the presentation.

James wanted them to go to Fort Myers that evening and avoid the need for early wake-up calls the day of the meeting. He suggested that it might be better to arrive the evening before, get a good night's sleep, and be fresh for the crucial presentations. There were no objections.

They'd leave their offices at various times, and then meet at the private jet section of Midway Airport for a six o'clock departure. Fitzgerald proposed they have a late dinner together on arrival, and his assistant agreed to find a good nearby restaurant, make reservations, and let them know where to meet.

The remainder of their two-hour session dealt with fine-tuning the presentation itself. Fitzgerald listened intently as his executives delivered their respective messages. He scrutinized all the PowerPoint slides as they rehearsed deliveries, and to finish preparation, he peppered each participant with dozens of reasonably anticipated questions.

In fact, last night James had spent almost four hours in the tranquility of his den thinking about questions directors might ask. Most importantly, he considered the most judicious responses. It was this area where James focused his input because team members were already adequately prepared with their answers. Now, he wanted them to be spectacularly primed.

He used his time and energy to suggest how they might fine-tune answers to the questions. He offered ideas to make responses more crisp and precise. Finally, he asked them to remember all the techniques they had acquired in those useful communications workshops.

By the end of the two-hour meeting, any lingering reservations he may have harbored about the change in schedule had evaporated. He was able to focus his attention on the big issue. The leader of their corporation was in serious trouble.

By now, it was abundantly clear Howard Knight was scheming to engineer a change in leadership at Multima Corporation. Each of James' discreet conversations with contacts over the past two days reinforced this conclusion. No one seemed to understand Knight's real motivation, but they all agreed that the brouhaha surrounding Mortimer's failure to communicate his illness was an almost transparent justification for a change in management.

Remarkably, it seemed Knight was winning this point. According to one of James' sources, Knight had the support of seven directors on the board. Fitzgerald decided to see what further snippets of information his favorite resource in business intelligence might have ferreted out.

He called Natalia Tenaz. When they last spoke, James asked her to continue investigation on the Internet. However, he realized it would be better for her to use a computer not owned by the company and not inside the company's facilities. Fitzgerald's assistant purchased a top-of-the-line HP laptop, paying with cash drawn from her bank ATM. The new unit was the fastest and most powerful personal computer manufactured by HP with incredible processing speed and an enormous memory capacity. Natalia had confirmed the purchase would be perfect for her task.

This conversation was productive. The ever-surprising young woman had spent hours with the new computer digging sites for information she might find about The Organization and VCI. She almost gave up after nine or ten hours. Then, Natalia suddenly discovered a link. Howard Knight's previously impeccable resume hid an ugly wart.

It showed a master's degree in business administration from Haarverde College, an MBA that opens doors and commands respect around the globe. However, Fitzgerald's favorite resource in business intelligence came across a surprising newspaper article during her research.

The Jewish Advocate, a special-interest newspaper established in 1902, published a one-column story. At last, Haarverde authorities had punished those students recently apprehended for vandalizing a local synagogue. According to the article, Howard Knight was among those arrested. Moreover, Haarverde subsequently expelled him and his three delinquent classmates.

As Natalia Tenaz continued her exploration, she confirmed that Knight's expulsion had indeed occurred. When she found and reviewed the published list of graduates for that year in a small local newspaper, Howard Knight's name was not among them. However, with further probing, she discovered his name was later added to the Haarverde website record of graduates.

Suspicious, Natalia continued her investigation. She uncovered a five million-dollar donation to Haarverde College in July of the year Knight should have graduated had he not been expelled. The donor was W.D. Knight. Further investigation determined that William Donald Knight was Howard's father.

When Fitzgerald's researcher from business intelligence started to dig deeper into available information about William Donald Knight, she learned he worked as an accountant with an obscure company in New York. Its reported sales were only a few hundred thousand dollars per year. How could an accountant with a firm generating so little afford to make a multimillion-dollar donation?

According to a respected blogger in the criminal investigation community, the obscure little company William Donald Knight worked for had strong connections to organized crime through an entity known to some as The Organization.

This discovery deeply troubled James. In fact, he almost forgot to thank Natalia until she interrupted his worried distraction by telling him she would really like to thank him.

Her college roommate from Fort Myers had called earlier that morning. She had just received an offer for a new job in corporate security and was very relieved. She would be moving to that section of Multima immediately. Natalia was sure James had something to do with that welcome new development and she knew her college roommate was grateful.

Mumbling his confidence that the young woman had earned her new role entirely with diligence and hard work, Fitzgerald ended that call to make another.

During this second call with Dan Ramirez in corporate security, Fitzgerald started to relax. Naturally, his long-time friend could not share all of the details yet. However, he could assure James they would finalize issues related to the hacking incident within the next forty-eight hours. Pieces of the puzzle were all starting to fit together.

Ramirez suggested they have breakfast before the board meeting on Wednesday when he might be able to provide more details. James wondered if he should divulge now what he had just learned about Howard Knight's background, or if it would be better to pass it along when they met for breakfast the next day.

He elected to do it right then, just in case.

The chief of corporate security reacted with unconcealed joy as James outlined his researcher's discovery. Profusely thanking him for providing such a valuable tip, Ramirez exclaimed that was precisely the sort of link he'd been seeking. "We can both sleep well tonight," he said, anxious to finish their call.

Before their conversation ended, James had just enough time to thank him for handling the other matter so expediently.

All that remained before flight time was to work his way through the stack of documents his assistant had deposited in the top left-hand drawer of his desk. As usual, he started with the first page on the top of the pile.

FIFTY-NINE

Multima Supermarkets' headquarters, Atlanta.
Evening, March 8, 2016

Her team was nearing exhaustion. More than twenty-four hours had elapsed since they got together in response to Suzanne's directive from the jet. Despite their hard work on the aircraft, and the team's diligent efforts during the two working days after their arrival, they still needed her leadership for the final push to completion.

The solution hadn't started to congeal until she laid out a more defined path for the team to consider. There had been a hodgepodge of good ideas on the healthy food initiative, but no common thread to bring them together. The intention to acquire a regional big-box retailer with a strong presence in the discount market appeared more encouraging. Still, a consensus about the most advantageous way to pay for the acquisition evaded the team.

With a couple hours' discussion, Suzanne had the teams on track again. Goals were clearly defined. Gaps in data were identified. Team members became eager to complete the analysis, formulate the strategies, crystallize the business plan, and develop a PowerPoint presentation to explain it all in thirty minutes or less.

Groups of three or four people worked on each of those tasks in the expansive conference room of Multima Supermarkets' headquarters, and she could feel the energy. Some were involved in quiet conversations while others focused on computer screens as their hands raced across keyboards in a blur of activity.

Individual team members took breaks when they needed them. Some took short naps. All the while, someone made sure there was a constant stream of fruit, snacks, and refreshments. The teams labored throughout the night Monday and the entire next day. They finally completed their tasks and rehearsed the presentation once. At that point, Suzanne glanced at her watch and realized they must stop right then to get sleep, or risk disaster when it came time to deliver presentations the following morning.

She was satisfied with the output. Their materials looked great, and the business plan was rigorous enough to withstand inevitable challenges. She would have liked the participants to have more time to rehearse, but they had accomplished the best possible outcome in the restricted time allowed. It was what it was. As John George Mortimer liked to say, they had played the cards they were dealt as adeptly as possible. They would soon learn if it was enough to satisfy the board.

Her team didn't have the luxury of traveling to Fort Myers the evening before the meeting like her colleagues from Financial Services. The logistics just wouldn't work. Instead, she'd dismiss them so they could sleep in their homes.

The three folks who would deliver the presentation to the board would need to rise about four o'clock in the morning. They'd prepare and dress for the occasion, pack clothes in the event of an unplanned overnight stay, then meet the Multima Supermarkets business jet for a six o'clock departure.

They would have breakfast on the plane during their short flight from Atlanta to Page Field in Fort Myers. They'd also have time for one more rehearsal. Suzanne made a mental note to quiz them with hypothetical questions to ensure everyone would be comfortable responding to probable tough questions posed by those high-powered executives who served as directors.

She too desperately needed rest. Her last sleep had been the brief nap on her flight from Quebec City to Atlanta on Monday evening. No thoughts of her mother's death, conversations with Monsieur LaMontagne, or the intriguing information the *notaire* delivered had surfaced on that arduously long day.

There had also been little time to consider that the board of directors might actually fire John George Mortimer. Now, she realized this once inconceivable possibility might occur as early as tomorrow. That left no time to ponder her personal issues. Such concerns would need to wait.

SIXTY

An office tower near Wall Street, New York.
Evening, March 8, 2016

Howard Knight's first indication there might be a problem was a lack of communication from either Klaudia Schäffer or Wendal Randall by the dinner hour. He had expected one or the other would call to update him on their progress with the game changer presentation tomorrow.

He had not specifically instructed them to call, but he hadn't thought it necessary given the punctual updates Schäffer typically provided with her assignments. About seven o'clock, he became concerned and tried to reach them by telephone. He tried Randall at his office. When no one there answered, he left a voice message.

Next, he tried Wendal's smartphone. Again, there was no response, and he recorded another message. Finally, he called Klaudia Schäffer's German mobile. There, he listened to a recorded message advising she was currently unavailable, outside the service area and calls could not be completed.

When he had not heard from them by eight o'clock, he remembered the early morning call Wendal had made to an associate from the VCI aircraft. He had used Knight's personal cell phone, and the number for that team leader would be in the call list. Knight couldn't recall the individual's name but tried the Miami number all the same.

Someone answered on the second ring. Knight identified himself and asked to whom he was speaking. The individual said he was Ricky Technori with Multima Logistics. Knight politely clarified that he was talking with the project team leader, and then asked to speak with Randall. To his abject horror, Ricky Technori replied that Wendal Randall had never shown up at the office. He was missing.

Aghast, Knight probed more deeply and learned a string of increasingly disturbing new facts. When Randall had not come to the office later in the day as expected, Technori had tried to track him down. There had been no answer at his home or on his smartphone. His assistant called the airport and learned that Wendal had indeed arrived in Miami just before noon, accompanied by a woman. They got into a waiting limousine and left the airport field right away. The airport staff couldn't provide any additional information about the limousine, the driver, or Wendal's whereabouts.

The blood drained from Howard Knight's face as he listened wordlessly and tried to piece the incredible story together. Gradually, he regained his composure. Of course, It would be a significant challenge should Randall be unable or unwilling to attend the meeting with the board of directors, but the situation was still manageable.

He first established that Technori knew exactly where Knight fit in the Multima Corporation pecking order. He was a director on the board and a major shareholder, he announced. Technori knew who Knight was, where he fit, and felt honored to have the pleasure of speaking with him.

Satisfied, Knight inquired about the project's progress and learned it was complete, sitting in his email box, ready for delivery the next day. He confirmed that a team had been selected to deliver their presentation but learned there were no plans to travel to the meeting. He instructed Technori to contact Wendal's assistant at home so she could arrange for a company jet to take them. They needed to be in Fort Myers by eight o'clock tomorrow and then make their way to Multima headquarters for the nine o'clock meeting, Knight stressed.

They should also both keep up their efforts to locate Wendal. Technori should ask Wendal's assistant to try his favorite restaurants, bars, and friends. They should all do everything possible to get him to the board of directors meeting.

Technori understood the importance of the instructions, pledged his full support and cooperation, and expressed how much he was looking forward to meeting Howard the next day. When the call ended, Knight felt unease greater than any he could recall.

He couldn't imagine either Wendal Randall or Klaudia Schäffer just running out on him. That would be totally out of character for both. Randall might be a little unstable after his confining weekend in Europe. But Schäffer, with significant responsibilities and long experience in The Organization, would not possibly try to escape. She knew what the consequences would be.

No, someone had intercepted his two crucial players in the plan to overthrow the management of Multima Corporation. He urgently needed to learn who and why. With profound apprehension but few alternatives, he called his usual contact in The Organization. Once more, he would need to ask for help.

SIXTY-ONE

*At his Fort Myers home.
Late evening, March 8, 2016*

John George Mortimer was at peace. His day of preparation before a crucial morning meeting with his board of directors was coming to a close.

The last several hours had been productive ones. During the early part of the afternoon, he prepared arguments for his defense in the event it became necessary to justify his judgment and actions. He also used precious time to access confidential Multima personnel records on a secure network.

Interspersed with those activities, he also called and quizzed Multima Supermarkets' IT leader Dieter Lehren about the hacking incident. More particularly, he delved into the innovative new tool embedded in the stolen software. He learned about its origins and posed dozens of questions about its development. Then, he explored other possible uses for it. Lehren seemed genuinely flattered by the keen interest shown by his CEO and by the amount of time Mortimer spent learning about it.

Later, he toiled industriously on a series of PowerPoint slides that included graphs, charts, and bullet points. It was rare for him to prepare such speaking aids. Consequently, it took a little longer than he expected, and his output lacked the polish and animation his communications specialists would typically create.

However, he was confident the storyboard adequately supported his message to the board. Whether or not he eventually used the slides would depend on which option the directors decided to follow. He remained hopeful he would be able to articulate and win support for the paths he intended to propose.

By the dinner-hour, he was able to power-down his computer. He retreated to his favorite wicker rocking chair on the outdoor lanai, pausing to fill a glass of fine Pinot Noir on his way. As expected, the sunset proved stunning. Combinations of brilliant reds and yellows of the receding sun contrasted with the softness of fluffy white clouds. It was simply resplendent. John George sipped his wine and gazed at the scene until the sun completely disappeared on the horizon and darkness set in.

Later, he enjoyed a simple fish dinner prepared by his house-keeper. She served the meal exactly as he liked it, a small piece of broiled grouper surrounded by mounds of steaming fresh green vegetables. He savored every forkful and was effusive in his praise as he let his house-keeper know just how much he enjoyed her culinary creation.

He asked her to join him on the lanai after she cleared the dishes and finished whatever she needed to do in the kitchen. When she arrived a few minutes later, she brought a pot of green tea and two cups. They chatted in Spanish for a half hour or so as they sipped the tea.

John George listened much more than he spoke. Of course, he was practicing his Spanish language skills, but he also genuinely enjoyed hearing news about the housekeeper's family and friends in El Salvador. He knew several of her relatives from his frequent short visits to the tiny Central American country, and his housekeeper was always happy to share news about them. She was keenly aware of the generosity he showed her family with the practical gifts he always carried there and the useful amounts of cash he left behind in unmarked envelopes.

When he realized the day had become tiring for his faithful house-keeper, he apologized and released her from their conversation so she could return home to spend time with her family.

Then, he read the Wall Street Journal and New York Times online and scanned newspapers in France, Spain, Germany, and Singapore. He had a genuine interest in happenings around the world, but also recognized the importance of broad awareness of current global affairs whenever he met with his board of directors. At the forthcoming meeting, some might check for signs of any inability to keep up with world events. Others might look for a signal of a reduced capacity to manage the company. He may not be aware of everything going on out there but was confident he was aware of the significant current global crises and issues.

The final task was his regular one hour of reading. That night, he read from a book of speeches by Nelson Mandela, the icon of leadership who waged a life-long struggle against apartheid. He found the speeches inspirational. It helped him put his own potential challenges into a more balanced perspective.

Despite that dose of inspiration, a gnawing concern resurfaced from the dark recesses of his memory, prompting him to think about it all again.

Alpharetta, Georgia is where it all began fifty years earlier. Using his inherited home as security for a loan, Mortimer had borrowed to buy the small independent supermarket where he worked when its ailing owner decided to retire.

Within only a few months, Mortimer took on even more debt to open a second location for Multima Supermarkets. Similar expansion continued with subsequent acquisitions of additional stores every few months. Over those early years, he repeatedly took on bank loans to acquire new locations and then diligently paid them off with the cash each store generated.

Over time, his business grew from that single outlet in Alpharetta to become a dominant regional chain of more than one thousand super-markets selling food and general merchandise across the Southeast. In fact, Multima completely dominated its competition in the states of Georgia and Florida within a few years.

Mortimer had used a simple formula to grow his business so suc-cessfully. He acquired other small supermarkets, then made the previous owners and store employees his business partners by giving them equity shares in Multima Supermarkets.

In the following years, Mortimer became renowned for attracting quality people, then empowering them to manage their individual stores expertly. Because everyone owned shares in the company, Multima Supermarkets developed extremely loyal managers and employees who worked diligently to keep the company successful.

Gradually, other private investors became anxious to share in Mortimer's success. He responded by selectively issuing small numbers of non-voting shares to them. With non-voting shares, Mortimer was able to expand Multima's working capital very inexpensively. Most importantly, since the non-voting shareholders had no direct influence on operating deci-sions, he was also able to retain absolute control over his company's strate-gic direction. Using this unique equity device, he remained the company's largest single shareholder, with the most voting power, for many years.

Later, when Mortimer created Multima Financial Services, he decided to separate the supermarket and financial services businesses. He restructured to create Multima Corporation as a legal entity holding all the equity. This entity oversaw operations and wielded the corpora-tion's financial strength. In due course, it became publicly traded on the stock exchanges.

When that rare opportunity to acquire Wendal's financially unstable company surfaced a few years ago, Mortimer immediately spotted the value. He could visualize how the tiny company's technology expertise could help to order, move, and track goods far more efficiently than practices used at that time. He knew that owning it would create an enormous competitive cost advantage for Multima in all aspects of supermarket operations.

He remembered being less enthralled with the intricate machinations necessary to eventually acquire the struggling company. At that time, the economy was suffering a period of profound weakness. Business conditions were worryingly unstable with slow growth and high risk in most industries and countries, all at the same time. There was a shroud of caution. Most lenders lacked confidence, with doom and gloom the business mantra of the period. Meanwhile, like most other publicly traded companies, the value of Multima Corporation was depressed amidst light trading activity on the stock exchanges.

When Venture Capital Investments approached Mortimer with the opportunity to buy Wendal's logistics company, he tried to arrange a loan with all of his usual sources. Every one of those contacts said much the same thing: Multima seemed already stretched to its financial limit with current debt obligations, especially in such a precarious economic climate.

Simply stated, investment bankers were not prepared to make additional loans to Multima despite Mortimer's previous stellar experience repaying debts well ahead of required deadlines.

VCI proposed a solution. Its owners were prepared to provide the financing necessary to acquire Wendal's company. There was one prerequisite: Instead of lending money, they wanted to become shareholders in his thriving enterprise, receiving new Multima Corporation preferred shares in return. Additionally, those shares must equal fifteen percent of the company's voting shares, and Howard Knight must join the board of directors.

Such an injection of new capital represented an investment far greater than Mortimer needed to acquire Wendal's tiny company. After the purchase, there would be hundreds of millions of dollars sitting on the corporation's balance sheet. Clearly, VCI was much more interested in getting an equity stake in Multima than just financing a minuscule acquisition.

Mortimer thought he understood the negative implications of such action. It would dilute the value of Multima shares for all existing preferred shareholders, himself included. Perhaps more importantly, he'd take on a powerful new partner who would have an equal say in the business direction. VCI would hold precisely the same level of ownership and voting control as Mortimer.

For several weeks, John George labored over that decision with multiple sleepless nights and careful deliberations by day. He knew this arrangement could have a profound impact on his latitude to make subsequent decisions. He knew about the checkered business reputation of VCI, and its tendency to support management for only as long as performance was above reproach.

He also knew an opportunity to buy a technology company like Wendal's would occur very rarely. The business media idolized young Randall as the technology genius of his generation. Those miniature GPS tracking devices, sophisticated software, and a network of satellites certainly appealed to him.

Countering his concerns about VCI were a lot of positives. With the added cash, his company would have a bullet-proof balance sheet. Plus, he knew the secret of success with supermarkets was to keep costs as low as possible with efficient storage and shipping, lightning-fast inventory turnover, and miserly purchasing policies.

After all the thought and analysis, he became confident he could contain any VCI aggressiveness with his superior management skills and ability to consistently grow profits. That should satisfy any shareholder. He decided to take the plunge. He allowed Venture Capital Investments to become a full partner in Multima and used part of its investment to buy Wendal Randall's struggling company and create Multima Logistics.

In the years since, the business accomplished everything Mortimer had hoped. VCI had been a docile and mainly silent partner. The strategy achieved all his established goals, and Multima Supermarkets was now the undisputed leader in the Southeast, with its massive inventories turning over more than twenty times per year!

———————————

There had been challenges over the years, and occasionally he'd heard gossip about VCI and its sources of cash, but he felt his decision a decade ago had stood the test of time. Now, it appeared his relationship with VCI might be tested severely. Perhaps it would even undergo a profound change. Regardless, with a quiet confidence and resolute clarity of purpose, John George Mortimer closed his eyes and promptly fell into a deep, energizing sleep.

SIXTY-TWO

Wendal Randall could not believe the horror of the past twelve hours. In just a few moments, it would be midnight and once again, he was confined against his will.

During the three-hour flight from New York, he had asked the pilots to arrange ground transportation in Miami and a black limousine was waiting in the private jet section of Miami International Airport. The luxury stretch limo first seemed more pretentious than Wendal typically used. Nevertheless, he felt no concerns as the well-dressed driver opened a door, greeted them, and politely shepherded both passengers into its cavernous rear compartment.

Conversation between Wendal and Frau Schäffer remained very limited up to that point. He was still not at all comfortable with the idea of a new 'life partner', even if this arrangement was only temporary. Klaudia Schäffer appeared to sense the wisdom of not disrupting his thoughts.

Wendal was somewhat relaxed for the first few minutes of the ride as he stretched out his legs and rested his still exhausted body. He even considered trying to squeeze in a short nap during the forty-five-minute drive to his home in trendy Coconut Grove. However, when the limousine suddenly veered off the expressway and onto an exit for a secondary route still near the airport, Wendal's interest piqued.

"Why are we leaving the highway?" he asked the driver. To his complete astonishment, the glass partition suddenly snapped closed and locked. Wendal heard the door locks activate with a definite 'thunk'.

The driver displayed a badge and glanced through the rear-view mirror. Wendal leaned forward to read the inscription. Federal Bureau of Investigation. He glanced at Frau Schäffer, who apparently felt the same terror he was experiencing. The color drained from her face, and she became a pale and panicked shade of white. Their eyes met briefly. Her expression projected confusion and fear, and Wendal expected it was a mirror image of his own.

"Do you see any way to escape?" he whispered a few moments later.

"Impossible," Frau Schäffer responded in a muffled voice. "We're traveling about fifty miles per hour. We're in the middle of a major three-lane road. Even if we could find a way to unlock the doors, we'd be killed if we tried to jump out."

"Watch the traffic signals," he said after a few more minutes. "He never has to stop. As we approach intersections, red lights turn green just before we arrive."

Before she could respond, the driver suddenly veered into a parking lot, tires squealing in protest. In fact, they barely slowed until they reached the end of that building. There, the driver stopped abruptly in front of a large metal door.

The door sprung open, and several armed men immediately swarmed out. A dozen quickly surrounded them, all shouting orders and pointing powerful weapons at the rear section of the car. They commanded Wendal and Frau Schäffer to get out, keeping their arms above their heads, and without making any sudden movements.

Their captors roughly cuffed their hands behind their backs and guided them by tightly grasping one arm. They led Wendal to a small room on the right side of the entrance. Frau Schäffer went in another direction. Wendal had not seen her since, and the past few hours seemed hauntingly similar to his confinement in Haarlem only a couple days earlier. This time, there was no explanation given.

Instead, there were unending questions. Hour after hour, they asked about his trip to Europe, his discussions with Technologie Bergmann, and his weekend in Amsterdam. The questions never seemed to stop. Multiple interrogators rotated in and out of the room. Over and over again, they asked similar questions, with only a slight nuance of difference. In fact, many didn't make sense to Wendal at all.

Continuously, he protested that he had rights as an American citizen, he was entitled to make a call, and he had a right to legal counsel. Every time, an interrogator gave the same terse reply. "This is a matter of national security. You have the rights we choose to give you."

A few minutes had elapsed since they last came to interrogate him. They freed his hands and he managed to eat some of the unappetizing food they brought. It didn't ease his exhaustion at all. Jetlag, stress, and the ill effects of his weekend confinement in the Netherlands all left him physically spent. Tears welled up in his eyes. Disconnected thoughts darted in all directions. His body started to feel intensely real physical pain. At that point, he had some sort of breakdown and lost all self-control.

Screaming in anguish, with tears blurring his vision and pain muddling his judgment, Wendal violently banged his fists on the door that held him prisoner. He continued to shout, cry, scream, and repeatedly strike the door until his hands were bruised and bleeding. Then, he kicked the door incessantly until his feet were also battered.

After he collapsed in a heap on the floor, five of his captors warily entered the room. Then, they circled him menacingly. On a signal, they pounced all at once to restrain him on the floor and roughly wrap him into a nylon device to keep him stationary and immobile. To protect him from further injuries to himself during this meltdown, one had muttered angrily.

They were no longer polite and courteous. One in rigid black boots stepped hard on Wendal's hand during the restraining process, audibly breaking bones in his fingers. When he cried out in shock and pain, another man punched him in the stomach so forcefully that he momentarily lost all sense of his surroundings. Satisfied, the men left him lying on the concrete floor, motionless.

As he gradually regained his composure, he no longer knew how many times over the past five days he had experienced such a feeling of complete and abject hopelessness. Each time it intensified. Restrained, imprisoned, and unable to communicate with anyone, he felt an isolation that was total as his tears continued to flow unabated.

SIXTY-THREE

A Multima Corporation headquarters' conference room, Fort Myers.
March 9, 2016

John George Mortimer strode confidently into the spacious conference room precisely twelve minutes before the scheduled nine o'clock meeting. He smiled, quickly surveyed the twenty-three other people waiting for him, and began his ritual tour around the gathering. He greeted each person with a warm handshake, a grin, a pleasant greeting, and a brief personal comment.

He spent thirty seconds with each. He didn't need a watch to keep track of the time; this routine was so practiced and polished, he could comfortably work the room with grace and ease. He felt penetrating observation from every person. He could sense each try to assess his current condition and seek any indication of reduced leadership capacity.

The scrutiny did not concern him at all. A man comfortable in his own skin, John George came to this meeting prepared to play all the cards in his hand. With the demeanor of an experienced poker player, his facial expressions and body language conveyed no more information than he was prepared to reveal.

He completed his greetings at nine o'clock sharp, took his seat at the head of the table, and called the meeting to order. Like many other chief executive officers, he was not only Multima's CEO; he also chaired the board of directors.

After standard opening formalities, he outlined the primary purpose of their meeting. "We are here to have a discussion about my leadership of the company," he acknowledged calmly. "And be assured you'll have all the time you need to discuss that subject after we listen to presentations from each operating division. If we deal with our business in that order, you'll be able to assess the current level of preparedness of each of them. Further, I expect these presentations about game changer projects to showcase the strengths and management skills of our second-tier management in each business unit.

"I hope you'll assess how well each management team is prepared to manage in the future. This will be particularly crucial should you

255

decide to promote a current leader to the position of chief executive officer, and that individual is no longer there to lead the business unit directly on a day-to-day basis.

"I think this order of discussion will help you to make the right decisions about both my leadership and my possible successor using your astute assessment of the presentations and your usual sound business judgment," John George said with a wry smile as he bent his head and looked over the top of his eyeglasses.

He asked if there was general agreement with that process. Several heads first glanced towards Howard Knight, who nodded, before they mimicked his gesture of acceptance.

"You've no doubt noticed that Wendal Randall hasn't arrived yet," he resumed. "We don't yet know the reason for this delay, but his team expects him to be here shortly. So here's the order we'll use this morning. Multima Supermarkets will start, followed by Financial Services. Logistics will make the final presentation. By then, hopefully, Wendal will be here to join them."

Several heads again glanced in Howard Knight's direction as Mortimer made his opening narrative. Knight continued to appear confident, relaxed, and completely focused on the chair's comments.

Mortimer finished his opening remarks by reminding presenters they would have thirty minutes to complete their presentations. He alerted directors that they would also have thirty minutes for questions and answers. In conclusion, he asked all participants to respect those parameters as he called for Suzanne Simpson to begin.

One of Suzanne's team members quickly circled the large table, distributing paper copies of Multima Supermarkets' presentation to each director, while Suzanne moved to the front of the room with her typical grace and self-assurance. Every eye followed her.

Right away, she announced the Multima Supermarkets divergence from Mortimer's directive for a single game changer project. "We varied from this parameter for only one reason: current market conditions demand that we undertake two significant changes to achieve a goal of doubling Multima profits during the coming five years. Our presentation will expand on that," she told them.

She then introduced the three presenters: Heather Strong, financial operations leader; Gordon Goodfellow, marketing leader; and Jeremy Front, the store operations leader. As Strong walked to the podium, Suzanne reminded directors that they were familiar with each of these people. She thought it unnecessary to use valuable time to highlight their expertise and long, successful backgrounds with Multima Supermarkets.

For the next twenty-five minutes, each of the presenters eloquently described their projects with confidence and enthusiasm. Each had previously presented to this board, and they demonstrated comfort with both the message and the opportunity to sell it to these powerful executives. Charts, graphs, and data supporting their recommendations were clear, concise, and conservative. Details included in their paper handout were comprehensive, well organized, and easy to follow.

Heather Strong outlined the planned acquisition in detail, including three funding options for the board to consider. She advised that investment bankers had already made discreet inquiries to the current owner. Their takeover target was receptive to an offer, the implied price range appeared acceptable, and the present owner had only one prerequisite. Multima Supermarkets must provide an attractive job, in a senior role, for the owner's son. If this could be achieved, together with the financial parameters tentatively outlined, their offer would be accepted. She believed such a requirement was both reasonable and manageable.

Gordon Goodfellow outlined their plan to refocus Multima Supermarket's orientation towards healthier food choices. His presentation included a description of the capital budgets necessary to make such changes, persuasive feedback from the focus groups, and other compelling new market research. He finished by reviewing a five-year business plan that explained how the current supermarkets business would grow, and ended with the anticipated bottom-line profits.

Jeremy Front presented a cogent argument for implementing both projects at the same time. He demonstrated expense synergies that would occur in warehousing and logistics. He outlined gradual purchasing efficiencies the team would achieve, with both existing Multima supermarkets and those of the new regional big-box retailer. He underscored the proven offshore buying expertise within their new acquisition. Most compelling of all, he revealed expansion plans for both retail channels during the coming five years to drive desired top-line sales growth and bottom-line profits.

Suzanne concluded their presentation with a brief three-minute summary asking for approval of the board of directors to move forward immediately.

Then she stunned everyone in the room. She wanted them to know that if the board ultimately decided to make a management change, they should not consider her for the role of CEO.

Instead, she preferred to continue leading Multima Supermarkets. During the coming few years, her division would undergo a dramatic transformation should the board approve her recommendations. She argued that she would make her most useful contribution to Multima's success right where she was.

Assembled directors were shocked with this selfless determination to do what she thought was best for the company at the expense of possible personal advancement. So stunned, in fact, they almost missed Suzanne's added recommendation that the board should approve her choice to become vice president and general manager of the acquired big-box retailer—Gordon Goodfellow. She also stated her desire to replace Gordon with Phil Archer, the highly capable son of the owner at their targeted big-box retailer.

She then checked her watch, confirmed that her team had used exactly twenty-nine minutes, and welcomed questions from the board.

There was a short pause of uncomfortable silence and shuffling of papers immediately after her invitation. It seemed the directors could not determine exactly where they should start to process the mountain of information just imparted. They also had to cope with genuine shock.

One of their three potential candidates to replace Mortimer had expressed her preference to *not* be considered for the influential role as CEO for one of America's largest companies! At least, not to be considered right now, one had whispered.

Once questions started, the board did not disappoint. Seven independent directors posed thoughtful and challenging questions reflecting their individual areas of expertise. Suzanne's team members handled issues according to their field of responsibility and capably addressed them.

There were no other surprises. To John George Mortimer, the mood of the room seemed acceptably positive as he called for a fifteen-minute break. During that short time, the room was abuzz with conversation about Multima Supermarkets' presentation. Directors spoke with each other about the benefits to Multima or asked further questions of Suzanne's team privately. He remained seated at the head of the table and surveyed the room with quiet satisfaction.

SIXTY-FOUR

Multima Corporation headquarters.
Morning, March 9, 2016

There was a small, unused office just down the hall from the large conference room attached to John George Mortimer's comfortable office. Reserved for members of the board when they visited, this was a quiet area where high-powered executives could make private calls. Howard Knight often used that room, but not this morning.

The calls he needed to make were too sensitive for even a private office. Instead, he preferred to step outside the building into the great outdoors. It was harder to record conversations with the background noise, especially in a downtown area near the river. He feared that Multima's corporate security department might have both the technology and motivation to pry into his private conversations.

He made three quick calls. All concerned the missing Wendal Randall, and all attempts were futile. None of his usual sources had been able to determine the whereabouts of the executive, and there were no traces of either him or Klaudia Schäffer since the time they had left the airport in a black stretch limousine. There was one added cause for increased concern.

A source in Miami had determined the limousine service first contacted to meet the passengers had subsequently received a call to cancel their pick-up. That company had not sent a driver to the airport. Therefore, some other unidentified limousine had met them. Neither Randall nor Schäffer had been able to make calls with their cell phones from the aircraft. Therefore, neither the request for a limousine nor a cancellation of that order came from either of them, he deduced. This glaring gap raised red flags.

Who canceled the original limousine? Who intercepted his passengers? More importantly, what did this curious turn of events mean for him? Perplexed, he made two additional calls before he rejoined the gathering in the conference room. One was to his assistant in New York, the other to a long-time friend with a small office on the perimeter of Palm Beach International Airport in West Palm Beach.

Still alarmed that Wendal had not yet been located, Knight returned to the meeting room where all participants were back in their seats and ready for the next presentation. They were all familiar with Mortimer's legendary penchant for punctual starts and finishes, with a demanding pace in between.

Making no preamble, John George invited Multima Financial Services to deliver the next game changer project overview. James Fitzgerald was already standing at the opposite end of the table with a projector illuminating the first slide of his presentation. Aides had distributed paper copies during the break, and directors were leafing through them as he introduced his team.

James didn't usually bring direct reports with him to board meetings. It was an occasional practice rather than routine. He also was aware some directors didn't view his subordinates with admiration. Apparently, some perceived them as typical finance executives, whatever that meant.

He used his introduction to highlight their credentials—their solid educations, long experience, and exceptional records of generating large, low-risk profits for Multima shareholders. Satisfied, he turned over the presentation to Douglas Whitfield.

He and his colleagues delivered a masterful performance. Their several days of preparation and rehearsal became apparent as they held their audience enthralled for the entire remaining twenty-six minutes. Normally mundane fiscal data, risk assessment information, and financial numbers seemed to come alive as the speakers delivered their message with enthusiasm, precision, and even a little humor.

Within minutes, directors stopped leafing through their paper copies of the presentation and devoted full attention to Whitfield and his team. Their proposal to create a new business unit to finance home mortgages was compelling. Directors' body language visibly shifted from initial skepticism to fully engaged curiosity, and then keen interest. Much of this occurred during Whitfield's first few minutes. His colleagues built on his initial impressive oratory. They added persuasive, fact-packed supporting arguments to solidify the directors' growing interest and discernible support for their project.

When the presentation concluded, there was a deluge of inquiries as directors sought to validate their understanding and test assumptions. In fact, interest was so high, Mortimer decided to let the question and answer period run a little longer than the allotted time. He knew well that permitting a few more questions at that stage, while data was fresh in people's minds, could save considerable discussion when it came time to vote on a proposal.

Moments later, John George would regret that decision. Just when he was ready to close the question period, one director asked about the bench strength of Fitzgerald's team to accomplish such an expansion. It was a soft question, one Fitzgerald would usually handle with ease.

Instead, to his amazement, James responded emphatically that his team bench strength was more than adequate to manage the expansion, even should he not be around to lead such an effort.

He didn't stop there. Should the director's question relate to the planned discussion about a potential successor to John George Mortimer, he wanted them to know that he also preferred they not include his name among potential candidates. A pall of silence gripped the room.

Again, several heads glanced towards Howard Knight, who still maintained a blank, neutral expression. Reading his personal feelings about this pronouncement was impossible. Without further comment, John George quickly concluded the question period, and again adjourned for a short break. Once more, the room was abuzz. This time, all conversations focused exclusively on their second potential CEO candidate's withdrawal from any consideration to succeed John George Mortimer.

Again, Howard Knight quickly left the conference room without comment, side discussions, or participation in any of the small group discussions. Meanwhile, directors sipped their second cups of coffee and compared personal reactions to this latest astounding turn of events.

For his second escape, Howard Knight took refuge in a black Mercedes-Benz limousine. The car's driver leaped from the vehicle when he finally noticed Knight's approach. He swiftly circled the car to open the rear passenger door, and then watched Knight slide into the rear compartment. The chauffeur returned, got into the luxury sedan, and started the air conditioning.

Knight asked the driver to close the sliding glass divider and pushed a speed-dial number on his smartphone as the window sealed shut. His dejected source in Miami had been unable to find any new information on the whereabouts of Wendal Randall or Klaudia Schäffer. He vowed to keep trying.

There was also a message from Knight's assistant displayed on the screen. After another press of a speed-dial number, his assistant responded almost instantly. He detected a tone of concern in her voice right away.

Moments earlier, she had received a call from an individual who claimed to be an agent for the Federal Bureau of Investigation. This man asked to speak with Howard Knight. When she replied that he was away from the office, the man inquired about his expected return. After she told him that he would probably return to his New York office tomorrow morning, the FBI man requested a meeting for eight o'clock.

Knight's assistant had taken some umbrage to him requesting a meeting at a particular time because Mr. Knight was such a busy executive. Apparently, the agent then became more assertive. He insisted she do two things: Contact Howard Knight immediately to confirm he would be available for a meeting at eight o'clock the next morning and then call back before noon to confirm the arrangements.

His manner had been polite enough, but firm and insistent. When the assistant inquired if she might advise Mr. Knight what the meeting concerned, the agent replied that it related to a hacking incident at Multima Supermarkets. When his assistant insisted Mr. Knight wouldn't possibly know about any hacking activity, the agent interrupted her. Tersely, he told her she should just confirm the meeting and do so before noon as he initially requested.

In a voice as calm and assuring as Knight could muster, he asked her to get back to the agent and let him know the time would be all right. She should also let him know that Knight doubted he could provide any useful information. However, he would be pleased to assist the FBI in any way possible.

Opening the limousine door as he ended the call, he realized his hands were shaking uncontrollably. Working to slow his heart rate and regain his composure as he stood up, Knight rechecked his tie, smoothed the front of his jacket and pants, and then slowly walked up the stairs to the large conference room.

With his usual precision, John George Mortimer reconvened the emergency meeting of the board of directors and made another observation that Wendal Randall had still not joined the meeting. He asked the Multima Logistics team if they were still prepared to present under the circumstances.

After a quick glance between Ricky Technori and Howard Knight, and Knight's barely detectable nod, the team leader affirmed they were ready.

Following the highly polished and carefully researched presentations of the earlier groups, the Multima Logistics effort paled in comparison. Perhaps team members were somewhat intimidated appearing before the board of directors. Wendal Randall had never deemed it necessary to invite other executive team members to board functions, so his direct reports were encountering these formidable business executives for the first time.

They were probably also apprehensive about presenting radical new concepts without the steadying influence of their leader. On the other hand, it might have been the extremely short amount of time allowed to prepare their project conclusions and presentation. Regardless, their thirty minutes of delivery was dreadful.

Individual presenters tried to make a good case for the automation of checkouts as originally conceived by Wendal. They worked equally hard to generate enthusiasm for that unique idea first articulated by the young systems engineer during their brainstorming meeting in Germany. Regardless, the dubious benefits of tracking each item individually in every Multima store using a razor-thin bar code did not resonate with their audience.

Each presenter became more tentative and uncertain. They repeatedly used words like 'might', 'maybe', 'could', and 'should' that lacked strong conviction and confidence. Their information lacked substance. Handout materials were meager, and supporting information was sparse.

To Mortimer, it was akin to a group of sheepish high school juniors reporting on a failed chemistry experiment. When the presentation concluded, at first there were no questions at all. Directors stared at or restlessly shuffled the useless handouts. After a moment or two of uncomfortable silence, Suzanne Simpson cleared her throat and turned towards John George to inquire if she might make a short comment rather than pose a question.

John George Mortimer agreed with a caveat; she should limit her comment to three minutes or less. Her face had become slightly pink as she listened to the presentation. He intended this time limitation as a subtle caution. She should tread carefully. Suzanne Simpson got the signal and delivered her scathing comment in less than one minute with an intonation that was calm, measured, and controlled.

"First, I want the board to know that this is the first time that I, or any of my direct reports, have heard anything about these projects proposed by Logistics. The technology sounds enthralling, and the presentation uses lots of impressive new terms. However, there has been no dialog with, or input from, Multima Supermarkets," she said as her eyes slowly looked around the table.

"I am not prepared to support any aspect of the proposals presented until we have a full and comprehensive discussion about assumptions used, the project costs and benefits, and any available market research. A fundamental value proposition is critical to assessing what impact such proposed notions might have on Multima Supermarkets' future.

"I'll add only a suggestion that the board of directors may want to delay consideration of these proposed projects until such conditions are satisfied," she ended.

The silence that followed enveloped the room. Even John George Mortimer was initially uncertain about the best course to follow. To his relief, an independent director suggested they follow Suzanne Simpson's recommendation. Defer both questions and discussion about the proposals until the two business units could meet and attempt to resolve their impasse.

With murmurs of agreement around the table, John George asked if that director would like to make her suggestion a formal motion. She did so. The board of directors voted, and there was unanimous agreement that consideration of the Multima Logistics project proposals should be deferred.

When Mortimer asked if there was consensus to discuss and vote on the remaining two division game changer proposals, Howard Knight immediately voiced an objection. It was worthwhile, even useful, to receive each of the presentations, he conceded, but in the event they ultimately decide to appoint a new CEO, would it be fair to saddle him or her with decisions of this board under the influence of the current chief executive officer?

Another director, one who tended to vote consistently with Howard Knight on the main issues, had a different suggestion. Perhaps the board should first shift the discussion to the primary purpose of the meeting and then decide later whether to vote on proposals from individual business divisions.

Without hesitation, Mortimer consented. Now would be an entirely appropriate time to address the issue of his leadership. He proposed that Alberto Ferer, as general counsel of the corporation and secretary of the board, chair the meeting while they discussed his leadership. Mortimer glanced around the room and saw signs of agreement. Even Howard Knight nodded.

Mortimer pointed out the rapidly approaching noon hour. He also declared that meeting participants who were not actually on the board must absent themselves from discussions about his leadership.

To satisfy both circumstances, he suggested his assistant make lunch arrangements for those who would not be present at the next stage of the meeting—perhaps an excellent restaurant on Fort Myers Beach. Directors would continue their meeting here, and sandwiches would arrive a little later. The business unit executives could rejoin the meeting once discussions about his leadership concluded, he declared.

Moments later, eleven senior leaders from the operating divisions were ushered to elevators, then whisked through the lobby to waiting limousines like middle school students dismissed from class. They were chauffeured to an excellent restaurant overlooking the Gulf of Mexico.

Without further ceremony, John George ceded the chair to Alberto Ferer, with an admonition that proceedings should start immediately.

SIXTY-FIVE

In a conference room at Multima Corporation headquarters.
March 9, 2016

Alberto Ferer was clearly uncomfortable with the role into which he had been thrust. First, it was completely uncharted water. In his entire career with Multima, there had never been a hint of dissatisfaction with John George Mortimer or his leadership. Rather, the exact opposite had been true throughout his tenure with the corporation.

Mortimer was a respected leader, admired, and genuinely liked by the majority of people with whom he made contact. Peers, subordinates, customers, suppliers, and even government officials thought highly of him and frequently heaped praise on him. That Alberto Ferer should chair a session that might depose the legendary business leader was abhorrent to him.

However, as an attorney, he respected due process. Some directors undoubtedly sought retribution for Mortimer's failure to notify the board about his cancer surgery. Others were more upset with his absence during crises that resulted in unwanted negative publicity. Of course, the twenty percent drop in Multima's market capitalization during the past few days had further compounded sentiments.

Diplomatically, Alberto asked the board of directors who among them might like to start the discussion. Cliff Williams, an independent director from Chicago, expressed concern about undertaking discussion of such importance at that juncture. He reminded directors that two of the three leading candidates for the CEO position had already withdrawn their names from consideration, and the third was missing.

Williams could not support any immediate nomination of Wendal Randall for the job. Randall hadn't made it to the meeting, and his current whereabouts were unclear. Maybe it would be better for the board to entertain a motion to support the current CEO. After all, John George had already announced his intention to step aside in less than six months.

Howard Knight immediately interjected. "Of course, it's appropriate to discuss leadership," he blustered. "The shareholders demand it. Multima's share values have plummeted under the current leadership,

266

and we have no way to calculate how much more the value might drop without decisive action."

"We have three clear options," he said. "We can discuss the contentious issues and perhaps vote to support the current CEO. The board might decide to remove the current CEO and name a replacement immediately. Or, we might decide to terminate the current CEO, and then name his replacement at some time in the future.

"I believe we have a fiducial responsibility to have a discussion. And, we have at least a moral and maybe a legal obligation to vote on one of those three motions," he added emphatically.

There were enough heads nodding and murmurs of agreement that Alberto Ferer agreed to proceed. Immediately after winning the argument to move forward, Knight again interjected.

"I don't think it appropriate for the CEO to be in the conference room while such discussion and voting are taking place," he thundered.

Ferer was almost panic-stricken by the request. Acceptance of Knight's proposal immediately reduced support for John George by one vote. Should the decision be a close one, such a tactic might become the decisive factor to remove Mortimer from his role as CEO of the company he founded.

Mortimer instantly recognized Ferer's discomfort. He quietly said he would accept that suggestion and withdraw to his office during the discussion and vote. He wanted directors to make their decision in the best interests of the shareholders. Further, he didn't want it ever suggested that he stifled discussion or thwarted the will of the board. Nonetheless, he wanted to make a couple of comments first.

Without hesitation, he took command of the room. Looking around slowly and deliberately, he made eye contact with each director and maintained a connection for some seconds.

Without the benefits of notes or presentation aids, he spoke for about five minutes. He explained his motivation for withholding information about his health from the board. He apologized, simply and sincerely, for all discomfort and embarrassment this caused for the directors and the management team. He acknowledged it was not the right decision. He expressed regret for the reduction in Multima market value that resulted and pledged to do everything possible to regain the faith and support of shareholders and the board.

He took only a few seconds to deal with his health. The surgery had been successful, and the cancer was gone. There would be further treatments, and his appearance might deteriorate for some time. He would experience nausea some days during the few weeks of treatment, and other days he might not feel the same passion for his job. However, his doctors assured him there would be no adverse impact on his mental health, and it would require only limited time away from work. Moreover, the prognosis for a cancer-free life for years to come was excellent.

With that, he urged members of the board to vote with their consciences. He assured them he would respect their decision and accept the consequences. His final comment was directed to Alberto Ferer, a request to let him know when they'd reached a decision. Until then, he would be working in his office. He walked purposefully from the room, his head held high and shoulders confidently squared.

As though on cue, when the door closed behind Mortimer, one of the board members who frequently voted with Knight's motions launched into a ten-minute diatribe. He vehemently denounced John George Mortimer for his lack of foresight, lack of consideration for shareholders, and disrespect for the board. Clever words from the CEO now were not enough, he proclaimed. The board should remove this arrogant CEO immediately and replace him with one with more respect for shareholders.

That initial salvo caused intense debate. Alberto Ferer kept score of the positions on a small piece of paper. No other director spoke as passionately as the first, nor was there another as vindictive in condemnation. Still, there was clearly broad support for the movement to oust John George.

In fact, tallies for the opposing views were precariously close. Some sought his removal, while others were more respectful of the enormous wealth he had created for shareholders over his career. One director even pointed out the tremendous contributions Mortimer had made to his country. As Ferer worked his way around the table, one speaker at a time, it became apparent the outcome of a vote would be extremely close.

During those discussions, a secretary slipped into the room, walking almost on tiptoes to maintain a respectful silence. She made her way to Alberto Ferer's place at the head of the table. There, she put a single sheet of paper on the table and waited for his nod of acknowledgment before she left.

Alberto would be the last to speak, if he should speak at all in his role as acting chair, and most of those around the table expected his loyalty to Mortimer. Accordingly, all eyes fell on the second last to speak—Howard Knight.

Undoubtedly, he had been keeping score of the comments as well. Before he started, he would be aware he had only seven votes, including his own and that would not deliver the two-thirds majority required by corporation bylaws to depose John George Mortimer.

Alberto Ferer waited for Howard Knight to reveal what other cards he might have. Other directors also appeared tense, almost as though holding their breath as they waited. Knight surprised them all.

He changed his tack altogether. They anticipated a passionate appeal on behalf of shareholders. Instead, Knight suggested it might actually be better to have some more discussion about a potential CEO of the company, in the event they should decide to remove Mortimer. Ferer was reluctant to let Knight control the agenda in such an obvious way. However, he was equally unwilling to alienate an extremely powerful preferred shareholder on a point of order. Consequently, he permitted the new diversion.

Almost immediately, another member of the board who often voted with Howard Knight, a woman this time, launched into passionate support of Wendal Randall. "It is indeed unfortunate Wendal isn't here to promote his interests today, but I'm certain there must be a good reason for his absence."

Without pausing for even a second, she also repeated the favorite mantra of American business media. "Wendal is perhaps the preeminent technology genius of our generation. He has the potential to revolutionize the entire business world. This is a point in time with a rare opportunity for us, an opportunity to promote an extraordinary individual who can radically improve Multima businesses and maybe even create new ones."

Before other members of the board could comment, Alberto gravely looked around the room. Then, in an unusually hushed voice, Ferer informed the directors, "Wendal Randall can no longer be considered a candidate for any senior position at Multima."

Howard Knight was the first to react, almost shouting, "What are you talking about?" Everyone else voiced some opinion or comments, some derisively, creating a sudden cacophony of noise that drowned Alberto out. Others raised their arms in gestures of frustration or waves of dismissal. Ferer was forced to raise both arms in a gesture of surrender to get their attention and return to quiet.

"I'm sorry to advise you that just moments ago I received a message from our chief of corporate security," he resumed. "Wendal is currently in the custody of the Federal Bureau of Investigation. There's more. They've charged him with interstate theft of computer data and several other charges related to hacking Multima Supermarkets' computer system. He's also a person of interest in the disappearance of an employee who was likewise implicated.

"Further, he's facing charges of harboring a fugitive from the law. Apparently, Wendal helped a woman wanted by Interpol, the international police agency, to enter the country using a false identity and forged documents. That woman has several arrest warrants outstanding for her alleged involvement in an extensive European human trafficking ring.

"It would be impossible to consider Wendal Randall for the position of CEO while he's facing such serious charges. Also, should one of those charges be proven in court, any conviction would exclude Randall from any executive position at Multima for the rest of his life."

The conference room fell eerily quiet. No one at all commented. Directors of the board exhibited all the physical characteristics of people experiencing extreme shock. Slowly, heads in the room turned towards Howard Knight. The blood had drained from his face, and it appeared the new information was as much a surprise to him as to everyone else. When he realized the attention now focused on him, he tried to recover.

"Certainly, this is an extreme disappointment. It's shocking to see such a promising executive face such severe upheaval in his personal life. We can only hope there has been some tragic mistake, and pray Wendal will be found not guilty of these charges," he said. Then he provided yet another unexpected jolt to the meeting.

"It looks like none of the current business division leaders can be considered for the position. There's also general agreement that our current CEO is not performing satisfactorily. Perhaps we should instead think about an executive holding a staff position at Multima. Someone like Wilma Willingsworth, our highly respected chief financial officer."

Again, there was total silence. The group of high-powered executives tried desperately to process both the unsettling news about Wendal Randall and the new, but intriguing, twist in the machinations of leadership change Howard Knight was attempting to engineer.

Heads shifted towards Wilma Willingsworth. When she looked around, she realized all eyes in the room focused on her. Stunned by both Knight's suggestion and the unusual attention, she was speechless. Alberto Ferer recognized her discomfort and proposed another break from their discussions.

SIXTY-SIX

A large corner office at Multima Corporation headquarters.
March 9, 2016

When she started to recover from the shock of Knight's suggestion, Wilma Willingsworth knew the most beneficial thing to do during the coffee break was chat informally with other members of the board of directors. That's probably what most men would do. It would be an opportunity for the directors to get more comfortable with her, and a chance to gauge what level of support she might have before making a decision.

Wilma knew her limitations well. One was difficulty making major decisions under pressure. As a result, she was more than a little uncomfortable with the current situation. Slow, analytical, and methodical decisions were much more within her comfort zone.

She politely extricated herself from the first director to approach her, just as the break began. She quickly invented an excuse to return to her office and strode from the room. Then, for a few moments, she stood by an enormous plate-glass window, gazed out at the Caloosahatchee River, and contemplated.

The position of chief executive officer at an enterprise like Multima Corporation would be the fulfillment of a life-long ambition. One of the largest companies in America, with high public visibility, Multima had also been one of America's most respected names until the last few weeks of turmoil. The latest episode with Wendal Randall would paint a further dark stain on the corporation's reputation and public image. Even so, Wilma supposed that would fade with time and careful nurturing of the company's many attributes.

A single mother of three, the result of a bitter divorce fifteen years earlier, she was entirely responsible for her family. Raising her boys had been a chore. They had now all finished their studies with postgraduate degrees from prestigious universities, but she still carried an uncomfortable load of personal debt.

Even with a good salary as CFO at Multima, Wilma had found it necessary to borrow large amounts to finance their expensive tuitions and housing at the finest colleges in America. Her salary as a CEO would certainly be higher, and would probably help her to escape the weight of that debt much more quickly.

She wasn't getting any younger. If she was eventually to become a CEO of any corporation, it probably had to occur within the next two or three years. Otherwise, most companies would consider her past her prime.

Perhaps the most convincing reason to accept the CEO position, should it actually be offered, would be as an example to other women. She could then prove that it really was possible to break through the infamous glass ceiling to achieve a pinnacle of leadership success in American business.

There were also concerns. This entire emergency meeting of the board did not feel right. Of course, she had an intense loyalty to John George Mortimer. Perhaps that contributed to her apprehension. She was also ill at ease with the apparent objective of replacing him. Termination for his error in judgment just didn't seem to pass the smell test. The whole series of events surrounding his illness didn't seem critical enough to warrant such drastic consequences as removal from office.

Sure, cancer is dangerous. Several of her friends and family had dealt with breast cancer. While it was an insidious disease, none of them had experienced any reduction in mental capacity. Most had experienced physical discomfort and some limitations for relatively short periods. In fact, recovery seemed almost predictable with today's technology and knowledge.

She was especially uncomfortable with the extremes to which some directors, especially Howard Knight, appeared capable of going to achieve their goal. Wilma had always harbored some unexplained unease when she was around Knight. Events of the past days and hours further reinforced that discomfort.

Perhaps the deciding factor in her quick assessment was significant doubt about Knight's ability to make it all happen. A week earlier, there may have been a chance. However, with events of the past few days, she could not visualize any scenario under which Knight could do it. Her decision made, she left the privacy of her office and strode with newfound confidence towards the conference room. If offered the position of CEO of Multima Corporation, she would decline.

SIXTY-SEVEN

A large conference room at Multima Corporation headquarters.
March 9, 2016

As soon as Wilma Willingsworth walked back into the room, Howard Knight sensed that he had lost her support. Her failure to make eye contact told him everything. Her more confident demeanor conveyed a suggestion that something had changed her mind during those few moments away. He chose not to risk a rejection.

Instead, he elected to change tactics one more time and felt a brief sense of satisfaction as he observed an almost undetectable twitch of Ferer's lips. He was feeling some pressure. That was good. Mistakes occur more often when people feel pressure, and it might help Knight's mission should Ferer make a mistake or two during the next crucial phase. He proposed another point of discussion as soon as Ferer reconvened the meeting. He laid out his thoughts with candor, detail, and simplicity.

"It might not be possible for two-thirds of us to agree on removal of the current CEO," he started. This recognition of the obvious seemed to refresh and energize a few directors. Knight noticed a shifting of postures, keen focus on him, and attention to the message he was about to impart.

"Bear with me as we review a few important details about Multima's ownership structure. Of course, there are two classes of voting shares. Class 'A' shares traded on the New York stock exchange determine virtually all issues that need shareholder approval. These are the shares everyone pays attention to, and it's the value of this class that dropped so dramatically these past few days.

"We also have 'B' class preference shares, held by only a few investors. In fact, only one hundred thousand of those shares have been issued, each with a fixed value of one hundred thousand dollars. Those voting 'B' shares have a combined value of ten billion dollars. That's about as much as all the class 'A' shares together.

"John George Mortimer owns fifteen thousand class 'B' preference shares. VCI holds another fifteen thousand. Forty-three other investors own the remaining seventy thousand shares," he explained. He thought

it crucial to remind the board of this important distinction because corporate bylaws gave extraordinary power to preferred 'B' shares.

"To remove a senior officer like Mortimer, it takes a board majority
of two-thirds. However, should only a simple majority of the board combined with a simple majority of class 'B' shareholders vote to remove the
CEO, a decision would become legal and binding upon the corporation."

At that point, he turned to Alberto Ferer and asked him to
concur with that important legal distinction. Ferer nodded, and
Knight continued.

"I anticipated that we might fall short of a two-thirds majority.
Proactively, I've contacted most of the preferred shareholders. I wanted
to know how they would vote, should there be only a simple majority of
directors favoring an ouster, and not two-thirds.

"I can report that 'B' shareholders with 50,544 shares are prepared
to support the removal of John George Mortimer from the position of
CEO. That's more than fifty percent of the 'B' shares outstanding." He
paused for dramatic effect.

There were quiet murmurs around the table. Directors realized
Knight need only call for a vote. Should a majority favor Mortimer's
removal, even without the mandatory two-thirds, Knight could demand
a vote among preferred class 'B' shareholders. It appeared that he could
win a simple majority in each scenario.

Initially, there was a mixed reaction around the table as some board
members sensed victory, others defeat, at precisely the same moment and
with varying degrees of intensity. Alberto Ferer calmly interjected that
everyone should wait just a minute before jumping to any conclusions. He
confirmed the legal distinction Howard Knight shared was accurate, and
the legal effect of those votes correct as Knight described them.

"However, there's one significant error with those calculations and
conclusions," Ferer said. "Actually, there are *not* one hundred thousand
preferred class 'B' shares outstanding. In fact, the correct number is one
hundred and eighteen thousand.

"Recently, some shares of a Canadian subsidiary were converted
into Multima class 'B' shares, as required by its corporate bylaws. When
that company was wound up, all shares were exchanged for class 'B' preferred shares. As a result, the total 'B' shares now owned by John George
Mortimer is thirty-three thousand," he said. Such a development defied
belief. For the second time that day, Howard Knight blanched in panic.

Although they had vetted the idea with two specialists, one in
Canada the other in New York, Alberto Ferer knew their scheme might

not be bullet-proof. He realized they might be on tenuous legal ground, even as he announced the correct current number of class 'B' preferred shares.

Howard Knight quickly regained his composure and reacted vehemently. He vociferously challenged the accuracy of Ferer's claim, while wildly waving around a copy of the corporation's last annual report.

"There's absolutely no mention of shares convertible to preferred 'B' shares in this report or in any Securities Exchange filings," he blustered.

Wilma Willingsworth leaped to Ferer's aid and chose her words judiciously. "Actually, there are notes about it in the financial statements. I draw your attention to the Notes section of the annual report, specifically regarding financial statements number thirty-one, section A, subsection xvi, paragraph ii. There we refer to 'goodwill' related to the acquisition of Countrywide Stores. The note explains the creation of a numbered subsidiary company as part of that purchase.

"I can confirm that personal funds from John George Mortimer provided the capital for that numbered company, which subsequently loaned funds to Multima to acquire Countrywide Stores," she explained with precise attention to detail.

"The note to the financial statements refers readers to the bylaws of that numbered subsidiary company," she pointed out. "Those bylaws explain that shares in the numbered subsidiary were all issued to a private Canadian citizen for the lifetime of that individual. Title to those shares reverted to the numbered Canadian subsidiary with the death of that person."

Wilma Willingsworth read the final paragraph of the note. "Upon death, title to these shares will revert to 976531 (Ontario) Holdings Inc. Said corporation will then cease to exist, and all shares will automatically convert to preferred class 'B' shares in Multima Corporation, retiring all debts to John George Mortimer."

Initially, several directors didn't grasp the legal jargon. One of them begged her to explain the financial statements' notations in plain English. With her most authoritarian body language, Wilma Willingsworth replied.

"To finance the purchase of Countrywide stores, John George Mortimer transferred most of his personal wealth to the Canadian numbered company. That company's only purpose was to pay the shareholders of Countrywide Stores, with a relatively small balance of cash left in the company to fund ongoing obligations. That remaining money paid a monthly dividend of three thousand dollars per month to a Canadian citizen for her lifetime. All the shares in a second numbered company were issued in that person's name.

"When she died, all shares reverted to the numbered Canadian company owned entirely by John George Mortimer. Those shares then converted automatically to preferred class 'B' shares. Four shares in the numbered company became one class 'B' share in Multima Corporation. These financial transactions all transpired before our initial public offering. All were legal, and all have been referenced in financial statement notes since the first filing of documents with the SEC," she concluded.

Alberto Ferer couldn't resist looking towards Howard Knight as the stark realization started to set in. During the negotiations to inject capital in Multima Corporation ten years earlier, Knight had insisted that VCI receive precisely fifteen thousand 'B' preferred shares. His strategy was to get precisely equal voting positions. Somehow, he had missed the significance of the deeply buried notations about those numbered Canadian companies. Knight failed to realize that Mortimer's effective control of the company was more than double what he had revealed publicly.

Legally, and consistent with accounting regulations in both countries, John George had structured a series of Canadian numbered companies to camouflage the true extent of his ultimate personal financial holdings in Multima Corporation. On a day-to-day basis, such greater influence had no effect. The only times such a larger holding might impact Multima would be upon the death of John George Mortimer or an attempt to depose him.

Members of the board turned to Howard Knight as each gradually realized his efforts to replace Mortimer had now become futile. Mortimer's hand in this high-stakes battle of power was stronger by far.

Knight regained his composure as quickly as was possible under such dire circumstances. He cheerfully requested another short break. Perhaps it would be a good time to enjoy those just-arrived sandwiches, he suggested.

SIXTY-EIGHT

Inside a limousine headed to Page Field, Fort Myers.
Afternoon, March 9, 2016

This time, Howard Knight carried his laptop with him as he left the conference room, marched to the elevator, and traveled to the ground floor seeking refuge in the parking lot outside. He realized he was not thinking as clearly as he would like.

His hands were again trembling terribly. He was nauseated. His knees were shaking and he felt physically weak. He cursed the bright Florida sun glaring down from its afternoon peak and shaded his eyes as he rushed from the building.

During the few minutes since Alberto Ferer's devastating announcement, Knight experienced fear more intense than he'd ever imagined. No explanation would suffice for a mistake of this magnitude. Back in New York, demanding people were waiting anxiously for a call to confirm that Mortimer was out and Wendal Randall installed as a pliable new CEO.

Knight might have been able to devise an excuse for the unexpected self-destruction of Randall and the need to find some new, equally malleable candidate to fill a vacant role of CEO. He also might have been able to convince them to be patient while Multima shares recovered their value squandered in the sell-off to weaken Mortimer. However, this calamitous oversight, buried deep within an annual report, would never be forgiven. More than a billion dollars had been invested for little useful purpose. Even if Knight were somehow able to recover those funds, The Organization wouldn't forget.

The message from his assistant about a meeting with the FBI the next day was perhaps even worse. He was confident the FBI couldn't pin anything on him for either the hacking incident or the murder of Willy Fernandez in Columbia, but there remained one important reality. The Organization had no tolerance at all for the FBI sniffing around their business affairs. Should The Organization attract any attention at all, its goal was to project only a squeaky-clean image of a respectable American corporation. No, they would not understand either his glaring oversight or the unwanted interest from the Federal Bureau of Investigations.

When the elevator reached the ground floor, Knight strode purposefully to the waiting limousine, arriving before the driver noticed his approach or could open his passenger's door. Knight got in and mumbled something about a change of plans. He asked the driver to take him to Page Field and the waiting VCI corporate jet. Please close the privacy window, he'd added politely.

Knight then made three calls from another mobile phone extracted from his bag. His VCI smartphone surely couldn't be used now.

His first call was to the pilot waiting at the VCI jet for his return trip to New York. Departure would be earlier than planned. He told him to start the engines and file a flight plan to Teterboro. Knight already knew this destination would change almost as soon as they reached cruising altitude, but he wanted that next step secret until they were in the air. It would be his only chance.

The second call was to his wife. In a voice as confident as he could manage, he informed her an emergency had occurred at a foreign subsidiary. He would need to visit it right away to manage potential damage. He'd probably be away for a few days, but would call her again tomorrow from São Paulo, Brazil. Then, he calmly said good-bye.

The third call was to his old friend in West Palm Beach again. They'd need an ambulance to meet the VCI jet in about twenty minutes. All overseas flights would be necessary. Flight plans should be filed for each segment at the last possible moment, each time with a different plane. The old friend clearly understood the cryptic instructions and assured all would be ready.

Moments before arriving at Page Field, he texted a director who consistently voted with his position.

"Urgent matter elsewhere. Can't return after lunch. Let others know & vote your conscience. Thx. H."

He sent the message just as the limousine came to a full stop beside his aircraft. The driver rushed to open the door for his passenger, and then shook hands in farewell. He appeared delighted with the five hundred dollar gratuity discretely slipped into his palm as Knight looked into his eyes and thanked him warmly. Howard then bounded up the aircraft stairway, had a quick word with the co-pilot, and entered. The door was locked, and moments later, the engine whine intensified as speed increased for takeoff.

SIXTY-NINE

A conference room at Multima Corporation headquarters.
Afternoon, March 9, 2016

The director who consistently voted with Howard Knight pulled aside Alberto Ferer for a whispered conversation as they glanced at the message just received on his mobile device. Alberto could barely contain his surprise and profound relief when he saw the news.

They concurred it would be best for that director to make the announcement about Knight's sudden departure once the meeting reconvened. Alberto dashed to John George Mortimer's nearby office for the second time in only minutes.

John George didn't express any surprise when Ferer relayed the news. Calmly, he suggested Alberto call for a vote on the issue of his leadership immediately after the director divulged the message from Knight. Then, Ferer would once more adjourn the meeting briefly and return to advise Mortimer of the results.

Alberto reconvened the meeting with a much more relaxed and confident demeanor. It was apparent to all. He could also sense a change in the mood of other participants, even before he called on the director who consistently voted with Howard Knight to make his announcement.

Once that director shared his text message, the mood of the room changed even more noticeably. It was as though some huge weight had been lifted from their shoulders. Postures straightened. Worry lines started to fade. There were even a few tightly suppressed smiles and brighter, more active eyes. Alberto called for a motion about John George Mortimer's leadership.

Cliff Williams, a director from Chicago, so moved. He proposed the board issue a press release that day to re-affirm that John George Mortimer enjoyed the full support of the board. Further, he recommended the release also include notification that Multima's board had invited him to remain chief executive officer until at least December 31, 2019. Williams also added that it might be best if the resolution was unanimous. All members of the board raised their hands in unison.

Less than five minutes later, John George glanced at his watch as he entered the conference room, followed by Alberto. It was just a few minutes before two o'clock. Mortimer was stunned when the entire board of directors suddenly stood and loudly applauded for several moments. He was surprised and warmed by the burst of applause greeting his entry. He basked in the praise with a self-deprecating smile, sensing that the timing was perfect for the radical leadership he was about to show.

John George Mortimer had already asked his assistant to summon James Fitzgerald and Douglas Whitfield from the beach restaurant where the division executives were eating lunch. They should leave the restaurant in twenty minutes using one limousine, he directed. The others should follow a few minutes later in the rest of the waiting cars. His assistant should make Fitzgerald and Whitfield comfortable in his office until his return.

Meanwhile, he walked to the end of the large, oval table, plugged his tablet into a digital projection panel, and turned on both devices. He humbly asked the directors to suspend their applause and take their seats. He had much to cover in a short time.

For the next half-hour, John George Mortimer controlled the room more masterfully than ever. Without notes, and without any noticeable pauses other than those used for dramatic effect, he outlined a series of measures he would ask the directors to consider and conclude with their votes that day.

He started by addressing the issue of Wendal Randall. John George made clear the entire matter saddened him. Nevertheless, there were few alternatives. He must suspend Wendal without compensation while the legal charges against him played out. It would be necessary to remove him as president of Multima Logistics. In the event Wendal was found to be not guilty of all charges, perhaps they could find another appropriate role for him in the corporation. In the meantime, John George wanted the board to consider his recommendation for a replacement.

When he finished his outline of the Multima Logistics leadership solution, he moved on to detail a series of proposed changes he wanted them to consider before any voting. Using his PowerPoint slides, he guided the board through proposed major revisions to the corporate structure. He shared his vision of Multima's business evolution and new business strategies that required capital investments. His presentation even included a high-level, five-year profit and loss analysis.

It was over in precisely thirty minutes as planned. He then asked the board to vote their support or denial. He handed Alberto Ferer a sheet of paper and asked him to make specific motions for the board to consider and vote to determine the outcome.

Alberto read each proposal to the assembled group and then requested that a director second the motion. By a show of raised hands, directors voted, with the corporate secretary recording the results. One by one all motions were approved unanimously, with only two slight amendments and the briefest of discussion. All in less than an hour.

As John George thanked the directors for their support and diligent efforts that long and stressful day, he apologized that he would not be available for any personal discussions after the meeting. Instead, he would start to execute their decisions immediately. Then, he suggested everyone arrive in Fort Myers the afternoon before the scheduled March 23 meeting for a group dinner. His assistant would get particulars to them as soon as possible.

With that farewell, he stood up and circled the oval conference table, firmly shaking hands with each director, making and holding direct eye contact. He expressed genuine, heartfelt gratitude for their support. Then, scooping up his tablet, he strode back to his office to start the first of several important conversations.

He glanced at his watch, noting that it was one minute before four o'clock.

SEVENTY

James Fitzgerald felt as though his head was spinning. He could not recall a more intense thirty minutes than those he had just experienced in Mortimer's spacious office overlooking the beautiful Caloosahatchee River. There had been little time to appreciate the magnificent scenery, though.

He and Douglas Whitfield had cooled their heels as Mortimer intended for about ten minutes before the board meeting ended. Mortimer burst into his office exuding energy and confidence. First, he asked Whitfield to wait in a nearby conference room for just another few minutes so Mortimer could meet privately with James.

There were no pleasantries to start, no discussion about lunch, professional sports, or their respective health. Mortimer lunged right into the purpose of the conversation. Some good news to share and some developments about which Fitzgerald might be less enamored.

While James braced for both with his best poker face, Mortimer informed him the board had voted support for his continued leadership and requested that he remain CEO for another two years. He also pointed out that he had not yet given the board his decision, but had agreed to think about it.

He briefly recounted events from the meeting. The board approved the Multima Financial Services game changer project with one important caveat. Rather than growing the business organically, the board wanted Fitzgerald to acquire a small, well-managed mortgage company to form the nucleus of the nascent mortgage lending operation.

Chuck Jones from Chicago made that suggestion. He said he knew of such a firm with an excellent management team, and they could acquire it at a very reasonable cost. The board authorized up to fifty million dollars for such an acquisition, and Mortimer suggested he get on with it as quickly as possible.

James immediately saw the wisdom of buying an already successful and experienced team as a foundation for the proposed new business and nodded his concurrence. He assumed that was the good news and braced for the bad.

Mortimer delivered the facts directly, without mincing words. James would need to give up a promising and valued young executive. Mortimer wanted to move young Douglas Whitfield over to Multima Logistics to replace Wendal Randall. One sentence revealed the unfortunate circumstances. "Wendal screwed up badly, is under arrest, and is out of the picture for good."

He then delivered a blow that had left Fitzgerald almost gasping for air, while doing everything possible to maintain his poker face. As much as he knew James would like to retire, he couldn't let that happen yet. He needed him to remain in his current role for at least two more years.

He wanted Fitzgerald's steady hand at the helm as Multima Financial Services embarked on this monumental new project. The board had agreed to make it worth his while. It issued fifty additional preferred class 'B' shares to him, subject to extension of his contract to December 31, 2019. Fitzgerald did the math as Mortimer spoke. The offer represented a signing bonus worth five million dollars—more than his base salary during the past five years combined!

Mortimer asked him if he would accept. James realized instantly that he could never refuse, even with his wife anxious to escape to their lake home in Wisconsin. The offer was just too attractive. More importantly, he was already more than a little intrigued by the opportunity to create another successful new business before he faced retirement. With no attempt to negotiate, James replied that he looked forward to an exciting two years in his current role at Multima Financial Services.

Mortimer then summoned Whitfield from the conference room. That discussion was even shorter. He advised Douglas Whitfield he needed to relocate to Miami for a couple years. He wanted him to run the Multima Logistics business, replacing Wendal Randall. There was no explanation of the reasons for the change in management, and Whitfield didn't inquire.

John George explained the board had decided to split Multima Logistics into two separate entities. The fifty percent of its workforce dedicated to Multima Supermarkets' activities would move to Atlanta and become part of that business unit. It made sense. Resources entirely committed to the supermarket business would be even more productive under the control of the Supermarkets' information technology team there.

This development meant Whitfield would start at Multima Logistics with a company about half its current size. More positively,

Mortimer explained that he needed him to grow the business. He wanted Multima Logistics to become exponentially larger. For John George had become convinced of an enormous untapped market for the ingenious software technology that had allowed Multima Supermarkets and the FBI to identify so quickly the perpetrators of their recent hacking incident.

The FBI and Multima corporate security were both impressed with the simplicity and efficiency of that software tool. They foresaw almost unlimited sales potential with governments and companies of all sizes, all around the globe. Mortimer wanted Whitfield to use his extensive network of contacts with banks and finance companies to launch the product and lay a solid business foundation. If Whitfield performed as well as Mortimer expected him to, there would be another more important role in a couple years.

Mortimer briefly outlined a new salary package for Whitfield, his proposed bonus, and reimbursement for relocation expenses. He asked Douglas if he could start the new job Monday morning. Whitfield requested only one clarification. He would like his children to finish their year in the current Chicago-area schools they attended. He would need to commute weekly between Chicago and Miami using the Multima Logistics corporate jet. Would that be acceptable?

Mortimer agreed as he rose from his chair. They exchanged warm handshakes and their discussion was over.

———

Along with the other division executives, Suzanne Simpson waited in the large conference room. She was soon summoned to John George Mortimer's office. Walking there, she recalled how headquarters staff lightly referred to it as the 'inner sanctum'. She'd still never figured out exactly why they used such a nomenclature.

On her arrival, Mortimer wasted no time with small talk. He reviewed results of the board decision about his leadership and the announcement scheduled for the media release. Then he delivered news about Wendal Randall and the board's decision to relocate Multima Logistics people dedicated to Multima Supermarkets from Miami to Atlanta.

Suzanne's smile grew broader with such welcome news. She'd long maintained those technology resources should be at the Atlanta headquarters under her control. She was gratified to see the development on two levels. First, her IT team would manage the brilliant technology employees more effectively and productively. Perhaps equally important, this move suggested an end to any consideration of the bizarre and ill-advised game changer project proposed by Multima Logistics that morning. Those marvelous technology minds could now be focused towards customer-centric thinking to blend better their technology dreams and ideas with the customer-driven and employee-valued business culture at Multima Supermarkets.

John George conveyed the approvals from the board of directors related to her game changer projects. Looking directly into her eyes, he congratulated her for the courage to disregard his directive limiting the game changer proposals to a single project. She had been entirely correct to resist this instruction. With a warm smile, he added his assumption such defiance would not be the start of some new *modus operandi*.

He affirmed that the board approved both projects to a maximum purchase price of five hundred million dollars. She would need to come back to the board should more become necessary to get the deal done. They'd also accepted Suzanne's proposed management changes, moving Gordon Goodfellow to lead the company to be acquired and replacing him with Phil Archer, the son of the acquisition target's owner.

John George closed their private meeting by expressing his desire to see the expansion of the big-box retail format accelerated even more quickly than she had proposed. He'd prefer to see it complete within the next two years, if Suzanne and her team could accomplish it prudently.

Curiously, something caused Suzanne to suspect his casual, off-hand delivery of such a message might mask his desire to make it more impactful. She was sure of it when he added that two years would be an excellent timeframe and probably allow a lot of positive convergence.

John George stood up as he delivered his last comment, signaling the end of their meeting. With a polite gesture, he motioned that she should lead the way from his office.

It had all happened so quickly, with so little time to digest the information, Suzanne entirely overlooked her private concerns. There had been no opportunity to inquire about those monthly deposits in her mother's bank account, nor had she solved the mystery of those preferred shares from a numbered company in Ontario. With the whirlwind of decisions and motion around her, it would all need to wait.

SEVENTY-ONE

A large conference room, Multima Corporation.
5:00 p.m., March 9, 2016

For the first time that momentous day, John George Mortimer started to feel the burden of his sixty-nine years. He was dreadfully tired. Pain in the area of his mastectomy had flared up again as he walked down the hallway from his office with Suzanne Simpson. He found it necessary to conceal a grunt caused by the sharp pain with a short, fake cough.

She didn't seem to notice, but it became necessary to cough again as he was taking his customary place at the head of the large oval table. Gathered were the rest of the executives who had not yet heard what had happened at the board meeting.

He began by announcing his intention to keep his comments brief. He realized it had been a long day for everyone, and he was sure they'd like to be back home with their families as soon as possible. He apologized for all the stress and disruption to their personal lives over the preceding weeks. He expressed his genuine hope the future could be less stressful and demanding, but shared his perspective that no one could foresee the future with accuracy.

Like him, despite their best-laid plans, they would have to play the cards they were dealt.

For about fifteen minutes, he summarized highlights of events over the past few hours and the decisive actions of the board. With particular care, he watched how the Multima Logistics team reacted to the dramatic news. They would have a new leader, would subdivide into separate business units, and some would have a responsibility to launch an exciting new software tool. Very significant changes.

With some satisfaction, John George observed that shock first registered on the faces of team members as he announced Wendal Randall's departure, but he noticed their body language improved as he detailed the business unit's future structure and direction. The team seemed to like their new leader too. Warm smiles followed his announcement about Douglas Whitfield.

When his brief overview of the day was complete, Mortimer mentioned the board's request that he stay as CEO for another couple years. Again, he smiled as he confided that he had not yet given the directors a response, but planned to see them again in just a few weeks. He asked each of the teams to join the board meeting scheduled for March 23. He'd like each business unit team to update the board on their progress with the game changer projects.

Finally, he wished each of the teams well and thanked them warmly for all they do to make their company a success. He also thought it helpful to make one final comment as he rose to signal an end to the meeting.

He probably wouldn't have any hair when they saw him next time, he pointed out. However, they shouldn't worry. Somewhere, he read that a surprisingly high percentage of women find bald men sexier than those burdened with hair.

With that lighthearted attempt to put everyone at ease about his cancer, John George Mortimer said quick good-byes as he circled the table. He stopped to shake hands with only the three presidents of business divisions—John Fitzgerald, Douglas Whitfield, and Suzanne Simpson. With each, he grasped hands firmly, looked directly into their eyes, and thanked them for their outstanding leadership.

He spoke with Suzanne last. To her, it seemed that he had just started his brief message when he suddenly stopped, smiled, and walked from the room. As he turned away, his smile transformed into a tight grimace from the pain he could no longer hide.

SEVENTY-TWO

In a Multima limousine heading towards Page Field, Fort Myers.
Late day, March 9, 2016

After John George Mortimer left the meeting room, Suzanne seized the opportunity to meet briefly with Douglas Whitfield. There were many issues to consider with the relocation of some Multima Logistics employees to Atlanta, and she wanted to set some parameters early in the process.

Their discussion was a good one. Both were great listeners and respectful of the other's challenges and needs. Within a few minutes, they drew other members of their teams into the discussions, agreeing on schedules and timing for follow-up conference calls. They named project coordinators and exchanged email addresses and cell numbers. It all started well, and they left confident that all would end well.

As usual, a car was waiting for Suzanne as she left headquarters. Usually, she would expect the limousine ride to Page Field to be relaxing, an opportunity to exhale after an action-packed day. Instead, she felt troubled over Mortimer's manner when he said good-bye. She was almost certain he started to add something to his word of thanks. Then, for some reason, he abruptly stopped. It was both unusual and curious.

She was also a little annoyed about the way he had directed the afternoon's events. She found it grating how he sent them all away to a restaurant while the board deliberated. Shuffling division presidents from office to office as he dramatically decreed sweeping organization changes caused concern. Most disconcerting was that she still had no answers to those gnawing questions about her mother's death, the bank deposits, or the shares for a numbered company in Ontario.

There was little doubt now. Those issues related in some way to John George Mortimer. Frustratingly, there hadn't been time for her to ask him even a single question. As the limousine neared Page Field, her thoughts raced faster and unease grew. Suddenly, she recalled a morsel of information Wilma Willingsworth had divulged in an unguarded moment as they walked together towards the elevator. Just as the door slid open, she conspiratorially whispered how fortunate their leader had been to tuck away another small company in Canada. They had both laughed as the elevator doors closed.

The potent significance of that comment finally struck her. Was it possible that company tucked away in Canada was the one that issued shares to her mother? Was it possible that same business paid three thousand dollars per month into her mother's bank account? Indeed, was it possible her mother's death determined Mortimer's boardroom victory?

Annoyance quickly turned into genuine shock. She felt her body chill as she speculated why Mortimer might do that. As they approached the parked aircraft, she asked the driver to stop and wait. She wanted to make one call before she boarded the jet for Atlanta. With a press of a speed-dial button, she connected with Sally-Anne Bureau and asked to speak with John George.

"I'm sorry, Ms. Simpson, but Mr. Mortimer has already left for the day. Would you like me to connect you to his cell phone?" Suzanne briefly considered but quickly decided against it. She told Sally-Anne she'd send an email or catch up with him later, and thanked her.

Instead, she decided to act on an impulse and asked the driver to take her to John George Mortimer's residence. The driver looked into the rear-view mirror in surprise. She assured him it would be okay. They should go directly there. With only a moment's hesitation, the driver accelerated and headed towards McGregor Boulevard.

It was rush hour, and Fort Myers' seasonal traffic was horrible, so Suzanne had more time to think. The more she thought about the possibilities, the more her apprehension grew. New questions came to mind. Disconcerting implications surfaced, but she realized all were nothing more than speculation. What she was about to do was completely out of character and well beyond her comfort zone. Regardless, as diplomats like to say, a full and frank discussion with her boss was now imperative.

A few minutes later, her driver drove up to Mortimer's magnificent home on Caloosa Drive. Out of the car the moment it stopped, Suzanne strode purposefully to the imposing front door and rang the bell. A few seconds later, the massive door swung open.

"You must be Suzanne Simpson," a small Latino woman greeted as she stepped out from behind the door. With a welcoming smile, she added, "Come in. He's expecting you."

ACKNOWLEDGEMENTS

Writing a first novel is a daunting mission. For me, it was possible only with unlimited support from a special team of people.

Charles Alessi, Ray Hardy, Cheryl Harrison, Dalton McGugan and Andre Morin all read early versions. Their incisive feedback and comments were valued beyond words.

Mariana Abeid-McDougall, Eric Anderson, Polly Cox, Paula Hurwicz and Elizabeth Siegel all helped me to polish the story with critical editing and proofreading that improved my work beyond measure. Any remaining shortcomings are entirely mine.

Tracy Kagan (our daughter), and Murray Pollard (a friend and former colleague) provided valuable insight about their personal experiences with breast cancer and inspired my goal to create more awareness about this insidious disease.

The team at FriesenPress performed admirably. Special thanks to Meaghan McAneeley for her outstanding design work, Hannah Monteith for her extraordinary promotions expertise, and Astra Crompton for seamlessly pulling it all together with professionalism, and unflagging good cheer!

Gratitude to my entire family and many friends around the globe for all providing a lifetime of support and encouragement. You are the ones who instilled confidence that anything is possible with enough patience, determination and perseverance.

Finally, it would be out of character for me not to 'ask for the order'. If you enjoyed *Three Weeks Less a Day*, please help me achieve commercial success by telling your friends and writing reviews wherever you buy books.

Printed in Canada